SJ HULL

The Crimson Script

This book is dedicated to my amazing wife Suzanne. Without her constant support and encouragement none of this would have been possible. She also brought me chocolate.

Contents

I

The Crimson Script

by SJ Hull

1

A Question of Luck

"Time to make your move, girl."

Lyra grinned.

She was enjoying the feel of the coarse and weathered cards that rested between her fingers, the smell of sea salt that lingered in the shaded confines of the room, and even the thin smile of the man seated before her.

"Just play your cards, sweetheart, we'll worry about the money later," said Stel. A sinister line of yellowed and broken teeth framed his words, as a murmur of laughter crept out from the other figures seated at the table.

Lyra's heart beat a little faster as she remembered to quickly wipe the grin from her face.

She was supposed to be new at this.

Lyra glanced back down at her cards with a concerned grimace.

"Oh, uh – I'm sorry, I've not played cards for money before..."

Stel leaned forward with a laboured grunt, the candlelight dancing along the grease stains spotted across his shirt.

"Like I said before, sweetie, the lads and I are here to help you," he said, his eyes widening with mockery as he gestured down to the four cards lined up across the uneven wood.

Lyra made sure to keep the look of confusion fixed upon her face, even as her hands began to tighten. Her eyes glanced momentarily down to the blades that lay scattered across the table.

"You just gotta make a set of cards with them that you has in your hands, and these here ones on the table."

"Right, uh, ok – there are just so many different numbers and colours. It's all a bit confusing," she stammered, staring at the crudely painted faces that looked up at her from the beer-stained cards.

"Ah, well, don't you stress, sweetheart, me and Kric and Limmy here will look after you."

Limmy, who was seated on her left, nodded with an awkward enthusiasm, casting bloodshot eyes across Lyra's frame.

She let out an involuntary shiver, but masked it by fumbling awkwardly over her cards.

Kric, who sat next to his leering associate, sat cool and still in contrast. His small, dark eyes fell upon her with cautious anticipation.

"No need to fret, darling, we's no threat to you. We's here to help."

"You're very kind."

Kric's gaze remained unsettlingly still. "There's no hardship in it, darling, not for a sweet thing like you."

Lyra felt her jaw clench involuntarily. "Oh, I'm really not that sweet."

"Sweeter than most," answered Kric, easing back into his seat. "Why? You're not the Lady, are you? Not going to slit our throats where we sit?" he laughed.

She blushed. "Slitting throats? Certainly not. Mr Stel, I didn't think that this was that sort of place," she said with a note of feigned trepidation.

Stel quickly jolted forward, slapping Kric on the shoulder. "Of course it ain't, sweet. Kric! Don't speak so vulgar to our guest. My apologies, miss, my friend here has just spent the last few months on a merchant brig. He must have lost his manners somewhere overboard."

"It's quite all right, Mr Stel. I'm just glad that there are still a few gentlemen around."

"A damsel like you deserves a true gentleman," replied Stel, chewing a lip,

4

as his eyes studied her face. Lyra nodded, sure in the knowledge that she was two stories up in a house that she had never been to before, and that the door was shut firmly behind her.

There was no way out, and she was very alone.

Yet, even as this knowledge brought a flutter to her heart, a question began to form in her mind that went against every word of her training. Lyra fought it back, willing it to be forgotten, but as she looked back at Stel's smug, lecherous face, she found that she could not resist.

"If you don't mind me asking, who is the Lady?"

"Some dumb whore."

Stel shot Kric a venomous look. "That she is, but that's no kind of language to be speaking in front of the young miss here."

"I'm sure our little lady has heard worse. What did you say your father was again? A spice trader? There's harsher words than mine flying about those ships," muttered Kric.

"Yes," answered Lyra, "we were fresh out of Aurel a week ago. We moored up this morning and Daddy said he had some business to take care of in the city. I was so bored left waiting all by myself on the docks, that is, until you fine men offered to entertain me."

"The pleasure's all ours," said Kric, his words suddenly more measured than those of his associates, and, as the lightest of breaths escaped Lyra's lips, she noted the tone of suspicion in his voice.

"So it is," exclaimed Stel, gesturing back down towards the cards. "Let's continue our game then, eh? No need to be worrying about the Lady here, we're safe as a magister's purse. Besides, she only goes after criminals and the like, so there's no fear of her turning up here. Not when we are blessed with such gracious company."

"She hunts criminals? How exciting, Mr Stel. What does she do when she's found them?"

The man Lyra knew as Limmy lowered his tankard to the table. "The stories say she strings them up, or slices them before throwing them into a canal. But not before she's tortured them for information."

Lyra cast an eye over to the bearded figure of Limmy, his breath heavy with the smell of beer and pork. He wore no mask but instead bore a series of strange tattoos, which almost seemed to dance around the corners of his eyes, meeting in a flurry of spirals just above the bridge of his nose. He had barely said anything since she had first been invited to take a seat at the table. When the brief sputter of words finally crawled out from between the greasy spirals of hair that framed his lips, Lyra detected a thick Fereli accent.

Irritation crossed the weathered features of Stel's face. "Come now, lads, this is hardly fitting talk for the young miss and besides..." he gestured to Lyra, who had placed a small pile of gold coins in front of her, "we have a game to finish before we escort our guest safely home."

"Right you are, boss," said Kric. "You're safe here, sweetheart," he muttered, spinning the blade before him. "Ain't no one getting to you in here."

She met his gaze. "I feel safer already. I truly believe that the Lady would be powerless against such fine, strong men."

Stel picked up his cards. "Aye, you're right there, the fighting's always best left to men. We wouldn't want lovely ladies such as yourself to bruise your pretty faces now, would we? Sweet as you are."

Lyra felt her charm falter, "Quite so."

Stel picked a few coins from his waistcoat pocket and added them to the pile at the table's centre. "There you go, sweet. Even more money to play for now. Plenty for a new frock or uh, a nice bag. All you need's do is play your hand."

"I do so love a nice bag," Lyra replied, with the briefest flutter of her eyelashes.

"How about you put your cards down then? We'd best walk you home before too long. Wouldn't want Daddy to start to worry now."

No, they really wouldn't, Lyra thought to herself.

"Can you put your cards down first please, Mr Stel. I'm afraid that I'm still not quite sure what all the pictures mean."

Kric let out an impatient snort of derision, earning a fiery look from Stel, before the older man lowered his cards.

"Sure thing, sweetie, wouldn't want you all confused now, would we?

Here's my cards."

Stel tapped one of the cards already lying on the table, laying his own alongside it.

"That's called trip aces, lovely, a high hand that one."

He leaned over the table, eying Lyra with a triumphant grin that he had kept reserved for this moment. She wondered how many others had suffered this same cruel leer.

"Oh uh, well – is this any good, Mr Stel?"

Laughter, harsh and loud, erupted from Limmy, as the three men looked over to see the worthless collection that was Lyra's cards.

"Pay him no heed, sweet. He's not from around here," said Stel. "These Fereli don't understand proper manners."

"Does this mean that I've lost, Mr Stel?" asked Lyra, her eyes widening with as much shock and disappointment as she could pour into them.

"Lost? No, no, my dear, that's not how cards work. You simply haven't won this hand, that's all. I now get all the coins that you put forward, but the good news is that all you have to do to win them back, is put some more gold forward for another round. A clever thing like you is sure to manage it."

"That is, if you have more gold?" asked Kric.

Lyra allowed the unspoken excitement brought on by the prospect of more money to hang still in the air for a moment. "Oh yes, Daddy gave me some coin for the purchase of a few supplies, but I'm sure he won't mind if I try again. I think I'm getting the hang of this now."

"That you are, sweet. You're a clever one, and no mistake."

Lyra dropped another handful of coins onto the table as more cards were dealt. She thought about the many hours that she had spent teaching her nephew to play cards and to work out the puzzles in his study books. She hoped deeply that she had never been as transparently patronising to him as Stel was being to her in this moment. Lyra then shook the image of her family from her mind. This dark place was not worthy of them and she still had work to do. However, she could not suffer this masquerade to persist much longer. These men saw her much like a cat does a mouse, to be taunted and tricked. Lyra did not doubt for one moment that Stel and his cronies believed they could overpower her and take whatever money and liberties they wanted.

And yet, they played cards for her money, toying with her at every hand. Lyra had heard tale of their cruel ways from their previous victims. It had not taken her long to find Stel and his fellows, and they had been easily baited.

This was going to be short, she thought to herself.

The door behind them was locked, and these men would soon be very alone.

Lyra looked down at her cards. They were as unexceptional as her previous ones, but she knew that it was not the cards that she needed to play.

"Daddy would be so angry to know that I was playing cards. He never lets me play with the men on the ship. What is it that you do, Mr Stel? Are you a sailor?"

"No sweet, not anymore. I'm a trader, of sorts," he answered, with a sly look to his companions.

"A trader? How exciting! I want to be a merchant one day. I dream of owning my very own ship. What do you trade in?" asked Lyra, making sure to be seen taking note of the cards that Stel placed face up on the table.

He looked back at her, amused. "Rare oddities, my sweet. Nothing that would interest you."

"Oddities? I simply adore oddities, Mr Stel. What sort of... oddities?"

"Trinkets, nothing more than trinkets."

Lyra flexed her right hand, allowing the rings upon her fingers to catch whatever meagre light crept into the room.

She decided to try again. "I collect trinkets myself. I've brought dozens from ports all across the Argenti Sea. Maybe I could use a few to bet on another round?"

Stel looked at Lyra. The thinly-veiled charm was now strained upon his face, his eyes narrow and lips tight. She had struck upon something, of that she could be sure. These were indeed the right targets.

"Ah, sweet, I don't deal in your simple rings. My trinkets have a bit more... life to them." Stel placed his final card upon the stained wood and gently pushed his pile of coins to the centre, readying himself for the end of the game.

"You mean magic?" asked Lyra, "Daddy says that magic–"

"Who exactly is your father? If you don't mind me asking?" interrupted Kric, slowly lowering his tankard.

"Oh, Daddy? He's a man of the city. Like you, he's got a few ships moored outside. Well, more than a few. He said I could have a look around the city while he sorted out some business."

A chequered toothy grin returned to Stel's face.

"Well sweetie, after our little game, me and the lads can escort you back to the docks, if you like?"

Lyra felt her fingers tense once again, as they creased the corner of one of the cards.

"Oh, that would be just lovely of you, Mr Stel, thank you," she replied, the corner of her mouth behind her half-mask curling in disgust.

Stel's eye traced the golden outline of hair which ran across the unmasked space of Lyra's brow. Keeping firm grasp of her cards, Lyra slowly lowered her free hand down towards her belt, offering as mirthful and innocent a smile as the dank, cramped room would suffer. This was becoming harder with every passing minute.

The three men's eyes passed to the gold, greedily drinking in the sight of the small cluster of shining coins now piled up at the centre of the table.

Covetous eyes moved from beauty to beauty, until Kric spoke again.

"You say that your father has many ships? Well I work at the docks, and I have seen few that I don't recognise. Which is his flag-ship?"

"The Aligri Verde," answered Lyra, slowly wrapping her unseen fingers around a pistol at her belt.

Kric made to speak again but was swiftly cut off. "There's plenty of time to socialise, but let's get these cards played first." Stel's voice brooked no room for disagreement, and a note of impatience harassed his speech.

Kric placed a particularly dirty thumb under his own splintered and cracked mask, relieving himself of a troubling itch. He was beginning to grow unsettled. Even Stel's awkward smile began to fade as time drew on and Lyra sensed that the game would soon be over.

More cards were drawn, bets were made, hands were folded, and before long the final stage had arrived. Lyra slowly pulled both of her feet to rest just under her chair, legs tensed.

She looked down to see that Stel had another pair of aces in his hand, which he now proudly displayed before the rest of the table.

How odd it was that his hand always seemed so flush with ace cards.

"Your turn, my sweet. All the money needs to go in the centre, now. Yeah, that's right. Now, what cards you got? They'd best be good."

Lyra revealed her worthless hand of cards with due surprise and disappointment. Stel chuckled and immediately began to console her with the least comforting language possible. Limmy once again fell into hysterics, descending back into the endless depths of his beer tankard.

However, Kric remained unmoved by this sudden loss and revelry. Pained concentration furrowed his brow, as he searched for the answer that for the past few minutes had eluded him, until now.

"Your father sails on the Aligri Verde, you say?"

"Yes," replied Lyra, and her voice hardened, less uncertain than before.

"Strange, that, because two months ago I heard that the Verde had gone down in a storm, with all hands lost," said Kric, locking eyes with Lyra.

Stel coughed out a sinister wheeze, obliviously piling the gold into a small brown bag. His laughter grew louder and louder, as he revelled in the success of the early morning venture. The clatter of coins rose joyfully to his ears, and soon it was all that could he could hear, as the rest of the room grew suddenly silent.

Stel's eyes remained fixed on the brief but enchanting shower of gold. There was no quiet void that the sound of swiftly falling coin could not fill.

"The Verde is sunk, you say?" Lyra mused, "Well, maybe Father and I are just strong swimmers. There's no shortage of new ships at the docks."

Kric's jaw clenched. "Maybe, but it's bad luck to name a ship after another that was lost in foul weather. I don't know any sailors that would sail on such a craft."

Lyra could feel her heart beating faster, as she withdrew her second hand to rest under the table. The only thing breaking the momentary silence between her and Kric was the falling clatter of golden coins and the slurping gulps of a very inebriated Limmy.

"I always found sailors to be a suspicious bunch, prone to all manner of flights of fancy."

A sudden paleness crept across Kric's cheeks. "Like believing in the Lady?"

Lyra grinned, "She does sound like quite the terror."

Silence fell, pregnant with threat.

"I hear she can cut a man up pretty bad."

"Cut, shoot, stab, I imagine it's much the same, all a means to an end."

A grimace marred Kric's lips, his hands curled into fists. "What end could a woman like that possibly have?"

Lyra breathed deeply, leaning ever so slightly forward. "Wiping scum from the streets. You'd be surprised how hard it is. You really have to put your back into it."

Kric nodded slowly, looking down at the knife that rested so close to his hands. "I expect some stains are harder to wipe than others."

"Sometimes."

In a sudden blur of motion, Lyra kicked her leg into the table, sending it flying into Kric and Limmy. Then there followed the crack of bone and the swift release of blood, as the Lady went to work.

Stel looked up, as a final gold piece could be heard landing within the meagre depths of his bag.

The crumpled form of Kric lay over by the door, his elbow jutting out at an angle that seemed anything but natural. Limmy was on his knees, wincing as a fine trail of blood ran down his head. The barrel of a finely-engraved pistol filled his mouth, as Lyra pulled back the flintlock mechanism resting just in front of his nose.

"Something wrong, Stel?" asked Lyra, keeping her second pistol levelled at his head. This weapon was different to the gun that was currently causing Limmy to choke a little. The firing chamber and flintlock had the appearance of finely-engraved silver, whilst the barrel gave off the shine of white pearl. To the right buyer, the weapon was worth more than the very building in which Stel's day was rapidly falling apart.

11

For a few moments he was rendered mute, looking slowly over to the collapsed form of Kric and the spluttering Limmy, before returning his frantic gaze to Lyra.

"No need for that, my good woman, no need at all!"

Stel slowly rose to his feet, keeping his hands high in the air.

"Really, Stel? Because if I didn't know any better, I could have sworn that you were just about to cheat me out of all my gold? Or did I simply misunderstand you?"

No youthful innocence hindered Lyra's speech, and her eyes had ceased their cautious wanderings around the room. The naïve merchant's daughter now spoke with a confidence and focus that brought a wave of unease to Stel's stomach – not that any merchant's daughter carried weapons like these.

"Misunderstanding? Yeah, love, all a big misunderstanding! Gold's all yours, plain as day."

Lyra nodded slowly, drawing the barrel of her pistol from Limmy's mouth and wiping it on his shaking shoulders.

Stel grabbed his small bag with a gentle clink of moving coins, and tossed it swiftly over to Lyra's side of the table. She parted the half-open leather with her first pistol, inspecting the gold inside.

Limmy rose to his feet looking nervously over to Stel, whose gaze had shifted back down to the knife resting upon the small table.

"So, Lady, what are you? A guild member? I ain't troubled no guild, I ain't stupid. Anyhow, I thought it was understood that the docks was neutral territory. Fair game for all and all that. That's unless Karrick wants another blood-bath on his hands," said Stel, edging back over to his side of the table.

Lyra looked up, keeping one weapon in hand, as she placed her winnings inside a larger bag hanging from her belt.

"Do you really think that Karrick sent me?" uttered Lyra, saying the name that could render silent any tavern on this side of Abys-Luthil, with an uncharacteristic solemnity.

"Uh well, no, no – I suppose not. After all, your ladyship, I ain't done nothing. Not to Mr Karrick. Not that there'd be a problem if you was representing the Pale Star Guild, I'm a local lad myself miss, always happy to help the community – "

Lyra saw the betrayal of thought in Stel's eyes, even before Limmy could make his final step behind her.

She spun on her heel, raising the butt of her pistol and slamming it into Limmy's nose. He staggered backwards as blood washed over his lips, struggling to steady himself against the wall behind and pulling down a poorly-assembled row of shelves behind him. He cursed and spat, barely able to regain his footing before Lyra's fist hammered into his windpipe, sending him reeling to the floor, desperate to catch what little breath he could.

A sudden blur of rusted steel erupted into view as Stel's blade passed mere inches from her face. Lyra felt the straps of her mask and the hem of her cloak tug against the air, as she spun swiftly away, raising her pistol and firing a shot at Stel's leg.

A horrid scream pierced the air and mingled with the brief roar of firing powder, and Stel's right knee burst in a flurry of blood and fractured bone.

Lyra's heart beat with the pace of a marching drum. The smell of the dark powder assaulted her senses and she began to feel her hands shake, watching whilst Stel's blood pooled between the rotten floorboards.

It really wasn't supposed to go this way. But she had to hold it together – she was on the wrong side of town, and even wounded, she couldn't let these men see her take a moment's pause.

Stel screamed and shook with pain, desperately trying to crawl away from Lyra. She knelt down beside him and placed the rim of her smoking gun next to the terrible wound.

"Now you're going to listen to me, Stel, or you're going to bleed out in this dank, forgotten corner of nowhere. Do you understand me?" asked Lyra, using whatever menace she could muster to hide the nerves which now wracked her heart, beating furiously in her chest.

There was no anger, no frustration left in the sweaty, pale features of Stel's face. There was only fear and the desperate need to survive.

"You've got the money! What else do you want? I haven't got anything!

Kric over there has a small amount of –"

Lyra pressed the steaming ring of her pistol against the bleeding remnants of Stel's knee. He cried out in a second howl of agony, and Lyra realised that she was now working on very limited time. She had to do this fast.

"I don't care about the gold, you, or the scum that you work with to lure innocent people into this rat-infested shell. All I want is the location of the shipment that you were paid to deliver this morning from Forely Docks. Where is it?"

Stel's eyes widened in surprise, as pain and confusion wrestled over the fractured remnants of his mind.

"H-How do you know about that?"

"Never mind how I know. Just tell me where it is, and maybe, just maybe, you'll be able to hobble down the street again one day."

What was she saying? Where were these words coming from? They seemed to seep out from some unbidden recess of her mind that lingered behind the fear and the nerves.

Stel grimaced, and for a few moments the pain became too much to bear.

Lyra turned towards the back of the staircase that led up to the room. Limmy was nowhere to be seen, having apparently summoned up enough breath to escape the room.

"Where is it!?" she growled, rising to her feet, holstering her used pistol, but keeping the second looming ominously over Stel's head.

"O-Ok, but you didn't hear it from me, I don't want that sort of trouble," rasped Stel between sighs of pain.

Lyra tilted her second pistol downwards, aiming the barrel directly between the squirming man's eyes.

"Oh yeah? What sort of trouble do you want?"

The gun slowly inched towards his face.

"Fine!" Stel exclaimed in bitter frustration. "We dropped it off at that abandoned manor house by the Castelli forges, the old Guilmino place. We was told to leave it under the grand stair, so that's what we did. Didn't see no one. Client was going to collect it later, he said. Didn't want to meet us face to face, apparently."

14

Lyra holstered her pistol.

"I wonder why? Lovely as you are."

The man spat on the floor and looked over to the doorway, as the sound of rushing feet echoed from the stairway beyond.

He smiled through the pain.

"Seems like you best be off, girl, unless you want to say a proper hello to the lads."

Lyra's eyes darted towards the window.

"You know what, Stel? I think I'll pass," she snapped, marring the repugnant grin on the man's face with a solid kick of her boot, before leaping over him, towards the window beyond.

It was small but easy enough to open. Lyra stuck her head outside, and saw nothing but a narrow waterway between the two high buildings. There was a small boat jostling between the swell of the water against the plaster walls.

"Oi you!"

She jumped.

Lyra landed awkwardly in the boat, catching her shin against one of the planks, which sent waves of pain shooting up her leg.

"She's jumped! Out the back, now!"

This really was not going to plan.

Another much larger window stood before her, and as she heard the number of angry shouts growing behind her, Lyra leapt through it and into the building beyond.

She fought through the pain coursing through her leg, as she ran through room after room. Most of them were abandoned, lined with row upon row of rusting machinery, which appeared to have been promptly abandoned once the old factory had begun to sink into the watery depths which made up most of the eastern part of the city's highways.

Not knowing how closely her pursuers chased at her heels, Lyra barged through doors and slid down any stairs that offered the quickest route away. Wet and rotted floorboards hindered her flight, and she passed through corridors lined with mould and chipped plaster. Soon enough, yet another door impeded her advance, with a large brass lock fastening it to an old wooden frame. In her haste she fired her remaining loaded pistol at the wood around the brass and gave the quivering door a solid knock with her shoulder.

The door flew open.

"Oh – uh, hello there."

Several young faces looked up with a collective stare of horror at the masked woman holding a gun, which was currently emitting fine tendrils of smoke.

They offered no reply, stunned into silence. One of them was standing up and holding a small brass cog a few feet away from a pile of other cogs, which were thrown haphazardly around a pointed wooden stick. Lyra was familiar with the game and saddened to see children of their age playing it in the decaying remains of a place like this. There was much wrong with this city, but she was hardly going to be able to heal its wounds this morning.

The sound of rushing footsteps resumed behind her.

"Right, you lot, scram now!"

They required little persuading and swiftly ran out of the room to find another place of refuge.

"Oi!" Lyra shouted.

The last child to leave the room, a young girl, no older than eleven, spun on her heel to face the masked horror.

"Take this, and run!"

Lyra threw the girl a small money pouch that she had kept hidden within the rim of her boot in case of emergencies. The child caught it with an awkward fumble, nodded meekly and hastily retreated into the darkness. *That would keep them fed for a few weeks, in the rare event that they weren't robbed of it first,* Lyra thought to herself. Dark thoughts clouded her vision, but not enough to stop her from pulling a small sphere of copper metal from her belt.

Virgil was going to kill her, but she was running out of options.

She pulled the fine wire cord from the grenade's spring mechanism and secured one end to the doorframe at knee level. Lyra then pushed the miniature lever next to a series of whirring cogs that would activate Virgil's bizarre prototype weapon. She very gently fixed the small copper ball onto the other side of the doorframe, before running with all the strength that she could muster over to the door through which the children had just fled. She could hear the panting of her own breath beating against the rim of her mask as she ran down the exceptionally wide service corridor towards the promising light of an open doorway.

She had set the grenade correctly, right? she asked herself, her boots striking a quick rhythm on the floor.

Virgil had definitely said to pull the wire before pressing the lever.

Or wait, was it the other way around?

Damn.

Well, she couldn't hear anything behind her, so maybe they had decided to—

Before Lyra could finish her train of thought, a resounding crash and burst of smoke erupted from the room that she had fled. She heard the distinct crack of electricity as the shock grenade tore through the room and echoed horribly down the corridor.

Virgil had insisted that they weren't lethal, that much she did remember clearly. They would simply give someone a rather nasty shock and knock them out for a bit. Lyra was now perilously close to experiencing this feeling herself, if Virgil learned that she had relieved his workshop of one of his precious inventions without asking.

But she could worry about that later. Not getting stabbed and left to die at the bottom of Abys-Luthil's watery depths would suffice for the moment.

Virgil would appreciate that. *Hopefully.*

The light sped towards her at a furious speed, as she leapt from the corridor and landed roughly onto the surface of one of the city's numerous stone bridges.

The sudden wash of light assaulted Lyra's eyes, momentarily obscuring her vision, as her hearing adjusted to the plethora of sounds around her. She could hear the heavy passage of a large barge traversing along the waterway under her feet, and the bustle of a large crowd teeming with hasty shouts and idle chatter.

As Lyra opened her eyes, she saw a large city square before her, alive with the journey of a thousand steps and the furious exchange of exotic goods. Ramshackle merchant stalls pocketed the vast expanse of the square, adorning it with vibrant colours and aromas both bitter and sweet. Trains of merchants traversed from stall to stall, haggling in languages both native and foreign. Strange voices and eager tongues emerged from faces decorated in a variety of painted masks and flowing robes. The stalls were flanked on all sides by an imposing row of grand colonnade structures, decorated with aged frescos and time-worn statues.

These monuments of past glory stood sentinel over the flurry of trade below. Weathered faces looked down on the moving figures with a muted solemnity that Lyra had always thought was rather sad. Figures of ancient legend, bearing weapons and texts of ages past, observed a spectacle of light and sound which almost seemed to mock the faded stone of their appearance. The rings of faded gold that sat above the lofty height of the grand columns glinted with the light of the rising sun, illuminating those below in a shower of glittering splendour. These timeless witnesses to the wealth of a once-great empire bestowed a crown of gold to all, whether noble, merchant or beggar.

Lyra smiled.

Each man and woman on that square was crowned by the titans of history that went before them, but, even as gold shone down upon their heads, so too did it fix their eyes to the ground, as the furious exchange of trade and coin continued ever onward.

The smile fell from Lyra's face as she submerged herself within the depths of the crowd's own heaving tide. She allowed the life of the city to envelope her, as she took refuge in the passage of strange faces and curious smells.

She took shelter in the light as she escaped from the dark, keeping her eyes fixed on the other side of the square and the promise of the path that would lead her to the empty shell of the old Guilmino manor, and her prize.

Lyra felt the edge of her mask press gently against the doorway as she gazed down the tall stairway. She could hear voices coming from the long-neglected grand entrance below. The size of the staircase was absurd, even for the aristocracy. Its finely-crafted bannister rail was designed to mimic the flow of tidal waves, washing down the room in heaving torrents that carried delicately-made ships of walnut wood and ash. It was truly a work of art in itself, and dilapidated and dust ridden as it was, it still warranted a moment's pause.

Then the sound of hushed voices called to her from the darkness of the depths below, and her mind began to focus.

Lyra placed the tip of her foot tentatively upon the first step of the stair. No eerie creak echoed from its surface and no shower of wood descended onto the floors below. It seemed stable enough to walk on, and keeping one hand upon the uneven surface of the bannister rail, she slowly made her descent.

With each step, Lyra felt a further weight fall upon the base of her stomach, and a slight shudder trouble the beat of her heart, unsettling the slow whispers of her breath.

Fear gripped her. The darkness hemmed her in on every side, and now the light seemed very far away indeed.

Why had she come to this place? Really?

In her head she knew well enough, and she could almost smell her prize which now sat between the growing pair of voices below.

But doubts now assaulted the certainties that she had once possessed.

What if her father found out what she was doing?

She did not fear his rebuke in the same way that she did Virgil's. Virgil would chastise her with a heat of rhetoric that closely resembled the fires of his workshop forge. She would feel the sting of his words and the shame of his weary stare, but she was no stranger to this and would soon recover.

But her father, that was a different matter.

He would not bluster or rage, he would not shout or stamp. He would simply look at her with a sadness that she had only been able to endure a few times in her life. He would utter a few quiet words, and her heart would sink.

He was not one for the shadows, and she felt that he would barely recognise her now, skulking about in the darkness.

He could never know that she was here.

She would not let that happen.

Before Lyra could ponder this any more, the image of his face now resting in her mind's eye became blurred, and was quickly dissipated by the darkness of the room, as the pair of voices below grew louder.

"Seems to be all here."

"Yeah, well, let me have a look. I ain't getting put on watch duty by the boss again. You know it rained for three hours last night?"

"Three hours?"

"Yeah."

"You was outside for three hours, in all that rain?"

"Yeah, like I said."

"Ah that ain't right, that ain't. You have a look 'ere then, looks to be all there."

Lyra leaned carefully over the bannister to see two robed figures investigating a small wooden box. She allowed herself to take a few more steps down the stairs before slowly drawing another copper sphere from the clasps at her belt.

"Did you have a break, when you was out on watch?"

"Nah, that's the thing! Groar had me out there for hours. I didn't even get me' tea," said the second voice despondently.

"What! No tea?" in disbelief.

"No, not even a little bit! An' it was really cold. Got me' fingers all numb and everything."

"Ah mate, that's not right, none of it."

"Yeah well, then I tried pouring some hot water on 'em, you know, but then they got all tingly and stung rotten," replied the man, putting the box down and displaying the red tips of his fingers.

"Ah mate, you gotta look after yourself. My wife makes the warmest gloves, ever. They're great, she can make you some up no problem," responded the first man, carefully offering his fellow a small woollen item.

"That's a mitten."

"What? No! They ain't mittens. This is the best quality gloveware is this," the man insisted earnestly.

"You sure? Co s' that really looks like a mitten."

"Nah mate. Look, try it on. It'll keep that cold out, no problem."

The other cloaked figure tentatively tried on the small object.

"Oh you're not wrong there, mate, that ain't half bad. You say Marion would make me a pair?"

"Yeah, no problem, she's great at the old stitching, my Marion. Feel the inside of that lining there, it's a real work of art that."

Lyra slowly placed the copper grenade back onto her belt. She just couldn't bring herself to do it.

"She makes a smashing pork pie as well."

"For the last time, Eric, you can't keep passing cat off as pork."

"You can if you've fed it a sausage."

Lyra pulled out a small pebble from one of the pouches at her belt. She looked towards the half-opened door by which the men had made their entrance, and threw the stone with an easy flick of her wrist.

Their conversation came to a sudden halt. The two figures made their way over to the building's entrance, pulling weathered short swords from their belts. Without a moment's pause, Lyra leapt from the bannister, allowed herself to fall a few feet, then caught the edge of the dust-strewn surface with her hands and landed with her boots to the floor.

"Evening, boys!"

The stunned duo turned upon their heels to face the masked apparition, who was bearing a long, dark cloak and finely made boots. However, what most captured their attention was the pair of finely polished pistols which she held pointed at each of them.

"Oi! Who are you then?" asked the one with what were clearly two mittens folded over his belt.

"Never mind who I am. I want that box that you're holding. Kick it over here, start walking up those stairs, and you and your friend get to live another day," said Lyra with more confidence than she had expected.

The two shared a nervous glance.

"Best do as the lady says, Eric, she's literally pointing guns at us," said the other one, as his sore, red fingers slowly sheathed his sword, before raising his hands.

Lyra pulled back the firing mechanisms on her pistols.

"This is about as literal as it gets, Eric. Kick over the box, now."

Needing no further motivation, Eric promptly shoved the box over with his foot. Lyra holstered one pistol, picked up her prize and edged towards the open door.

"Much obliged, gents. Now, if you wouldn't mind heading up those stairs and keeping those eyes of yours forwards, you never have to worry about seeing me again."

The pair moved over towards the stairs, hands raised.

"Sure thing, miss, but you do know who we work for, right? Maybe you should reconsider, not that I'm threatening you, you understand. Just a friendly warning."

Lyra knew exactly who they worked for, but Karrick would have to enter her side of town if he wanted to catch her. Karrick's guild was not to be trifled with, but he wasn't that stupid.

"I'll bear it in mind. Now, up you go, eyes forwards."

The two shuffled up the stairs, happily averting their eyes from the armed stranger.

"That's gonna be another two nights' watch for us now, mate."

"Ok look, I'll get Marion to knock up a few gloves, maybe a flask of tea, and we're right as rain."

"Honestly mate, they still look like mittens to me."

Lyra holstered her weapons, box in hand, and made for the door, easing out of the darkness and into the light. Her prize had a satisfying weight to it as it knocked against her thigh. She made for the busiest city barge that she could find. For her, the crowd and the noise promised safety, discretion, and most importantly, anonymity. Qualities which were going to be in short supply in an hour's time. She considered extending that travel time to over an hour. Hopefully, Virgil would be less inclined to shout at her if his mouth was full of the cake that she planned on buying him. It was a thin hope, but in this city of shadows and masks, hope was always a rare commodity.

The sweet smell of fresh icing sugar rose through the air, as Virgil eyed the greasy brown paper bag with no small degree of suspicion.

"What have you done now?"

Lyra looked back at him with her large eyes, a feigned look of confusion and innocence etched across her face.

"Done? I haven't done anything, Virgil. Except to buy my favourite artificer some iced buns."

Virgil's eyes wandered down to the twin pistols at Lyra's belt.

"Lyra, I can smell the firing powder."

"Yeah, well I took them out for some target practice. A few bottles on a wall, that sort of thing."

"A few bottles on a wall," the older man replied slowly, eyeing up Lyra's scuffed boots and torn shoulder cloak.

"I don't suppose that these particular bottles fired back, by any chance?"

Lyra produced another bag of sweet-smelling rolls from behind the folds of her cloak.

Virgil's weathered eyebrows quickly fell into a scowl, but his free hand grabbed the treasured brown bag all the same.

"You think that you can buy my silence with cake?"

Lyra placed her hands dramatically over her heart, letting out a sudden, indignant sigh.

Virgil's scowl narrowed further.

"Now, Virgil, how can you say such a thing? I may have taken to wandering the city a bit. But only with the best of intentions."

The artificer with the ash-strewn face let out an exasperated sigh of his own.

"The best of intentions? That's exactly what worries me."

Virgil placed the small bags on a nearby table before holding a hand out to Lyra.

"The grenades?"

"Ah, yes. Well, I do have a grenade for you."

Lyra placed a single copper ball into a strong, calloused hand.

"A grenade?"

Lyra cast her eyes down, unable to look her mentor in the eye. She felt the familiar glow of the forge fire warm her cheek.

"Ok, so I may have encountered one or two unsavoury characters on my walk—"

"You? Run into some unsavoury types? Surely not, Lyra!" replied Virgil with a hearty dose of sarcasm.

"Ok Virgil, I was just—"

"A woman of such culture and noble standing as your good self, could surely never have dealings with those of ill repute," interrupted Virgil with a mocking grin.

"What they had was dangerous, we just can't let them trade it on the street. If the guilds get hold of power like this—"

The grin dropped perilously from Virgil's face.

"Danger? Yes, my girl, there's plenty of danger out there, on those streets!"

Lyra was about to speak in her defence, but the tone in the artificer's voice brooked no quarter.

"I cast a blind eye when you took those grenades this morning, in the hope that if you did find danger through some foolishness of your own making, you'd have some way of getting out of it."

As Virgil's voice grew louder, the very fires of his forge appeared to dampen down in submission.

"And don't think that I don't know what you and Katerina have been "liberating" from the streets. That kind of power is dangerous, Lyra! Even for those who know how to wield it!"

Virgil's eyes moved over to the small box that Lyra had placed gently on his work surface upon entering the forge.

Most of the room's light was emanating from the roar of the nearby forge, sending dancing trails of orange and red across the cluttered spaces of the large room. However, as Virgil looked across to Lyra's prize, he saw a fine trail of blue light creep out from the rimmed lid, crowned with a thin, white mist.

"Magic is not to be trifled with, Lyra, especially not now. This city is a powder keg waiting to explode as it is, and having you and Katerina take on every guild in the city is hardly helping matters, let alone my sleep."

Lyra ran her fingers through her long blonde hair, before crossing her arms in defiance.

"I'm sorry, Virgil. I just – we just want to get this stuff off the streets. Karrick's guild has more influence on the docks than ever, and people are getting scared."

Ever since Lyra was a child, she had viewed Virgil with a sense of awe and wonder. Not only was he a close friend of her father, but he had the ability to bend the elements of the world to his will. He had practically been a father to Katerina, his apprentice, ever since her parents had died when she was but a child.

He was not a man whose word was easily ignored.

"I know, Lyra, believe me, I know. I have my own people keeping an eye on those docks, and I've heard more than one report of a young woman garbed in a green mask leaping through tavern windows and breaking into warehouses and more than a few stately homes."

Lyra's cheeks grew a deeper shade of red.

She said nothing. Virgil let out an exasperated sigh and wiped a thick layer of sweat and ash from his brow.

"Virgil, I – I'm sorry, I was just trying to help. I was just trying to do something other than lounge about on Father's estate, while there are people out there barring up their windows at night for fear of what might be lurking outside."

The artificer smiled, and his kind face looked gently at Lyra from the layers of dirt that bore testament to his morning's work at the forge.

"I know you do, Lyra."

He placed a reassuring hand on her shoulder and gave it a gentle squeeze.

"I know you mean well, my girl. But think about your father, if he knew what you were up to and where you were going. At the moment, it might just break the poor man. Maellon means a great deal to me, you both do. I would hate to have to be the one to tell him how his daughter died in some back alley because she pushed her luck just a little bit too far."

Lyra met his gaze once again.

"So, you want me to stop?"

Virgil smiled and retrieved one of the iced buns with a satisfying rustle of brown paper.

"I want you to be careful. If you and Katerina want to experiment with whatever small magical artefacts the guilds have managed to cobble together, then so be it. Katerina has the makings of a great artificer, and I won't deprive her of the opportunity to learn, within reason."

He bit into one of the small cakes with a smile upon his lips, comically at odds with the weight of his words.

"If some thug captures you and learns that you're a magister's daughter, and not only that, but the daughter of Maellon Alpheri himself... well, he might just be stupid enough to ask for a ransom."

The bag rustled once more as Virgil, the greatest artificer in the land, searched for another iced bun.

"Which means that I soon become the idiot arming other idiots to save your idiot behind from some idiot thug. Not a terribly attractive prospect, that."

As he spoke, a familiar face, wearing small rimmed spectacles sitting perilously upon the tip of her nose, edged around a half-opened door.

"I hope I'm not interrupting–" began Katerina.

"You know fully well that you are," answered a weary Virgil. "But come in anyway. You can deal with the fire for me. I'm off for a bath, anyway."

Katerina edged slowly into the room, having spent the last few minutes eavesdropping on their conversation.

Her eyes darted over her glasses until they came to rest upon Lyra's newly-acquired prize, and the eerie blue light which shone from the midst of its aged wood.

Her eyes met Lyra's. Lyra gave her an enthusiastic nod as Virgil collected his things, making sure to take the remainder of the buns with him.

"Yes, yes, you can play with your new toy. But, Katerina, I want your monthly project finished in two days, in addition to whatever you shape the contents of that box into. And, if you do manage to blow my forge from its foundations, rogue magic will be the least of your concerns. Do we have an understanding?"

Katerina raised an eyebrow and walked eagerly over to the box.

"Sure thing, boss, I'll keep the tumults of fire and destruction to a minimum. Provided that Lyra can keep her mitts off the forge controls," answered Katerina with a wry grin.

"Hey! That was just the once! And besides, the forge hardly blew up, it just got rearranged a little..." replied Lyra defensively.

Both master and apprentice gave her death stares before looking at each other and shaking their heads.

"Ladies, all I ask is that when I return in the morning, the forge is still in one piece, and my home is free from the intrusion of city guard officers enquiring as to why there is now a large death crater in the middle of the city," said Virgil, stuffing another bun into his mouth and making for the door.

Katerina nodded slowly, eagerly reaching for the box, her hands twitching with anticipation.

"No death craters, sure thing, boss."

"Now why doesn't that reassure me? Lyra, I'll have my pistol, if you please. Best that you keep the other one hidden as well. It wouldn't do for your father to see it."

Lyra sighed and nodded with mute reluctance, handing the beautiful pearl white weapon back to its designer.

"You won't need to borrow it again for a while. Your father has more speaking engagements this week than ever, and he'll feel a good deal better for having you by his side. You'll be serving the city a great deal better by supporting him, rather than skulking about the Water District," said Virgil, taking hold of his weapon and stepping over to the door.

Katerina rolled her eyes, and gave Lyra a quick wink.

"Night, night. Don't stay up too late," and with that, Virgil walked out into the room beyond, closing the door loudly behind him.

"Thanks Dad," muttered Katerina sarcastically, running her fingers over the smooth wood of the mysterious box.

At this, Lyra couldn't help but smile. Both Virgil and Katerina had sharp tongues, of that there could be no doubt. There had been more than a few times when she had walked into a heated argument between the two of them, or a tense moment as Virgil corrected his apprentice on her forge technique. They bickered like family, despite the fact that they shared no common blood.

Katerina's parents had died when she was a child, and she had found herself an orphan in a place with little care for those who didn't have the coin to pay their way. On a mercy mission to the poorer parts of the city, Lyra's father Maellon had set up medicine posts and housing for those in desperate need of both. One day, as Maellon and his retinue made their rounds, Virgil had accompanied him. The artificer had found the orphaned Katerina, alone and scared in the midst of a terrible famine, and with Maellon's patronage, he had taken her in and employed her as an apprentice. He had clothed her, fed her, and been every bit the father to her as it was possible to be.

Virgil could not be called a hasty man. He was careful, methodical and not prone to making rash decisions. But on that day, all those years ago, he had seen something in Katerina that had compelled him to call her out of the crowd and grant her a position in his forge. It was either with great luck or an uncanny sense of foresight that Katerina had proven to be a skilled junior artificer, even from a young age.

The two were an odd pair, to be sure. Katerina was impetuous, spontaneous and ever seeking adventure and a means to improve her craft. But even in this, her loyalty and respect for Virgil were beyond question. No matter how often they fought, or how much guidance Virgil was required to give her, Katerina's devotion to Virgil was clear. They were as much a father and daughter as Lyra had ever seen, in the good times and in the bad.

"Any problems with the pick up?" asked Katerina.

"Hmm? No, no, it all went as planned."

"Lyra."

"Yes, Kat?"

"Did you know that you're a terrible liar?"

Lyra grinned.

"In spite of the company I keep, yes."

Katerina looked up, meeting her friend's eyes.

"Yeah, well, Virgil's not all that bad."

The two laughed as Katerina slowly opened the box, and they both peered inside.

"Well, the intelligence you got from Virgil's men turned out to be pretty good. Stel didn't take too much convincing to give up its location," said Lyra.

"There's not a lot that you can't learn with enough gold, beer, and flattery. As for Stel, I trust that he didn't give you too much of a chase?"

"No, though he won't be running anywhere for the foreseeable future."

Katerina paused her inspection.

"Wait, you didn't..."

Lyra tore her eyes away from the box's contents and back to her friend.

"Didn't what?"

"Well, you know. You didn't umm – deal with him, right?"

"What?! No Kat! Nothing like that! It's just that one of his knees now has a few more holes than might otherwise be considered natural," replied Lyra, slapping Katerina playfully across her shoulder.

"Oh, that's a relief, good. Anyway, it's my turn to go out next. Half the streets in the city are plastered with pictures of your father's face. It won't be long before people start to recognise you."

Lyra nodded thoughtfully in a few moments of silent contemplation.

Her father had been taking more public speaking engagements than ever recently. As a member and magister of the Council of Five, the city's governing body, under the leadership of the High Magister, Maellon Alpheri certainly held the right to address the people in a public forum. He was the most gifted speaker that Lyra had ever heard, even if he was her father. His words carried with them a weight that reminded her of the grand statues that presided over the city's old market squares. But lately, his speeches had grown increasingly critical of the High Magister's decrees. Maellon repeatedly found himself outnumbered within the Council of Five, and even in the grand voting chamber itself, which consisted of hundreds of lesser magisters. His political status ensured that he was entitled to speak openly on such matters, and none dared try to hinder the free speech of any magister. But even now, Lyra could feel a tension forming at the base of her stomach. She had noticed how the mood of the streets had changed in recent months. There was unease and a restlessness in the air, with discontent and bitterness mingling in a noxious brew that was slowly poisoning the city. It couldn't remain this way much longer.

"Father has it under control," she lied to herself.

"Yeah, well, just in case he doesn't, let's have a look at this," replied Katerina, lifting a fragile handful of paper out from within the box, which on closer inspection turned out to be a small, well-worn book. Its pages had turned brown and spotted with age, and its binding consisted of only a few strands of string. Katerina's hands began to shake as she gently lowered it onto the table, finding the cleanest space possible, which was no mean feat.

"Do you know what this is?" she asked, her voice uncharacteristically hushed.

"No. Is it an instruction book of some kind? Like the ones before?"

Katerina smiled, her hands shaking as she gently opened the first page.

"My dear Lyra, this is a memory codex. I can't believe it, I've only ever seen a couple of them in Virgil's study. Not that he lets me read any of them, of course. To have one of my own to study – there's so much that we could do with this."

Lyra leaned in closer and saw the fine ink script that was scrawled across the aged pages. It was unlike any ink that she had ever seen. It was blue for one, and shone with an intense light that made it hard to look at for longer than a few moments.

"So, what exactly is a memory codex?"

Lyra turned her eyes away from the pages, and wiped them as they recovered from staring into the bright light.

"It is knowledge, Lyra. Knowledge from the old times. Magic, and old magic at that, written by master artificers many centuries ago. I will need to acquire some cypher glasses to read it properly – not that those will be easy to find, but I can begin making some discreet enquiries," answered Katerina, the excitement in her voice palpable.

"Maybe you should tell Virgil about this one. If it's that old, it could be trouble," said Lyra with uncharacteristic caution. Both women had "rescued" a number of magical items from the city's underworld over the last year. They had found a whole plaza of thugs brawling over a sliver of magical parchment, and they had even sneaked their way through several turf wars to locate small ingots of precious metals imbued with ancient power. Katerina had experimented on the small pieces that they had recovered, and was slowly forming them into projects that she might one day present to Virgil, and hopefully use to set up her own forge.

Katerina looked over to her friend, hearing the unusual note of trepidation in her voice. Lyra was gazing at the eerie blue light which emitted from the ancient script, as it danced across Katerina's spectacles.

"No need to trouble Virgil with this one, Ly. He saw the box. If he was worried, he would have taken it off us. Besides, look at it! Who knows what we could do with this? Who we could help with this!?"

Lyra looked over to the magical script and shuddered inside. The two of them had indeed encountered the power of the old world many times before now. However, as she looked at the book containing who knows how much ancient lore, she began to wonder where a power that had lain dormant for so long could lead them.

"I don't know, Kat, this time – it just doesn't feel right."

Katerina smiled her easy smile, which had always contained more than a hint of mischief.

"I've never known you to be superstitious, Ly?"

"Kat, you said yourself, even Virgil doesn't let you touch his memory codices." Lyra paused. "Did you know that it was Karrick's guild that were after this?" she asked, staring intently at her friend.

Katerina's smile slowly faded, and her eyes dropped to the floor.

"There might have been some rumours concerning that, yes."

"Thanks for the warning," replied Lyra, in a heavier tone than before.

Katerina took a few steps forward, and placed both of her hands firmly upon her friend's shoulders, looking her straight in the eye.

"You are Lyra Alpheri. The daughter of the famed Maellon Alpheri. You're the second-finest swordswoman in the city after my good self, naturally," spoke Katerina, as her signature taunting grin returned.

"Except for the old man himself, no one shoots better than you. No one can talk themselves out of a bind like you can, and more importantly – no one is a more loyal friend. I knew that you could handle yourself, and you have brought both of us a tool – a weapon like no other."

Katerina pointed back over to the box and the thin sliver of metal that rested underneath the aged book.

"If that metal is what I think it is – with this codex, I can fashion us such artefacts that no gang would dare come within a mile of us." Katerina spoke with a passion that Lyra had only heard a few times since their first meeting. She did not plead and she certainly did not beg, but one of the many gifts that Katerina did possess was the ability to compel. Her passion and her energy washed over the waning defences of Lyra's doubts like a great, unstoppable tide.

Lyra sighed, casting her eyes slowly between friend and ancient tome.

"You know what's going on out there, Ly. The injustice, the poverty, the hunger. Scum like Karrick's band of thugs preying on the lost and the desperate. The wharf companies paying children with scraps of meat to clean their vile machines."

Katerina's grip became tighter and Lyra saw within her friend's eyes the haunted echoes of her past.

"We can stop it! Me and you, Ly – against the whole damn lot of them. Your father can fight them in the light of day in the forum, and we can bring them judgement at the dead of night, on the same streets in which they abandon the poor to starvation and death. We will bring them pause, and they will think twice before abusing the people of this city ever again."

Katerina's eyes had narrowed, and her voice was strained under the weight of memories of which even Lyra was not fully aware.

"What do you say, Ly? You and me together. There's nothing that we can't do!"

If Lyra was being completely honest, that was exactly what she was afraid of.

She thought back to the dank tavern in which she had been playing cards only a few hours previously. It had hardly gone to plan, and she had, more than once, come close to using the lethal shot of Virgil's pistol on one of the men that had so willingly invited her into their trap. She had trusted that Stel had survived the leg wound, as men like that always seemed to have a way of clinging onto life. However, she could not be sure that he hadn't simply bled out onto the floorboards, in the same place in which he had most likely brought suffering to so many others.

In her heart, she knew that she was only one wrong move away from needing to fire that killing shot. Every time she walked the streets in the hope of acquiring another prize, she risked not only her life, but also the lives of everyone that she came into contact with. There were only so many times that she was going to be able to roll the dice before she had to make the call. She knew that, but had yet to come to terms with it.

Katerina had no such quibbles. The streets were a dark place, and sometimes the light needed the cover of darkness before it could make its move.

Maybe Kat was right.

"All right Kat, all right. Let's do it. But on one condition!"

A grin sat happily upon Katerina's face.

"Why, anything for the good Lady Alpheri," she taunted.

Lyra rolled her eyes.

"At the first sign of trouble, you show the book to Virgil. Do we have an understanding?" asked Lyra, in the most authoritative voice that she could muster.

"You have my word, Ly," replied Katerina, embracing her friend in a tight hug.

"Any time, Kat. They won't know what's hit them."

Katerina nodded, swiftly wiping the corners of her eyes before moving back over to the work table.

"Right, let's get this lot packed away. I'm ready for some wine. You in?"

Lyra shook her head as she helped pack some of the tools away.

"Afraid not, I've got training in the morning and I'd better not be late. Castel isn't exactly the forgiving sort."

At this, Katerina chuckled.

"Well, do send him my love, and remember, if he bruises you, you hit him right back. I don't care how many wars he's fought in, you can match him with a blade."

"Yeah well, we'll see. Want me to shut off the forge controls?"

Katerina scowled playfully, as she moved over to the dying forge fire.

"I think not, Ly, we're still finding debris from the last time you tried to help."

The two laughed before they heard the swiftly rising voice of a rather angry Virgil.

"Lyra! Why is there blood on my gun?!"

2

Friend & Foe

"**S**tand up!"

Lyra's stomach tensed and burned, and she spluttered helplessly as she tried to speak, wheezing desperately for the breath that had just been forced from her lungs.

"I don't want to hear your complaints, because frankly, I couldn't care less. Now stand up!"

She began to raise her arms, slowly adjusting her weight onto her hands and wrists as she pushed her upper body from the ground.

"Despite my ravishing good looks, Alpheri, I can't actually wait around for another forty years. So get on your feet! Now!"

Lyra felt the rasping air of her own breath tear across her lips, as she placed more weight upon her struggling arms. But no sooner had she done so, than her elbows began to shake, the strain of fatigue ran across her shoulders, and she collapsed once more to the ground.

However, as she fell down for what must have been the third or fourth time, no angry shout or harsh rebuke followed her failure. The training ground sat silent and still, disturbed only by the noise of the streets beyond and the laboured draws of her breath.

Until, without the sting of harsh and bitter command, Castel's voice rolled smoothly and calmly through the air.

"Lyra, make a decision."

Lyra wiped the sweat from her face with her sleeve. She looked up at the man who had only this morning run the same miles that she had run, lifted the same weights that she could only just bear to hold, and fought the same number of practice bouts as her. Nonetheless, Castel stood in a manner as unshakable as the grand house of the Alpheri family that dominated the ground behind him. Sweat stained his brow, and the dirt of the training ground marred the otherwise immaculate surface of his boots. Yet he looked back at her with eyes alive with the kind of focus and determination that only came through many years of training.

"The choice is yours, Alpheri. You could stand up if you really wanted to. You could pick up your weapon if you really wanted to. You could fight if you really wanted to!"

Lyra's boots scraped along the ground as once more she tried to stand, but the unrelenting pain still burned across her stomach and she fell back into the dirt.

She had parried his strikes with the blunted steel of her training blade as fast as she could. She had even landed a solid blow on his shoulder, as she sidestepped one of his attacks. However, as the two had recommenced their starting positions, Lyra had found herself pushed to the brink, forced to parry again and again until her footwork began to fall apart. As she raised her blade to fend off the fall of Castel's sword across her chest, she had forgotten to maintain her guard position, leaving her abdomen exposed. Even as she heard the clash of their steel, Lyra had crumpled under Castel's savage strike to her stomach, with a sudden blow from his fist.

"The only thing stopping you is yourself! You're tired, so you don't keep your feet moving like I told you to. You're distracted, and so you don't hold your sword properly. And now, you're hurt, so you're lying in the dirt. Stop fighting the pain, Lyra! Embrace it! Hold it! And get on your damn feet!"

Lyra looked up at Castel, the captain of the Alpheri family guard, and, for the last few years, her very own weapons' instructor.

After years of watching Castel train his men and women into the fiercest protection unit in the city, well, at least in Castel's opinion, Lyra had finally plucked up the courage to ask him to train her. There were all manner of duelling instructors throughout the city that attended to the offspring of the noble families. Many of them were highly skilled, leading their young charges forward to win all manner of shooting prizes and duels, committed to the defence of some thinly-veiled veneer of honour. Lyra had little passion for either of these pursuits, and after spending years listening to Katerina talk about the fighting that occurred in the streets, especially in the ever-treacherous Water District, she had decided to be trained by someone who had fought in an actual battle.

Castel continued on in his taunts and rebukes, and Lyra could feel the fire welling up in her chest, being stoked by the pain that now echoed across her body. Her hands tensed, her eyes narrowed and she offered Castel a rare snarl of aggression, as she met his stare.

He grinned in return, kicking her neglected sword over to her with a tap of his boot.

"Alpheri, if you want, I can call one of your father's servants over here to pick you up, set you up in a comfy chair, feed you fruit from a silver plate. You like that sort of thing, don't you?"

Lyra's hands curled into fists. She beat them into the dirt, as her arms tensed and her shoulders strained to lift her body.

A mocking smirk crossed Castel's face as he leaned down and pressed every button he could see written in the frustration of his young student's face.

"That must be what you want! Because you clearly don't want to be here! Stop using the pain as an excuse and get some fire in your belly, get some grit, and stand! That's unless you want to find some nice young man to fight your battles for you? Yeah, no need to put up with this pain, just find some fella or a servant to do it for you. You can stay comfy at home, spend your time keeping the furniture in order. How's that sound?"

Lyra felt her lips curl in anger, as the bruised skin of her knuckles dug deeper grooves into the dirt. She grunted in frustration as she slowly rose to her knees, looking over to the sword lying at her feet.

"Make a decision! Let the pain keep you in the dirt, or use it to rise to your feet!"

Lyra grabbed her sword and desperately lifted herself to her knees, biting her lip as she tensed her thighs in a strained effort to stand.

The fire of her eyes held Castel in view, drawing his mocking grin into the fore.

"You know, I can see it now. Lady Lyra Alpheri! A dutiful wife and mother, mindful of her duty to birth a son and adore her husband. Keeping the house clean and the servants in order, which you'll have to, what with all the dinner parties you'll be hosting."

The knuckles on Lyra's sword hand grew white, and she rose unsteadily to her feet.

"This is just my opinion, but corsets don't look mighty comfortable. But with all those rich, noble folk to fawn over I guess you won't have too much time to dwell on it. Tell me, Alpheri, how many curtsies can you do a minute? At least, the ones that you can fit in between lovingly hanging off some powdered boy's arm?" asked Castel, easing into the guard position, slowly shifting his weight onto his back foot as he watched Lyra approach.

"I imagine he's the sort of fella that likes his women quiet. Not that that will be hard for you. Nose stuck in a book all the time. Wouldn't daddy be proud of his mute princess?"

The pain took hold of her. It coursed through her veins and numbed the dull ache of her lungs. It gave movement to her legs and strength to her arms. She saw Castel, the stupid grin on his face and the mocking light of his eyes, and that was all.

Lyra roared, raising her sword high and striking savagely at Castel's shoulders. At first, he parried her blows with ease, but as Lyra continued to push forward with a new and unseen ferocity, Castel soon found himself at the edge of the practice ring. He quickly spun on his heels, blocking another strike to his chest with a sharp clash of steel. But, as he did so, Lyra swung the full force of her arm into the guard captain's jaw. Castel staggered back, dazed from the unexpected blow. Yet even then, he managed to block Lyra's attacks, one after another. However, with each passing blow he grew slower, shaken by yet another assault on his face.

The two locked blades and Castel leaned forward, using his greater weight and strength to push Lyra away. She stumbled backwards.

The war veteran wiped a thin trickle of blood from the corner of his mouth.

"What's wrong, Alpheri?"

He grinned.

"Something I said?"

No roar now rose from Lyra's mouth, but her blood pumped in a rising tide of rage, all the same, as she charged once again.

She hated the way that Castel spoke her family name. For many in the masked city, the name Alpheri was one to be respected and honoured. It was an old name, adorned with the weight of a noble and prestigious heritage. For most of her life, whenever Lyra walked into a room, she was not received as Lyra the passionate swordswoman, Lyra the eager reader and writer, or even as Lyra, a young woman of some potential. No, she was always Lady Alpheri, daughter of the great poet and orator Maellon Alpheri, and sole heir to the legacy of a great and aged family name. To all that met her, Lyra was but a name and a legacy, predestined in all that she did to pursue what was honourable and dignified with no question of failure. Such was the power of the name that overshadowed her.

She was of the nobility, and as such, expected to seek such ends as would best support the standing of her class and the great city of Abys-Luthil.

This certainly did not include regular brawling matches with a mere guard captain in the dirt, but that was precisely why she loved it. She fought because she liked it, because she was good at it, and most importantly, because she chose to.

Whilst Lyra had never much relished the thought of injuring others, with a few notable exceptions, she had found that there was something brutally honest in the violence and dangers of both practice ground and alleyway, that no noble pageantry could ever hope to rival.

The real world was fear, hunger and desperation. She would bring it what comfort it was in her power to give; she would no longer live in fantasy. Castel used her name against her as a weapon, a provocation. But she would overpower his mockery.

She would overcome her name.

Steel hammered against steel, and Castel was responding with his more restrained and measured attacks, poking at Lyra's weak spots, as her anger surged forth and her swings became all the wilder. Suddenly the guard captain lowered his blade, and Lyra saw a clear chance to strike. Castel's trap drew her swiftly forwards.

Lyra lunged. Castel flicked his sword hand, striking her steel and effortlessly knocking her blade away. Then without warning, he dived forwards, wrapping his arms around Lyra's waist and spear-tackling her to the ground. Lyra felt her back slam into the earth, and a flurry of dirt suddenly flew into the air around her. Her breath was torn from her chest, as the anger in her heart died, and for a few moments, all her thoughts centred on the desperate need to breathe.

Lyra felt the blunted edge of Castel's blade rest against her throat.

"Anger is useful, Lyra, no doubt. But if you let it rule you, it will get you killed."

He rose to his feet, wiping away the streaks of blood that splattered his cheeks with one hand, and offering her a hand up with the other.

"Yeah, I'll bear that in mind, next time," she muttered, wincing as her stomach muscles objected to the sudden movement.

Castel raised an eyebrow as he handed her a water canteen.

"This can stop any time you want, Alpheri. You can tap out whenever you like," said the old soldier, taking a large swig of his own canteen.

Lyra's dirt-stained brow furrowed, and she eagerly drank the deliciously cool water, before pouring the small remainder over her face.

She noted the fatigue evident on Castel's face, and the laboured breaths which shook his words, even as he spoke. Sweat poured down his cheeks, and his posture was less steady than usual, his knees bent and his back not entirely straight.

She had really pushed him this time. He had bested her, of that there was no question. But she had never seen him quite this fatigued before, and neither had she been able to strike him so many times in the practice ring.

"Stop? What, are you getting tired, old man?"

Castel grinned, returning the sparring blades to their weapon racks.

"Careful girl, this old man can still knock you onto the dirt with one hand tied behind his back," he replied, pulling off his training armour with a grunt of pain, as Lyra followed suit.

"Don't worry, Lyra, that's what he says to all the girls."

Lyra removed the final strap fastening the boiled leather armour to her shoulder and looked over to see the approach of Alina Jarro, Castel's lieutenant and the second in command of the Alpheri family guard.

"Oh yeah, like you'd know," replied Castel, splashing his face with water from a nearby basin.

"Never had the pleasure myself, but one hears stories. I'm told that the barmaid from The Stallion still hasn't recovered," said Alina with a wink to Lyra.

"All I did was offer her a drink," answered Castel, turning to face Alina, hands on his hips.

Alina readjusted the large rifle that rested on her shoulder, and the noonday sun glinted off the polished steel of the twin pistols hanging off her belt. She gave her captain a mock glance from head to toe.

"After that offer she probably needed one. Poor young thing." Alina pretended to squint as her eyes traced the fine series of scars that marked Castel's face. "I know taverns are dark, but damn, they ain't that dim. I hear that the sorry lass nearly fainted, laying eyes on a colourful face such as yours."

Castel smiled, nodding his head as he gave his lieutenant the dirtiest look that he could muster. Which coming from Castel, was on par with the local sewer.

"Oh yeah? So, how's your latest lad doing? Aaron was it? Or, am I thinking of Aiden?" Castel took a few steps forward. "Bit hard to remember, what with there being so many of them. How do you remember all of their names? Or do you have them on a rota? At this rate I'm guessing it's going to have to be updated weekly? Daily?"

Alina spat on the ground and flexed her hands as she took a few steps forward, her face now mere inches from Castel's.

"It's honestly like looking at a map. One of those distant, foreign ones, covered in mountains and caverns. You could hide a small village in that one," she muttered, gesturing up to an old rapier scar on his forehead.

"Where do you find them all, Alina? Is there a centre you pick 'em up from? You know they're not like horses, right? You don't get paid for breaking them in," replied Castel, leaning his head forward and rolling his shoulders.

Lyra's face turned bright red and she took a few steps back from the duo. Alina cocked her head to one side.

"I'm surprised they let old men into The Stallion anymore. Gets awful crowded and noisy in there. With all that business and confusion, we wouldn't want someone mistaking your ugly mug for an old wineskin now, would we?"

Castel's nostrils flared.

"I ain't as well used as some are, lass. The rate you're going, you should start charging. You'd be able to buy your own tavern before the week's out."

Lyra took a few more steps backwards out of sheer awkwardness, as the air grew dangerously silent.

Hands clenched and eyes locked, and the guard officers stood their ground, tensing their muscles and shifting their weight onto their heels.

For a moment, silence invaded every part of the training ground, appearing to rout even the noise of the street beyond the Alpheri estate's walls.

Suddenly the snarl that had begun to form upon Alina's lips broadened into a hearty smile, as she laughed, punching Castel on the shoulder.

The guard captain broke only a moment later, laughing loudly and embracing his colleague in a firm bear hug.

"It's good to see you back," said Castel happily.

"A pleasure as always, Cap."

On seeing this, Lyra slowly exhaled and relaxed.

She had spent enough time around the pair to know how close they were and how dearly they actually cared for each other. But that didn't mean that

42

she had learnt to endure what she thought was rather savage banter any better. She feared that she never would understand their sense of humour.

Maybe it was a combat thing?

Both Castel and Alina were the only members of the family guard to have served and fought in the city's last war. As a consequence, their bond was special, unique, baffling, and often downright terrifying.

Alina patted her fellow soldier on the back and her gaze shifted over to the young noblewoman.

"Don't take anything this one says too seriously. He's getting even odder in his old age."

Castel followed her gaze and offered Lyra a mock bow.

"Not so odd that I don't remember how to treat nobility. Apologies for the language, m'lady," said Castel with an exaggerated wave of his arm.

Lyra rolled her eyes.

Alina grabbed her captain's shoulder and pulled him up, causing him to grunt in protest.

"So how's our girl doing?" she asked, looking straight at Lyra with a gentle smile.

The mocking grin slowly faded from Castel's face, his back straightened, arms crossed and he simply offered a gentle nod.

"Better, she's still got to train some more on her footwork. But, dare I say it, we might have a half-decent soldier on our hands." These final few words came with a respectful bow of Castel's head and gave Lyra's heart a warm glow of pride. The only people she had ever heard the grizzled war veteran openly compliment were Alina and Virgil, and he had never done so in their presence.

"Good to hear. If she's to take on half the city's guilds with young Kat, she'll need all the training that she can get."

Lyra felt her face turn a shade redder.

"I didn't think you knew–" she began, before the two guards turned to one another and once again burst out laughing.

"My dear Lyra, we happen to be patrons of enough fine drinking establish-ments in this city to hear about what you two have been up to. Don't think that we don't recognise the tales of the young women in the decorated green masks sweeping ruffians from the streets," replied Alina with a knowing look.

"And then there's Virgil," muttered Castel.

"Oh yeah, him. You know, I never would have guessed that he could be so sentimental. Keeping us up all hours on watch, talking about how worried he is about you. He might act tough, but the man's soft as toffee on the inside, at least when it comes to you two," said Alina.

"Virgil, really?" asked Lyra with genuine curiosity.

"Oh please, like you didn't know!" Alina chided.

"Well, he was pretty angry the last time I saw him."

Castel let out a heavy sigh.

"Yes, exactly! I thought you noble lot were supposed to be smart? Look, Katerina's practically his daughter, and you're pretty much the same, all told. You know those trinkets of his aren't cheap, right? He doesn't let you run off with them into the night on a whim! The man's terrified something might happen to you, and he knows he can't stop you. So he keeps you safe as best he can, by giving you the best equipment," said Castel, glancing over to the immaculately polished rifle that Alina had swung over her shoulder.

Lyra followed his gaze, observing the beautiful weapon. It was a remarkably designed artifice. Rare and powerful items such as these could only be fashioned and designed by a select few. These artificers of great skill and renown were specially licensed by the office of the City Arms Registry to develop weapons, armour and other articles of power for the noble houses of the city.

The Alpheri family guard held only six artifices, two of which lay in the hands of Alina.

Alina smiled as she saw their covetous eyes resting on the shinning barrel of her weapon.

"Virgil does indeed make the very best," she said.

Suddenly, in a frantic blur of motion, the rifle was brought to rest in Alina's hands, and she placed the butt of the gun against her shoulder. She levelled her weapon against a row of straw targets standing at the other end of the training ground and fired.

Smoke erupted from its barrel and the firing pan of her rifle, casting a thick smog of black powder across the space around her. Yet even with her vision obscured, Lyra clearly saw a spark of blue light mark the flight path of Alina's bullet. Her eyes desperately followed the intense magical light, but failed to keep pace. As the moment passed, Lyra spun her head to see not one, but three swaying straw targets with large holes torn through their quivering frames.

For a few seconds Lyra looked on. Fine traces of white flame were dancing across the straw.

Castel gave Alina a respectful nod, before looking back over to the targets.

"Not bad, not bad. Would have thought you'd get four, but I guess three is all right," he said with a grin.

"Still quicker than most, old man."

"Yeah, well most ain't everyone, my dear."

"Oh, is that so?" spat Alina, eyebrows raised.

Without warning, Alina grabbed a leather training helmet from a nearby table and threw it with all her might at Castel.

The guard captain, smiling his weathered smile, reached for the hilt of the trusty steel blade at his belt.

To Lyra's eyes, time itself seemed to slow its pace; but even in those drawn out moments in which the helmet arched towards Castel, a flash of radiant light crossed her view, and in what seemed no more than the blinking of an eye, the helmet was cleaved in two.

Alina winked at Lyra.

"There's life in the old dog yet."

A faint magical light danced through the air, and Castel returned the blade to its scabbard with a flourish.

"Show-off," chided Alina.

"The word you're looking for is masterful."

Lyra looked down at the sword hilt, which even now appeared to be glowing slightly.

How long would it be until Kat could forge something like that?

A new knot of discomfort formed in her stomach, and this time, it was not from sword practice.

As Alina and Castel resumed their banter, a new figure made his way across the training ground. He cast a nervous eye over to the laughing guard officers before turning to Lyra and bowing.

"Lady Lyra, Lord Alpheri requests your presence in the house, in preparation for your journey to Magister's Square," spoke the youth, with no small degree of nerves.

Castel's laughter ground to a swift halt and a grimace crossed his face. His hulking frame loomed over the messenger.

"Lord Maellon's address is not scheduled until this afternoon. He has a number of other engagements before then - I've seen to the security details myself," growled Castel.

The young man, dressed in the dark green typical of a servant of the Alpheri household, took a few steps back, desperately attempting to avoid eye contact with the guard captain.

"Yes sir, but the public forum has been called forwards."

"Called forwards? On whose authority!?"

"The High Magister, sir," answered the quivering shadow of green.

Silence took the scene, as Castel grunted, before sharing a troubled glance with Alina.

Lyra took a step forwards, gently placing a hand upon the young man's shoulders.

"Tom, you don't have to call me lady when my father isn't around – Lyra is just fine" she smiled, gently squeezing his shoulder.

"And you certainly don't need to call this one sir," she said softly, looking over to Castel, who still dwarfed the young servant.

Tom smiled back, finding some comfort in Lyra's kindness, despite the towering threat.

"Return to the house and inform Lord Maellon that his daughter will be with him after her bath, which I want prepared for her before we reach the house. Do I make myself clear?" rumbled Castel.

Tom's smile vanished. He nodded, bowed to Lyra and mutely withdrew, back to the safety of the house.

For a few moments the trio watched him go, allowing the weight of what they had just heard to settle in their minds.

"Lyra..." Castel began.

"You don't have to be so mean to him, you know. He means well, and he works pretty hard–."

"Lyra..."

She turned to face the two guards and her heart sank, as she looked into their eyes, each in turn.

There was going to be no escaping this.

"It's bad, isn't it?"

Alina stepped forwards, nodding slowly.

"For the High Magister to interfere in a public forum? It's not good, Lyra." Alina turned to her captain. "He would not have dared do so, even a year ago."

Castel nodded, looking at nothing in particular.

"No, no, he would not."

Lyra took a few steps towards her family's guards.

"I know my father. He's still going to continue this campaign. He won't back down, not when he thinks there are innocent lives at stake."

Castel smiled, a rare, gentle smile.

"Most like, my lady, you're right. But we'll be standing beside him, all the same." He turned to Alina. "Given the state of the city, the Vox Militant will be present at the forum in force."

Alina shrugged. "Not a problem, as long as they remember whose side they're on."

The guard lieutenant's concern did nothing to sate Lyra's fears.

It was the duty of the Vox Militant to provide security at the Magisters' Chambers, protect public forums, and investigate serious crimes, as well as to keep an ever-watchful eye on the city guilds. But above all else, the Vox Militant enabled the people to freely express their views and question their leaders in open forum. Even the High Magister could not command them to do otherwise. However, as High Magister, Nihilo continued to interfere in more and more public addresses. He was beginning to find himself at odds with the Vox Militant. Some rumoured that this ancient order planned to unseat the High Magister, whilst others speculated that they would soon join him in overthrowing the Chamber of Magisters and proclaim him emperor. Amidst the rumours and the lies, all anyone could know for sure was that this tension could not hold for much longer.

Something, or someone, had to break.

Castel placed his hand instinctively upon his sword, running his fingers along the familiar pattern of its hand-guard.

"Get the troops together, I want them ready in twenty minutes. And double the guard on the house before we leave. I don't want to come home to any surprises."

Alina hurried to her task without a moment's pause, as Castel guided Lyra back to the house.

"As for you, young Alpheri, let's get you ready to face the city."

3

The Vox Militant

Sergeant Aequo winced.

He was no stranger to the scene unfolding before him. He had even been party to it, more than a few times. During his many years of soldiering, policing, and protection of the city, he had hammered hundreds of new recruits into shape.

However, there were still those rare moments in which even the tired ghosts that haunted his memory, clothed in blood, gunpowder and tortured limb, could not stop him from averting his gaze, as the senior officer of the Vox Militant began to shout.

"Why, Private Lumnus, am I once again finding dirt on your bayonet? Eh? Is it that you're leaving it in the mud, Private? Because if that's so, I promise you that that's exactly where you'll be sleeping once I boot you out of here!"

The young man recoiled from the officer's rage, looking desperately over to the familiar face of Sergeant Aequo.

"Don't look over at me, boy! Face the captain and answer the question!"

Aequo's voice was iron, his glare a roaring fire, and yet he felt his heart melt a little, as the young man stared hopelessly back towards the unyielding glare of Captain Rillo.

"I cleaned it yesterday, Sir, but I guess- "

Captain Rillo's eyes narrowed.

"You guess!? Sergeant, are soldiers of the Vox Militant trained to guess?"

"No, Sir."

"What are they trained to do?"

"To be the best, Sir. Ready to face any threat, at any time."

Aequo watched the nervous Lumnus recoil as the captain looked back at him.

"Any threat, at any time!" Rillo shouted, waving the bayonet back and forth.

"Sorry, Sir. I'll be sure-"

"Not sorry enough, Private! For the next week, your kit will be inspected at every morning muster and every evening parade! And so help me, Lumnus, if I find so much as a single speck of dirt on any of your gear, I'll have you doing solo patrols of the Water District for a month." Rillo leaned forward. "If you make it that long."

Private Lumnus stood mute, holding onto his rifle for dear life, and not daring to meet the officer's gaze.

He could hear the sharp intake of the captain's breath, but before another rebuke was uttered, his sergeant took a step forward.

"Head back to the barracks, Private, and get your sorry excuse for kit clean, now!" Rillo scowled, placing a hand up, as Lumnus began his eager escape.

"One moment, Sergeant. I have one more question for our new recruit."

Aequo said nothing, simply giving his superior a knowing look. He could not yet bring himself to openly contradict Rillo in front of another soldier, especially not in times such as these. But he sensed that there was more turning the wheels of his old friend's mind, than a simple kit infraction.

"You've already failed one practical test, Lumnus. So let's try something a little different. What are the three duties of a soldier of the Vox Militant?"

Lumnus closed his eyes for a moment and stuttered as he spoke, eager to avoid yet another torrent of threats.

"Uh, to defend the great city of Abys-Luthil, protect the Magisters' Chamber Rooms, and to keep the voice of the people free," he replied, as confidently as he could.

This time, Sergeant Aequo openly sighed, rubbing the corner of his eyes with calloused fingers. He felt bad for the lad, but he really wasn't helping himself.

He watched as a familiar twitch crossed the captain's right eye, and the scene grew unbearably silent. Rillo took another step forwards, leaning in uncomfortably close to Lumnus' face.

"Oh Lumnus, my lad. You've got the three duties right and no mistake, but..."

It was a speech that Aequo had heard countless times before, but that made it no less uncomfortable to hear, and the pregnant pause that now hung in the air seemed to wrack Lumnus more than any amount of shouting.

"I'm going to put those duties in the right order for you now, lad. Best that you listen close, because if I hear you get them wrong again, I'll string you up above the gatehouse myself and leave you up there until there's nought left but rags and bone," Rillo hissed.

The soldier said nothing in response, devoting all of his remaining energy to resisting the shaking sensation that now gripped his arms and legs.

The fiery glare of Rillo's eyes dampened and a look of steely determination crossed his face. His words were slow, measured and landed in Lumnus' ears with all the threat of a falling anvil.

"The first duty of every soldier of the Vox Militant is to protect the voice of the people, above all things. No standing army is allowed within Abys-Luthil, and every prancing noble man and woman in this city has a family guard with artifice weaponry. This is especially true of the magisters."

The anger had now been drained from the captain's voice, but his words lost none of their weight and his tone brooked no moment for levity.

"Our order was formed in the ashes of the tyranny of the last empire. A time when kings and queens enslaved the people to toil to death in their workhouses and slaughtered them by the thousands in their petty wars. We guard the Magisters' Chambers, yes. But only so that those elected by the people may air the grievances of those on whose behalf they serve."

Aequo looked around the stone courtyard in which they stood, centred right in the heart of the Vox Militant's headquarters. He watched as soldiers went about their daily business and stable hands tended to their horses, noting that none of them were within earshot. He knew that this should not concern him and that everything Rillo was saying was written in the very ink of Abys-Luthil's constitution.

It was not sedition, it was, in fact, the very letter of the law.

And yet, as his officer spoke these words, it made him nervous. The city was not what it once had been. It had always been an uneasy union of two different empires, both now lost to the pages of those books that ever since Aequo had been offered the chance to read, in his late teens, he had relished in reading.

The ancient city of Abyssus had once ruled the waves as a mighty naval empire. It had grown rich in the trading of spices, exotic ships and crates full of coloured silks, adorned with pearls and rings of gold. Nations beyond count had fallen in the wake of its great fleet of ships, and numerous trading posts had been established across the known world. Before long, the city of Abyssus was awash with music and foods from cultures hitherto unseen, even as the very air itself was scented with foreign spices. But as trade brought life and colour to the city, built half on land and half along lavish decks and waterways spiralling out into the sea, it also brought ruin.

With trade came money, however, as those eager for gold filled the narrow alleys and waterways of a city that had once declared itself the very envy of the sea, disease ran black cords of death through the streets. Houses, built upon great platforms that rose out of the very waters themselves, filled with workers so desperate for a share of the wealth that green-eyed landlords crammed room after room to capacity. These buildings then crumbled into ruin, choked with the bodies of those who had succumbed. War had soon followed, and conflict wracked Abyssus from without as well as from within. In one particularly disastrous assault upon its shores, arcs of fire had come sailing through the sky, launched high from enemy ships. A maelstrom of flame and smoke had swept through the city, scorching its grand buildings and laying waste to its once-thriving market squares. Whole districts had been choked in ash, and noble houses fell tumbling into the sea, their fires only quenched by vengeful, raging torrents, as the waters fed hungrily on the fiery ruin of Abyssus' pride.

And yet, with its colours muted and the navy a shadow of its former self, Abyssus endured. That is, however, until the arrival of the mysterious Empire of Luthanril.

The people of Luthanril had long watched Abyssus with envious but cautious eyes. Yet when their own home fell to ruin amidst a mysterious calamity, and the fires of Abyssus had faded, the Luthan people impatiently came forward to conquer it.

This was a people of magic, who had been masters over other nations back in their homeland, far to the north. The empire that the Luthan people would build, with newly-titled Abys-Luthil as its capital, would not reach the size of that of Abyssus, but in grandeur, none would surpass it. The new cultural structures of Luthan design rose high on the city's skyline. Grand colonnades of pale stone, crowned with carvings of statues of Luthan heroes, were built on the land from which the Abyssus waterways ran out into the sea. Great libraries were constructed across the city, and both the people of Luthanril and Abys were encouraged to further their learning.

The Luthan people ruled not by the power of their navy, but through their skill in the arcane arts. The tread of their armies rang heavily as their constructs of war strode purposely towards their foes, all but invulnerable, their metallic forms marching ever onwards. Great ships of war, powered by a concoction of machines spouting columns of steam and winds of an unnatural source, poured fire and ruin on the enemies of Abys-Luthil from dark guns.

As the power of the Luthans' sorcerers rose, so too did the fortunes of their empire. Yet as the power of magic began to retreat into the corners of the world, the city's rulers resorted to despotism and tyranny. The poor of Abys-Luthil saw a chance for change, and discontent with the rule of a particularly cruel queen soon grew into full-scale rebellion. Thus the new republic of Abys-Luthil was born. The people of the twin city now elected magisters, who ruled with a High Magister at their head. With some foresight, these first magisters feared the resurgence of tyranny, especially in a city where gold was valued over so much else. So they established the order of the Vox Militant, who would not only guard the debating rooms of the Grand Magisters' Chambers, but more crucially, would ensure the freedom of speech and assembly for every citizen of the city. They were a check against the power of the guilds, the merchant houses, and any others who sought to gain influence over the magisters and thus deprive the people of their voice. It was a life and a calling which the members of the order, most of whom were recruited from the poorer districts of the city, especially the waterways of old Abyssus, took very seriously. Especially Captain Rillo.

"We keep the people safe from assaults from the noble houses and the criminal guilds," said Rillo, knowing full well that the young man he was addressing probably had little choice between joining a guild or applying for the Vox Militant. He had passed the rigorous training necessary for becoming a member of the order, but he still had a lot of learning to do.

"We then protect the magisters in their council chambers, so that the voice of the people is not suppressed. By doing so, we keep Abys-Luthil safe from enemies both inside and out."

Private Lumnus nodded, remembering the instructions he had received at the start of his training a few months ago.

Rillo gave Aequo his own knowing look, which was something that the sergeant had seen far too many times before to take any comfort from.

"A quick scenario for you, Private Lumnus - let's see how you do. You're at a public forum, the magisters are spouting whatever they need to say to get re-elected, and the crowd are starting to get a bit restless."

At this, Aequo shot his captain a sharp glance. *Where was he going with this?*

"The magisters mention a new conflict in the far East, and a new war means new taxes. The crowd of exhausted factory workers don't take too kindly to this, and start to get a bit...lively. The overpaid and undertrained guards that these fine-speaking noblemen and women surround themselves with, start to advance on the crowd. You're present at this forum with ten soldiers under your command, Lumnus. What do you do?"

There was a momentary pause. The private gripped tightly upon his rifle, almost drawing upon it as a source of strength.

"Captain, maybe this is not the best place to-", Aequo began.

"Thank you, Sergeant, but the private will answer the question," snapped Rillo, his gaze locked upon the hesitant soldier.

"Come on, Lumnus. You have an angry crowd, and noble guards with artifice weapons advancing on them."

"Sir, this really isn't-"

The captain's glare now fell upon his sergeant, who in turn locked eyes back with his commanding officer without so much as a flinch.

"That's enough, sergeant!"

"Rillo, you can't say this, not out here! If Nihilo and his officials heard of this-" hissed Aequo, leaning forward.

"Enough, Aequo! Private, answer now!"

Lumnus avoided eye contact with either of them, as he offered his best reply, in the desperate hope that he might soon be excused.

"I would muster the Vox Militant to form a line between the forum stage and the crowd, sir, instructing alternating soldiers to face both the magisters and the people, in order to distance both groups. I would not give the order to fix bayonets without some provocation aimed at a soldier of the order from the noble guards, sir," Lumnus barked.

Captain Rillo rolled his shoulders back, looked Lumnus up and down, and began to slowly nod.

"Well, Private Lumnus, it seems that you learned something during your training. Very good."

The cold, hard stare set in again.

"We protect the people, Lumnus, at all costs. If we lose their right to speak, then we defend nothing. Do you understand?" There was no anger in this question; Rillo's voice was low and his tone calm. For the briefest of moments, an almost compassionate expression washed over his face, as he watched the young soldier nod enthusiastically.

"Yes, sir!"

A smile rose to the corners of the captain's lips.

"Good. Now get back to the barracks and clean your kit. I don't want to have this conversation with you again, Private."

Needing no further encouragement, Lumnus marched hastily away. He headed for the barracks, his boots beating a steady pace across the smooth sandstone surface of the parade square.

Rillo's smile faded.

"Sergeant, follow me."

Aequo met his old friend's gaze without so much as a hint of shame or apology, and marched two paces behind him towards the captain's quarters. These were situated across the other side of a canal from the towering dome of marble and glass that was the Grand Magisters' Chambers. Both landmarks sat on the very edge of old Abyssus, overlooking a wide waterway. This were flanked by a great plethora of shops and market stalls which ran beside the canal, filled with the sound of music and eager conversation, each fuelled by the sweet aroma of imported coffee. As the sun rose high in the sky, and the sparkling water lapped across the aged stone, smoothed by the timeless tread of merchants and sailors, it could truly be said that some part of old Abyssus was still alive.

In stark contrast to the colours lavished upon the surrounding scenery, the headquarters of the Vox Militant were built in the style of the Luthan Empire. A towering white stone colonnade formed its entrance, and high walls, marked by statues and dedications to battles long past, ran the length of its exterior. Its colours were muted, but Aequo had nonetheless always believed that it carried an air of authority and dignity in its character. A place of order and structure, in a city in dire need of both.

The two entered the office of the captain of the Vox Militant and Aequo closed the door quietly behind them. Rillo walked past his ink-blotched desk and over to the large glass windows that gave the order's commander a towering view of the bustling Grand Canal. Light flooded the room as the captain placed his officers' cap on his desk. He sighed and rubbed his battle-scared face.

"Damnit, Aequo, I have enough troubles as it is without you adding yet more to the pile."

The sergeant removed his military shako from his head and placed it next to Rillo's cap.

"You know, whatever troubles you bear, I more often than not end up carrying them with you," he answered.

"I know. But the Order is stretched more than ever, and Lumnus was in need of correction. I can't have soldiers out on the streets unsure of what their first duty is."

Aequo slowly nodded his head in agreement.

"That you can't. But you have to be more careful, Rillo, you must choose your words more wisely. If even one magister's servant was to hear that, we could have more trouble on all our heads than we can bear."

At this, the captain offered a bitter laugh.

"I don't fear him, Aequo, and neither do the men and women outside. Whatever Nihilo does, whatever he says, he is the High Magister and we are the Vox Militant. We are a check to his power, and we will do what is necessary."

Rillo turned on his heel, walking over to the table and looking earnestly over to his friend.

Aequo smiled his own grim smile.

"You know I don't give a damn about Nihilo or his veiled threats. The man's a snake and a greedy one at that. But he has friends in the right places, money, and position. We must tread with caution, my friend."

Rillo's hands clenched as his knuckles rested on the leather surface of his desk.

"I won't give in, Aequo. I won't let that man bring ruin to over three hundred years of free speech."

The captain shook his head. He watched as the light glistening from the surface of the water outside danced across his desk.

"No one's talking about giving in. I'm just saying, if you want there to still be a Vox Militant to keep watch on the magisters, then you must watch your words, especially in front of the new recruits. That is my concern."

"Yes, well, your concern is noted. And that's the last time I want you questioning me in front of the others!"

"I meant no disrespect, Rillo."

"The last time. I mean it."

Aequo's posture stiffened as he met his captain's gaze.

"Yes. Sir."

The two words cut across Rillo's ears, as sharp as they were curt.

A slight pause hung in the air, as the officer's eyes scanned the powder burns that marked the sergeant's cheeks. He knew that he himself bore the same scars, received in the same battles, in the same long war. A fleeting host of memories rode across his mind, before he swiftly pushed them back into the shadows.

"Dismissed."

Aequo thought of a response but decided against it. There was nothing more to be said, for now. He grabbed his shako from the desk and quietly made his way over to the door. However, before he reached it, three loud knocks rang out through the aged wood.

"Enter!" snapped Rillo, his tone unchanged.

A familiar face now stood in the doorway. Corporal Griss, his uniform as spotless as ever, met the officer's gaze, whilst noting the obvious tension in the room.

"Sorry to disturb you, sir. The High Magister's chamberlain, a Mr Silo Rees, is waiting in the courtyard and wishes to speak with you."

Rillo looked over to Aequo, who promptly stepped back to stand beside the captain's desk, needing no further instruction.

"Is he, now? Very well, Corporal, send him in."

Griss nodded and departed the room, and an uneasy silence sat between the two men. Aequo could not leave now and neither would Rillo ask him to, this much he knew. He had never once abandoned his friend in the face of an enemy advance, and he certainly was not going to start now, even as he heard the polished boots of the chamberlain make their way slowly down the corridor.

"Captain, a pleasure to see you, as always."

Rees stepped gracefully into the room, dressed in his typical dark suit, high boots, and embroidered silk shirt adorned with unashamedly frilly cuffs. Whenever Aequo laid eyes upon the man and he started droning on, the sergeant liked to imagine Rees trying to survive an hour in the Water District, especially on a few choice streets. He found that it helped dampen the rage that he felt building up inside him whenever the unbearable man uttered a word.

"Master Chamberlain, to what do I owe the pleasure of this sudden visit?" Rillo's tone suggested that this was anything but an honour. In response, the thin man in the austere, classically Luthan suit, simply smiled, almost appearing to feed off the officer's distain.

"Oh, I always enjoy dropping in to see how my fellow public servants are doing, Captain. We must look out for each other, mustn't we?" he replied, casting a cursory eye around the room.

"Indeed," Rillo answered flatly.

Aequo stood mute, his eyes alone attempting to bore a hole into the clerk's face.

"So, how are the fine men and women of the Vox Militant? I saw a number of your guards on patrol outside, or wait, should I rather say officers? Soldiers? I never quite know how to refer to them."

The captain's nostrils flared, as words dropped bitterly from his mouth.

"Soldiers will do fine. But should you ever find yourself...in distress, out in the streets, Master Chamberlain, simply cry for help. I'm sure someone will find you. Maybe my troops will get to you first, maybe not."

"That is indeed a comfort, Captain. Some say that the streets are more dangerous now than ever, for everyone. It's best that we all remain vigilant."

"On that we're agreed. But unlike the City Watch, my soldiers lack the means to properly patrol the city, so low are our numbers. I would be cautious of any further budget cuts imposed by the magisters, if the streets are to remain safe."

Aequo felt his hands tighten, clasped behind his back.

Careful, Rillo.

Silo Rees smiled and slowly eased himself into one of the seats in front of the captain's desk.

"Your concerns have been noted. Of that I want you to be reassured. The High Magister himself has commented on your...pleas."

Rillo did not sit, but rather, stood straight, allowing rays of light from the world outside to cut across his form and rain down across the room.

"I'm glad that Nihilo is keeping up with current events. Has he also noted the large number of Fereli mercenary visitors that we have been receiving?" Rillo leaned forward, his expression as cold as stone. "Now, rumour can be an ugly thing, but it seems to be public knowledge that Nihilo is personally entertaining some of their leaders. A bit awkward, that. Especially given the last war we had with Ferelian."

The chamberlain's eye scanned Rillo from head to toe, as Rees noted the epilates of rank that sat on the captain's shoulders. His mouth adopted an almost feline grin.

"You are correct, Captain."

He leaned forward.

"Rumour is an ugly, ugly thing."

Rillo offered a snort of derision in response, crossing his muscular arms across his chest.

Rees continued. "But I did not come here to waste time as precious as yours with talk of rumour, Captain."

The clerk's unsettlingly blue eyes swung round to face Aequo, before turning back towards the looming figure in front of the window.

"Might we continue this discussion alone for a few minutes?"

This time Rillo offered his own thinly-veiled sneer.

"Men in our profession know that we are never truly alone, Rees. There's always someone listening. Wouldn't you agree?"

The chamberlain sat mute for a few moments, and the grin now spread so far across his cheeks that Rillo could almost swear it would soon touch his ears.

"Very well. I am here to inform you that the Vox Militant is being summoned to appear at a public forum in precisely..." With an exaggerated flick of his wrist he reached into the folds of his jacket and consulted a small, golden pocket watch. "...ah, yes, in precisely one hour, at Magister's Square."

Rillo's arms tensed. He did not reply immediately, but instead looked over to Aequo before staring intently down at the clerk.

"So, Nihilo is moving Lord Alpheri's debate forward. At the last minute, it seems. You know that custom dictates that the Vox Militant are to be informed of the time of any public forum a day before its commencement."

"Yes, custom does indeed, Captain, but sadly the word of the constitution does not. The High Magister retains the authority to adjust the times and locations of forums as needed. He was hoping to observe this one himself, and his afternoon has quickly been filled with affairs of state."

Rillo nodded. "Affairs of state," he repeated slowly.

The grin remained. "I'm glad that you understand."

Suddenly, the chamberlain's face relaxed, and what to Rillo's eyes looked like a fleeting attempt at sympathy crossed his eyes.

"Captain, I want you to know that the High Magister values your service and those of your order. Really, he does. This city owes you a great debt of gratitude for your years of service. And in these times of...change, it would be most unfortunate if the Vox Militant were to misunderstand just how much it is appreciated."

The clerk stopped for a moment as if waiting for a response. None came.

Rees sighed. "The city is restless, Captain. Recent speeches by certain magisters appear to have disturbed the people. Shipments from the docks have been delayed, work in some factories has stopped completely. This cannot be allowed to continue. For the good of the people."

"So, Maellon Alpheri really has got Nihilo worried," growled Rillo.

The briefest flutter of frustration crossed Rees' face. It was there only for a moment, but Aequo saw it.

"Magister Alpheri has the right to say whatever he wants," replied the clerk.

"Yes. He does," snapped Rillo.

"But for the good of the city, we must be united. You know as well as I, Captain, that there are rumours of war in the north, and a disruption of trade to the west. We are approaching dangerous times, and it would greatly reassure the High Magister if he knew that the Vox Militant will stand beside him in the trials to come."

Aequo's eye widened in shock. Silo Rees, a man who wielded words even as Aequo himself fought with his rifle, was close to approaching constitutional treason. The newfound boldness with which the chamberlain now spoke concerned Aequo more than a midnight patrol in old Abys.

Rillo kept his eyes locked on Rees, and made his way around the desk, standing at an uncomfortably close distance.

"Tell Nihilo that the Vox Militant will do whatever is necessary to protect the people of this city."

Rillo took a further step forwards, the open snarl upon his lips almost seeming to meld with the old battle scar that sat upon his right cheek.

"The Vox Militant will guard their right to speak and will safeguard the city from threats from abroad and at home. And Rees, if I find so much as one shred of evidence that a magister, any magister, is recruiting Fereli mercenaries to operate illegally in Abys-Luthil, I will arrest them," uttered Rillo as he leaned down, his nose hovering only a few inches from the clerk's face.

Rees' lips formed a smile that bore a greater threat of blades than the whole of the city's armouries combined. He stood up and began walking back towards the door, before suddenly turning around upon his expensive heels.

"That is your final decision?"

Rillo offered one simple nod.

"I made it a long time ago."

Rees' lips curled further as he appeared to share some private joke with himself.

"You know, Captain, it is a dangerous man, who does not for one moment sit down and consider the possibility of error in his own convictions."

Aequo opened the door of the office to hasten Rees' exit, and Rillo took a seat at his desk.

"Well, how fortunate it is, Master Chamberlain, that you are afforded the right by the constitution of this city to openly and freely offer me correction. The corporal outside will escort you the rest of the way."

Rees stopped in the doorway for a moment, as his eyes darted between the two soldiers.

"Until next time, Captain." With these last words, his elegantly tailored jacket disappeared from view, and the sound of his fine leather boots processed back down along the corridor.

Silence quickly consumed the room. Aequo took a seat beside the desk, staring intently out of the window before him, and watching the gentle lapping of the canal water wash against the cobblestones of the market street. Without warning, the moment was broken. Rillo's fist slammed into his desk, his knuckles striking against its ink-blotched surface in frustration.

A void of silence soon fell upon the room yet again, as the sergeant sat mute, waiting for the words which he knew were soon to be uttered once more by his closest friend.

"What am I going to do, Aequo?" sighed Rillo, running his bruised hand slowly through his hair.

Aequo did not answer straight away. He sat silent, whilst all manner of thoughts, hopes and fears for himself and his friend raced through his mind.

"What do you want to do?" he asked simply, and as he did so, the officer's fist once again stuck the desk, sending pens and drops of ink flying from its surface.

"What do I want to do!? I want to march across that bridge outside, right up to the High Magister's chambers, and arrest him, Rees, half of the Council and more than a few city guard officers on charges of high treason! Then I want Nihilo hung in a cage across the steps of the Noctus Bridge, as a warning of what this city does to tyrants!" Rillo raged, stamping across the room.

"And as for Rees, that silk-swaddled, serpent-tongued worm! I'll make it so that he can never talk his way out of anything ever again! Let's see how fine he can talk when his mouth's filled with molten gold, or fire-beetles, or even–"

"Ok, ok. I get the picture," interrupted Aequo.

"The picture!?" spat Rillo, turning back towards his sergeant. "The picture we're facing, Aequo, is not so finely framed as I would like. I have to keep watch on the growing power of the corruption of the High Magister and his Council, with less than eight hundred troops at my disposal, in full knowledge that there are well over double the number of mercenaries in the city. Most of whom are in Nihilo's pocket!"

Rillo went to strike the table again but fought against the urge. Instead, his hands once again curled into fists, and he blustered over to the window.

"And that's without dealing with the city guard. When they're not drunk, they're escorting the would-be emperor around the city, like he's some damned folk hero. All because their officers can be bought with a handful of pathetic titles, and most of their men are sated with a pint of rum. Useless bunch of ingrates!"

The complexion of Rillo's face now resembled the bright shade of red that marked almost every roofing tile adorning the buildings of old Abys. Most of the Water District was composed of a series of brightly-tiled squares, and each building practically sat upon its neighbour, connected by a series of bridges and canal networks. These waterways bustled and shifted with a steady stream of trade, in much the same way that a large vein was now angrily throbbing upon the captain's forehead.

Aequo remained silent, content to watch Rillo as he paced the room. Soon enough, the officer's voice tempered, his pace slowed, and he was once again in his seat, his head clasped between both hands. A few moments passed and Rillo sighed once more, leaning back in his chair with a satisfying creak of wood. His eyes finally rose above his fingertips.

"He's going to make a grab for power, Aequo. He's going to do it. The swine is going to do it in broad daylight and we won't be able to stop him."

The sergeant cleared his throat, leaning forward. He had spent many years watching Rillo deal with countless burdens, most often when both of their lives had teetered on the brink. He would rage, he would spit, kick, shoot, and even cry, but never had the battle-weary sergeant seen him give up. In this moment, as they both sat there in the wake of Rillo's rage, Aequo found to his surprise that he missed the simplicity of war. This was not to say that in the heat of battle there were not hard choices to be made, far from it. Both he and Rillo had made more than their fair share of difficult decisions in their time, and they lived with the consequences of those decisions every day. But in this arena of politics, trade and secret meetings were not a battleground that Rillo took to well.

Nonetheless, since their mutual transfer from the military into the ranks of the Vox Militant, both men had come to be respected amongst its ranks. Rillo, as a somewhat unusual member of the officer corps, had risen quickly to become the order's commander. His swift elevation had been aided by the fact that whilst he could sometimes be harsh and quick to chastise, he was fair, able, and commanded the full respect of the men and women of the Vox Militant. Such a commander was rare, and this was an abnormality that appeared to concern more than a few experienced magisters.

Aequo met Rillo's gaze.

"Most likely you're right, but we needn't be alone in this battle. There are others who would help us."

Rillo shook his head.

"If you think that I'm turning to your criminal friends in the guilds, Aequo –"

"Friends is unfair, and you know it."

"Oh, come on. I've seen you at the pub with some of the dock-side lads, and that place you took us to last time was full of the Pale Star Guild. I'm happy to cast a blind eye to your little meetups, but don't think for one second that I'm going to go crawling to them."

Aequo bit his lip and swallowed his pride for another minute.

"Fine. But as you say, if the High Magister tries to pull anything, there aren't enough of us to stop him. There are other people beside the guilds who are concerned about Nihilo's rise."

"Like who?" Rillo snapped.

Aequo thought about framing his words carefully, but soon found that his patience was wearing thin.

"Not every magister is a supporter of Nihilo. Maellon Alpheri and others have spoken out against –"

A mocking look of triumph crossed the captain's face.

"Well, well, I never thought I'd hear you support a magister! World must be turning on its head."

Aequo felt his hands clench as his last shred of patience tore away.

"Look! If you want to fight this mess all on your own, then fine! But take a moment to think about all the soldiers outside who you'll be dragging along with you."

"This is what they signed up for!"

"No! They did not sign up to be slaughtered by mercenaries in the middle of a public square! You know what I think of the magisters! Don't you dare suggest that I relish the idea of asking them for help!"

Soon, Rillo's own voice grew louder, and he rose to his feet.

"I do, and it's no wonder that you'd rather reach out to the criminals first!"

As Rillo shouted, the warrior within Aequo awoke, and his instincts drove him towards the killing blow.

"Just because you've sacrificed your life for this job doesn't mean that they have to as well! Don't punish them because you're alone. They weren't the ones who drove her away!"

At the very last word Aequo's voice faltered, and his anger faded as he looked up at Rillo's face. A feeling of regret ran through his body like a cold stream.

The aggression on the captain's face faded like melting snow, and the colour slowly drained from his cheeks.

"Ok, Rillo, look I'm sorry – "

"Get out."

"I shouldn't have brought her up, all I was trying to say was – "

"Get out now, Aequo." Rillo did not shout or bluster as he spoke. His words were uttered with a terrible solemnity that told the sergeant that the conversation was over.

Now more frustrated with himself than he was at Rillo, Aequo grabbed his shako and made for the door.

"Sergeant."

Aequo turned within the now-open doorway.

"I want three hundred of the troops ready to march out in five minutes. See to it," ordered Rillo quietly, looking down at his desk.

Aequo stood still for a moment, trying to think of the right words to say but finding none. This particular battle was over, and much like the ones Rillo and Aequo had fought together during the war, there had been no winners.

"Yes, sir."

4

A Noble Endeavour

"You shall be safe!"

Salaris Bremmer waved across the surface of the wooden podium as he observed the great crowd of people before him.

"We will make you safe!"

Lyra had mixed feelings about public forums. As the daughter of a long-standing magister she had attended more than she could remember. For her, they conjured both pride and fear, mixed in equal parts. She was immensely proud of her father, not simply because of the eloquence of his speech, or even the manner in which he had supported the rest of the family by himself, ever since Lyra's mother had died. What really made her heart warm, whenever she saw him, was the passion that her father held in his convictions.

In Lyra's opinion the man now standing before the crowd, her father's opponent at this forum, possessed few of his qualities, if any.

"Great people of Abys-Luthil! Your safety is of the greatest concern to myself, the Council, and the High Magister Himself. None shall be allowed to harm you, or speak against you!"

However, despite the pride that Lyra felt, she could never quite shake the niggling quake of fear that scurried across her mind whenever a forum was in full swing. She did not fear the crowds. Lyra had become accustomed to walking unseen amongst the tide of people too many times for that. She did not even fear the many armed guards that littered the forum squares. She trusted Castel and Alina; they had never let her family be troubled by danger. No, Lyra's doubts came from the history books that lined her father's library. The history of the city was full to the brim of noble officials being toppled, removed or even murdered by their opponents.

"With your help, we will make this city a haven of peace and safety for all. The harsh tongue of mockery and criticism will not touch the ears of our fair citizens."

With these words her attention was drawn to Magister Salaris Bremmer, the Master of Blades. Magister Bremmer was a member of the Council of Five, the senior ruling body of the Grand Chamber of Magisters, which sat under the governance of the High Magister. The Grand Chamber itself was composed of five hundred magisters, who elected five of their own number to serve on the Council of Five. Each member of the Council held their own title and was responsible for the order and maintenance of different aspects of city life. The Master of Blades was in charge of mustering an army in times of great need, supporting the running of the city guard, as well as liaising with the Vox Militant. Next came the Master of the Fleet, who commanded the city's navy, and saw to the maintenance of its docks and the order of its incoming trade. The Master of Coin oversaw the finer points of trade within the city itself as well as the collection of taxes, the payment of officials, and the distribution of currency. The Master of Stores saw to the supply of food and water to the city, and this was a post that Lyra's father had held some years ago. Lastly, but by no means least, was the Master of Words, who initiated foreign trade, entered into diplomacy with other states, and kept a wary eye on threats within and outside of the city. Currently, there was a vacancy for that particular post on the Council, and much rumour and speculation surrounded the new appointment.

"Under the guidance of High Magister Nihilo, we will no longer permit the publication of materials or the organisation of movements which threaten your safety or peace of mind. No longer will slander or wanton criticism plague our city streets."

Lyra smiled, noting the continual stream of irony that ran thick and fast throughout the magister's speech. It was clear that some in the crowd agreed with Salaris, especially those seated amongst the other members of the nobility to Lyra's right, but more than a few were shaking their heads in opposition.

"Lyra, Lyra!"

She felt a tugging upon her sleeve, as she strained to hear the conclusion of Salaris' speech.

"Lyra!" came the eager voice once again.

"What is it, Nathan?" she hissed back, keeping her voice as low as possible.

"I'm bored. When is Uncle Maellon going to speak? Can we go home then?"

Lyra smiled as she ruffled her young cousin's hair, and picked up the illustrated story book that he had dropped under his chair.

"I'm afraid not, but if you can finish your book before we're done, I might be able to smuggle you a cream cake from the kitchen again."

The young boy's eyes widened with interest.

"Only if you finish the book though, and you can tell me what happens at the end. Do we have a deal?"

Nathan nodded enthusiastically, and grabbed the book eagerly with both hands.

"Good boy," said Lyra with a grin. She looked affably over to Nathan's mother, her aunt Mara, who offered an apologetic smile and began following her son's reading of the book, her finger tracing slowly across the page.

Soon enough, the affairs of state caught Lyra's attention, and she looked back towards the speaker's podium. Family life and politics were rarely far apart from each other in the Alpheri household.

"Therefore, my good people, I commend to your discerning ears the wishes of the Council and the High Magister himself. If you support your loyal magisters in this endeavour, no longer will citizens bear the burden of slander from the press houses. Your businesses will be free from the assaults of those who spout lies and speculation, which bring only harm to city trade and commerce. Your places of learning will be conformed to a unified purpose, and those who seek to scold and attack with vitriolic prose will be barred from school and university grounds alike!"

Salaris' speech came to an end. Many of the common folk stood mute in the face of the applause resounding from the merchants and a healthy portion of the magister class seated next to Lyra.

"Thank you, Master of Blades, Magister Salaris Bremmer. Would Magister Maellon Alpheri care to ascend the stage? We will now hear your thoughts on this matter," wheezed an elderly clerk in charge of the proceedings, struggling to be heard above the murmur of the crowd.

This murmur slowly grew into a series of cheers and cries of support, until much of the square clapped and shouted in welcome of the man who was celebrated in council chamber and tavern alike as the voice of the people. Lyra knew that it was not a term that her father cared for, as he insisted that every aspect of the magister system should support the voice and opinions of the people. She watched her father approach the stage, dressed in a modest crimson gown and wearing a ring of oak leaves upon his head. Every picture of his face plastered across the city featured this gift, which was offered by the people to mark his end of term from the Council of Five.

Maellon disliked wearing it, but he recognised it as a present from the people he served and would not deny them sight of the gift that they had so earnestly bestowed upon him.

His fair features now rose above the podium, as he laid his hands down to rest upon it. He did not, like many of his fellow magisters, speak from a script, but rather he had before him a few scrambled notes. Lyra had no idea how he was able to present a whole speech from a few seemingly random sentences, scribbled across what looked like the back of an envelope.

"Good people of Abys-Luthil." Maellon's voice rose above the cheers and soon the entire square was drawn into a reverent silence.

"I have had the honour of serving you for many years. During that time in your service, I have experienced both success and failure, and times of both great joy and deep concern. I have witnessed you endure wars, famines, treachery, and I have never seen you falter. You have endured storms the like of which would destroy nations and empires, and for your strength of character and spirit you have my everlasting respect."

Maellon's bright green eyes looked around the square, coming to stop at Lyra. She smiled back, offering him the briefest nod of encouragement as he glanced back towards his notes before surveying the crowd before him.

"This respect that I hold for you compels me to stand here and reject the proposals offered by my colleague, Magister Bremmer, and other members of the Council. By wiping so-called "topics of contention" from the public sphere, they wish to restrict the publications of the printing houses, and to limit the number of public forums."

Maellon leaned forward as he offered his audience an audible sigh.

"To seek to protect the citizens of this city is a most noble endeavour. But it cannot and must not come at the price of limiting the right of any citizen to express his or her opinion by written word or voice."

Lyra watched as her father's posture straightened and his voice rose yet further, touching every corner of the grand square.

"Those who offer this proposal have sadly and lamentably underestimated your strength and resolve by claiming that you need protection from yourselves! My friends, you require no such protection. You are the proud inheritors of a tradition of freedom and democracy, the like of which other nations can only dream of!"

At these words, a loud cheer arose from the crowd, and proud banners were waved vigorously in the air. A few cries of protest arose from the noble stalls, but most of these were rendered inaudible by the enthusiastic applause. The only figures that stood still and silent throughout the proceedings were the various noble guards, watchful around their respective charges. However, more striking than these heavily-armed figures was the thin green line of soldiers that stood between the magister's stage and the large crowd, the Vox Militant.

Most of their number faced the stage, their rifles held at ease, the polished brass buttons of their uniforms glinting in the bright sunlight. These uniforms were of a similar colour to those of the guards of her own household, Lyra mused.

As a teenager Lyra had dreamed of joining the Vox Militant. She had even been found practising with one of her family guard's rifles more than once, much to the displeasure of her father. She had taken to running a few laps of the family home's training grounds every morning, in preparation for the Vox Militant's gruelling selection process. It was on one of these runs that she had quite literally run into Alina and Castel, and only a few weeks afterwards both Kat and she had first ventured out into the darkness of the Water District and old Abys.

An occasional cheer from the crowd sounded as Maellon spoke.

"Your freedom is built upon your right to speak, to criticise and to oppose. What my colleague Magister Bremmer calls mockery and lies, are in truth the foundation of healthy debate, on which the freedom of this very city stands. Your magisters work tirelessly in your service," continued Maellon, as he looked over towards Bremmer.

"But they are not without fault. We suffer from the same error that afflicts all men and women. We need your help, your voice, and the voice of the printing press houses." Maellon paused as he surveyed the square once again. His voice dropped and he turned to one side to look at Lyra once more before returning to face the now silent crowd.

"My friends, you know better than I that there will always be those who seek to rule over others with wickedness and vice. If we hope to halt the grim advance of people of such evil ambition, by silencing their right to speak, it is not them that we shall disarm, but ourselves! If you consent to the proposals put forward today by the Council, then you and your magisters will remove the very shield of freedom that protects you."

Maellon's voice rose as he raised one arm in the air and waved it across the crowd.

"Freedom of speech is for everyone or no one! The moment that we deprive our opponents of it, we set one another on a path at whose end we shall lose it ourselves. I do not think you weak, and as an elected magister, I trust in your courage to meet a world where every opinion may be met with ridicule or applause. Call upon your magisters to reject this proposal, and ensure that your safety is not robbed from you!"

Thunderous applause poured from the depths of the crowd, and before Maellon could even step away from the podium, great chants of "Alpheri!" echoed across the grand square. Lyra looked on in awe as a thousand voices chanted her family name. She watched as a man with a tattered tool belt wrapped around his waist lifted a young girl upon his shoulders and shouted triumphantly.

However, as the same elderly man that had introduced Maellon to the stage invited both magisters to come forward, shouts of applause quickly turned to cries of anger, and a slow murmur of unrest spread across the crowd. Fists waved in the air, as Salaris Bremmer resumed the stage, and the voice of the crowd grew bitter.

It had not gone unnoticed by the press houses that the Master of Blades' personal fortune was built upon the production of farming machinery that was used across the farmland that spread out far and wide beyond the walls of Abys-Luthil. For workers involved in this manufacture, the shifts were long and the environment dangerous, as heavy machinery and plumes of steam would race across the workhouses, sweeping up their attendants in vicious waves of heat and the heavy strikes of tempered steel. The press houses' criticism of Bremmer's factories had been widespread, prompting many farming barons to shun his business for fear of aggravating their workforce. This had at least brought a sense of justice to those who would return hungry and tired to their homes after a long shift.

Lyra watched as Magister Bremmer slowly backed away, and his own family guard formed a protective circle around him. Much like those of the Alpheri guard, these men and women wore the family colours of their lord: a weathered orange and yellow, covered partially by breastplates marked with a lion's head, the patron symbol of the Bremmer household. The approach of the guards did nothing to ease the crowd's protests, and out of its heaving depths flew an apple core, bouncing harmlessly onto a polished breastplate.

A tall woman with flowing black hair, her face partially hidden by a traditional Abyssus golden half mask, drew her sword, lowering it towards the crowd and gesturing at her fellows to do the same.

"Stand down!"

Lyra turned her head to see a tall man of Luthan heritage, with a pale complexion and short brown hair, marching across the thin line of the Vox Militant. He bore the uniform of a captain; his green coat and steel bracers were in immaculate condition. He had an ornate-looking short sword at his belt, and kept a large pistol strapped across his chest.

"Sheath your sword!" he ordered, placing no hands upon his own weapons.

The woman in the golden mask shook her head, and her fellow guards took their positions beside her.

"Get that rabble in order first!"

Even from this distance, Lyra could see the captain's face contort with anger. This tension appeared only to feed the frustrations of the crowd, as yet more angry voices cried out into the square. Nathan became distracted from his book, so his mother swiftly put an arm around his shoulders and pointed him back to the coloured pages, eager to ensure that whatever was unfolding before them, he would not see it.

Bremmer stuck close to his guards, and one of them placed a hand on a silver-engraved pistol at their belt. Lyra watched as the captain took a few steps closer towards the speakers' stage. She could see his face more clearly now. He appeared to be in his late thirties or early forties, but it was difficult to tell exactly because of a series of small scars that ran across his face, the largest of which cut across his left cheek. However, the most striking feature she noticed was the man's eyes. Lyra had never before seen a person that looked so alert and yet so very tired in the same moment. The hazel hue of his eyes was framed by a weary melancholy that only enhanced the unflinching stare of aggression with which he was eyeing the guards before him.

"Stay back now, my lady." The tone of Alina's voice permitted no room for objection, and Lyra's view was momentarily obstructed by five Alpheri guards that now stood around her, her uncle and aunt, and Nathan.

She shifted in her seat to see the figures of Castel and seven other guards ascend the stage and take position between her father and the line of Vox

Militant before them. A large number of guards were now at their stations all across the stage, and it was clear to Lyra that Castel's attention was not focused so much on the crowds, as on the ever-advancing line of the Bremmer family guard.

Lyra's heart almost skipped a beat as she watched rotten fruit land upon the stage. The more the magisters were obscured by a row of artifice armour and swords, the more restless the crowd became. In that same moment, all she could do was watch as one of the Bremmer guards drew his pistol.

"Vox Militant, stand to!"

In one unified, swift motion, the thin line of soldiers stood to attention and drew their bayonets, fixing the sharp blades, which shone in the sunlight with an unnatural red gleam, to their rifles. Their captain drew his own pistol, and the line of soldiers lowered their weapons towards the stage.

Alina's rifle was ready in her hands within moments, and Castel spun on the spot to face a figure dressed in the uniform of a sergeant of the Vox Militant, commanding a unit of twenty soldiers standing directly in front of him.

"You will lower your weapons and withdraw from the stage, now!" bellowed the Vox Militant officer, gun in hand.

"How dare you point weapons at a member of the Council! Stand down now, Captain!" came the shrill cry of a masked face, the leader of the Bremmer guard.

"You have precisely ten seconds to lower your weapons, or according to the laws of this city, you will be placed under arrest!" replied the scarred officer.

Lyra leaned forward, staring intently at the pistol in the captain's hand. Even at this distance, she could clearly see that it was an artifice weapon. She would have spent longer wondering about what power it contained if her focus had not already been drawn to the sharp line of bayonets pointed in her father's direction. The urge to find a weapon and draw herself alongside him pulled at her heart, but she knew that there was nothing she could do. There was no way that Alina would allow her to leave her seat, and even if she did find a weapon, what was she going to do against two hundred armed soldiers in broad daylight? Many rumours surrounded the future of the Vox Militant. Were they really secretly taking orders from High Magister Nihilo? Was this the excuse they needed to open fire on one of his most outspoken opponents?

Lyra felt her hands shake as the stand-off continued. It was one thing putting herself in the line of fire, but quite another to see another member of her family face a line of loaded weapons, even when he was surrounded by guards. She heard the audible click of the firing mechanism on Alina's rifle, as the guardswoman pulled back the flintlock with her thumb and brought her gun to the ready.

"Back off, Captain! I won't warn you again!" yelled the guard commander. The officer did not so much as blink.

"Advance!"

At his command the thin green line took five steps forwards, beginning to ascend the stage. A few of their number remained behind, their bayonets drawn, facing the crowd, ensuring that the angry mass of people did not follow.

"Very well!" snapped the voice behind the golden mask, her one visible eye glaring at the advancing captain. "Guard, present your weapons, on my order–"

"Silence, Yalda!" snapped Castel, standing directly in front of Maellon, his hand resting upon the handle of his own pistol, but with no weapon drawn.

"You look after your own lord, Castel! I won't be intimidated by some idiot soldier, threatening violence in broad day–"

Castel took one step forward.

"Yalda, for the last time, be silent, or I swear if the Vox Militant don't shoot you, I will!" He turned back to face the soldiers standing before him, making eye contact with their leader.

There were two hundred soldiers in front of him, each bearing artifice weaponry and ready to open fire in an instant. No matter where the allegiances of the Vox Militant now lay, this was not a fight that he and the noble guards could win.

"Captain," began Castel.

The officer turned to face the Alpheri guard, his gun kept low. Castel slowly lifted his hand from his pistol and took another step forward, careful to ensure that he still remained between his lord and the soldiers.

"None of us want to see blood this day. We will lower our weapons if you remove your troops from the stage. We will make no attempt to harm the people, but you must allow us to stand beside our lords." Castel's voice was steady and calm as he looked at the man he knew as Captain Rillo of the Vox Militant. He made it his business to be informed of who held the senior positions in the other noble guards, the city watch and, most importantly, the Vox Militant.

Nathan grew more restless as an unsettled silence fell on the scene.

"Lyra, what's going on? Who are those men?"

She took his hand. "It's going to be ok, Nathan. Look down at your book, just here," she pointed. "There's a good boy."

"Where is uncle Maellon?" Nathan stuttered nervously, trying to find sight of his uncle between the guards.

Lyra heard the fear that coursed between his stammered words and gave his hand a gentle squeeze.

"Father is going to be just fine. Castel is with him, you know Castel."

Nathan looked up at her with wide, fearful eyes.

"The scary man?" he asked, sinking back into his seat.

"Yes, Castel, the scary man."

"I want to go home," muttered Nathan, clutching his book to his chest.

"Me too, Nathan. But everything is going to be ok," replied Lyra, looking out towards the glittering wall of bayonets. "...everything is going to be ok."

She held her nephew's hand all the tighter as she watched the captain take a few steps towards Castel, his troops halted.

"This is a public forum and you stand in a public square. You will put down your weapons, or you will be relieved of them," replied Rillo.

Lyra flinched as she watched the head of the Bremmer family guard, whom Castel had called Yalda, raise her pistol.

"No, Yalda! Don't be a–" began Castel, but was cut off as the sergeant standing before him gave the order and nearly two hundred rifles were aimed in their direction. Alina responded in kind, even as Castel held out his arms wide.

"Hold! Hold, damn you!" he shouted, backing away from the soldiers.

"Captain, there are children and other civilians behind us. Please lower your weapons."

The square became quiet, as the crowd, their anger sated by the show of strength from the Vox Militant, watched the stand-off with bated breath. The green-coated sergeant that stood on the steps moved across the line of soldiers, and began whispering in his officer's ear. In this same moment, a figure clothed in dark crimson made his way from between the ranks of the Alpheri guard. Castel began to protest, but Maellon would not hear of it.

"Captain, I am a servant of the people, and I fear neither their words nor you, their weapon. Here I stand; I shall not hide from them," spoke Maellon calmly, but with an authority that still from time to time caused Lyra to involuntarily straighten her posture.

Her father could not be called a small man, but neither was he a warrior, and as Lyra watched him face down hundreds of loaded guns, she felt the sensation of her heart rising to the back of her throat. Fear gripped her and laid terrible, unshifting slabs of stone at the base of her stomach.

Rillo listened intently, casting an eye over to Yalda.

"Very well. Sergeant, keep ten with their weapons trained on this one. Have the rest lower their arms," responded Rillo, pointing towards the yellow-coated guard, Yalda. The order was given, and the Vox Militant and the Alpheri guards stood at ease. They watched those few protectors who still stood around the Master of Blades.

Lyra exhaled and sat back into her seat.

Castel was about to offer Yalda another rebuke when Maellon took a step forward.

"I am certain that my fellow magister will join me in this gesture of goodwill immediately," said Maellon, his voice underlined with a sense of urgency.

Slowly, with a noticeable delay, the not-insignificant figure of Salaris Bremmer crept out from between the ranks of his household guards, and edged across the stage towards the weapon-free space of Maellon Alpheri.

"Certainly...it is a pleasure to serve the people," spoke Salaris, with an awkward stammer, towards the crowd. Lyra watched as Maellon gave his colleague a quizzical look and resisted the urge to roll his eyes.

"We thank you for your vigilance, Captain, on behalf of the people of this city. We magisters will strive unceasingly to serve you all with humility. This is why I must repeat what I have said before, that the right of free speech must be protected. We must never again see the rise of tyranny or the shedding of blood in our city streets!"

The crowd cheered and Lyra stood to her feet in applause, having rarely been quite as proud of her father as she was in this moment. Rillo gave the order for his troops to fall back towards the crowd, and a gentle wave of relief washed across everyone in the square.

"He certainly is a very brave man. An admirable quality for a magister."

Lyra froze, and her hands ceased mid-clap. This was a voice she had heard before, with its sickly, honeyed tone, and she did not relish the thought of the conversation that would follow.

She painted a smile upon her lips and turned around.

"A pleasure to see you again, Master Chamberlain."

Silo Rees offered her an exaggerated bow.

"The pleasure is all mine, Lady Lyra."

"Are you here on official business, Mister Rees?"

Rees shrugged off the informality of Lyra's address, knowing full well that where titles were concerned, he was out-ranked. His pale, shaven face grinned back at her.

"In truth, my lady, I am indeed here on business; but I must say, in greater truth, that it is always a joy to listen to your father at a forum." Lyra saw Alina make to grab the chamberlain and pull him to one side, even as the words were twisting and crawling from between his thin lips. Lyra slowly shook her head, Rees pretended not to notice, and the two took a seat.

Despite this unwelcome presence, Lyra was pleased to hear that to her right, Nathan had settled down and was happily reading his book, closely supervised by his mother.

"You are a supporter of my father, Mister Rees?"

The grin sat upon his face as if carved in stone, and the clerk slowly folded his hands upon his lap, casting his eyes back to the stage where the magisters continued their debate unobstructed.

"Oh indeed, my lady. One cannot but help but admit that Lord Maellon is one of the finest public speakers that this city has ever known - certainly, to my memory, though thankfully that does not stretch too far back."

Lyra watched as faces in the crowd seemed to brighten, looking on as her father provided yet another rebuttal to his opponent.

"It seems that you and the people are of one mind, Mister Rees. They too applaud him."

Rees' eyes narrowed but the grin remained.

"What a pleasant thought. It is such a joy to see the crowd so...enthralled."

"Has the life of a magister ever appealed to you?" asked Lyra, still observing her father.

At this question the clerk allowed a moment's pause, tapping his fingers gently across his knee.

"Alas, my lady, I'm afraid not. I lack the required...qualities. I fear that I am not the right man for a stage. I suspect that it is my lot to perform forever behind the curtain."

"You perform, Mister Rees? I would have thought that the rigours of public service were a rather sober affair, what with so many responsibilities laid upon you? I cannot imagine that the High Magister's personal chamberlain has much time for performance," replied Lyra, turning to face Rees.

His eyes met hers, alive and piercing.

"Oh, on the contrary, Lady Lyra. I find myself repeatedly fatigued by the rigours of performance. I serve, and in doing so, I must perform."

Lyra's brow furrowed.

"I'm not sure that I understand you."

His grin faded and Lyra observed the very first look of sincerity that she had ever seen upon the clerk's face. It was a far from reassuring sight.

"You should know better than most. Or maybe you are too close to him to be able to tell," he began, glancing over to Maellon.

"It is all a performance. Every word of it." Rees looked back to see Lyra about to object, and was quick to cut her off in a rare moment of hasty speech.

"I mean no disrespect to your father, really I don't. I mean only to compliment him. He is a fine speaker and a dedicated public servant, that much cannot be denied. But in order for any of us to serve for long, my lady, we must perform. Even with words of honesty we must persuade, and to do so we must appeal, we must sometimes even...insist. And that's what they really want," said Rees, gesturing towards the captivated crowd.

"They want to be enthralled, entertained."

"Entertained? By their magisters?" Lyra asked suspiciously.

"Oh yes, especially so. Everyone wants to be entertained by their leaders. If governance was based purely on logic then the city would be run by accountants, and that sounds frightfully dull," Rees laughed to himself as Lyra sat unamused, but intrigued all the same.

"I can't help but feel that you're trying to make some sort of point, Mister Rees?"

The clerk sighed.

"Not especially, my lady, I merely offer an observation. However..."

Rees leaned closer.

"If any of us aspire to serve, or even lead, we must learn to perform. It is only by doing this that for good or ill, one can hope to bring change."

A brief silence hung in the air whilst Lyra considered his words.

"Thank you, Chamberlain, I'll bear that in mind," replied Lyra, with the distinct feeling that she had far from grasped whatever subtle message Rees was trying to convey.

Although the chamberlain to the High Magister had never spoken to her in hostility or even been anything other than cordial, in his words at least, Lyra had never warmed to the man. His performance, whatever that was, had certainly not enthralled her.

She had once asked her father about the man. At first, Maellon had seemed amused by the question, before offering an uncharacteristically brief answer.

"Lyra, that man is a consummate civil servant."

It did not sound like a compliment.

"Lady Alpheri, I hope that my chamberlain is not distracting you from the proceedings."

Where Rees' voice seemed to pour like honey, this new voice was deeper, more resonant, but flowing freely, no more objectionable to the senses than silk is to the touch.

Lyra rose to her feet and greeted the High Magister of Abys-Luthil.

Nihilo did not smile, but neither did he frown. On the many times that Lyra had seen the man in passing conversation or across a dining table, he appeared unnaturally restful. Her eyes examined his face, unremarkable in its composition but by no means off-putting, with his large eyes, high cheekbones and finely trimmed hairline resting under a modest but well-tailored cap. It was difficult to imagine Nihilo as either happy, or melancholy. He appeared both content and composed at all times, never more, never less.

"Not at all, High Magister. In any case, I believe that the debate is almost at an end."

Nihilo nodded slowly, casting a malign eye across to Rees who promptly fell in line alongside him.

"So it seems. Though from what I have heard, it was not much of a debate. You must be very proud of your father. He is a gifted man," uttered Nihilo.

"I am. We all are," replied Lyra, looking back towards the members of her family now standing behind her. She suppressed a smile as Nathan stood before his mother, holding his book over his face, paying no attention to the High Magister despite his mother's best efforts.

"Quite so, quite so. Tell me, Lady Lyra. What do you think of this matter? I would like to hear the thoughts of the younger generation on this great question," asked Nihilo, his eyes scanning her face, his hands held behind his back.

Lyra knew that more lay behind this question than mere curiosity and thought for a moment, not allowing herself to break eye contact with Nihilo. She found speaking to him difficult. Talking with Silo Rees felt like throwing one's words into the sea, with the expectation that they would be tossed and turned in the waves and soon be returned back to shore with an altogether different meaning. But with Nihilo, Lyra felt as if she were speaking into a great chasm. A vast, empty space, dark and unyielding, that took her words and devoured them in the depths, never again to see the light of day.

She could delay no longer.

"I must agree with my father, High Magister. The freedom of every citizen of the city must be protected. Without full freedom of speech, it appears that all civil liberties might soon be erased. All of us must be free to be able to proclaim what we feel to be right."

Not a flicker of emotion crossed Nihilo's face.

"Well said, my lady. Yes, freedom. It is truly a goal to be protected. On that we all agree. Your father once wrote a treatise on the nature of freedom. It made for interesting reading. You should ask him about it. I believe it might be as illuminating for you as it was for me."

"I will," Lyra replied simply, struggling to imagine that anything might arouse the High Magister's interests, so still were his eyes.

"Good. You are right to defend freedom, my lady. One must do so unashamedly and without regret. There can be no greater purpose for which we strive than that."

For a moment, the tone of Nihilo's voice became firmer, and his eyes widened with a rare display of conviction.

"I hope you understand that in this goal at least, we may be in agreement."

"Yes, certainly," replied Lyra hesitantly, more than a little confused.

"Good. I am pleased," spoke Nihilo, as he lowered his head in acknowledgement. "Please excuse me." Without pause he turned smoothly upon his heel and began ascending the stage.

The stage was a calmer place than it had been only minutes ago, as the magisters continued their exchange and the Vox Militant kept their uneasy vigil. Salaris Bremmer was now at the podium desperately trying to offer a response to his opponent, but faltering in the face of an unconvinced-looking crowd.

"Thank you, Master of Blades. Your thoughts on this matter have been greatly appreciated."

Salaris looked around to see the steady approach of the High Magister. He lowered his head in acknowledgement, and without uttering another word he withdrew from the podium, seating himself between Maellon and his muted guards.

Nihilo stepped forward.

"Good people of Abys-Luthil, I hope you will join me in applauding the work and passion of these fine magisters," spoke Nihilo, with a voice that was suddenly much deeper than a man of such slim build would be expected to project. He led the applause for a few moments with light taps of his hands, as a row of darkly-clad family guards filled in behind the stage. Nihilo's personal guard were dressed in a similar manner to himself, adorned in dark blue robes. They bore a host of weapons around their belts, with black and silver checked half-masks worn over their faces.

The High Magister settled the crowd with one wave of his hand.

"I wish to echo the words of those who have gone before me. Your freedom and security are of the highest importance." A rare vein of emotion ran through Nihilo's voice, and a sincere note of sympathy framed his words.

"I promise you that the prosperity and security of this city are foremost on my mind. So much so, that I would have it that no one is in a position to take them from you. But alas, there will always be those who seek to oppose you, the people, wanting to place unnecessary stumbling blocks in your path to fulfilment. I understand that your lives are busy and your burdens many. This is why your government and your magisters wish to relieve you of at least some of your heavy load."

Nihilo cast a benevolent eye across to Maellon.

"My honourable friend, Lord Alpheri, is of course correct when he seeks to protect your freedom of speech, and is to be applauded for doing so."

The High Magister faced the crowd, and spread his arms open wide as if to embrace the entire square all at once.

"Nevertheless, my good people, I could not bear to see your peaceful lives troubled by the aggression of others, by vicious criticism, or by the restless seeds of anarchy that a great number of the printing press houses have sought to sow. I would have you enjoy your days in happiness, not fear. To that end, a balance must be struck."

He raised his arms higher in the air, his voice rising across a now silent square.

"I would not have you settle for a freedom in which you are made a target for mocking voices, or persecuted by those who think in ways which harm you. We will protect you from the voices that can so easily turn upon you, and so you shall be free. So encourage your elected magisters to support the new Public Censor Act, and you shall be truly liberated."

Applause, scattered but audible, greeted his words. It was neither as thunderous as it had been for Maellon, nor as subdued as it had been for Salaris. Nihilo waved to the crowd, casting an eye down to the line of Vox Militant facing him. His eyes finally focused upon the figure of Captain Rillo.

"The time of the old order of things will soon pass away. For too long have we hung on to the traditions of the past. A brave new future awaits."

With these last words the forum was brought to a close. The nobility rose from their seats and made their way to their carriages, whilst the crowd wandered back through the streets.

Silo Rees offered one last smile towards Lyra, before withdrawing behind the wall of Nihilo's guards.

Nathan let out an exaggerated yawn, stretched his legs and wrapped his arms around his mother.

"I want to go home" he muttered wearily.

"I know, baby boy. Once your uncle makes it back through his sea of fans we'll be in the carriage home," replied Mara, lifting her son from the ground and gently rubbing his back.

Alina and the other guards kept a small perimeter around the family, and maintained a watchful eye upon the ranks of the Vox Militant marching away across the square. Lyra followed her gaze, wondering just how close they had really come to a full-on fight, before her uncle Alfred moved next to her.

"I say! That was all rather tense! The boys in green were getting rather boisterous, I thought," he exclaimed, a thick moustache resting comically above his plump red lips, both hands clasped on the edges of his jacket.

Lyra simply smiled and nodded along, watching the last few ranks of the Vox Militant march out of sight.

"Lucky for us that we have such fine guards, eh? Never one to shy away from a bit of a scrap, ey, Alina?" he proclaimed to anyone nearby who would listen.

"A pleasure, sir," the guard sergeant replied with a strained smile and furrowed brow.

"Good show, good show. Back in the day, I would have enjoyed showing them a thing or two myself. Not so today, the life of a merchant banker does not make for a good soldier, eh? Haha!" he boomed, rubbing his not-insignificant stomach with hearty satisfaction.

Lyra turned around, a look of amusement painted across her face.

"Indeed, Uncle. I'm sure you were quite the warrior."

She had almost forgotten that Alfred's current occupation was merchant banking, especially as his chosen career varied from month to month. Only six weeks ago, he was still trying to gain a profit from his business in trading dyed goat furs overseas. Whatever the colour, no matter the pattern, Alfred's goat fur firm could provide for whatever goat-related apparel a customer could wish for. Sadly, this particular business venture had not been successful.

Alfred was not the wisest or the most informed of businessmen, but he was at heart good-natured and had been tireless in trying to build a business empire that his son would one day inherit. However, at the moment, as for many years past, his brother in law Maellon had provided for the family, taking Alfred, his sister Mara, and Nathan into his home, until Alfred got himself back on his feet.

This was likely to take a few more years, and for this, Lyra had to admit that she was thankful. She enjoyed their company, and relished coming back home to Nathan's happy voice after her visits to the streets. They were her family. They were home.

Her thoughts were broken on hearing a light chuckle from Mara.

"A warrior?! Oh, my dear husband, let's get you home before you enlist. And if it's a soldier's life for you, then we'd best have Tom find your old running shoes. I'll tell the cooks to replace the cake with celery. We'll have you fighting fit in no time."

A concerned twitch ran across Alfred's face, ruffling his moustache.

"Now, now, my dear. There's no need to do anything drastic. Your husband is happy at home," replied Alfred, smiling his sweetest smile and placing an arm around his wife's shoulders.

Mara gave Lyra a sceptical look and rolled her eyes, handing Nathan over to her husband.

"Good to know," she replied with a sincere smile, giving him a kiss on the cheek. "Now, where is that brother of mine? I am in dire need of some tea."

A familiar voice eased its way between the ranks of the bustling nobility.

"Ah yes, some tea would be a welcome sight. Fear not, sister, we will be home soon."

Maellon Alpheri approached, followed by the familiar faces of the family guards, including Castel who was busy gesturing over towards a few green carriages.

"Very well, brother, if we could make it there without you inciting half the city into a brawl, that would be appreciated," Mara replied, her eyebrows raised, hands on her hips.

"Ah, Mara, what would I do without your words of wisdom?" Maellon laughed, embracing her. Lyra watched as Mara's hands gripped at the folds of her brother's coat to the point where her knuckles turned white. She whispered something into his ear, holding him close.

He placed a hand gently on Lyra's shoulder, and his voice became lower.

"So, how did I do?"

She put her arms around his neck without a moment's pause, resting her head upon his shoulders.

"Wonderfully."

"Well, I could wish for no higher praise." Maellon looked into his daughter's eyes for a few moments, the worry that underlined his words evidenced in his weary eyes. But he smiled all the same.

"My lord, the carriages are ready. We'd best get you home," said Castel.

Maellon let out a tired sigh and nodded slowly.

"Very well, let us be away. I cannot say that some food and rest would be an unwelcome sight. Lyra, after you."

She began making her way to the carriage door, just before it suddenly flew open and a familiar face appeared.

"Kat!" Lyra exclaimed in surprise, as her friend leapt nimbly from the depths of the carriage before pulling out a large wooden box, filled with vegetables and sweetmeats.

"Hey Ly!" replied Kat cheerily, before quickly looking over to Maellon and bowing her head slightly.

"Forgive me, my lord. Virgil and I were on the estate and we needed to head this way..." A sudden look of concentration crossed Katerina's face as she desperately thought of the right words to say. "...and we caught a lift."

"In my one of my carriages?" said Maellon with a raised eyebrow.

"...in one of your carriages."

"Did you say we?" asked Castel, less than amused.

"In my defence, my lord, she did insist," came the sheepish voice of Virgil, his head now leaning around the door.

Castel stepped over to the carriage.

"Right, the circus is over. Can everyone please step out of the carriage so that we might be on our way," insisted the now-irate guard captain, finding no humour in the situation, unlike his master who now eyed the veteran artificer with no small degree of amusement.

"I never thought that you were one to be cajoled into anything," mocked Maellon.

Virgil grunted in irritation as he exited the carriage, carrying his own box of food.

"Yes, well. You know how insistent young ladies can be. Anyway, I couldn't let her walk this far alone and it is not a quick journey," replied Virgil.

"No," said Maellon knowingly, remembering that one fateful evening that the two of them had made a similar journey through this part of the city towards the streets and waterways of old Abys, and found young Katerina. "No, it is not a short journey." In the busyness of the day's affairs he had forgotten about the young lady's annual pilgrimage back to her place of discovery, in memory of those that she had long since lost. In the same moment that he remembered, Maellon suddenly grew very tired, and he slowly patted his old friend on the shoulder.

For a moment, Maellon cast his eyes to the ground.

"I hope the visit goes well, Virgil. As well as it can."

Virgil smiled as he stood beside his lord.

"Enjoy a rest at home, Maellon. You've already had a long day and you deserve a break."

"Thank you," replied the magister, looking into the interior of the carriage and following the path that his eyes set before him. He turned back towards his daughter, whom he now knew would not be joining him.

"I will see you at home. Don't be out too long."

"I won't, Father. I promise."

Maellon nodded and entered the carriage, and the rest of the family and their guards did the same, along the small train of Alpheri carriages. They were soon on their way, lost within moments in a sea of moving horse-drawn carriages, travelling across the winding streets and bustling squares of Abys-Luthil.

Virgil placed his box on the ground and stretched his back.

"I saw that, you know. Our dear Alina is not quite as quick as she thinks she is," he said, looking at the pistol that poked out from between the folds of Lyra's cloak. This was the very one that Alina had subtly handed to her as she had mounted the second carriage, eager that the young Alpheri would not walk the streets without a weapon.

"I think it's sweet, shows that she cares," winked Kat, briefly pulling back her own cloak to reveal a pair of pistols hanging from her belt.

Virgil rubbed his eyes.

"No, no, no. We'll have none of that today!"

"Virgil, relax! We're just taking a few precautions, that's all," snapped Kat, unhooking one of the daggers at the top of her boots and handing it to Lyra.

"No! Right, give that here," muttered the artificer, snatching the dagger from Lyra's grasp and turning back to his box. Kat began to object but Virgil paid her no heed, as he moved small pallets of carrots and cabbages from his box to reveal two short swords hidden at the bottom.

"This is for you, and this one is for you. If you insist on using a blade, it's best that you only need to strike with it once," said Virgil, handing both Lyra and Kat two short swords, subtle in their design, but each with a small gold band forged into the base of the blade. Lyra took a moment to examine the blade as she pulled it two inches from its scabbard. She watched as an eerie blue light danced across the metallic surface. Virgil had armed both her and Kat for the last few years that they had made this annual pilgrimage, but never before with artifice weaponry. She had learned enough from Kat over the years to know that the blue light meant that this blade was as likely to crush an opponent as it was to cut them.

"Since when do you give us artifice blades for walking through the Water District in broad daylight?" Lyra whispered, eager not to be overheard in their corner of the still-busy square.

"You know as well as I, Lyra, that there's no such thing as broad daylight where the Water District is concerned. Besides, given your little escapades, I think it best that we move with caution. Karrick's guild is said to be looking for a woman dressed in a green cloak and mask, so let's try and keep our heads down, shall we? Put these on." Virgil handed them each a full-face mask, and placed a faded orange one of simple design over his own face.

"Know a lot about the Pale Star guild's movements do you, Virgil?" asked Lyra, with a twinkle in her eye.

"I keep an ear to the ground," answered Virgil, with narrowed eyes that were barely visible behind his mask. "It's called doing your research, Lyra, you should try it. It's far less likely to get you shot."

"Research, oh, that's what you call it," smirked Kat, putting on her mask.

"Must be quite a bit of research that gets you such rare metals and artifice tools. Good to know that it's just research though, nothing as onerous as black-market trading or anything like that," said Lyra, joining in.

"Well, it's enough to keep you two alive, which is quite a feat in itself. And I can't say that I'm sorry to hear of the frustrations of the guilds as more of their shipments go missing," muttered Virgil, lifting his box of food from the ground.

"Wait, was that a compliment, Virgil? I think he just complimented us, Kat!" exclaimed Lyra, placing both hands dramatically over her heart.

"I know! One minute, I need to record this moment for posterity. Now, where's my notebook?" Kat immediately began patting herself down in exaggerated sweeps, in a feigned search for pen and paper.

"Ha. Ha. Why, aren't you both quite the comedians? We could head north and sign you up for the theatre, or we could get on with our business for today and then I can go back to my forge. What do you say?"

"Hmm, now that question deserves a moment's consideration, wouldn't you say?" mused Lyra, looking over towards her friend.

"Indeed it does, Ly. I can see it now! The Noble Theatre! A big stage! With me, in a wonderful dress, classy, but with a touch of seduction..."

"Oh please, just stop–" began Virgil.

"A nice red number, and of course the beautiful Lady Alpheri will make a fitting assistant."

"Assistant!? Please, you're crazy if you think for one moment I'm letting you try to saw me in half."

"Can we just move on, please–"

"Don't worry Ly, we'll find you a fetching hat, something that goes with your eyes. And for me, I was thinking something with a bit more song and dance."

"Oh! Like that cabaret we saw last week!" replied Lyra.

"Exactly, though I think we'll skip the whole bear costume bit. We'll go straight to the ball room scene."

"For the love of–"

"I loved that bit! All except for the lead's jacket - I had no idea where they were going with that."

"If you're both quite done–"

"I know, right!? It completely clashed with the rest of the stage design. What were they thinking?" exclaimed Kat, throwing her arms in the air.

"Ladies!"

Lyra bit her tongue, halting her reply, as the two women observed the fuming artificer. Virgil breathed out slowly, shaking his head, and began walking across the square.

Lyra tapped Kat on the back, as the trainee artificer picked up her own box of food.

"We'd best catch up with him. Wouldn't want him to get lost."

"I heard that!"

With that, the trio made their way across the square and along a trading street, which led directly to the looming structure of the Grand Magisters' Chambers, also known as the Old Palace.

Virgil grunted as he weaved around market stalls, panting horses and eager traders. It was on the exceptionally long street in which they now found themselves, the one known as Nation's Way, that the twin parts of the city, old Abys and noble Luthil, had truly begun to merge. The vast array of the city's many colours were on display here. The fine and fashionable suits and flowing robes of proud Luthan tailors sat side by side with the ornate and vibrant shades of traditional Abyssus cloaks and painted masks.

This was one of Virgil's favourite places in the city, so full of life and colour. It reminded him of home, but that was a very long way from here. His eyes lingered briefly on a bowl full of spices, its rich smell filling his nose, even behind his mask. The half-masked trader behind waved vigorously at him, speaking of a special offer and a rare deal. Virgil paid him no attention, drawing his eyes upwards as he continued onwards, observing that as they made it further down the bustling street, the cream coloured brick of Luthil suddenly gave way to the dark crimson brick and slate of Abys.

They reached the end of the street without incident, now walking past the great structure in which all the great matters of the city were discussed and debated. The Grand Magisters' Chambers had once been the home of some of Luthil's greatest emperors, and were built upon the foundations of an ancient Abyssus palace.

Virgil observed the towering gates which marked the entrance to the chamber, lofty with bands of steel around the sides, and polished to a fine sheen. He looked up to see the twin horses, who stood forever charging into the sky, their bronze forms running relentlessly into an unknown horizon. The one on the right represented noble Luthil, proud and tall, its head continually pointed towards the rising sun. The other bore the image of ancient Abys, smaller but running with frantic speed, adorned with an exotic headdress, and charging desperately into the quiet twilight of the setting sun.

The trio continued onwards, and with some significant prompting, Virgil finally got his companions to the other side of the Grand Canal. Upon crossing the bridge, Virgil readjusted the weight of the box in his arms, and led Kat and Lyra into old Abys.

The faces of creatures that had long since passed from the face of the world lined each chipped plaster wall and well-trodden bridge. Lit candles surrounded these walls, their flame fighting against the wind as they stood in memory of lost relatives. There was little space for horse and cart in these narrow waterways.

With each passing bridge and painted square, Katerina's voice became quieter. Soon she walked in silence, her eyes cast low, the box of food weighing heavily upon her arms.

The waterways grew narrower, and the walls closed in. The noble houses of Abys were soon behind them. Light shone between broken tiles and the fractured skyline of winding alleyways, and yet in the depths of the Water District, the creeping shadows overwhelmed whatever golden rays had made it this far.

The sounds of the city changed, submitting to the darkness. Laboured creaks moaned across rotten wood, sprawled haphazardly across derelict bridges. The eager cries of trade faded into hasty shouts and distant screams, muted by the scuffle of tavern brawls and the cries of hungry infants. Silent figures wrapped in weatherworn coats stood in long-forgotten doorways, staring out hopelessly across broken patterns of plaster and chipped bricks. Each building bore the story of a hundred years, every scar of time and storm visible on its broken form.

Shivering bodies, both young and old, moved across this dark warren. Their passage was fleeting, their faces hollowed and wearied, and they paid little heed to the plethora of guild markings that lined every waterway. In a place where even the Vox Militant rarely walked, the guilds were a part of daily life. There was no escape from their rules or their demands, except for the depths of the water below.

The trio turned along what was now for all of them a well-known corner, and they came to a sudden stop. Lyra placed her hand on Kat's shoulder, and Virgil stepped reverently to one side.

Kat took one deep breath and stepped forward, approaching a door which was for her the entrance to so much more than just an old house. She handed Lyra her box of food, and gently tapped on the door.

A small elderly face answered, a pair of yellowed eyes peering out from the darkness within.

"Yes?" squeaked the woman, seemingly unsure of what to make of her visitors.

"It's me, Mrs Magorin, it's Katerina."

The elderly woman peered closer, pulling some dusty spectacles from out of the black depths behind the doorway, and placing them perilously upon her nose.

"Who's that, now?" she asked.

"It's me, Katerina, Mrs Magorin. Kat Darrow, you remember?"

The woman leaned closer, straightening her spectacles with one crooked finger.

"Why, yes! Young Kat! You've grown so much since I saw you last," replied Mrs Magorin, repeating the same sentence that she had greeted Katerina with every year of her return.

Kat took the box of food from Lyra. "I have brought you and the children some gifts."

The elderly woman smiled and welcomed the three of them inside, holding the door for them as they processed in, before shutting it quickly behind them.

Now that they were inside the room, it suddenly seemed less dark. Lyra observed a scattering of candles dotted around the interior, their gentle flames melding with the light that poured in from a half-boarded window on the other side of the room.

Even in this confined space, Lyra could still feel the cold bite at her fingers. The sound of lapping water could be heard from all around, and the ceiling sagged with warped timber beams.

Three small figures under three layers of blankets looked up at the visitors, their tired eyes watching with interest.

"Don't mind these," said the old woman, gesturing down at the three young children. "Their parents make them labour in the machine works by night, poor things. I let them sleep here during the day and feed 'em what food I can. Don't I, young ones?"

"Yes, Mrs Magorin," they muttered sleepily, pushing themselves up from their makeshift beds.

"Why don't they sleep at home?" asked Lyra.

"There's nowhere that they can sleep, dearie. Their parents have no home, and they work during the day. At night they sleep where they can find a floor, and then the little ones go off to work."

Lyra met their gaze, watching as their fearful eyes were rubbed awake. They could only have been a few years older than Nathan.

"And you more than earn your keep, don't you, my dear?" muttered Mrs Magorin, handing a glass of water to the nearest child. "Not that you should have to, mind, not in that awful place. But Mummy and Daddy need to save up for that rent money, and then you'll get a warm bed for a few evenings. Won't that be nice?"

Lyra felt her heart break as the child enthusiastically nodded his head, his eyes widening at the thought of a warm night, away from the damp streets and the rising steam of the factories.

"Two sleeps more, Mummy says. Only two sleeps more," spoke the young boy, his words shaken but his tone hopeful.

"That's right, sweet one," replied the old woman.

Lyra knew very little about Mrs Magorin. She was something of a mystery, this elderly custodian of the most broken and wretched people of a city that had no shortage of either. What she did know was that Mrs Magorin opened her house to needy children from all across old Abys, offering them free room and board for a few nights each, and her house soon became overwhelmed by the wearied steps of the poor and needy. She herself survived on the sale of whatever knitted clothes that she had the time to make, and from the offerings of what little the community had to spare. Lyra also knew that Kat devoted a good portion of her earnings to supporting this fragile place. This shaken house of worn bones and quivering limbs, which she had once called home.

A sudden series of taps rattled across the windows, and the sound of a brick breaking against the plaster wall of the house ran across the room.

The children looked up and Mrs Magorin settled them with a smile, before looking back over to Kat.

"We pay the guilds for protection. Same as everyone else. But we don't seem to get much. We hear much more from that rabble outside and I'll have to find money for another window, won't I, little ones?"

The smallest child leaned forward, whispering something into her ear.

"What's that? No, no, Alun. I'm not going to sell you for the money. I wouldn't get enough for you, my boy, skinny as you are. Got to get some meat on your bones before then. But don't be giving an old woman ideas like that, especially as I'm hankering for a new bed." Mrs Magorin grinned, rubbing some greasy hair away from the young urchin's face. She looked up at the trio, her grin fading as more jeers could be heard outside, alongside the distinctive breaking of beer bottles.

Even from the corner of her eye Lyra could see Virgil's hands slowly curl into fists.

The artificer gave the old woman a respectful nod of his head.

"Please excuse me for a few moments." Without waiting for a reply, Virgil took a step outside, and closed the door promptly behind him. Lyra listened as his entry into the street was met with a flurry of drunken shouts, which suddenly fell silent.

Kat leaned down towards the child closest to her.

"Hey there, my name's Kate. What's yours?"

The young girl hid for a few moments behind her elderly guardian, before cautiously leaning around to peek at Kat.

"Constance," she replied, her voice weak, her eyes fearful.

"What a pretty name you have, Constance. I have a present right here for little girls with pretty names." She lifted a blanket from her box of food and pulled out a fresh green apple, handing it gently over to the child.

For a few moments Constance's eyes darted warily between Mrs Magorin and the apple. Hearing no warning, and seeing food freely offered, she took it gladly, biting into it with enthusiasm. On her second bite three loud thuds rumbled in from the street outside, along with a chorus of painful yelps. Momentarily distracted away from the offer of food, the children looked over to the window, hoping to catch a glimpse of what was going on.

Standing between the children and the window, Lyra and Kat promptly began handing out more food, eager to keep their attention within the room. A sudden flash of blue light crossed the window pane, and it was at this moment that Lyra thought it would be a good idea to hand out small squares of chocolate. Mrs Magorin now also looked outside, her interest peaked by the strange noises.

"Are there any more children upstairs, Mrs Magorin?" asked Lyra, gently placing herself in front of the old woman. "We have some food for them as well."

The older woman paused and smiled happily, forgetting the noises outside and happy to be able to call the children down with some good news.

No sooner had she walked towards the stairs than Virgil once again entered the room, straightening his cloak and the cuffs of his jacket. He winked over at Lyra and began to help handing out food. The street behind him was now perfectly silent, with the exception of the gently lapping water.

Mere moments after Mrs Magorin called out with the promise of food, the room was filled with hungry mouths and young, dirt-stained faces. The trio happily portioned out fresh fruit and sweets. Laughter, mixed with the satisfied chewing of these rare gifts, filled the room, and for the first time in a long while, Mrs Magorin brewed herself some tea, took a sip and sat relaxed in her chair. She watched content, whilst the children enjoyed the food, and took some rest as her guests filled the pantry with pallets of fresh food. Once the sweets were utterly devoured, Virgil sat on the floor and opened a small box that hung on his belt. He entertained a crowd of smiling faces that spanned across most of the room. Sparks of light and shining figures danced between his fingers.

Lyra and Kat sat beside Mrs Magorin. Virgil's tricks and trinkets held no wonders for her. Even as the tail of a fiery red dragon curled around Virgil's thumb, her eyes remained fixed upon the smiling faces of the children. Lyra had rarely seen someone grin with such glee as Mrs Magorin did now, and in only a few moments, years of fatigue and worry lifted from her face.

"Thank you for coming again, young Kat. Your visits always bring me joy," spoke the old woman as another gasp of surprise erupted from Virgil's audience. Her voice was a tone lighter; it was steadier and more assertive. The haze of forgetfulness that had greeted Kat's arrival seemed lifted from Mrs Magorin's mind, and the hot tea was emitting spiralling tendrils of warmth across her wrinkled fingers.

"I know that this is a difficult day for you. This house is home to more than a few ghosts."

Kat nodded slowly, remembering the day that her parents had died and the very hour in which Virgil and Maellon Alpheri had stepped into her home. She still remembered clutching on to her mother's coat when they had opened the door, and she could feel the coarse cotton lining under her finger nails to this very day. Only in the heat of the forge did this particular phantom fade away.

On their tour of mercy across the Water District, Virgil and Maellon had simply been handing out food to those in dire need of it. They had not been expecting to return with the distraught figure of a young child who no longer had a place to call home. However, on seeing the terrible fate that awaited the newly-bereaved Kat were she to be left there, Virgil had felt that he had no other choice than to rescue her from the endless depths of the Water District. Mrs Magorin had taken on the rent of the property soon afterwards, and with the passing of its landlord, it had been left to her, freely given to support the work that she did for the community.

The room was now full of the noise of joyful children who eagerly watched Virgil's display. Nonetheless, when Kat had first laid eyes upon the artificer, she had just emerged from hours of deathly silence.

"I still think of your parents, often," smiled Mrs Magorin, turning a friendly eye to Kat.

Kat could not quite meet her gaze, not in this moment. She listened to one of the younger children laugh as Virgil pulled a contorted face between a pair of sparkling flames.

"Your father was quite the character, though, not to be outshone by your mother. They were very kind to me."

Kat looked up.

"Could you tell me about them?"

Mrs Magorin sipped her tea once again and told the same stories, in the same way that she had for many years past. Each year Kat listened intently, responding as if she were hearing them for the first time, just like always. Lyra sat beside her and the hours passed like minutes. Each word that fell from Mrs Magorin's lips mattered more to Kat than all the gold that lined the domes of the Magisters' Chambers.

With each passing tale, the light in the room grew darker, and before long the trio knew that they would soon need to leave. Virgil's fingers grew dim as he returned the magical powder that he had taken from the box at his belt. The children, happy with the display, were content to return to their beds and dream. A wearied contentment soon settled once again on Mrs Magorin's face. She rose from her seat, helped settle a few of the children, and bid her visitors goodbye.

"Thank you again, all of you. This short time that you have given us will mean a lot to them."

Virgil cast a watchful eye up and down the narrow street, before turning back to Mrs Magorin and handing her a small bag of golden coins.

"For you and your charges. If your home is troubled again you can reach me through the usual channels. I will deal with it," he said intently, holding her hand briefly before setting off with Lyra in the direction of a small canal, leaving Kat and the old woman alone for a few moments.

Lyra saw Kat hand Mrs Magorin a small cloth bag filled with what Lyra knew was a good proportion of her wages. They shared a brief goodbye before Kat wrapped her cloak around herself and made her way over to the watchful pair.

"You all right?" Virgil asked, a warm smile settling on the weathered features of his face.

Red lines of sorrow criss-crossed across Kat's eyes, with small pools of tears welling up.

"I'll be ok."

The artificer stepped forwards, crossed his arms, and slowly nodded.

"Good, you have some forge work tomorrow, and as it happens I might have some tools you can use on that new memory codex of yours. It's time that you started forging your own gear."

Kat's eyes now twinkled with both interest and tears. Virgil tapped her reassuringly on the shoulder, before leading them back the way that they had come. Lyra placed an arm around her oldest friend and they made their way home.

5

A Family Matter

L yra sighed, massaging the sole of her foot before turning her attention to the next set of laces that ran across the leather frame of her other boot.

"I've said it before and I'll say it again."

"Don't say it," Lyra replied, rolling her eyes.

"I'm going to say it."

"Uh, Virgil, they're fine!"

"But they look so uncomfortable," muttered the artificer, pulling off his rain-soaked coat and handing it to Tom. The young serving boy was dressed in his servant robes, with a clean, white apron worn over the top of his emerald green jacket.

"They look nice, ok?!" snapped Lyra, her fingers unravelling the knot that sat just under her knee.

Virgil looked down at the boots and scowled, eyeing them with no small degree of suspicion.

"There must be something more comfortable that you can wear. Look at those heels! How do you even walk in those?"

Before Lyra could offer a reply, Virgil picked up a boot from the floor and held it in front of Tom's face.

"Look here, lad. Does that look comfortable to you?"

Tom's eyes widened with embarrassment and he stood mute, held still by Virgil's commanding tone.

"Don't bring Tom into this!"

"Where you, Kat, and bizarre footwear are concerned I'll take all the allies that I can get. Now, Tom, would you wear those?"

Tom eyed the boots for a moment, his brow furrowed with confusion.

"No, sir."

"Smart lad. Now, do you think that any sane person would walk around in them?" Virgil asked, with a twinkle in his eyes.

"Uh, well, I...um" Tom stuttered.

Lyra kicked off the offending boot, its laces now untied, and rose to her feet. She threw a glare towards Virgil, before smiling over at the serving boy.

"Don't listen to him, Tom. He's been breathing in too much steam from his forge. Thank you for taking our coats," she said softly, looking down at the apron. "I take it that dinner is ready?"

"Yes, Lady Alpheri –"

Her eyes hardened in playful reproach.

"Yes, Lyra," Tom corrected himself. "The rest of the family are seated and I believe that Miss Katerina is –"

"Absolutely starving!"

Kat turned the corner, a dark, leather notebook gripped tightly in her hand.

"You had half a chicken for lunch!" laughed Virgil, removing his own considerably smaller boots, before settling into a pair of slippers that Tom handed him with his free hand.

"Well, it's been a busy day," Kat answered, waving the notebook triumphantly. "It's not every day that I get to decode a memory codex," she continued with a wink and a skip across the marble floor of the mansion's foyer.

It had been a week since she had made her annual journey to her former home in the shadows and ruin of Abys. Lyra had kept a careful eye on her friend, the same as every year. She had recovered from the visit, she always did. But this year it had been different. The gift from Virgil of the tools needed to read her memory codex had brought a smile to Kat's face every day without fail. Lyra doubted that the memory of Kat's scarred childhood and her passion for decoding the old book were unconnected.

Memory codices were a remnant of ancient Luthanril, an empire which could trace its heritage back before even that of old Abyssus. It was, like its prodigy the empire of Abys-Luthil, a civilisation of magic. Luthanril was a great and powerful nation, stretching across the vast plains and mountains of the north. Its sorcerers and knowledgeable artificers interwove the disciplines of technology and the arcane to field fleets of vast ships and armies of walking, mechanical goliaths. Or so the chronicles said, but all that was left of their records was locked away in the city's two universities and the lofty heights of the Aquin tower near the Magisters' Chambers.

After the fall of Luthanril into ruin, the exodus of its people, and the subsequent conquest of what remained of Abyssus, what was left of their knowledge was recorded in what came to be known as memory codices. These were the frantic scrawlings of magic users long since passed, and they were very difficult to read, let alone decipher. They were all written in haste, as the sorcerers who wrote them were still reeling from the sudden and disastrous destruction of their home. Their desire to record all that they could from the vast libraries of their burning civilisation meant that the old Luthan text of the codices were often barely legible and contained errors leading to fatal mistakes for eager artificers. Worse still were the magical wards and protective enchantments laid upon these books, only enhanced by the rare and arcane-imbued metals that often accompanied them. Given these spiralling levels of complexity, memory codices could only be read with special tools, often in the form of glasses made for this singular purpose, designed and produced by only the very finest of Abys-Luthil's artificers. Thankfully for Kat she just so happened to work for one of them.

"I want that on my desk first thing tomorrow. It would be a bit of a waste if you blew your hand off trying to read a codex," said Virgil, looking at the notebook which contained Kat's transcription of the aged tome.

"Aww, it's nice to hear that you still care," replied Kat.

"Oh I care, my girl. I'd care greatly if you blew up part of my forge, believe me."

With that Tom handed their coats to another servant and led them from the foyer to the dining room. To say that the home of the Alpheri family was vast would feel like an understatement. Marble columns lined the front corridors and rooms of the great mansion, standing beside lines of servants and guards. Rooms decorated with oak panels and chairs of burgundy leather were dotted between these ornate colonnades. Great frescos of famous battles and revered scholars greeted each passing guest and family member who walked by, each telling the story of a proud city and a noble family.

Lyra had spent countless hours staring into these paintings of her fore-bears, searching for traces of a family resemblance. She had found them many times, but much more often in the lineage of her father than that of her mother. He carried the same blonde hair and high cheek bones that she herself bore, and these family traits were well reflected in the paintings that lined the venerable house.

It was not long before they passed the picture of her mother that hung near the library. It was a large painting and Lyra could not help but look at it every time she passed it. Her mother's face was kind, her auburn hair falling in fine locks across the side of her face with a gentle smile resting upon her lips. She held a book in her hands, which appeared to be rather old, with a weathered spine and uneven pages, yellowed by many years. Her eyes were the one point of resemblance that she had passed to Lyra, as her father often liked to mention.

Her gaze lingered upon the painting for a few moments, before she recovered her steps as the group made their way to dinner.

"Lyra! Lyra!" came an eager cry further along the hallway.

She smiled, even before the appearance of Nathan, who sprinted as fast as his little legs could carry him.

"Lyra! Lyra!" he exclaimed, arms open wide. She knelt down and scooped her nephew up in her arms, placed him on her shoulders, and continued her journey to the dining room. This was not the first time she had been greeted by Nathan in this way and for her, it was often the highlight of a long day. The lavish décor of her house, and its marvellous frescos, vibrant paintings and antique furniture, were nothing to her compared to the sweet cry of young Nathan welcoming her home.

"Mr Salmons said that I got a ten out of ten in maths today, Lyra! Look! Look what he gave me!" said Nathan, promptly thrusting a small woven badge, bearing a large gold star, in front of her face.

Lyra, her vision momentarily obscured, narrowly avoided walking into a large statue, as Virgil rolled his eyes and pulled her to safety.

"Wow, Nathan! That's fantastic! What did mummy and daddy say?"

Nathan smiled with unashamed glee.

"They said that I get extra pudding after dinner!"

"Extra pudding! You're a lucky boy, Nathan. Keep that maths up and you could be an artificer one day," smiled Kat.

The prospect of this seemed to please Nathan, and he spoke happily of his studies and his hopes for pudding for the rest of their short journey. It seemed that chocolate ice cream was at the top of his list, which gained further support from Lyra and Kat.

They soon reached the dining room, their journey disturbed only by Nathan's retelling of his day and the occasional rumble from Virgil's stomach.

Maellon, Mara and Alfred greeted them on their arrival beside a vast host of servants, and the Alpheri family and guests sat down for dinner. Lyra had never considered either Virgil or Kat as guests. For her they had been part of the family for as long as she could remember, but as Luthan custom dictated, they were served first, as guests of the family. The scent of roast duck soon filled the room and trays of freshly cooked vegetables were laid beside bottles of wine and lemon water.

"All looks rather marvellous to me," exclaimed Alfred, rubbing his hands together happily, before he tucked Nathan's napkin into the young boy's collar.

"Best not leave it to get cold then," said Kat, who swiftly piled roast potato after roast potato onto her plate with wilful abandon.

"Ah, Nathan, stop trying to put your broccoli back on the tray. You're going to be eating some more of that, mister," chastised Mara, placing two more pieces of green food onto her son's plate, ignoring his protests.

Maellon looked over to Lyra and grinned, observing the unfolding domestic comedy with muted contentment.

"You're never going to eat all of that," whispered Virgil, leaning over to his apprentice.

"Oh, no?!" spat Kat, her mouth half full of food, the indignant tone of her reply further obscured by yet more crisp, golden portions and a sliver of duck.

Despite the fact that Kat and Virgil usually cooked for themselves, Virgil often taking meals into his forge and Kat making the best possible use of his small kitchen as she could, Maellon insisted that the pair share a meal with the family at least once a week. He often took this opportunity to take counsel with Virgil with some wine after the meal, and given the continual unrest in the city, Lyra suspected that the two had a great deal to discuss. However, thankfully, the strain of politics was not brought to bear at the table, and the group enjoyed a pleasant, if noisy meal.

Once dinner was concluded, with as generous a portion of chocolate ice cream as a young boy could wish for, Maellon and Virgil retired to the study.

"Come on, Nathan. Let's see if I can't beat you at dominoes again," said Kat with a wink, guiding the young boy to the sitting room as Mara followed suit.

Lyra began to rise from her chair to join them, until Alfred, wiping one last drop of ice cream from his moustache, sat beside her.

"Lyra, old girl, I wondered if you had a moment to spare for a quick chinwag," he asked, easing slowly into his chair.

"For you, Uncle, any time," answered Lyra, pouring herself another glass of water as a servant removed her empty bowl.

"Wonderful, wonderful. The matter rattling around the old brain box is, well, I'm not so sure if I'm cut out for the new job, as it were," muttered Alfred awkwardly, rubbing the side of his head. "You know, this merchant-banking lark. Not as simple as it looks, lots of records and numbers and all that." He cast his eyes down, his greasy fingers fiddling with the cuff of his jacket.

"Not that I'm bored, no! In fact, a lot of it is jolly interesting stuff. But when I'm staring at all that paperwork, oh, there's piles and piles of it, dear girl, well, I'm not so sure that I can do it."

He glanced up at her, his face downcast, eyes strained with worry.

"Uncle, I'm sure you're doing the best that you can. Aunt Mara knows just how hard you work," replied Lyra, pouring him his own glass of water, which he sipped noisily for a few moments.

"Well that's just the thing, Mara's a wonderful lady. She's kind, patient and beautiful; the finest woman that a chap could ever hope to marry. Well out of my batting average," he answered before taking another sip.

Lyra had spent enough time talking to Alfred to understand what he meant, though it still brought her some amusement.

"You make her very happy, Uncle. Nathan too."

"You see old girl, I'm just not terribly sure that I do. I can't say that I'm very good at sticking to a job. In fact, one might say that I've been downright awful at it. I know that I made a right pig's ear of the old goat business."

Lyra resisted the urge to cringe.

"You weren't to know that the last shipment was full of cows, in a certain light... dim moonlight, they looked kind of similar," she said in as reassuring a voice as she could muster.

"That's very kind of you to say, my girl. But I can't help but feel if I fail at this banking endeavour, well, I'll just be letting them both down again," he uttered despondently, cupping his glass in both hands.

Lyra placed her drink back onto the table and leaned forward.

"I know just how hard you're working at this new job, and so do Father and Aunt Mara. If you keep doing that, then you won't ever let her or Nathan down. I've seen how they both look at you. They love you very much and I have no doubt that if you keep working as hard as you have, you'll be just fine and you won't make a... pig's ear of it."

"You really think so?"

"I do."

A smile stretched merrily across Alfred's lips, crowned by his fiery red moustache.

"That's jolly good of you to say, Lyra. Very good indeed. I appreciate it, I really do!"

Without pause Alfred gave her the greatest bear hug that he could muster, and the two made their way to join the other family members.

She watched for a moment. Alfred looked on whilst his son happily played with Kat and his wife.

"I'll do whatever I can for them."

"I know you will."

Alfred smiled and entered the room, giving his wife a kiss on the cheek before ruffling his son's hair and sitting down beside him.

Before she had a chance to join them, Lyra heard a familiar voice a few steps behind her.

"He wants to see you."

She turned to see Virgil, glass of wine in hand, walking towards her.

"What about?" Lyra asked.

Virgil shrugged, taking a hearty gulp of wine.

"Ah, now that would be telling. You're going to have to find out for yourself."

She offered him a playful scowl. "Did anyone ever tell you that you can be a right pain sometimes?"

Virgil considered this for a moment, taking another, rather large sip of wine.

"Yes, but most of those people are dead, so I don't feel too bad about it."

Not attempting to offer a retort, Lyra made her way to her father's study, thanking the Alpheri family guard who opened the door for her.

She was not sure why, but each and every time that she entered this particular room, she was always caught off guard by how chaotic and messy it seemed. Opened books filled with page markers lay piled beside perilously-stacked sheets of paper, each adorned with a plethora of scribbles and hastily recorded notes. A roaring fireplace flanked by desks laden with ink and charts stood at the far end of the room, next to the seated figure of Maellon Alpheri.

109

Lyra noticed the spiralling tendrils of steam that emitted from a fresh pot of coffee beside her father's flagon of wine. He regularly drank the two together, comforted by the sweet taste of the wine and energised by the bitter tang of the coffee. She often mocked him for it, having never acquired a taste for drinking both at the same time. She settled for pouring herself a small cup of coffee.

"How was your day?" he asked softly as she took her seat.

"It was fine. I spent some time at the forge. Kat will soon have made her first shield, which is really exciting."

"A shield? Seems a bit old fashioned for Virgil, let alone Katerina," said Maellon.

"That's what I thought, but Kat says that there's something different about this one. Even Virgil hinted that if she's done her research properly, it will be able to stop a bullet or two."

On hearing this Maellon nodded slowly, taking a sip of coffee. "Impressive. I should like to see it when it's finished. Katerina has indeed come a long way. If she keeps this up, she'll make a fine artificer one day."

"She's very thankful for what you and Virgil have done for her," replied Lyra encouragingly. On hearing this, her father quickly shook his head.

"Whatever Katerina has already accomplished or will go on to do so, is because of her hard work. I have done very little for her." Maellon placed his coffee down on a small table adjacent to his chair. "Far less than I should have."

"You know that's not true."

Maellon sighed, rubbing his hands gently before the fire. "Lyra, the older I get, the more I am convinced that I actually know very little."

Lyra's brow furrowed in a mixture of irritation and confusion.

"There is no one who does more for this city than you do."

Maellon replied with a bitter smile. "Yes, Lyra, but that is not always a good thing."

"Why do I feel like I'm missing something? What's wrong?" she asked.

Her father did not answer straight away, but instead leant back into his chair, clasping his hands together.

"Nothing. Well, nothing new. Troubles rise and troubles fall but rarely are they new."

"So now you're reciting poetry at me."

"Alas, not even good poetry at that," he muttered, eyes gazing lazily across the room.

"Father, what is it?"

Maellon sighed once more, picking up a small piece of scrap paper from the nearby table and casually folding it between his fingers.

"The vote of the Public Censor Act was today."

The sound of his words was broken only by the crackle of the flames which devoured the large pieces of wood piled at its base.

"Yes I heard, as has most of the city. It was rejected. You won!" Her words were followed only by the splutter of flame. "That's good news, isn't it?"

"That it was rejected? Yes. That is very good indeed. But what the people on the street are probably not talking about is the fact that it was rejected by a margin of fifty. Fifty magisters, out of five hundred." His hands suddenly clenched, and the delicately folded paper became a small crumbled ball within his fist.

"Nihilo's last measure was rejected by a margin of over three times that many. I am losing ground, Lyra, and the momentum of power is moving swiftly against me. A tide that I cannot, at this time, easily swim against."

"But you have lots of friends at the Magisters' Chambers. Surely they'll support you. They always have in the past."

The ball of crumpled paper became smaller and smaller between his fingers.

"In the past, yes. But now, they grow tired of fighting. Their passion for defending the people wanes. They spend more time in their palaces or on the Grand Canal than they do in the voting chamber. Their lives become easy, sedate, as does their politics. There are still a few good magisters that I can count within their number, but they grow fewer with every passing year."

Lyra, not sure what to say in response, returned to her coffee for a few moments, watching as her father's hands curled in anger. To say that seeing him this upset was unusual was an understatement. Her father was the most controlled and measured man that she had ever known, and impressively he had done this without ever becoming cold.

"He's going to try again," he muttered rolling the paper in his hand.

"So what are you going to do?" she asked.

"Same as I've always done, Lyra. I'll keep fighting. Nihilo knows that he faces a fight each time that he tries to place a censor on free speech. While the printing presses still operate, I'll find some support."

With a flick of his wrist, Maellon tossed the ball of paper into the fireplace, watching it dance amongst the flames.

"I won't let Nihilo drive this city once again into the fires of tyranny. While I draw breath, I won't let him drag us down into the inferno."

Lyra followed his gaze, seeing the paper blacken and burn, swiftly consumed by a writhing sea of flame.

"While you were on the podium, at the last forum, Nihilo spoke to me. He said something strange," she said, her eyes still looking into the fire as waves of orange and red ran across the corners of the room. Maellon's hands suddenly relaxed. He took the goblet of wine into his hands and looked back over towards his daughter.

"What did he say?" asked Maellon, his words slow and steady.

"He said that he agreed that freedom should be protected, and that it was the most important thing. Then he mentioned that he had once read a treatise that you wrote on freedom, and that it had greatly influenced him."

She watched as her father's face grew darker on hearing these words, until a strange smile formed upon his lips.

"Yes, it does not surprise me that he mentioned that. I have heard him quoting it more than a few times in the forums. He does so out of context, of course, but it appears to be sadly effective all the same." Lyra felt badly for her father, hearing a note of concern in his voice, and yet the same curiosity that had propelled so much of her life welled up within her.

"What did you write about freedom in your treatise?" she asked, before draining the last drop of coffee from her cup and reaching over to the small table to pour some more.

"I wrote it a long time ago. Though in truth, it feels like a lifetime ago."

With no further pause Maellon explained the premise of his treatise on freedom, as his mind wandered back to his days as a new university lecturer all those years ago. He spoke with a gentle wave of his hand upon reaching every central point of his argument. Lyra listened intently as always; she relished these conversations and now that the recent voting process was over she sincerely hoped that her father would have more time for them. However, as Maellon continued to speak, she could not help but scowl slightly as she tried to reconcile what he was saying with the speech that he had delivered at the last forum.

"Wait, so you wrote that freedom doesn't actually exist?" she asked with hesitation.

Maellon swapped his wine for coffee and continued.

"Yes."

Lyra breathed in, attempting to object, before her father continued.

"And no."

Lyra sighed, giving him a sideways look.

"Clearly I'm missing something. Would you care to enlighten me, Father?" she said rolling her eyes.

Maellon grinned. "Certainly, Daughter."

"Lyra, it is not simply that freedom, well, more specifically, absolute freedom, does not exist. To even say that it does, to claim that you can live and act with the belief that you can possess freedom absolutely and without hindrance, is in fact a terrible, terrible crime."

Maellon leaned forward for a moment, pouring himself the last of the coffee.

"It is both a crime against nature and against every person whom you come into contact with. Any man or woman who claims to possess such freedom is a tyrant, whether peasant or king. There can be few darker ambitions than that of the desire of freedom without restraint."

"Then why do you defend the voice of the people and the printing press houses? If freedom is so wrong, then why fight for it? And who, dear Father, gets to decide how much freedom each person should have?"

At this Maellon laughed heartily.

"There lies the hard questions! You always ask the hard questions, just like your mother did. She kept a loving watch on my freedom. I loved her for that." His voice grew quiet for a few moments, and he sat silent whilst memories still raw after all these years leapt out at him from the flames.

"To claim to have absolute freedom, Lyra, is to claim to be free from all responsibility or constraint. It is to brazenly declare that your will matters above all others, and that you are at liberty to make your own laws and your own moral code. Like a god."

Lyra thought about this for a moment, reflecting on the weight of her father's words.

"So we leave the state to decide the limits of our freedom for us?" she asked sceptically.

"Certainly not. The state is not fit to do that, not as long as it is comprised of people. No, the voice of the people must check the state, the press houses must be free to print and to publish, but most of all, to criticise."

A sudden crackle of flame sparked from the fireplace, illuminating Maellon's face and casting thin shadows across his cheeks.

"The sad rule of politics, Lyra, is that the government exists, in part, to limit the freedom of the people, and the voice of the people will always strive to check the freedom of the government. Which is why censorship, any censorship, cannot be endured, or very soon, the freedom of the government becomes limitless."

"People will always think and say terrible things. No amount of censorship will change that. I would rather that such people are offered the chance to air their ridiculous views so that I may be sure that I always keep my right to oppose them. The serpent that you can see is always less dangerous than the one hiding in the grass, well, in most cases, at least, anyway."

To this Lyra offered no response, taking some time to think upon his words.

"Nihilo abuses my words, twisting them to limit the freedom of the press houses so that the state may wield power without criticism. This cannot be allowed to happen. He deliberately ignores my conclusion. The only freedoms that may be endured in their totality, are those of freedom of thought and free speech, and that is only because without them, great power will always roam unchecked, and then tyrants will claim power in the name of freedom."

Lyra rubbed her head slowly, wishing that there was more coffee left in the pot.

"I think I understand what you mean."

"That's reassuring, because sometimes even I'm not terribly sure."

Lyra smiled, reminded of why she so admired her father, even if the two did not always agree.

Lyra grabbed the nearest piece of paper that was to hand and began inspecting it.

"Ah, yes, I was planning on showing you that particular design. Virgil has only just approved it, and if I recall correctly, you wanted one for your birthday," Maellon said, finishing his wine.

It took Lyra a few moments to figure out what she was looking at. She turned the paper around more and leaned closer, paying close attention to the intricately-drawn diagram, examining the fine ink lines that ran across its surface.

A sudden realisation brought an instant grin to her face, but only prompted more questions. It was a pistol, of that she was now sure, but the barrel seemed to be made entirely of metal, and it lacked a flintlock. In the place of the usual firing pan found on other guns, there was a rotating wheel consisting of six chambers, each holding a small cylindrical object labelled "bullet".

"What do you think?" asked Maellon. Despite the fact that he was not an artificer, Maellon and Virgil's friendship spanned many years, and he had learned a considerable amount from his friend. Whilst he had little knowledge of the technical aspects of forging artifice tools, weapons and armour, Maellon was very gifted at offering new conceptual designs for all manner of projects.

"I must admit that I'm not sure I completely understand it. But I love it already," she replied with genuine excitement.

"Funny, that's what I said on the day you were born," Maellon laughed.

Lyra joined him, making a small ball of paper of her own and throwing it in his direction. It bounced harmlessly from his shoulder, as he rose to his feet and offered her a hand up.

"I know that I can trust you, Lyra. But I want you to be careful with this gift. It is for practising on the training ground under Castel's supervision, and self-defence only. I know that you won't take my words lightly."

"I won't, Father," she replied, wrapping her arms around him.

"Good, and tomorrow we need to have a conversation about your future, young lady. I need a trade envoy to represent the family company at a meeting in Aurel next month. I think that it's about time that you presented your own trade pitch."

Lyra looked up, her heart beating a little faster. "You think I'm ready?"

"I know you are," Maellon answered, leading her from the room. "Now, it's time that you got some sleep. We have a busy day tomorrow and I can feel my eyes closing already."

"Goodnight, Father."

Maellon rubbed her gently on the shoulder before turning towards the house's grand stairway. "Goodnight, Lyra."

She watched as her father cast a wearied eye over to the painting of her mother and walked out of sight. Lyra yawned, as tiredness set in, and decided to make a quick visit to the sitting room before she made her way to bed.

Kat had to hear about this.

6

The Last Cry

T he ring of the doorbell reached Castel's ears as he stepped out of the kitchen.

"Don't forget to drink all of it. If you pour it down the sink, you'll be the one paying for it on the training ground later," he said, pointing at Lyra, who could not have looked less enthused to drink the strange concoction that he had prepared for her, especially at this time in the morning. The energy drink was an early morning ritual that was easily Lyra's least favourite thing about training, but with Virgil and Kat absent, their having returned to the labours of the forge, she had no one to distract her from its inevitable consumption. Castel left her to it, knowing that she would finish it, eventually.

"Tom, door!" snapped Castel, watching the young servant scurry down the long corridor.

"Yes, sir. I'm right on it," spluttered Tom, nearly running straight into Alina as he turned around a marble column.

"Are you on your way to see Lord Alpheri?" asked Castel, approaching his fellow guard.

"Yeah, I'm going to relieve Evans and Krell. They've been on duty for the better part of six hours. I'm taking Milo with me."

"Good, he's mostly in the study today. But he has a meeting at the Aureli Embassy with Lyra in three hours. I'll meet up with you before we leave."

"Very good, Cap," replied Alina, with a wink and a quick step towards the other end of the corridor.

A sweet scent flew through the air as she passed by and Castel loudly sniffed.

"That's a new one, smells like caramel, lots of it. Is that what the lads are chasing these days? A woman with the aroma of a cake shop?" he mocked.

Alina spun on her heel and offered him a smile that was anything but sweet.

"Men are like women, Cap, they tend to prefer most scents over that of a damp brewery. You should give it a try sometime," she yelled back, before turning around to take up her post.

Castel chuckled to himself, making his way over to the door that Tom was struggling to open. "I wouldn't mind guarding a brewery."

Spurred on by the looming figure of the guard captain, Tom opened the door slightly ajar. Castel waited in the foyer, nodding at the two guards who had kept watch on the room throughout the early hours.

He could hear voices outside, as rays of sunlight flooded in through the open door.

"How can I help you?" asked Tom, less assertively than Castel would have liked, but the lad was getting there.

"City guard! Here to speak with Magister Maellon Alpheri. Is your master in?" growled a loud voice from the other side of the door. Castel began to step forward, whilst motioning for the other guards to join him.

"Yes, my lord is in the house," replied Tom.

"Good."

Castel had just enough time to see the young servant's eyes widen in terror, when the barrel of a pistol emerged from the doorway and fired, showering the room in a violent red mist. Castel pulled his pistol from his belt in the same moment that Tom's body fell lifeless to the ground, and a host of armed men stormed the room.

Lyra's glass fell crashing to the floor. She froze, not knowing what to do, or where exactly the sound of gun fire was coming from. However, as shot after shot rang out and the desperate cries of the wounded screeched across the corridors, she picked up a bread knife lying on the table beside her and stepped out from the kitchen.

No sooner had she done so, than a man dressed in the bronze armour and purple robes of the Abys-Luthil city guard charged at her from behind a marble column. He swung wildly with his sword, missing her in his desperate attempts to land a blow. Without thinking, Lyra grabbed his sword hand and twisted, feeling his wrist contort under the pressure, and the man cried out in pain. She pulled him down, batting away his free hand with her knife before watching him stumble, and sunk the full length of her blade into his neck.

Blood gushed from the wound, washing in thick red waves across her arm. She saw a look of horror on the guard's face, and the life drain from his eyes. Lyra let him drop to the floor, her hands shaking as she stared down at his bleeding form, still and unmoving.

Her mind raced with thoughts and feelings too numerous for her to process. Her heart beat faster than it ever had before, and a rising feeling of sickness rose from her stomach.

Screams once again assaulted her ears, and soon she could hear the frantic tread of heavy boots running down the corridor. Another city guard, his bronze armour stained with blood, and face scorched with powder burns, was running straight at her.

Lyra froze once more. Fear wracked the shaken thoughts of her trembling mind. Her blade, soaked in crimson, fell from her grasp, and her feet remained unmoved on the bloodstained floor. The man raised his sword, screaming at the top of his lungs.

Then without warning, a shot rang out. Blood splashed across Lyra's face, emitting from a terrible wound that now sat where the man's left eye had once been. He collapsed to the ground, his voice cut short.

"Lyra, run!"

Castel's voice boomed down the corridor.

"To the back of the house, now! Go!"

The guard captain ran towards her, his clothes torn, his sword drawn, and his left arm covered in blood, still holding the freshly-fired pistol.

Yet Lyra stood unmoved, save for the shaking sensation that ran uncontrollably across her arms, her eyes fixed upon the sight of the man she had killed.

Castel grabbed her shoulder with an unyielding force and pulled her down the corridor.

"Lyra, run, now!" He snarled, turning his head with his last breath. More city guards were pouring through the front door, leaping over the bodies of the two Alpheri guards whom only moments ago Castel had been fighting alongside. Pistol shots echoed down the corridor, throwing up chunks of marble and stone as they struck the elaborate columns and decorated walls.

Feeling the pull of Castel on her shoulder, and the screeching sound of passing bullets, Lyra suddenly came to her senses, and ran like she never had before. The two of them leapt from room to room, knocking aside furniture and throwing open doors. Eager gasps for breath tore at Lyra's lungs, as she kept pace with Castel, and the distinctive smell of flame and smoke tainted the air.

Where was her family?

Where was her father?

Was Nathan safe?

Questions and fears lay shrouded across her mind.

The clash of steel lay before them as the blast of musket powder fired behind, and they were soon within sight of a fierce melee around one of the mansion's many grand staircases. A thin line of green stood against a wavering tide of bronze, and Lyra watched as Alina rammed the pointed tip of her bayonet into the chest of a charging city guard. The man grabbed hopelessly at the guard sergeant's artifice rifle and screamed out in horror, before Alina thrust once again with her bayonet, twisting it twice before the scream faded away.

"Father!" Lyra cried out, seeing Maellon standing behind his guards upon the stairway.

"Lyra!" His voice was shaken but clear, his eyes looking out at her from between the guards that surrounded him.

Without pause, Castel joined the fight against the intruders, who appeared to be launching their assault from multiple points of access across the grand house. His sword shimmered with blue energy, carving through man and armour with ease, and quickly felling two of the city guards. His presence appeared to rally his comrades, who brought the full weight of their swords and guns to bear, dispatching the rest of the intruders with brutal efficiency. Two Alpheri guards lay dead on the ground, surrounded by many more sundered opponents.

"We must get the family out to the carriages," said Alina in haste.

"Agreed," nodded Castel, his eyes surveying the room.

"Nathan, we must find Nathan! Aunt Mara, Alfred, where are they?" asked Lyra, running over to her father.

A shaky hand wiped the sweat from Maellon's brow. "The last I saw of them was in the dining room! They must still be there." His words were framed by the lingering presence of smoke which was now spreading rapidly through the house, and within a few moments each of them could hear the distinctive crackle of fire.

Castel pointed towards Maellon and Lyra.

"Get these two in a carriage now. I'll take Milo, Evans and Tyren, and head to the dining room."

Maellon pushed himself forward, his gaze momentarily distracted by the slain forms of his former guards that now lay at his feet.

"I'm not going anywhere without my sister and–" he began.

"Oh yes you will, my lord. Alina, see it done!" Castel's eyes settled on the two guards standing beside her. "If either of them linger, you drag and carry them to get them out of this house. Do you understand?" snapped Castel, motioning over towards Maellon and Lyra.

"Yes, sir!"

Maellon made to speak, but Castel was already on his way, with Milo, Evans and Tyren following swiftly behind.

"I'm coming with you," Lyra pushed past her father and one of the guards to follow Castel.

"Lyra, no!" cried Maellon, but this alone could not stop her. It was only when Alina stepped out in front of her, and another guard placed a hand on her shoulder, that she came to a stop.

"I'm not going to walk from here without the rest of my family, Alina!" yelled Lyra. The more blood that sullied the sight of her home, and the greater the sound of the encroaching fire became, the sooner the fear in her heart was overwhelmed by anger.

"I know, Lyra. Which is why you won't be walking." Without a moment's pause, Alina nodded towards the guard known as Krell, who lifted Lyra off her feet with both arms. Lyra protested with every beat of her hands upon the tall man's back, but to no avail.

"Let's move!"

Alina led the way towards the back of the mansion, her loaded rifle kept ever at the ready, followed swiftly by half a dozen guards and the two shaken nobles.

"Keep those corners tight! Watch your corners!" she hissed at the guards beside her, each one of them turning from room to room with their rifles and pistols held before them.

The small company made their way through three rooms and saw no one, but remained alert for any threat that would present itself. Yet violence nipped hard on their heels, and the sound of rifles and the cries of the wounded passed from room to room, in an unrelenting symphony of death. Lyra saw the bodies of several slain servants littering their way, faces contorted in pain and fear, but now forever still, their eyes locked in a state of horror.

Suddenly the screaming passage of bullets filled the air. The party had reached the grand chamber that marked the rear entrance of the Alpheri household, where large parties of carriage-riding guests were often greeted.

But not today. The green-clothed bodies of Alpheri guards and servants lay lifeless in bloodied heaps across the floor, staining a dark emerald carpet with their blood. Bronze corpses littered the same space, rendered forever motionless by the desperate efforts of the few household guards who had been stationed there during the attack.

However, many more bronze figures were moving amongst the six huge marble columns that supported the vast ceiling of the vaulted chamber. The light of the morning sun shone through the glittering panes of glass that lined every wall, illuminating every corpse and pool of blood with a golden hue.

"Move right!"

The roar of blasting powder once again assaulted Lyra's senses, filling her nose and stinging her eyes.

One of the Alpheri guards to her right dropped suddenly to the ground, his head snapped back by the blow of a rifle shot.

"From column to column, advance! Cut them down!" ordered Alina. The remaining guards needed no further instruction, angered by the loss of their fellows and eager to reach the hope of escape promised by the sight of the carriages outside.

The Alpheri guards moved forward, slaying their foes with the harsh crack of rifles and the swift thrust of bayonets. The intruders fell in droves, their overeager advance cut short by Alina's counterattack, as they left themselves exposed in the room's vast expanse, or took shelter in a position that was soon overwhelmed by their remaining opponents. Lyra saw with her own eyes that they were shown no mercy.

"To the doors, move!" came Alina's voice, melding with the blast of the guns, as another city guard fell to the floor.

The green coated guardsman beside Alina stepped around the nearest pillar, about to make his final advance for the doors, but suddenly a great force wracked his fleeting form, knocking him back, reeling, into Alina.

Lyra, now standing beside Krell, who kept an uneasy watch beside her, pistol and blade in hand, looked over at the large axe that protruded from the dead Alpheri guard's chest. It was clearly no weapon of Abys-Luthil. Even a cursory study of war would have taught any citizen of her city that this weapon was forged far to the north, wielded by an old enemy. She looked up to see the bitter snarl that now formed across Alina's lips as her own eyes lingered on the weapon, before looking around the pillar to see the advance of a dozen large, fur-clad figures.

The Fereli warriors walked beside the city guards, their muscular arms wielding large axes and swords of no shape or design that Lyra had ever seen before. Alina spat on the ground. "Make ready."

On her order, each guard reloaded their guns and gripped their swords tightly.

"Let's make the scum pay!" grunted Alina, glaring over at her foes of old. Chunks of stone flew around her, and the shots of the city guards that covered the Fereli's advance whistled past her face.

Alina took in a great breath, leapt out from the safety of the pillar, and rolled across the floor.

She brought her rifle up to rest against her shoulder and slid her finger across the artifice rune that sat beside the trigger.

"Open fire!"

A roar of smoke and flame filled the scene, with Alina's own weapon leading the fierce volley. Three of the Fereli flew backwards, their bodies falling with unnatural speed, reeling from the beads of blue light that shot from Alina's rifle. Two more of the strangely adorned warriors fell, and Alina charged, spearing one with the tip of her bayonet before swiftly turning upon another with her sword.

Krell and the other Alpheri guards joined her, speeding into the fray. Lyra suddenly found herself alone, kneeling behind the pillar, looking over to catch sight of her father, whose figure was obscured by a remaining household guard at his side. She leaned to her right, watching as Krell removed the tip of his blade from one Fereli and moved onto the next, stepping quickly to one side, and narrowly avoiding the mighty swing of a large axe.

However, the man that he had left bleeding on the floor began to stir, and Lyra watched the fur-clad warrior rise painfully to his elbows, reaching over to grasp a throwing axe that lay by his side. His fingers slowly wrapped around its handle, and the bloodied man looked over to Alina, who was already locked in a desperate combat with two foes.

Lyra ran with all the speed that her shaky legs could muster. Within moments she was upon the Fereli warrior, hammering her fist into his face before wrenching the axe from the man's grasp, sending it sliding across the carpet. He grunted in anger, punching her across the jaw with a bloodied fist, and knocking her sideways. Dazed from the blow, Lyra crawled to her knees, spitting blood before throwing herself on him once more, lifting her elbow and falling with all her weight upon his throat. A terrible, gargled splutter of rage emitted from the Fereli's mouth, veins pulsing angrily across his head as he struggled to breathe.

His fist flailed wildly in the air, but to no avail. Lyra dodged to one side, and, looking down, saw a large dagger that hung from the man's belt. She pulled, lifting the blade from its leather scabbard, and avoided another desperate swing of a tattooed fist before thrusting the dagger down. A scream of pain pierced her ears as the man's fist got in the way of her intended strike, the blade cutting clean through his hand, protruding from the other side. Lyra quickly raised her other hand and launched blow after blow at the dagger's pommel, hammering the blade down towards the man's eyes. Terrible cries now filled the air, but again and again she struck the dagger's handle, forcing it through the quivering hand and into the warrior's eye and further still with every passing blow. His body flailed, his fingers tore at her hair, but still she forced the blade down, leaning upon it with all her weight until the screaming stopped.

Then came a cry more horrible than any she had yet heard.

"Lyra! Lyra!"

His small form was running towards her, but he was far away. So very far.

"Lyra!"

She saw him running down one of the long corridors that led into the chamber. A crown of smoke, gathered from a sudden eruption of flame that was spreading across the house, loomed over Nathan. Rising to her feet, Lyra could see other figures running just behind him. They were garbed in strange furs, their skin covered in tattoos, axes and large swords held in their hands.

"Nathan!" she screamed, speeding towards the young boy, dagger in hand. She ran, but he was still at the other end of the long corridor, and she had not yet exited the chamber.

She could not reach him in time.

Suddenly, one of the corridor's many doors flew open and a large man, wounded, but sword still very much in hand, stepped forward.

Castel urged Nathan to keep running, allowing the boy to pass him as he alone faced down the oncoming Fereli warriors.

Dazzling fire flanked Nathan on every side and the flames grew and surged with unnatural speed, tearing away at the structure of the grand house. This was no normal fire. Lyra saw one of the distant Fereli pull a few glowing stones from his robes and throw them down the length of the corridor.

She watched Castel charge forward, cutting off the Fereli advance with sweeping arcs of his blade, the shimmering blue light cutting down foe after foe. Yet, whilst three of the Fereli fell before him, another figure stepped out of the smoke. This one was larger, his chin and neck covered in a black beard that ran across his chest. He wore tattered mail and leather under a dented silver breastplate, with a wolf skin thrown across his shoulders. Even at this distance Lyra could see that a large tattoo of a crow covered half his face, and he bore an axe of tremendous size, which was imbued with fiery rubies, shining with a great red light.

The huge warrior raised his terrible weapon, and its rubies shone all the brighter, pouring out a great torrent of flame that flew over Castel's head as he ducked to one side. Lyra shielded her face from the heat of the flames, but between the gaps of her fingers, she watched as the ceiling of the corridor began to collapse and a large timber beam, wreathed in flame, blocked the corridor between them.

"Nathan!" she cried, but her scream died in the flames, consumed by the terrible heat. She could see the young boy rising steadily to his feet, and in the distance, she watched Castel trade blows with the huge Fereli, the blue light of his artifice sword running between the flames.

Yet as the fires grew in size, Lyra saw, between the unyielding tide of smoke, Castel's body fall under the blow of the axe.

"No!"

She ran forward once more. Aunt Mara and Alfred were nowhere to be seen, and even now she could barely see Nathan through the shroud of flame. The only thing that she could clearly discern was the looming figure of the Fereli warrior, who made his way towards her nephew.

More timber beams fell and the fire grew, shooting out great waves of heat.

"Nathan!"

She tried to move forward, willing herself to step towards the fiery torrent of the inferno, but the very air itself seemed to oppose her as the flames licked at her hair.

Lyra reached her hand out, grasping for the collapsed timbers. Suddenly, she felt herself being pulled back and looked down to see Alina's arm wrapped across her chest, dragging her away. Lyra tried to step forward once more, but she began to choke on the rising sea of smoke. She fought against Alina's grip, but the guard sergeant refused to yield, drawing her towards the light of the open doors at the other side of the chamber, and the carriages outside.

"I have to get Nathan!" Lyra yelled desperately, pulling at Alina's arm.

"Lyra! We have to leave! There's nothing we can do, we must go!" replied Alina, dragging her into the light.

Lyra's reply became lost in a coughing fit and soon the vast chamber became filled with smoke.

And then she heard it.

"Lyra! Lyra!"

His voice cried out from the flames, shaken by fire and fear.

The cry reached her ears and placed within Lyra's heart a weight that would never leave her.

"Lyra! Lyra!"

His desperate cries swamped her heart and mind, even as rays of sunlight fell upon her face.

"Lyra!"

Tears ran from her eyes and washed away the blood upon her cheeks.

"Lyra!"

She placed her hands over her ears and screamed.

7

Parade's End

"**V**ox Militant, attention!"

Aequo's voice rose clear and crisp over the parade ground. Yet not even his steady cry of command could mask the sense of unease in the air, or obscure the dark pillar of smoke that arose from the western part of the city.

He had heard the rumour, as had every soldier in the order. The home of the Alpheri family had been set ablaze.

Aequo looked over to Rillo who stood five feet in front of him, with hundreds of men and women of the Vox Militant standing to attention behind him, their rifles resting upon their shoulders.

Beyond these ranks of green, on the other side of the parade ground stood High Magister Nihilo and his entourage, and behind them, a further one hundred magisters.

The High Magister was, as always, flanked on both sides by his personal bodyguards, dressed in their distinctive blue robes and black and silver checked masks.

"Soldiers of the Vox Militant, you will now be addressed by the High Magister of Abys-Luthil!" proclaimed Silo Rees, gesturing to his master as Nihilo took a few steps forward, surveying the men and women on the parade ground.

"Soldiers, I have summoned you here today to share a message of hope! A great hope, that rests at the very heart of the future of our great city! Freedom is soon to be brought to you!"

Aequo cast an eye around the rest of the square. No traders were present, no civilians walked on their daily journey across the large square on their way to the trading stalls of the Grand Canal. An uneasy quiet framed each of Nihilo's words, a quiet that was most unnatural to this section of the city at this time in the morning. He could see the occasional city guard patrolling the very edge of the square, their bronze armour shining in the early morning sun.

He looked around to the other side of the square, past the Grand Magisters' Chambers and the lofty Aquin tower, and readjusted the heavy rifle that hung over his shoulder. A sense of unease gripped the sergeant, and he was glad to have his weapon by his side.

"Our great city has come under attack. An attack so insidious and corrosive in its execution, that it sought to strike at the very heart of our state unnoticed."

Nihilo's face suddenly twitched and a seemingly involuntary snarl crossed his lips, in an almost unprecedented display of emotion.

"In a most vile and treacherous union! The slanderous press houses, in collusion with numerous criminal guilds, have forged an alliance with one of this city's great noble houses."

A cool and eerily dispassionate stillness suddenly settled on the High Magister's face.

"The Alpheri family, who can count many of their ancestors as some of this city's most ardent defenders, have betrayed us. They have betrayed you and the people you protect!"

Aequo's eyes widened in shock, his heart beating all the faster as Nihilo continued his speech.

Surely this could not be true?

Aequo knew of Maellon Alpheri and his family. The man was the most gifted speaker and writer of his generation. Aequo had learnt to read by examining one of Lord Alpheri's early books of poetry. He had since bought many more copies, and had always respected the man, even if he was a magister. He heard the rumours surrounding Lord Alpheri when he was Master of Stores, years ago, but those had been dark times and it was difficult to know how responsible he had been for the suffering that had once fallen upon the city.

"Such betrayal cannot be allowed to fester, and so the Council of Five and myself agreed that immediate action had to be taken. Therefore, just two hours ago the city guard has launched an authorised raid to arrest the Alpheri family. This family plotted to inspire the vulnerable people of our fair city to riot, so that Maellon Alpheri himself could seize power in the anarchy that followed!"

There were several audible gasps from the ranks of the Vox Militant, and many turned their heads looking over to their officers and sergeants for orders. Nihilo had just admitted to breaching the constitution which they were sworn to defend.

No magister was allowed to muster armed forces to assault the residence of another magister, no matter if they were a member of the Council of Five or even if they were the High Magister himself.

Without pause, noting the sense of unease running across the ranks, Rillo stretched one arm out, demanding calm.

"Steady! Steady! Stay in rank!" his voice carried easily across the parade square, resolute and unshaken. Aequo felt his heart beat all the faster, knowing the very words which were about to fall from the captain's mouth.

"You have overstepped the mark, Magister," spat Rillo, pointing directly at Nihilo. "No matter what suspicions you held, you may not assault the property of any citizen without the express permission of the Vox Militant." Rillo stepped forward, his hands curling into fists. "You have broken the laws of this city!"

A thin, terrible smile, curled along Nihilo's cheeks as he cocked his head to one side, leaning forward ever so slightly.

"The laws of this land, Captain, are in the hands of the people, not you."

Nihilo spread his arms wide, gesturing to the many magisters behind him.

"We are elected by the people and we stand for them. And now, Captain, comes the time for us to protect them from any that would bring them harm. The printing press houses are to be destroyed. No more will they sully pages with their hate and their lies, offending the minds of our people." With every word that Nihilo spoke, more of the masked, blue robed guards stepped out from between the clustered group of magisters, taking a stand beside their master.

"Those members of the Alpheri family that escaped arrest this morning will be hunted down, so that they may not conspire further to harm our city. The known whereabouts of any and all criminal guild activity will be brought to ruin, to eradicate all treason and sedition!"

Rillo took one more step forward, seemingly unperturbed by the sudden appearance of the many guards that now stood beside Nihilo.

"Your public censor act failed, High Magister. You may not overrule the vote of five hundred other magisters by enforcing it through force of arms."

This time it was Nihilo who advanced, followed by the many guards forming a ring around him.

"Captain, the world has changed and, I fear, it seems to have passed the Vox Militant by. War builds to the north. Even now the Fereli people flee their home and seek shelter in our city for fear of a great armed host that is laying waste to the nations of the north. More and more artefacts of the old Empire appear on our city streets every day, and even the most cautious of our artificers report that magic appears to be returning to the world in a way unseen for millennia!"

Nihilo's voice soon grew silent and his posture relaxed, his feet drawing to a halt. He now looked at Rillo with utter sincerity, with no hint of mockery or anger.

"Captain Rillo, if our city is to survive the changes which will soon be wracked upon it, we must be unified and we must be strong, and sadly to achieve this, decisive action must be taken," uttered Nihilo before he paused, appearing to struggle under the weight of his own words. "Do not think that I relish doing what must be done to keep Abys-Luthil safe, but a stand must be made." His tone was quiet, his words bitter as he seemed to force them painfully from his lips.

"Our current democracy, beautiful in its ideal but fatally flawed in its practice, will not secure the safety of our state."

Rillo's face hardened, locking eyes with the High Magister.

"I will not allow you to deprive the people of their freedom, Nihilo."

On hearing these words, the High Magister smiled and yet his eyes were downcast, offering the floor at Rillo's feet an expression of grim acceptance and regret.

"Captain, there can be few darker ambitions than that of the desire for freedom without restraint. A wise man once taught me that." A look of sorrow washed across the Magister's face, and a deep melancholy twinkled in the corners of his eyes.

"Freedom without restraint makes a man a tyrant, and I would rather that this city suffered the rule of just one tyrant rather than many thousands." Nihilo looked back up at Rillo. "The Council of Magisters is to be suspended with immediate effect. Myself and the Council of Five will rule this city and secure its safety until such a time that we deem fit."

Rillo took a deep intake of breath, ready to give the ranks of soldiers behind him their orders, before Nihilo quickly cut him off.

"Captain, the Vox Militant still have a place in this city. If, that is, you are willing to adapt as we have. Join us, keep your status as the guardians of the people. It is a noble pursuit and it may be your duty still, if you would only accept that times are not what they used to be and that there is now need for a new order."

A pregnant pause hung in the air. Breaking the High Magister's gaze, Rillo looked around the square to see that over the past few minutes, numerous contingents of city guards had made their way into the vicinity. His thin ranks of just over six hundred Vox Militant troops were now surrounded by a ring of bronze armoured guards.

Rillo rolled his shoulders and slowly exhaled, looking back over to Aequo who simply offered him one solemn nod.

"A new order, you say? Well, I never did like change." He raised one arm suddenly in the air, placing the other upon the pistol holstered across his chest. "Vox Militant, stand to!"

The outer ranks of the Vox Militant fell down to one knee, bringing their rifles to the ready in one fluid motion. Behind them, a flurry of rifles and polished bayonets bristled from the order's ranks, pointing in every direction across the square, aimed directly at the encircling wall of city guards and the blue-coated guardians of High Magister Nihilo.

Aequo stood beside the men and women of his unit, keeping the sights of his weapon focused on one of the guards that now stood in front of the High Magister with his own weapon drawn. Rillo's pistol was pointed at the head of the other, whose face was covered by an elaborate mask.

The sergeant kept his finger lightly pressed against the trigger, ready for any sudden movement. Yet he still felt the sweat trickling down his brow and a familiar quiver flutter across his heart. Fear began an assault upon his senses, and it was a feeling that he knew all too well. The Vox Militant were the best trained armed force in the city, of that there was no question. If it came to a fight, the city guard would fall in their hundreds and Nihilo's guards would be decimated, but that alone did not guarantee their survival.

They were surrounded. Even with their superior training, if the order were to be given, he doubted that many of the Vox Militant would be walking out of this fight. He cast a quick eye over the rooftops surrounding the square on three sides, with the fourth flanked only by the Grand Canal and the historic bridge that rose above it. It took a few moments, but it was not long before Aequo could see rays of light dancing along the barrels of finely-crafted rifles leaning out from balconies and windows across several different buildings. He looked forwards and up to see that several figures stood amongst the domes of the Grand Magisters' Chambers, their crouched forms silhouetted against the shimmering domes of gold.

They were trapped: outnumbered and exposed in the middle of an open square. The order could indeed wreak a terrible cost for their lives, but odds of their survival were low, even for a man of Aequo's experience. Nevertheless, he would act as ordered, as always. He would not abandon Rillo or his city.

"You're under arrest, Nihilo! Tell your people to stand down, or we will open fire!" bellowed Rillo, his weapon steady and voice resolute.

Obscured by the many guards that now surrounded him, Rillo heard Nihilo sigh in the silent void of the square. Just to the side of a black and silver mask, the captain caught sight of a sinister smile that now sat on the High Magister's lips.

"I'm afraid not. You're a soldier, Captain, you know how to read a dangerous situation, and I fear that this situation is far more dangerous than you may have supposed."

Nihilo's face was once again obscured, but this time, it was not one of his personal guards that stepped forward, but a far stranger man altogether.

With broad shoulders and a long black beard, the towering figure of a Fereli chieftain emerged from the ranks of the blue guards. His eyes were narrowed and focused, and his lips curled with anger and hate, framed by an ornate tattoo of a crow that covered half of his face. Rillo did not recognise the man, but on sight of the many layers of fur that he wore, and the large axe in his hands, the captain's muscles began to tense.

On many battlefields, in a war too long in the waging, Rillo had seen countless figures dressed in such a fashion, charging towards him with fire and fury. He had slain many of them, and had been wounded by more than a few such warriors in Abys-Luthil's last war with the Fereli people. He had never expected to again see one of them armed, and staring down the Vox Militant.

A chorus of guttural cheers now rose from across the corners of the square, and a vast host of fur-clad warriors covered in tanned leathers and wolf skins, bearing weapons of great size, made their way forwards from between the ranks of the city guard. The sound of their eager war cries rang across the square, assaulting the ears of the Vox Militant, whose rifles shifted to aim at this new threat.

A writhing sea of anger and fear surged across Rillo's mind and he let out an involuntary snarl.

A face, released from its hallowed chains by the sight of the many Fereli that now filled his vision, ran fleetingly across his mind, beautiful and

135

painful in its memory. A sharp sting of pain raced through his heart and Rillo gritted his teeth and shook it off, his finger pressing lightly against the trigger of his pistol.

"Stand down!"

Not one of Nihilo's guards responded to Rillo's words. They remained eerily still, many of their weapons now pointed at the captain of the Vox Militant. The Fereli chieftain leaned forward, grinning at Rillo with a ring of broken yellow teeth.

"None of us want to see blood spilled in this square, Captain." Nihilo cast a cursory eye across to the looming Fereli, "well, most of us, anyway."

He continued. "No one needs to die here. Withdraw your forces and you and your soldiers may live. You may even keep your weapons, well, those not of artifice design, of course. The Vox Militant will be disbanded, but you may keep your lives. A slaughter in this place benefits no one."

Rillo's mind was now awash with the ghosts of his past, each dragging his conscious thought further and further down a darkness that still lingered in his dreams, but now dared to stand in the light of day. For a moment he offered no reply, his thoughts broken, his mind lost in a sea that he was not yet ready to sail. Until a light shone, and a moment of clarity settled upon him.

"The Vox Militant exists to fight tyrants, and we will not allow you to take this city unopposed!" Silence followed his words, and slowly, but with purpose, Nihilo stepped around his guards and stood alongside the towering Fereli warrior. His unnaturally dispassionate face suddenly became contorted with frustration and his almost ethereal sense of control gave way to a visible anger that burned in his eyes.

"Lower your weapons, Captain, or your order shall be purged from the annals of history in this very square. I shall ensure that your slaughter will not even warrant a footnote in the history books. The very memory of you will be burned away with fire and blood, and I will bring such ruin to you and those men and women behind you that you will wish that you had fled a long time ago!" Nihilo hissed, his eyes hardening with an unsettling glare, and Rillo felt, in that moment, that he was finally seeing the High Magister for the first time as he truly was.

"Make your decision. Death or life. Choose poorly, and not even the waters of the Grand Canal will be able to wash away the blood that I will shed in your destruction." Nihilo's voice was low, piercing and bitter in its speech, specks of spittle flying from his lips like venom from a snake.

"You will not endanger the type of freedom I have promised, or the future I have planned."

The chieftain grew restless as the High Magister spoke, running his hands across his axe in preparation for the fight he so dearly wanted. Rillo looked over to the warrior and the terrible weapon that he held in his grasp, its heavy blade gleaming with a series of finely-cut rubies. He cast his eyes back over to Aequo and held his gaze for all but a moment. The sergeant sighed and slowly shook his head, his rifle aimed directly at the chieftain.

The captain of the noble order of the Vox Militant looked back at the High Magister of Abys-Luthil and glared with barely-restrained hate, as every fibre in his body willed him to fire a shot at the usurper that stood before him. He knew not what magic artefacts and artifice armour protected Nihilo under his dark robes, but his mind burned with frustration and the knowledge that even a shot to the magister's face would likely be stalled by some unseen power or another.

And yet, the shot was clear and the chance of a clean kill lingered.

Maybe it could end right here, right now. Even at great cost, a would-be tyrant could be felled.

Then once again, ghosts, launching unbidden from the depths of his mind, surged across his thoughts, scattering them to the winds of his imagination. A voice, long suppressed, spoke to him, an unwanted spectre of echoed memory.

"*You're a good man, Rillo.*" He could hear her laughter and smell the sweet scent of lavender oil.

"*They follow you because they love you.*" The soft caress of a feather cushion held his head, and the light touch of her hands gently rubbed his arms. Her smile shone out between the rays of golden sunlight streaming in from clear glass windows.

"They know that deep down behind all that bluster and discipline, you love them too."

Rillo's breathing rattled slowly across his lips and the square fell utterly silent, a void that tipped on the edge of a far darker precipice, as the Vox Militant waited for the order to fire. He looked back at them, row upon row of men and women who would gladly lay down their lives if he gave them one single word of command.

Her smile faded from his mind's sight, and the weight of many hundreds of lives rested on his shoulders. The threat of loss layered upon loss and the promised howls of suffering that would ring through the night as over six hundred families would mourn a terrible loss.

Rillo stared Nihilo dead in the eye and lowered his pistol.

"Very well. If my people are allowed to withdraw unhindered, you will have your city, Magister."

The anger slowly drained from Nihilo's eyes, receding into a disarmingly gentle smile.

"A wise decision, Captain, or should I say, Mister Rillo. You may leave this square with your weapons and of course your lives. But you must leave your uniforms and artifice weapons behind, after which..." a shallow grin now stretched across the High Magister's lips as he spread his arms out wide, looking across the ranks of the Vox Militant. "You may return to your lives, unhindered, and look forward to the coming age of freedom. I wish each of you the very best." His calm and settled manner restored, Nihilo gave Rillo the lightest nod of his head and swiftly disappeared behind his guards.

Rillo looked over once more to the Fereli chieftain, who offered him the merest mocking laugh before following behind Nihilo, his axe resting across his shoulders, eyes dark and full of malice.

He turned around and gazed across the sea of green.

"Vox Militant, dismissed!"

The beer flowed freely and the tavern was alive with the same sounds, smells and sights that had marked many a drinking establishment that Aequo and Rillo had visited over the years. A fluttering amber light washed across the small booth in which Rillo was now sitting, his elbows resting upon the chipped varnished wood.

His eyes traced the labyrinth of swirls and scratches that marked the oak table, drawing elaborate patterns across its stained surface. Voices rose in anger and mirth filled the room, as numerous figures jostled for a space at the overcrowded bar.

Out of the chaotic throng emerged Aequo, carrying two large tankards of beer.

"Drink up, I've opened a tab," he said before unceremoniously thrusting one tankard in front of Rillo and taking a few hearty gulps from his own.

Rillo eyed the beer suspiciously before grasping the wooden surface of the tankard with both hands and taking a swig.

"This is awful," he muttered with a grimace.

Aequo shrugged his shoulders, wiping a thick streak of beer foam from his upper lip.

"Yes, but it is very, very cheap." He took another swig before continuing, "and given our recent unemployment, cheap and strong will do for the moment."

Rillo sighed, "Might need something stronger than this, mate."

"Indeed, which is why I grabbed this," replied Aequo, pulling a sleek bottle full of a clear liquid from out of his coat, and pouring a little into both of their drinks. "This can hardly make the beer taste any worse."

Rillo's eyes narrowed, "I take it that that bottle didn't simply... fall off the shelves? You put that on the tab, right?"

Aequo feigned his best attempt at indignation. "Naturally, of course I did. What do you take me for?"

His friend scoffed, leaning back into the booth, "A would-be guild master, who, because of a soft-minded judge, found himself in the army, where a young, unsuspecting officer befriended him, securing him a position in the Vox Militant so that he wouldn't turn to his roguish ways once more."

Aequo took another quick swig of his drink and smiled, "Yeah, sounds about right."

They shared the type of bittersweet laugh that can only be heard after the longest of days in a smoke-filled tavern between old friends.

They drank in silence for a few minutes, keeping a careful watch on the shifting crowd in the room around them.

"He did it, he's taken all of it, and we didn't even fire a shot," spoke Rillo, pouring more of the clear liquid into his tankard. Aequo offered him no reply, pulling out a small pipe from the depths of his coat and scraping out the old pieces of tobacco within.

"He took the city in broad bloody daylight, with me standing right in front of him."

His words were met by the scratching of wood as Aequo fished out a few stubborn pieces of ash.

"We lost it all, in the blink of an eye." Rillo's grip on his tankard became tighter, the wood creaking under the pressure. "It's all gone, everything."

Aequo looked up, absentmindedly placing a small amount of fresh tobacco into the pipe. He saw Rillo stare into the varnished wood of the table like it was some great mountain range far off in the distance. It was no longer anger that furrowed his brow, it was something that Aequo had seen far too much of in his lifetime. It was deep, unshakable loss. The kind of loss from which you could never recover, you simply learned to carry it with you, and as Aequo knew all too well, it was a wound that went far deeper than the events of this morning.

"I have nothing."

Weariness settled into the lines which now grew under Rillo's eyes, words falling from his lips like some terrible bile that had formed at the base of his stomach.

"I sacrificed everything for that job, for the Vox Militant, for the city."

Aequo leaned forward. "Don't go down this road, mate. Don't do this to yourself."

Rillo stared back at him, his face contorted with regret. "How can I not? She's gone, Aequo. She's gone and I'm never going to get her back."

"Rillo, come on now –"

"Now? Now, what? What do I do now that I have lost the very job which forced us apart in the first place?" He paused for a moment, eyes cast back down to the table. "I excused what I did by claiming that it was for the good of the Vox Militant, for freedom." Rillo sighed as bitterness curled his lips. "I abandoned her for some stupid ideal which was taken away from me this morning right in front of my face."

"You did not abandon her, and you know it. She left."

"Like I left her much of a choice? Look at me, Aequo and tell me that it wasn't my fault," snarled Rillo, his anger seeking to bite at himself rather than at the man opposite, and yet, there was a note of pleading in his tone, an uninhibited plea for absolution for a wrong that still plagued him from day to day.

"You both made mistakes," Aequo replied simply, unshaken by Rillo's emotion, staring him straight in the eye. He knew that this reply would cut him, but it was the truth, and there was no changing that.

"I could hear her today, in the square. I could see her."

"You did what you had to do. You saved hundreds of lives in that square today."

The former captain bit his lip, slowly shaking his head from side to side. "If any lives were saved today, it was her doing not mine, and she did it a long time ago."

"Rillo, you're a good man," replied Aequo, with the most supportive smile that he could muster.

He finished his drink before calling over to a nearby barmaid to bring them two more.

"Neither of you have lost everything. Last I heard, she was still living in the city, and there is still a fight to be had over the future of Abys-Luthil."

Rillo sighed dismissively, taking the next tankard in hand. "Not a fight for us to lead. We failed, and by the time Nihilo is finished there'll be nothing left to fight for."

Aequo placed his drink down and gave Rillo a hard stare. "You know that's not true. I'm sorry that Evelyn left, you know I am. She was, and is, a fine woman. I hated seeing what happened to you two. But you are not the only person to have lost something today."

Rillo failed to meet his friend's gaze and looked back down to his drink.

"If it's all the same with you, Aequo, I'm not really in the mood right now."

The former sergeant took a hearty swig of beer and slammed the tankard back down onto the table. "From what I've heard, Nihilo had his Fereli mercenaries and city guard virtually wipe out the Alpheri family this morning. Their house is just ashes now, and the bones they found of those slain were scorched black. Nihilo took out both of his opponents today in one swoop."

Rillo grabbed the bottle of clear liquid once again. "My point exactly. There is no one left to oppose him; we should have acted sooner and we didn't. I failed. This is where the story ends."

Suddenly, Aequo grabbed the bottle from his grasp and pointed it at him, splashing specks of pungent alcohol across his coat. "No, I'm not having this. I've spent too many years protecting this city, fought too many battles, walked too many streets, same as you. Look, I know you're hurting and I'm sorry about that. Have a little bit of a cry if you want, there's no shame in that, I should know. But at some point either you're going to pick yourself up and get back in this fight, or I swear I will drag you up!"

Rillo sat mute, taken aback by the sudden outburst. He felt his hands curl into fists and the warm glow of the beer and spirits he had ingested spread throughout his body. He stared at Aequo and his mind filled with sorrow and pain, his senses numbed slightly by the drink.

"You know, today I saw the Vox Militant disbanded. Hundreds of years of tradition, gone. Hundreds of fine soldiers sent home, without a second thought. My rank and position taken away from me in a matter of minutes, but here I am still sitting in front of a sergeant."

Rillo then fell into uncontrollable laughter, a strange sound concocted of equal parts sorrow, alcohol, irony and mirth. "I do swear, that you could be out of uniform for a decade and yet you'd still be as much of a sergeant as you were a day ago," spluttered Rillo, his outburst obscured by laughter and the intake of beer.

Aequo rolled his eyes, holding back a grin. "And you'll always be that wet-behind-the-ears officer I found in the woods outside Draynoth, who had got his squad lost in the forest," he replied, drinking straight from the bottle.

"Ah yes, Draynoth, I still hate the smell of pine trees. What was it you called me again, that first time we met, when you found me and my squad?"

"A bloody stupid git."

"Yup, that rings a bell."

Aequo handed Rillo the bottle with what little remained of the clear spirit inside, before calling for more beer to be brought to the table.

"But I distinctly remember saying sir at the end, which made it ok," he replied, waving over to a waitress, who was now considerably blurrier than she had been ten minutes ago.

"I still reckon that I could have had you put on a charge for that."

Aequo snorted derisively, "You could have tried."

The conversation quickly centred on what it did most evenings; their escapades in the war to the north. The beer flowed and spilled as they remembered the highs and lows of a long campaign which had, in many ways, defined and saved them both.

That is, until a small doubt sown by Aequo's words fought through the noise and the alcohol and rose to the top of Rillo's mind.

"Wait, you said "virtually" wiped out?"

"What?" asked Aequo mid-way through recollecting the time that the two of them had disguised themselves as fishermen in order to sneak onto a Fereli ship.

"The Alpheri family, you said that they were virtually wiped out. So there were some survivors?"

Aequo took a few moments to think about this, his memory desperately trying to pull together pieces of information which were now submerged under considerably more beer than he had drunk for quite some time. "Yes, uh, there were reports of a carriage escaping from the attack. Some of my sources suggested that both Maellon and his daughter were on the carriage, but I don't know how reliable that is."

Rillo allowed himself an indulgent smirk. "Those wouldn't happen to be guild sources by any chance?"

Aequo simply grinned back and shrugged, knocking a considerable amount of beer onto his leg in the process before swiftly consuming the rest.

"So Maellon and his daughter may be out there somewhere. Now there's a thought. If they have any sense they'll be staying far away," muttered Rillo.

"Indeed, though I doubt that the people will take the disappearance of their hero so easily," replied Aequo.

Rillo took another sip from his own tankard as his brow furrowed in thought. "The sight of a few Fereli warriors on their doorsteps might dampen the people's protests somewhat. Besides, we both know that Maellon Alpheri's no hero. Man's got blood on his hands, same as the rest of them."

"True enough. But he was not the only one to oppose Nihilo, there are others."

Rillo sat back in his chair. "Somehow I don't think that I'm going to like this next bit."

Aequo smiled. "And yet you're going to hear it anyway." His voice suddenly grew hushed as he leaned closer across the table. "I have contacts across the city, through some old connections, who are not exactly fans of the High Magister."

"You'll excuse me if that doesn't fill me with confidence. I believe that we just spent a few years putting some of your old contacts in jail."

Aequo ignored this. "I know a guy, he and some friends have a meeting point not far from here. He says he can introduce us to a group of people planning an attack on the High Magister. They need some extra help. It could be worth a shot."

"Who exactly are these people?" asked Rillo, quick to bite, but with a tone of caution in his voice.

His friend looked around the room, noticing the numerous groups of tavern patrons who were standing close to them.

"I can't say here, but they're meeting a week from now. I don't know about you, but I don't have any other plans and I wouldn't mind getting back at Nihilo."

The former captain of the Vox Militant leaned forward, his mind awash with the numbing effect of beer.

"Ok, let's meet this contact and see what he has to say. Let's hope your trust in them is not misplaced."

His friend grinned, arms held high in the air, now with a fresh tankard of beer in his hand.

"Now, Rillo, when have I ever led you wrong?"

8

A Requiem of Flame

The wind swept gently across her face, kissing her cheek before blowing across the vast fields of corn that lay in front of her. Row upon row of golden corn bent and swayed, silhouetted against a clear blue sky and the gentle slope of rolling hills. Aged carts and humble cottages sat amongst the fields, joined by the hasty tread of horses and the wearied tread of farm labourers.

To the north it seemed as if the fields of gold and green would continue on forever. To the east, the rich harvest was cut in half by a series of roads and houses that spun through the landscape, leading towards the city of Abys-Luthil that was in this moment, beyond her sight. Once again, the wind brushed the hair from her eyes, but was unable to shake those tears from her cheek which had yet to fall, now locked away behind eyes which had little time for tears, so filled were they with visions of smoke and flame.

A small piece of corn rode through the air, coming to rest against the back of her hand. She grabbed it, holding it for a moment, examining its many folds and facets. It felt rough and coarse between her fingers as she spun it, pulling it up to her face and watching fine rays of sunlight dance across its surface. She turned it once more before her fingers tensed, her thumb bent down and she crushed it, balling up the corn inside the tight embrace of her fist.

"Lyra."

Her hands balled into fists again in a sudden tensing of muscles, and soon the rising smell of smoke lingered under her nose. Even now, she could feel the flames running along her fingertips.

"Lyra, they're here."

She turned around to see Alina, offering her no rely, not that one of the three surviving members of the Alpheri family guard had expected any. Lyra had now been almost completely silent for the better part of two weeks, ever since their narrow escape from the city. She had muttered a few words to Kat and Virgil, but when they were not present her efforts were divided between walking the grounds of the farm, lost in her own thoughts, or in earnest conversation with her father, who, as far as Alina could tell, spoke little more than she did.

Alina Jarro led the way and Lyra followed, walking along the same dirt path she had paced for many hours already today, until they both reached the humble stone dwelling in which the remaining members of the Alpheri household now took shelter.

They stepped over the threshold, the squeaking of the aged door's rusting hinges announcing their entrance, and stepped into the small kitchen. No sooner had Lyra entered the room than Katerina's arms were already around her. This had been the same greeting that her friend had given her every day since the attack. At first Lyra had felt unable to respond, her arms hanging by her side like lead weights, but now both her arms were also around Kat. No tears fell from her eyes, even though they rolled freely across Kat's cheeks.

Virgil stood behind his apprentice, greeting Alina with the same handshake that he always did. He placed a large bundle of food on the kitchen table and Alina filled a nearby kettle, placing it on a warm stove.

Kat rubbed her friend's shoulder reassuringly as the artificer took a step forward, looking Lyra in the eye. "Where is he?"

"In his room, same as every day."

Virgil sighed, rubbed the corners of his eyes, and took a seat at the table.

Alina made four cups of hot tea and placed them across the scuffed table as the others took their seats. For a few moments the group sat in silence, taking some comfort from the warmth and flavour of their drinks.

Alina broke the quiet mood of the kitchen, as she had done most days, by holding her cup in both hands and leaning forward in her chair. "What news from the city?"

Kat looked over to Virgil, who offered the first reply.

"Much the same. The Grand Council has been disbanded. Many magisters voiced their opposition, but as more Fereli have entered the city their voices have quickly grown silent. Nihilo and the Council of Five now rule unopposed, the city guard is fully under his command, and with the Vox Militant now out of the way, there is no one left to oppose them."

Alina glanced down at her tea. "Then it is as we expected."

"That is not all," replied Virgil who looked over at Kat to see that silent tears were still falling from her eyes. His face hardened and Lyra followed his gaze to see that the grief which wracked Kat's face was more than just empathy.

"What else? What's happened?" Lyra asked.

"Nihilo is a cunning politician, but he has yet to win the love of all the people. His talk of freedom and safety has attracted many, of that there can be no doubt. Public forums are no more and the press houses have been shut down. He's fulfilled his promises about public criticism. The universities and public libraries have been placed under government control, and any text which is thought to incite debate or encourage outspoken critiques is to be burnt. There are entire squares filled with burning books, and their ashes are thrown into the waters of the Grand Canal."

Virgil now shook his head, his face grim, his eyes bearing a mocking grimace. "Nihilo has called these public book burnings "The Purge of Hate", which means that to be found in possession of such books is not only illegal, it is to be hateful. He's a clever one, I'll give him that."

Lyra looked once more over to Kat. "But there's more, isn't there?"

"Yes." The artificer finished his tea and leaned forward. "Like I say, not everyone has been so easily convinced by Nihilo's words. There have been protests but sadly these have all ended in blood, and the state has declared them to be hate riots. The protest leaders were either arrested or fled into Abys, only to be followed by the city guard."

For a few moments Virgil's voice trailed off as he took in a deep breath, preparing himself to continue. "The guards ransacked whole streets and houses in Abys, and anyone suspected of sheltering state fugitives has been arrested and put to work in the factories. The old part of the city is now crowned in smoke as the factories run almost ceaselessly. But they manufacture more than just goods for trade. It seems like the High Magister is forging a grand arsenal, and entire warehouses have been cleared, prepared to store the huge number of weapons which the city is now producing. He warns the people of a great war that is coming, and he builds an army on the backs of slaves whom he calls criminals. According to my sources in Abys... Mrs Magorin's street was one of those targeted, and city guards were seen entering her house. I have heard nothing from her in over a week."

Silence followed his words, a terrible empty void that left the weight of this knowledge looming over all those in the room.

Kat sniffed and Virgil poured her another cup of tea.

"So the city is truly his. With the Vox Militant gone I can't see any hope of opposing Nihilo," Alina said bluntly, her voice wracked with hopelessness.

No silence followed these words as Lyra turned to face her. "What are you saying?"

Alina sighed. "Without the Vox Militant, Nihilo has free roam over the city. There must be thousands of Fereli mercenaries inside the city by now, paid by Nihilo. If he's truly building an army then his power and influence will spread, and his greatest opponent is currently sitting in a farmhouse bedroom with only three guards protecting him."

The war veteran sat forward in her chair and cupped her hands around her face. "We cannot stay here." She looked over to Lyra. "We have to get you and your father as far away from here as possible."

"You want to run away?" asked Lyra, her words sharp and bitter in their utterance.

"No. No Lyra, I don't. But this isn't about what I want. This is about keeping the two of you alive," replied Alina.

"She's right. With things the way they are in the city, this hiding place will not be safe for long," spoke Virgil, picking up his second cup of tea.

The young Alpheri snorted in derision, her tone uncharacteristically aggressive as she turned to face the artificer. "So what? We give up now? Nihilo murders my family, burns our house to the ground, and now we run?"

"Lyra." Alina's voice was calm but unwavering as she met the young noblewoman's gaze. "There is no fight to be had here, no battle to be won. Nihilo has thousands of armed guards and mercenaries at his side, and, I suspect, more than a few artificers on his payroll," said the former soldier, looking over to Virgil who nodded in response.

"I know you're upset, but there's nothing we can do here. For you and your father's sake we must leave."

Lyra now stared at Alina, her eyes narrowed and her fists balled once again into fists.

"Upset? Everything is gone! All of it! Mara, Alfred, they're both dead. Buried under the ruins of their own home! The same as..." Even now she could not say his name. "The same as..." She could see his face and hear his voice, framed in fire and smoke. His cries haunted her mind and choked her throat, stopping her from even speaking his name.

"Lyra..." began Virgil, his voice insistent but calm.

"No!" she shouted, rising to her feet, speaking more words in a minute than she had in a week. "He has taken everything! He burned our house to the ground with my family still inside!" Anger, hitherto unknown to Lyra, boiled in her heart and raged across her thought and speech. "I will not run and hide while that man takes over our city, my home, without anyone even firing a shot!"

"Some did, Lyra. Some did." Now Alina stood, her cup cast upon its side on the table. "Too many good men and women gave their lives so that you and your father could escape that house. I'll be damned if I'll see their sacrifice go to waste."

One of Lyra's hands uncurled as she jabbed a finger towards her own chest.

"I know, Alina! I watched Castel die, and I won't repay him by simply running away, fleeing into the shadows! I saw him standing in the fire!"

"So did I!"

Alina's voice seemed to shake the very kitchen itself and she stared down at the young noblewoman. "I was there, same as you!" Waves of anger and grief poured from the guard, who spoke as if the only thing holding back the tears were towering walls of rage and bitter memory. "I've stood and fought beside that man for ten years! I've walked through fire and death with him." Alina took a few steps forward and both Virgil and Kat quickly made their way over to that side of the table.

"I know you lost family that day, Lyra. But so did I!"

Lyra did not back away, but stood motionless, save for the words which fell from her lips. "Then let us avenge them!" Her voice grew steadier and she stared hard into Alina's eyes. "What would Castel want? I didn't know him as well as you, but I know that he was not the sort of man that would run away from a fight!" Her words were not now driven by anger so much as pleading, and an almost feverish desire to rally Alina to her side.

Suddenly the fire faded from Alina's eyes and the anger subsided as quickly as it had come. She drew a deep breath, closing her eyes for a moment.

"Lyra, Castel was the sort of man that you are only likely to meet once in a lifetime." A strained but sincere smile formed across her lips. "He was a rude, foul-mouthed, egotistical old tyrant, and one of the best men that I'll have ever known." The older woman stepped forward once more, slowly this time, and gently placed one hand on Lyra's shoulder. "As for revenge? Well, Castel and I spilled much blood for many years in the name of many causes. For home, for money and yes, for revenge. But it never made us happy and it certainly never satisfied us, well not as much as a bottle of whiskey, and that never lasted too long with Castel around." A wearied but happy smile now beamed from the guard's face, born aloft by many years of memory and lessons learned.

"He wouldn't want you to walk that same path, Lyra, not for him, not for anyone."

"So what should I do? Just walk away?"

"If it's a choice between that and fighting a man like Nihilo, then yes. There's a whole wide world out there just waiting for you, Lyra. Better that, than hunting for blood in a city that is falling into the depths. It won't bring them back and..." Alina's face hardened once more, "...if you walk that path, you may not recognise yourself at the end of it."

A tumult of thoughts tossed and jostled in Lyra's mind like ships caught in a great storm. Fear, anger, love and grief swept along the waters of her conscious thought, her mind swallowed and wracked by emotions that towered like high inescapable waves. Yet even these raging waters could not quash the fire that now sat forever in her mind's eye and the terrible screams that rose ever higher above the thunderous gale. She closed her eyes, and still the visions lingered, memories as clear as glass and haunting in their visage.

She shook herself and pulled away from Alina's grasp. "No! I won't run! I'll make Nihilo pay, no matter what the cost!"

Lyra stormed from the room, ignoring Kat's plaintive cries for her to stay.

"Lyra! Lyra!"

She slammed the door behind her and made for the stairs, heading towards her father's room. As she reached the door, she came upon Krell and Peter sitting at a table next to it.

"Lady Lyra, is something wrong?" they asked her, but before they could even rise to their feet, she opened the door, stepped into the room and closed it with an almighty thud. For a moment she leaned against the door, and her hands gripped tightly around its handle until her knuckles strained under the pressure. Her teeth ground against one another and her heels dug into the floorboards at her feet, but still no tear ran down her cheeks.

"Lyra, what's the matter?"

She relaxed, her hands loosened and her teeth ceased to grind. Leaning on the door, she slowly slid down to the floor, looking over to the figure of her father, who was seated on a chair by the window.

"They want to leave. They want to run away." Her fist hammered into the wooden floorboards, again and again, with her form slumped weakly by the door.

"And what do you want to do?" he asked, now standing over her, his hand reaching down towards her. She rose to her feet, taking his hand, and looked up into his wearied face.

"I want to fight!"

To this, Maellon offered no response. He had already spoken more words to his daughter in these few moments than he had in four days. Lyra looked around the room, watching him walk back to his chair to see a work space that was a dark and shadowy reflection of Maellon's former study. Only a few books lined the walls, on the few little rickety old shelves that could be trusted to bear their weight. There was a fireplace, but it was little more than a hole in the wall flanked by small columns of slate, and framed with varnished timber beams. The window allowed small rays of light to enter the dusty room, but its surface was marred and obscured by dirt and aged by the elements outside.

Lyra paced the room.

"You want to kill Nihilo?" her father asked, simply and dispassionately.

"Yes!"

The reply came to her lips before she had the time to think about her answer. A fervent energy moved her, and yet many sleepless nights had left her drained and wearied. All manner of faces haunted her dreams and compelled her to wake from sleep. Most of these faces she recognised, after all, they were family, in one way or another. As for the others, they were strangers to her, and yet she saw them clearly. They came to her as a pair, each of them crying out in pain and covered in pools of their own blood. On sight of them, in the dread hours of the night, she could feel her hands around the blades that she had thrust and sunk into their screaming forms. The city guardsman and the Fereli warrior looked out at her from the depths, crying out in agony, their hands clawing at her face. Such terror moved through their eyes as she dealt the killing blow, over and over again, that Lyra felt herself tremble at the thought of what she had done in the halls of her own home.

And yet.

Not even this spilling of blood could quench that anger and the fear that burned within her.

She was afraid, more so than she had ever been in her life. Fear kept her from sleep, it deprived her of food, and even the company of those who were closest to her. She had fed upon fear in these last few weeks and it had made for a solitary companion, but it was one which she could not shake. Strength was needed, she decided, and she would be strong.

"I will kill him for what he has done."

Maellon rubbed his temple with ink-stained hands, and looked up at what little remained of his world.

"I fear that may be so. But it should not be you, my daughter, not really," he muttered weakly. A look of irritation crossed Lyra's face. She did not understand his words, and was becoming more and more vexed by her father's speech, which became more veiled with riddles as each day passed.

"Would you rather that we fled? That we forgot about our home? Forgot Mara, Alfred and... and..."

"Nathan," he said bluntly, concluding her sentence. A sharp grimace furrowed her brow and Lyra turned away, angered by how easily the name of her cousin came to her father's lips.

"I would rather that we all lived, Lyra. I would rather that there were no flames, no swords, no guns, no fire. I would rather that the world were different, that the skies were clear, the oceans calm, and wind but a gentle breeze. I would rather that in its fullest form, the world was not as it is. Yet in doing so, I would rather that all were a dream, and alas, I can dream no more, for too violently have I now been roused awake."

Lyra turned suddenly upon her heel, smacking aside a small tower of books from a nearby shelf with the back of her hand. "What are you saying?! That the world is the way it is, so we should just move on?"

Maellon looked out of the window, paying no heed to the books now strewn across his room. "We will move on, that is the only certainty. What we move on to, and who we move forward to be, is yet to be decided."

"Stop!" Her shout reverberated across the room as the door swung open and Krell stepped inside, before quickly withdrawing at a dismissive wave of Maellon's hand.

"Stop speaking to me in riddles! Stop it!" She marched over to him, slamming a fist down upon his desk. "Tell me what we are going to do next! Where are we going to go? How are we going to fight back?"

"Fight back? You think that there is some battle to be fought? Some war to be won?" he replied, still not facing her.

Lyra leaned across the table. "If there isn't already, then I will start one, and I will finish it."

On hearing these words, Maellon's gaze broke from the window and he looked up at her, before swiftly looking back down to his desk.

"How often it was that you used to speak to me of peace. Of the need to fight only in defence of one's own safety, and even then, to act with the greatest of restraint. How much has changed within you already?"

Lyra's jaw dropped in disbelief. "How have I changed? How have I changed?! They murdered our family! Our home lies in ruins, and no one is doing anyone about it! I would rather fight than run away!"

"So would everyone, Lyra," answered Maellon, his voice firmer this time. "Those same people who once sought wars and blood, which you in your comfort once condemned as tyrants and butchers, oft felt how you do now." With each passing word Maellon's face hardened, and bile flavoured his every utterance, as burgeoning wrath hastened his speech.

"The debt of blood has rarely demanded any other payment than that of yet more blood, which in turn, only indebts others to demand the same. History is the story of one flowing crimson tide, as debt has piled upon debt, blood for blood."

He finally looked up at her, with eyes that had aged years in a matter of weeks.

"I was a fool to believe that the future promised anything different than what we knew of the past."

She turned away from him, grabbing one of his books and launching it across the room. "I don't care about your riddles or your history lessons!" She faced him once more, hands locked by her side, curled into fists. "I only want to know what we should do next?" Her words now pleaded more than they accused, and Maellon saw that behind her eyes, her mother's eyes, a great wall of anger had been raised.

His face relaxed, and his words resumed their steady pace, even as a single tear ran down his left cheek.

"Lyra, in my lifetime I have suffered more loss than I believe my heart can bear the weight of. But now, my greatest fear is not for my own life. It is the fear that you have already made up your mind, and there is nothing I can do to stop you."

Lyra could feel her hands shaking, driven by a tumult of emotions, not all of which she could name. A snarl began to distort her lips, but she did not suppress it. She did not even try.

"You're hiding! You have already run away, in there!" she rasped, pointing at her father's head. "You can't rationalise this! You can't think this away. It's not a debate, it is not a sum to be worked out, it is not a problem to be solved. It was murder! They murdered our family!"

"I will take my revenge, Lyra, I am too broken a man to resist the urge not to. But I cannot do it in blood." Maellon looked down at his hands, which were marked by many splashes of ink and bitten finger nails.

"I cannot delve into blood any more, not again. I will fight with the only weapon that is left available to me. The written word." He reached back over to his desk, and brushed aside a small pile of loose papers, upon which were written a hasty script of corrections and jumbled notes. Under these, he found a book, which was newly-bound, its pages pale and its leather smooth. He held it for a few moments in his hands before passing it to her, his thumbs pressing gently against the brown, leather surface.

"This will be my revenge, or part of it. It is the first of three volumes, and my daughter, believe me, into its pages I have poured every drop of malice and anger that my mind could channel." With each passing word the room seemed to grow darker, and to Lyra's eyes the flames which moved within the fireplace seemed to grow in size, shifting into spiked tendrils that formed contorted faces, screaming and crying out to her in agony.

"Never before has the writing of my hand ever spoken of such torments, or such terrible, unceasing punishments. There is fire in those pages, and it is such a raging torrent that for the past few weeks it has consumed me. I have never written at such speed of so many macabre horrors, issuing such spectres that my mind could not hold them for long, and I was forced to commit them to the page. There is all my hate, and there is the beginning and end of my revenge, I can do no other."

She looked down at the book and held it close to her chest, wrapping her arms around it as if seeking to find some comfort in its cold embrace. Lyra still felt the anger burn within her, but as she looked down at her father and saw the sorrow and fatigue that had hollowed his cheeks and wrecked the fraying mantle of his eyes, sadness overwhelmed her.

"I will read this, but words were never my tool in the way that they were yours. I will repay Nihilo for what he has done, and I will do it, no matter the cost."

She could not bring herself to look at him on speaking these words, and without delay she left her father and retreated to the solitude of her room. During the many hours that followed, a plethora of different voices knocked at her door, each calling her to come downstairs and take some food, or simply to join them for a walk outside. However, she paid them no heed, ignoring their eager cries as she opened the pages of her father's book and read the many pages that followed the title of "*The Crimson Script.*"

Hours passed through the night, and soon the darkness retreated before the advance of the rising sun. The blazing orb rose and waned as it always did, and before long, the small farm once again found itself cloaked in shadow, the only light to be found radiating from the lofty stars above, as night descended once more.

The knocking at her door had ceased some time ago, not that she would have noticed if it had not. She was currently walking under the light of a very different world altogether. The words that ran across her father's manuscript jumped out at her with visions of fire and pain. Murderers, thieves and muggers walked under the drudgery of an ashen sky, as flames licked at their heels and serpents poured venom into their blistered limbs. It was a vision of horror and piercing, unceasing dread, shrouded by smoke and flanked by rocks and lakes of fire. Great chains, spiked and burning red with heat, wrapped around the legs of those accused of arson, and dragged them down into heaving fields of fiery coal. Down and down these forlorn men and women were pulled, further into the roasting depths. After a few minutes they would struggle out of this burning prison, only to find that as they walked free, the chains would find them once more and drag them down into the flames, again and again.

In this frightful after-world were the souls of those whose mortal lives were marked by crimes both dark and terrible, and there was only the inescapable light of scorching flames and the wailing of the lost.

Each soul, by no means divorced from its material body, but rather locked within a prison of quivering, tortured flesh, paid the cost of the crimes that they had committed in their life when they had walked in the world of the living. Fraudsters found themselves robbed of every possession, both bodily and otherwise, as every sinew was poked and stabbed by cackling monstrosities, wielding long, iron spears. Thieves were robbed of their hands and feet by large, vicious hounds, which chased them through forests whose thickets and branches tore at their flesh with every passing scratch. These torments ran in circles, for only mere moments after the dogs caught the fleeing thieves, rending them apart with every bite, then their hands and feet would grow back and the chase would begin anew.

Those guilty of the crime of gluttony, too full of their own desires to have helped another living soul in want of food or drink, were tied to vast tables and served an unending banquet of horrors that no worldly kitchen could have endured.

So the circles of dread ran down into a tortuous abyss, and as Lyra read on, she recognised the names of some familiar figures. Members of the Council of Five, Salaris Bremmer, and his cohort suffered amidst the flames. So too did Silo Rees and High Magister Nihilo, each brought to tears by punishments which darkly mimicked their crimes. Whilst walking this dark path, and turning page by page, Lyra failed to hear the fresh cries which echoed from the other side of her door. So engrossed was she by the descending circles of punishment, and so eager to commit the pains of familiar faces to memory, that she didn't even hear the sound of her door being kicked in.

Suddenly, with a great splinter of wood her bedroom door flew open, and hammered into its adjoining wall.

"You're going to have something to eat, or so help me I'll force feed it to you!"

Lyra's eyes glanced over to the paragraph which spoke of the punishment for gluttons, and for a moment she felt mildly sick.

"Not now, Kat."

Her words were met with bitter laughter, "Oh yes now, very much now." A plate of steaming meat landed beside the book, throwing specks of gravy across Lyra's hand. She snapped the manuscript shut and glared at Kat.

"I said, not now."

Katerina crossed her arms and glared back. "You've been up here for over two nights. Either you eat some of that beef, or I will ram it down your throat. In the politest way I know how."

"I said I'm not hungry," snapped Lyra, rising to her feet.

"Yes, you are, you're just too tired to realise it," answered Kat, standing between Lyra and the doorway.

"Get out of my way."

"Nope."

"I'm not hungry!"

"Yes, you are, Lyra. It's just that hunger is a new feeling for you," said Kat softly, looking her friend straight in the eye. "You've never felt this way before, but I have. I have been there and back again and I can promise you that if you carry on like this, that hunger will never leave you."

Lyra could feel her hands tense up, but in the blink of an eye they relaxed, and she let out a wearied sigh.

"Look, I'm really not in the mo–"

"Sit. Down."

Too tired to fight any more, she obeyed, and as Kat handed her a freshly-cleaned spoon she began to eat. With each warm mouthful she grew more satisfied and yet more tired, and it was not long before sleep took her.

Before she knew it she awoke to the rising of the morning sun. Light filled the small expanse of her room, and she looked around to see that she had not made it to her bed, but had rather fallen asleep at her desk. Lyra leaned back in her chair to find that someone had wrapped a large blanket over her shoulders, and before she had a moment to collect her thoughts, a small, steaming cup of coffee was thrust under her nose.

"Rise and shine."

Too weary to answer she took the cup and sipped. A bemused expression crossed her face before she took another, rather tentative sip.

"Is that caramel? Where did you find the ingredients for caramel?" she asked, genuinely bemused.

"I know a guy that had some going spare."

"You know a guy?"

"Yup," she replied simply.

Lyra rolled her eyes, rising to her feet and heading over towards the door. "You're beginning to sound like Virgil."

"Oi! I know it's early but there's no need for that kind of insult."

Lyra ignored Kat's grin and made her way downstairs. She felt surprisingly hungry. For the first time in weeks she had a desperate desire for food, and her nose led the rest of her body towards the kitchen, following the smell of fried bacon and sausages.

She entered the room to see Krell walking outside via the back entrance, holding a bacon sandwich in his hand, with a rifle slung over his shoulder.

"Ah, good morning, Lyra. I thought that the promise of bacon might bring you downstairs. That, and Katerina seemed rather insistent on you having some food."

Virgil smiled his gentle smile from across the room, wearing a small green apron and rolling half a dozen sausages across a frying pan, next to a small pile of bacon. Lyra took a seat at the table, managing to take only one more gulp of coffee before a large plate of sizzling meat and fried bread was thrust under her nose. After thanking Virgil with the briefest of nods, her subsequent words of gratitude were muffled by many mouthfuls of crispy bacon. This continued for almost five minutes, without pause, as Kat and Virgil shared more than one look of concern, looking on as plateful after plateful was furiously consumed.

Lyra caught one of these shared glances whilst looking up to grab more meat.

"What?" she asked indignantly, as grease and small specks of bread swept across her lips and cheek and a small sliver of bacon sat neglected upon her chin, kept in place by a drop of warm butter.

Kat stared at her through spiralling tendrils of steam rising from her tea. "Nothing. Nothing. You just look so lovely this morning." Lyra followed her gaze and picked at the bacon resting on her chin, holding it between finger and thumb for a moment before consuming it with a healthy cut of sausage. This continued for a few more minutes, but before long the remains of Virgil's cooking were demolished, and the three of them sat in silence at the kitchen table.

Lyra stared down at the last dregs of her second cup of coffee, her hunger satisfied and mind more stilled than it had been for the past three weeks. She looked out of the window above the sink, staring off at the mountains in the distance, wondering what might lie beyond them. Soon, however, her mind wandered back to the concerns of the little house in which she now took refuge, and she glanced around the room in the search of more food, though not for herself.

Virgil answered her question before she could ask it. "I took some food up to him this morning."

"Thank you."

The room grew silent once more and Lyra sat content, listening to birds outside and wiping crumbs from her fingers.

"Did they find any bodies?"

Kat's posture suddenly froze, and Virgil stared back down towards his plate. Lyra's question cut across the room with all the shock and ferocity of cannon fire.

"Lyra..."

"Virgil. Did they find any bodies?" she asked pointedly.

A fleeting grief washed across the artificer's face and he slowly shook his head. "No, Lyra. There's nothing left. I wish that I could say otherwise, but they burned the house to the ground. The site has been cordoned off, and there are city guards all over the ruins."

Kat placed her hand upon Lyra's, only to feel it slowly turn into a fist. The kitchen was silent, the light of the sun shone through the windows, and the vast expanse and beauty of nature surrounded the house, pouring in through every window.

Lyra tried. She desperately tried to look beyond the dusty glass, out towards the world outside, and wonder what new home might await her and her father beyond the horizon. She thought of ports, cities, towns and mountainsides. Her mind drifted across the many maps that she had looked upon in her father's study, of Aurel, Dargestan, Corrunstone and Vaillenthorn. There were forests, mountains, valleys, and cities both prosperous and abandoned that she had spent years dreaming of exploring. She and Kat had spent years talking about the many sights they wanted to see, and adventures on which they hoped to embark.

However, as each passing vision crossed her mind, no sooner did she glance at a future that promised a new home than it was immediately consumed in flames. No city, no field, no forest that her memory or imagination could conjure escaped the fires. The raging maelstrom of flame consumed everything, and soon the visions faded into descending circles of ash and destruction. The fire led her back to Abys-Luthil, which burned and yet stood tall amongst the flames, and try as she might, she could not escape it.

"The night before...before the attack. My father showed me a picture of a gun. A design that you were working on, as a present for my birthday. When will you have that completed?"

Virgil sighed, "I don't think that's what you should be thinking about right now. I know you're angry, Lyra. But you cannot take on Nihilo, not even with a weapon such as that."

"Are you saying that you're not going to make it?"

The artificer shook his head and leaned forward. "I'm saying that I know what you're thinking, and this is not a problem that you can simply shoot your way out of."

"Who said I was limited to shooting?" replied Lyra, reaching a hand around her back, pulling something from her belt, and slamming the Fereli knife she had taken from one of the warriors during the attack down onto the table.

"Where did you get that?" asked Kat, her eyes wide with shock, looking over at the savage blade.

Lyra cocked her head to one side. "I knew a guy who had some going spare."

She heard Virgil snort derisively as he ran his fingers through his white hair. "So, what? You're going to stab and blast your way to Nihilo, through his army of guards and mercenaries? And then what?"

"You'd rather I ran away?"

"I'd rather you think, Lyra. Going after Nihilo won't bring your family back."

Lyra toyed with her cup, forcing the little remaining coffee to swirl in circles at its base. "I don't just want Nihilo. I want all of them: him, the Council of Five, the city guard, the lot."

"Fighting is not always the best option, my girl. Not by a long shot. Sometimes...running away is the right thing to do," exclaimed the artificer.

"Oh please, like you've ever run away from anything!" accused Lyra, with a wave of her arm.

Virgil leaned forward, and his eyes narrowed. "Believe me, Lyra, I've run away before. I've run away from plenty," muttered the artificer, his mind's eye momentarily lost in a myriad of memories.

"I can't just run, because this isn't just about me. You said that you've had no word from Mrs Magorin, right?" Lyra asked, looking at both of them. Neither Kat nor Virgil offered a reply, their faces strained, their thoughts conflicting, even within themselves. Lyra could see the conflict they were both enduring, both battling against. Behind all the goodwill, all the good intention that they held for her and her father, there was anger. Such anger that Lyra knew all too well, that even a small spark would ignite it. They wanted to keep her and Maellon safe, of that she had no doubt, but really, they too longed for revenge, the same as her. She just had to make them realise it.

"What about Mrs Magorin? What about the children she looked after? Where are they now, Virgil?"

"We don't know for sure what–"

Lyra cut him off, slamming a fist on the table. "Yes you do!" She glanced over to Kat. "You know exactly where they are, and what's happened to them!" She watched her best friend wince and saw as Virgil scowled, faced with the terrible prospect of a grim reality which they were desperately willing Lyra to flee from.

"Someone has to do something! You've said it yourself. Nihilo has robbed everyone of their speech! The press houses, the universities, the forums! Without those the people have nothing left to protect them. If Nihilo is so afraid of hate, then let us fight him with it."

Lyra sighed and now pleaded more than she railed, her hand clasped across Katerina's. "It is right to hate evil, it is right to fight against it! Let us voice our anger with our deeds, even with guns if only for a moment! If we give the people just one day to rally, if we can resurrect just one press house, then the voice of the people will topple Nihilo swifter than any blade!"

Kat nodded, "Your father aside, I can't claim to have any love for the magisters." She turned to her mentor. "Things in the city are getting worse. Either we start fighting back or we leave, and I for one have no intention of leaving just yet."

Virgil's fingers drummed across the table.

"You sound just like your father," he muttered, turning back to Lyra.

The light of hope sparked across her eyes. "So you'll help?"

Virgil sighed and cupped his head in both hands, rubbing his brow with his fingers.

"Of course I'll help. You two will only get yourselves killed otherwise," he said reluctantly.

His ward glanced over to her friend, "We'll make them pay, Ly, we'll go after Nihilo and the whole damn lot of them." Lyra clasped Kat's hands in response, feeling tears begin to well up in the corner of her eyes for the first time since the attack, but she managed to hold them back.

"We'll burn down everything they've done. All of it," she answered, almost to herself.

Virgil felt a small trembling flutter across his heart. "Lyra." She turned to face him, but the eyes he looked upon now seemed so very different from that of the young woman he had watched grow up.

"I will help you. I'll even forge that new gun of Maellon's for you. But if you're going to do this, then it must be for more than just revenge. It is a dark descent that you are soon to walk, and I will guide you through it, as best I can. But only if you remember that there are other lives at stake, and that at the end of all this, one way or another, there will be a city in dire need."

"You have my word, Virgil," she replied steadily, her words slow and considered, her eyes fiery, still framed by wearied lines of hate.

He looked back at her for a few moments, seeing more than he wished.

"Very well. Kat, fetch Alina. The three of you have a long day ahead of you," he said, to his feet.

"What do you mean?"

The artificer cracked his knuckles and strode over towards his muddied riding boots. "Because it will take me some time to forge this new-fangled design of Maellon's, and no doubt it will require a few tweaks along the way. In that time, I want you training with Alina every day. That woman knows how to fight, and if you two want to live for more than a week in Abys-Luthil, you'll need to be sharp." He placed the boots upon his feet and began tying the laces.

"We all have a long road before us, and there'll be more than fire to face us before we reach the end of it."

9

Unlikely Allies

R illo reached for the glass of stale water by his bed and took a sip. He had not slept well, but that was nothing new. Even before the dissolution of the Vox Militant, sleep had often eluded him, and now, with fresh spectres and new worries to haunt his thoughts, a quiet night's sleep was looking less and less likely.

Rillo thought of many things. He gazed around the tired and worn boarding room that he now called home. It made him think of his childhood, though for the life of him, Rillo could not understand why. His former house could not look any more different from the surroundings in which he now found himself.

In those days he had awoken to the sight of white plastered walls, adorned with ornate gold filigree, and complemented by finely-polished oak furniture. He would have needed only to ring a small bell that hung by the door and one of his father's maids would have brought him a freshly-cooked breakfast.

He looked over his shoulder to see a small plate, chipped and stained with age, that bore a crust of bread and a half-eaten apple. For a moment he thought he could almost see a steaming pot of coffee sitting next to it, with a delicately crafted cup bearing a silver teaspoon. But this mirage faded quickly, and was replaced by a large pewter mug, filled with the same unappetising water.

If only Father could see me now.

He never thought it was possible to disappoint the old man more than he had, but this might just about do it. He could still see his father's face, framed forever in his mind's eye: red, angry, and blustering with rage. Wearing one of his finest suits, his boots were polished to a fine shine and servants stood ready at his side. Rillo had faced him down without so much as a blink, leaving the halls of his family to join the army, to fight a war which he knew nothing about, and which he had no business in fighting.

Rillo had known that his father would not approve. He never did. But he had needed to escape, he had to do something. He could not bear the thought of sleepwalking through life under the heels of a tyrant.

He looked around the room, noting how the sunlight poured in through the numerous holes that lined the curtain. After years of fighting tyrants both at home and abroad, this was where he found himself. He wondered how his father would respond. Would he grin that terrible, arrogant grin of victory across the shadows of his son's failures? Would he mock and jest?

Would he show pity?

Rillo shook off these redundant questions and rose to his feet. He dressed quickly, knowing that he and Aequo had scheduled a meeting in less than an hour. Thinking about the past never did him any good, but in truth, it was not the bad memories that chased his sleep away.

Thoughts of past joys haunted him relentlessly. Faces and laughter swam in circles in his mind, each lost and far out of his reach no matter how much he might wish it were otherwise. No lingering failure could possibly hurt as much as the ever-present weight of past joys lost.

He left his room, closing the door quietly behind him, and made his way down the tavern stairs. Aequo's room was further along the hall, but Rillo had no intention of waking him. Today was going to be a difficult day. If he was to face it with any hope of energy or sanity he needed coffee.

The bar was in much the same state that he had found it last night, except devoid of people. Well, almost.

A solitary figure sat at the bar, facing away from him, scribbling something upon a piece of paper. He paid the figure no heed and looked around for some sight of the proprietor, but found none. This was not unusual, so he simply placed two silver pieces into a small bowl behind the bar, set a small stove alight and hunted for the coffee box which he knew resided somewhere in the drawers under the bar.

"You won't make it right."

Rillo's head jerked in surprise, smacking against the varnished wood of the bar.

"What?"

The voice came again, young and fleeting, but no less confident for that.

"You always heat the water too much. It burns the coffee and it doesn't smell very nice."

Rillo raised his head and stood up, a small bag of coffee held in his hands.

Sat across from him, but not looking up from her scrap of paper, was a young girl of no more than ten years old.

"How could you know that?"

The girl brushed her hair away from her face and drew another line across her paper. "I come here in the mornings. My aunt gives me sixpence to clean the stove and I always do it after you've gone," she replied, still not glancing up.

"And you think that you could make it better, do you?" asked Rillo, rubbing the back of his head.

"Yup."

Rillo smiled, his eyebrows raised. He selected a small handful of coffee beans and began grinding them. Coffee was a rare and expensive commodity, especially in this end of town. He had developed a taste for it on his return from the army, and had often mused about how much of his savings would eventually disappear on the precious beans. Though admittedly, when morning came each day this concern was fleeting. The owner of this particular establishment had been more than happy to reveal the location of their small supply once Rillo had produced enough coin.

"Your aunt, she owns this place?"

"Yup, and she thinks that you pay too much for coffee. But she also thinks that your friend drinks too much."

"Observant woman, your aunt," replied Rillo, taking careful note of the water beginning to warm atop the stove.

"Why do you drink so much coffee? It smells horrible."

"It helps me wake up."

"Well, maybe you should go to bed earlier."

Rillo turned around and leaned forwards, looking down at the girl's scrap of paper.

"What are you writing?"

Now she looked up, her eyes briefly scanning his face before she sighed dismissively and returned to her work. "It doesn't matter, you won't understand."

"Oh really? Try me."

She rolled her eyes, lifting up the paper and turning it lazily between her fingers. He looked at it for a few moments, following the short sentences of her uneven prose.

"I told you that you wouldn't be able to understand. You need to able to read to understand it, and none of you ever can," she muttered, flicking specks of wood from the end of her pencil.

Rillo smiled, impressed by the girl's boldness, and by the fact that she had spelled most of the words correctly. Neither the pencil nor the clean paper would have been cheap, and no doubt she had more of both stored up somewhere else. A number of the noble families of Abys-Luthil had set up various literary charities across the city, helping the poor of both Abys and Luthil to read and write. This had been largely successful, but there were still significant portions of the city's population who had no access to these lessons, and so he did not blame the girl for her scepticism. After the past few weeks of moving from tavern to tavern, he doubted that he looked particularly respectable, and yet the figure sitting before him was far more perplexing.

"What is your name?"

"I'm Mia, you spell it with an M and an I and–" she replied, counting off the letters with her fingers.

"And an A," he said with a wry grin, snatching the paper from her hand and laying it down on the table.

"Lucky guess," she pouted, watching carefully as Rillo's finger ran slowly across the paper.

"Well here's a few more lucky guesses. Hope starts with an H, and the word ship only has one P in it. Put in a capital letter just here and you'll have yourself a proper sentence."

Her eyes widened and she snatched back the paper, examining his corrections closely, her tongue pressed lightly against her cheek. She eyed him suspiciously, laying the paper flat upon the wooden surface.

"Where did you learn to read?"

"School," he replied simply.

"School? It must have been a long time ago. You look pretty old. My aunt says that only nobles go to proper schools," said Mia, looking him up and down. He did not dress poorly and from the pallor of his skin she could tell that he hadn't grown up hungry, but he certainly didn't look like a noble, to her at least.

"Yeah well, sometimes failed nobles go there too." He turned back to his coffee.

"Ok then, if you can read and write so well, prove it and write your name here," demanded Mia, pushing her pencil forward and gesturing down to the paper. Rillo sighed and began to turn around before Mia spoke up again. "But take that pot off the stove before you do, otherwise your coffee will burn, again." Rillo's eyes narrowed and he offered the girl an exaggerated nod of his head, before lifting the pot from the stove and placing it to one side. "Whatever you say, coffee expert."

She ignored the jibe, pushing the pencil another inch towards him. He picked it up and held the paper steady, writing his name in his very best cursive, with an extra flourish. He grinned and pushed the paper back, taking a moment to see the girl's eyes widen further before adding the finishing touches to his coffee.

"Wow, that must have taken a lot of practice," spluttered Mia. "You must be really old."

He rolled his eyes in response, looking through the cupboards for his drink's second rare commodity, sugar.

"Rillo," Mia read slowly, tracing each letter with her finger.

"That's my name," he said, holding a newly-discovered cup of white sugar in his hand, but no sooner had he placed it down on the counter than her voice rose again.

"That's the wrong sugar, you want the brown one. It will taste better." Rillo slowly looked back at Mia, his expression stone, and she simply stared back unapologetically, looking as unintimidated as it was possible to be. He grabbed the small cup of sugar, thrust it back into the cupboard, and retrieved the second container.

He looked back over to Mia, whilst stirring the brown sugar into his coffee. She had just pulled out a second piece of paper and set it down beside the first, drawing careful, deliberate letters across its creamy surface.

"What are you writing about, anyway?" he asked, just before taking his first sip.

"A story," replied Mia.

She leaned forward, watching closely as Rillo took another satisfying slurp.

"Tastes better, doesn't it?"

"It's ok, I guess," he swiftly replied.

It tasted much better.

Rillo placed his cup to the side and sat on a stool beside her.

"What is your story about?"

Her pencil paused mid-vowel, not that Mia had quite worked out what all the vowels were, but she was getting there.

"Do you really want to know? Or will you just make fun of me?" she asked hesitantly.

Rillo took a sniff of his coffee, followed by a healthy gulp.

"I want to know, really," he replied with a smile, relaxing his shoulders for a moment. A mirthful grin crossed Mia's face and she began to pull other carefully-folded pieces of paper out from a small satchel that hung at her side.

"It's a story about a girl who goes on exciting adventures in faraway lands with a band of warriors and smugglers." Without pause a host of fantastical tales spilled forth from the pages that she presented him. It was an impressive narrative, full of exotic and wonderful places, ranging from icy, windswept mountains, which housed long-forgotten mines, to vast cities with towering buildings soaring high above the clouds. She placed her papers to one side and spoke to him of great battles that her band of adventurers found themselves in, and more than a few close escapes.

"They sound like a perilous bunch," Rillo mused.

"Yes, they go on lots and lots of adventures! I was hoping to write more this morning, but I have to go to the doctor," Mia replied despondently, sighing and cupping her head in both hands.

"Oh, not a fan of the doctor's, are we?"

She looked up at him with as much contempt as her scowl could muster, "No, I hate the doctor. He's stupid, and I hate going."

Rillo was unable to restrain himself from smiling as he leaned back onto the bar.

"You know, I hate doctors too. I got shot once, right here," he said, pointing to his shoulder. "The doctor had to use a knife to pull the bullet out and it hurt like...well, it hurt a lot." On hearing this words Mia's face became contorted with equal parts horror and fascination, and just before Rillo could offer any assurance that today's visit to the doctor would almost certainly not include knives, another voice spoke up.

"That's enough disturbing Mr Rillo, Mia. Go and grab your coat. Your appointment's in twenty minutes."

Rillo turned to see the approaching figure of Marion, the proud owner of the Broken Sword Tavern. She was a tall woman of a similar age to Rillo, with rosy cheeks and long blonde hair that she kept tied up in a small bun.

"Come on now, we'll have no time wasting if you want to earn a few more coppers today," she said, giving the young Mia a very deliberate look.

The girl considered protesting, but even as the thought entered her mind it was quickly snuffed out by the iron will that even the merest glance from her aunt could convey. She quickly gathered up her papers and stomped upstairs, her unhappy footsteps audible as she made her way across the floorboards.

"And we'll have less of that attitude, young lady!" yelled Marion after her, before she made her way behind the bar.

"So do you make a habit of terrorising young children with your war stories? Or was this more of a one-time thing?" she asked, collecting the two large silver coins that Rillo had previously deposited in the bowl by the counter.

"She seems like she can handle it. But I never was much of a morning person. I'll make sure to have two cups of coffee next time," he answered, gently massaging the site of his old war wound.

Marion held one of the coins up to the light and inspected it closely, placing her other hand upon her hip. "That's fine by me, you do that and I'll be able to pay the doctor's bill with your custom alone. Most of the other nobles go to the proper coffee houses."

"Who said I was a noble?" asked Rillo, looking her dead in the eye. Marion leant down onto the bar and met his gaze.

"Battle scars or no, I've served enough old squaddies in this place to see that you're no simple soldier. To my eye, it doesn't seem like you've missed too many meals."

"I'll take that as a compliment."

Marion shrugged. "You can take it however you like. Enough gossip runs through this tavern that I know more than I care to about most of my patrons. Anyway, you speak too fine to be one of us."

Rillo finished the last dregs of his drink. "One of us? And who might you be, exactly?" he asked.

The owner of the Broken Sword stowed the coins away in a small bag that hung by her side and turned her back to Rillo, rearranging the contents of a small shelf in front of her.

"The common folk, master noble, the lowly masses."

Rillo sighed and rose to his feet. He had heard similar statements from Aequo and was rarely moved by them. "Sounds like a fun club, do let me know if any openings come up. Is there an entry fee?"

Marion paused. "No. No fee, there's few of us who would be able to pay it."

Rillo offered a strained smile, rubbing the point where the wound still ached, even after all these years. "Well, if there was a fee to pay, be assured that I've paid it more than once," he muttered, heading back towards the stairs. It was time to check where Aequo was.

Marion's voice bid him stay.

"On the subject of fees, it is my understanding that even the lowliest of nobles can put pen to paper, and my niece has a burning desire to write proper. If you could see yourself giving her and myself a few lessons come evening time, then maybe I could overlook the money you owe me for all that sugar you've had, and even make you the odd cup of coffee for free, here and there."

Rillo came to a stop mid step. "You want me to teach you two how to read and write correctly, in exchange for coffee?"

"And the sugar. If not, then you're free to pay with coin, just like everyone else," she replied.

Rillo thought about it for a moment, his interest piqued. He had never enjoyed school and as a child he had not been particularly gifted in the learning of his letters. But as he grew older, he had learned the true value that there was in being able to write one's own name, and he had spent more than a few hours teaching the soldiers of his old regiment how to sign a document with more than a simple cross to mark their signature.

"Very well, this lowly noble can give you a few lessons. I appreciate the offer of coffee, believe me, but shouldn't the girl's parents be paying for her education?" he asked, now leaning against the wall.

A spike of pain crossed Marion's face as her brow furrowed with sadness and raw memory. "No chance of that, I'm afraid. Mia's mother died of the coughing sickness some six years ago, though that was more because of want of food than anything else. Her father was a city guard, but he died a few weeks past, trying to arrest Lord Alpheri." As Marion spoke, Rillo's heart skipped a beat, but his face remained as steady as ever.

"I'm sorry to hear that."

Marion looked down to the ground for a moment. "So was I. They were good people, desperate, but good people all the same. They loved their little girl."

For a few moments Rillo said nothing. He'd heard such tales before.

"Well, she's lucky to have you looking out for her. I'll be back from my business sometime this evening. If you want, we could get started today?"

Marion looked up and smiled for a moment.

"Yes, we'd like that."

"Good," said Rillo, only realising that he was smiling long after it had spread across his cheeks. That is, until a familiar voice could be heard making a speedy entrance down the stairs.

"Good? What's so good? My head feels like several horses have been stamping over it during the night," muttered Aequo with a wince, holding his head with both hands.

"Yeah, there's a cure for that," yelled Rillo unnecessarily, "it's called drinking less beer and more water." To this Aequo snorted derisively, and muttered something that Rillo thought it best not to repeat.

Marion chuckled to herself and made her own way up the stairs in search of Mia. "I'll leave you two fine gentlemen to the rest of your day. Mia! I better find you tying your shoes and ready to leave, my girl!"

The former sergeant's pain was not eased as the two of them exited the tavern, and walked out into the light of day.

"She's got a right voice on her, that one. What were you two chatting about, anyway?" he asked, shielding his eyes from the sun.

"Nothing important," answered Rillo. "So where are we meeting this contact of yours?"

"On the end of Sovereign Road, by the corner of the old library."

Rillo swiftly pulled Aequo from the path of a moving cart. "A library? Are you sure you'll spot it once we get there? They look quite different to taverns, you know."

"Ha. You're a funny man, Rillo, you know that? A right comedian, and not just when you're trying to march straight. I'll have you know that I was reading a book only yesterday."

"Aequo, you're from Abys. What were you doing reading a book?" Rillo jibed before spluttering as the back of his friend's hand smacked into his stomach.

"You're getting slow, you Luthan toff, best that you sharpen up and look after that pretty face of yours. It might be just about the last money-maker that we have left."

The conversation continued in its usual tempo for the next half hour as the pair of them made their way to the meeting point.

Despite the tumultuous year that had marked Rillo's departure from his family home, Luthil still held a place in his heart. It did not move with the same palette of colour that ran thick and fast through much of old Abys. Neither was it host to the same vast array of meats and spices which flowed through the older district's scented air. Luthil had always had a certain magic to it that Rillo could never quite put his finger on. In a very real sense it contained vast libraries of magical tomes that were often consulted by the city's artificers and scholars, and yet, there was more to it than this.

Rillo looked up to see rays of golden sunlight warm towering spires of yellowed sandstone. The faces of noble emperors and fantastical beasts looked down on those below, and aged doors of solid oak were dotted across Luthil's many streets. There were no waterways here, since this part of the city was constructed entirely upon dry land, but there were many bridges. Finely-crafted arches ran from building to building, and Rillo could see groups of robed figures walking within the sheltered walkways of the bridges. There were many rumours surrounding their construction. Some claimed that they were built so that nobles could traverse between buildings without having to mix with the common folk. Others maintained that it was simply an easy way to transport books and materials without exposing them to the outside elements. Rillo did not know which of these was true, but as a child he had enjoyed looking at the heraldry of the noble families decorating each bridge.

Before long, the pair found themselves at the old library. It was a vast building, adorned with many towering spires. Whilst making their way inside, the duo were passed by a group of six city guards who were holding a group of three men, their hands bound with iron chains and their shoulders covered with scholars' robes. They were shoved forward without ceremony, and escorted away from their place of learning. The squares were open to the public, but as Rillo glanced around, he could see that every entrance to the library was flanked by bronze-armoured city guards.

On entering the largest of these squares, the towering walls of the library were obscured by a great pyre that had been constructed in the centre of the square. Countless books and manuscripts were being haphazardly thrown onto a pile of wood, torn out of the very hands of scholars, who were being dragged from the library by armed men and women, garbed with furs and great axes.

A Fereli warrior held a knife to a quaking figure wearing what Rillo recognised to be a lecturer's hat and scholarly robes, and holding a small book.

"Drop it, now!" she hissed in broken Luthan speech.

"It's just a book on the errors of a free society! It contains nothing seditious about the magisters, nothing on Nihilo!" the scholar wailed. The Fereli snorted in response, pushing her knife closer to the man's chest as a city guard stepped in from one side.

The guard leaned forward, sneering down at the lecturer. "The errors of a free society, eh? Sounds like a noble sort of book to me, good for treading down the common folk, good for keeping us as slaves."

A sudden look of bitter frustration crossed the scholar's face. "Yes, its message is terrible, its prose vicious! Many of its pages are abhorrent and thus it is all the more important that we should study and discuss it!"

The guard grabbed the book and wrenched it from the man's hands as the blade moved up towards his throat. "It's illegal, and must be burned. From the sounds of it, not a moment too soon. High Magister Nihilo would have us free from such things!"

He threw the book onto the pyre and ordered the Fereli warrior to allow the scholar to stand to his feet.

The man rose unsteadily, clearly shaken, and yet he took a few moments to straighten his robes and brush the dust from his mortarboard.

He spoke again, his voice now untainted with fear but rather laced with grim certainty. "If you start banning and burning the works of anyone whom you disagree with, no matter how unpalatable or how vile their opinions may be, you will only place yourself one step closer to the fire, book by book."

Rillo heard the guard laugh in mockery as both he and Aequo left the scene, making their way past one of the library's great wooden doors. Outside, another guard was reading an announcement.

"Any lecturer or public speaker wishing to teach or address members of the universities or libraries must first be examined by the newly established Board of Public Protection. Those found to be expressing any views which mock, improperly examine, or offend the views of any other person or group of persons, shall be barred from this city's schools, universities and libraries. Those found to be in breach of this law will be sentenced to prison and public service in the foundries."

His voice carried clearly across the square and even as he spoke a few figures in the surrounding crowd cried out in protest, continuing to do so until several Fereli warriors pushed their way through the mass of people and dragged the protestors away.

"Ok, it's just around here. We were told to wait in that archway over there."

The pair leaned against one of the many pillars which ran across the outer dome of the ancient library. They waited nearly an hour before three figures appeared. They were walking amongst the multitude of travelling students and lecturers, and they slowed their path and started heading towards the pair. Two of them were dressed in humble and slightly moth-eaten clothing, and Rillo could swear that both of them wore a pair of mittens by their belts. They each carried a small pile of books, walking dutifully behind the third figure. She was dressed very differently indeed.

A scholar's robe, laced with a dark blue trim, hung from her shoulders and flowed down to her ankles. This meant nothing to Aequo, but Rillo could recognise the academic uniform of a lecturer when he saw one, especially given the doctoral cap that sat upon her head. She was short with dark brown hair, and approached with a smile, glancing across Rillo from head to foot.

"Captain Rillo, it is a pleasure to meet you at last," she said, offering her hand. Rillo shook it, surprised by the strength of its grip, and looked quickly over to Aequo, but frustratingly his friend looked just about as confused as he himself was.

Surely this could not be their contact?

"Good morning. I am afraid that I am no longer a captain, but the pleasure is all mine, Dr..?"

Her smile broadened as her eyes studied every aspect of his face. "Dr Schumon, and yes, while I have indeed heard that lamentably the Vox Militant is no more, please be assured that for many of us, you still bear the title of Captain," she answered.

Rillo, unsure as how to respond, simply smiled in return, though far more awkwardly than he intended. "I appreciate that, Dr Schumon, and thank you for your greeting. However, I'm sad to say that my friend and I were waiting to meet some old acquaintances and would be most upset to miss them."

Dr Schumon took a step forward, staring intently at both of them. "Yes, Karrick did seem rather insistent that I speak to you both, and the Pale Star Guild likes to be punctual if nothing else." Her smile finally came to rest upon Aequo as she offered her hand once more.

"Sergeant Aequo, I have heard a great deal about you. It is good to meet you face to face."

Both men looked utterly confused, and so surprised were they by the unexpected identity of the guild's contact that they were unable to hide it. A fact which Dr Schumon seemed to notice all too well.

"Is there a problem, gentlemen? I was informed that you were both eager to meet a representative of the Guild."

Her two assistants remained behind her. One of them had placed his pile of books on the ground and was slowly stretching his back, whilst the other faced away from the group, keeping watch on the steady trail of people that walked past them.

"Eager might be putting it a little strong, Doctor, but we are still happy to meet. However, I'm sure you'll forgive me if I say that you're not exactly who we were expecting," replied Rillo, casting a fleeting glance across the library grounds before looking back at her.

This comment did not appear to deter the short academic who held the old soldier's gaze with the same ease that one might hold a pencil. "I appreciate your honesty, Captain. I am aware that I'm not what a Vox Militant officer would consider a typical guild member. But believe me when I say that I speak for Karrick."

Rillo's eyes narrowed ever so slightly. "Very well. But once again, I am no longer a captain, and the Vox Militant is no more."

Schumon cocked her head to one side and nodded slowly. "Yes, I suppose that is the case, for the moment."

Aequo took a step forward, thrusting his hands into his pockets. "I've heard word that Karrick and his guild are in a position to inflict some harm on the magisters. The rumour is that he's looking for volunteers?"

"You have heard correctly. The Pale Star Guild has many members within its ranks. But Karrick feels that a large number of them will be most unsuitable for this next assignment," replied Dr Schumon, examining Aequo closely as she played with the hem of her gloves. "How fortunate it is that you hear so many rumours, Mr Aequo. I was most surprised to hear of how many friends you had both outside and within the Guild. A most unusual trait for a member of the Vox Militant. It is indeed impressive that it did not split your loyalties at all," uttered Schumon, directing this last statement towards Rillo.

The former captain's expression hardened. "The loyalty of my friend here is beyond question. He has spent years risking his life for this city, rather than lining his own pockets by murder and thuggery," spat Rillo.

Schumon listened intently to Rillo's every word before grinning outright in amusement.

"Murder and thuggery? Terrible things indeed, if only they were limited to savage guild members like myself. Alas, recent events suggest that both the city guards and the magisters like to dabble in them as well. I'm sure that you won't be surprised to hear that many of my fellow guild members are former soldiers from the last war with the Fereli. I hear plenty of war stories of murder and thuggery from them too."

She watched as Rillo's hands curled into fists and he turned to his friend.

"I told you this was a mistake," he said, walking around Dr Schumon and making to head out of the square. Her two associates blocked his path, and between the folds of their cloaks Rillo could clearly see the hilts of several daggers at their belts.

"Move," Rillo uttered in a low, threatening tone. He could feel the satisfying weight of his pistol hanging by his hip, but before he had the chance to reach for it, Schumon's voice rose from behind him.

"They'll move when I tell them to move, and if you really wish to leave then I will not hold you here."

"Good," replied Rillo sharply, stepping forward.

"So, you have given up? Leaving the city to Nihilo and his thugs?"

The former captain turned on his heel, his eyes now burning coals of rage that stared directly at Schumon. "The man has the city guard and a whole host of mercenaries in his pocket. My order is gone and there is no standing army. I'll find a way to get to Nihilo eventually, but not with you."

Dr Schumon stood unshaken by his words and sighed. "That's a shame, because if you were willing to listen to the offer of the Pale Star Guild then I could have you standing before a member of the Council of Five in..." she glanced down at her watch, "...just over three hours."

Rillo grimaced shaking his head, "Thank you for the offer, but a botched assassination attempt is not really what I had in mind. I didn't plan on dying bound and gagged today."

She looked up at him, pulling out a small slip of paper from a pouch at her waist.

"You won't be bound, either of you. You'll walk into their home as clear as day," she spoke softly, her large brown eyes sparking with energy and intrigue. "I can make it so that you'll be escorted in as an invited guest. If you wish, the magister will even arm you and offer you a job. If you play your part correctly, there should be very little danger involved."

The scene became quiet as two competing voices battled for supremacy within Rillo's mind. He despised the guilds, he always had done. Years of watching over the streets and witnessing more than a few gutter fights, streaming with pain and blood, had taught him all he needed to know about the guilds.

"How? How will you get us so close to one of Nihilo's councillors in so little time?" he asked.

Dr Schumon smiled, her expression filled with confidence and something else, something that Rillo couldn't quite put his finger on.

She handed him the piece of paper that she held in her hand.

"This contains the address of the meeting place. My friends and I shall walk you a small part of the way there, and if you're willing, we'll inform you of our plan and your part to play in it. For the good of the city."

"For the good of the city," Rillo muttered, his scepticism sitting unveiled across his face.

Dr Schumon smiled once more with no hint of guile or deceit, her words steady, her eyes set. "Yes, Captain. In that goal alone at least, I feel that we may be united."

Rillo saw Aequo nod in agreement. "Very well, let's hear this plan of yours, and along the way you can tell me how a university lecturer ended up joining the Pale Star Guild."

That same spark of intrigue that rested in the corner of Dr Schumon's eyes gleamed once more as she took the lead, walking across the cobblestones.

"Certainly, all will be revealed in time."

A few hours had passed since Rillo and Aequo had stepped into the grounds of the old library. The room in which they now found themselves could not have been more different.

Lavish tapestries lined every wall, and a large balcony hung over the back of the room, adorned with gold leaf carving and flanked by towering statues. Nonetheless, the main thing that grabbed Rillo's attention was the many guards that stood on either side of the red carpet down which he and Aequo were now walking. They were heading towards a large seat that sat atop a raised dais.

"His Excellency, The Master of Blades, and Governor General of Luthil, Lord Salaris Bremmer," exclaimed the servant with a wave of his hand.

Rillo and Aequo bowed their heads in acknowledgement, as was quickly becoming customary under Nihilo's new regime.

Even from the corner of his vision, Rillo could see the outline of a heavily-armed figure standing beside the man who sat seated upon his throne. Yalda, the captain of the Bremmer family guard, was dressed in the faded yellow garments of her lord's heraldry, wearing half-plate armour, with a sword and pistol at her belt. Her gaze bit like a hungry dog as she glared down at the two of them. Rillo did not meet her gaze, keeping his eyes fixed upon Lord Salaris.

The Master of Blades was in deep discussion with a woman who leaned casually against his throne, dressed in the finest array of silk robes that Rillo had ever seen. The noblewoman wore a half-mask across her face that was decorated with interweaving patterns of purple and silver, and the end of each glittering spiral was encrusted with diamonds. She was flanked by her own guards, each of them wearing the purple livery of her family heraldry. On hearing the servant's proclamation, the noblewoman spun gracefully upon her heel, but Rillo did not need to see her face to know exactly who she was.

Lady Aayla Farris, Master of Coin, was not a woman who was easily forgotten. Her dark, brooding eyes looked down at him, examining him, measuring his worth. The Farris family were famed for their great wealth, having amassed a large fortune from their sugar plantations founded many miles away from the borders of Abys-Luthil. Lady Aayla had continued in the aggressive mercantile tactics of her predecessors, and only two years after taking over her family's vast business empire she had bought up one whole quarter of the city's docks. She was notorious for hosting lavish balls and dances, and rumour had it that she refused to wear the same dress twice, and employed a whole host of dressmakers and tailors who worked around the clock, replenishing her ever-expanding wardrobe.

Aayla tapped her fingers across the varnished wood of her fellow council member's throne and smiled.

"My dear Salaris, it appears that you have some guests." She spoke softly, her words gentle and yet laced with purpose.

The servant that had escorted Rillo and Aequo through the house took another step forward.

"My lord, may I present Mr Rillo and Mr Aequo who wish to offer their services to your lordship," he said with a bow.

Salaris leaned forward in his chair, running his fingers along the tips of his long moustache. His small, beady eyes scanned them both intently, pausing for a few moments upon Rillo. Salaris' brow furrowed in concentration, but no realisation dawned. Rillo's face may have been familiar, but he could not yet give a name to it.

However, the same was not true for the captain of his family guard.

"Mr Rillo," cackled Yalda, walking down a step to stand between the two newcomers and her lord, her every word laced with venom. "Yes, it must be Mr now, I suppose. What with the Vox Militant having been disbanded. What's life like, without your little band of toy soldiers to parade around with?"

Rillo said nothing, feeling his teeth grind together and an involuntary snarl form across his lips.

"What are you talking about, Yalda?" asked Salaris, leaning further forward.

"My lord, this is...was, Captain Rillo, commanding officer of the late Vox Militant. He made to attack you at your last forum with the traitorous Lord Alpheri," she replied, her eyes now glaring down at the servant standing beside the former captain, who thought it best to answer the question which he knew was coming before it was asked.

"They have been searched for weapons, my lord, but they were found to be unarmed."

Salaris leaned back into his chair with an amused grin. "So, former Captain Rillo, what brings you to my humble home?"

Rillo gritted his teeth before proceeding with the plan that Dr Schumon had so carefully explained to him. "I come here to offer you my service, my lord. Yalda is correct, I was the captain of the Vox Militant, and my friend Aequo here was my sergeant. We served in the last war together and we trained hundreds of men and woman for combat. We would like to offer ourselves to join your household guard."

Yalda snorted in amusement, but Salaris placed one hand thoughtfully under his chin, glancing over to Aayla. "What think you, my lady?"

"What an exotic prospect." Lady Aayla took a few steps down towards the pair, holding a set of gold plated spectacles up to her eyes. "Not many magisters could boast of having a Vox Militant officer in their personal guard, Salaris. He and his friend would make quite the addition. A bit scarred here and there, but the older the wine, the better the vintage," she said, running a gloved finger across Aequo's shoulder. "I must say that I'm rather jealous of you, Salaris."

The Master of Blades drummed his fingers slowly upon the arms of his throne, making deliberate eye contact with Rillo. "Lady Aayla has been helping me redecorate my house. She has found all manner of strange and wonderful items with which to decorate my home," he said, gesturing over towards the room's many tapestries.

Aayla sighed, "But alas, despite all the beauty I have brought, you persist in having that monstrosity glaring down at us. I've said it before, my dear, it's very large but utterly hideous." She pointed up towards the room's most imposing feature, a large skull of a great beast of prey which had once skulked along the waters beyond Abys-Luthil.

The skull of the great fish was truly massive, with many teeth protruding from its opened jaws, some of which were as long as a man's leg. It had been hoisted up by a number of large robes and loomed above Salaris' throne, staring menacingly down at all who entered the room.

"Yes, my lady, you do truly have an eye for beauty, but beauty without strength is vanity and I would have the whole city know of my victory over such a great and mighty creature."

On hearing this, Aayla chuckled, pulling a piece of hair from Rillo's coat and examining it closely, "and that is not vanity?"

"No, it is truth. Strength is the purest truth there is. But I would not expect a lady such as yourself to understand," blustered Salaris, looking happily up towards his prize.

Aayla immediately ceased her examination, and a thin strained smile crossed her lips, as she looked up at her fellow council member.

"Is that so? Well, in order that I might be better informed on the matter, why don't I employ these fine men myself? I've been looking for some more guards. Nihilo may trust those Fereli brutes to keep things in order, but I have no interest in such savages. Besides, I had forty dock workers organise a strike last week, or wait, was it a riot? Well, whatever it was, it was clearly seditious anyway. I had to have ten of them shot, and I could do with a few good and well-paid men keeping a watch on the area for me."

Salaris suddenly jolted in his chair, "Hang on a moment, they offered themselves into my service. You can't just steal them from under my very nose."

Aayla grinned. "Oh I do contest, my dear, you know how trading works and you have Yalda to protect you. What more could you want?"

The captain of the Bremmer guard leaned forward, "With respect, my lord, both of these men were part of the Vox Militant, a criminal organisation disbanded by the High Magister himself, I do not think employing them would be wise."

Aayla supported her words of caution with the lightest of nods. "Exactly, you should listen to your captain. No need to bring any danger upon yourself, my dear. But as for me, well, I don't mind dancing with a bit of danger," Aayla replied, winking over towards Aequo. Even from this angle, Rillo could clearly see Aequo's face begin to go slightly red.

He remembered Dr Schumon's words and the great need there was to infiltrate the Master of Blades' household. At this moment in time there were very few other places that Rillo would not have preferred to be in, but after hearing Karrick's plan, he knew that he had no better option. He could never leave the city, not like this, not after Nihilo had seized power on his watch. This regime needed to topple, and despite his deep hatred for the guilds, this seemed like one of the few ways to achieve it. Karrick wanted some spies present amongst Salaris Bremmer's guards who could smuggle his guild any information they could find, such as the number of guards in the Council of Five's employ, the location of key Fereli deployments, and the shipment and development of arms and armour. The Master of Blades would have access to all of this information, and with it in their possession,

Karrick's guild could launch targeted strikes all across Abys-Luthil.

This seemed to be the only way.

He turned towards Lady Aayla, "Your interest is most appreciated, my lady, but Mr Aequo and I would like to offer ourselves solely to the service of Lord Salaris."

"Ha! You hear that, Aayla, these men recognise a fine master when they see one!" scoffed the Master of Blades.

Aayla rolled her eyes. "Ridiculous! Now see here, I can pay you twenty gold a week with your own bed and board, plus the finest weapons that money can buy. What say you to that?"

Suddenly Salaris rose from his seat, stomping down to stand directly in front of Rillo. "I'll not be out bid in my own house! Look here, Rylo or whatever your name is, I'll pay you and your man here thirty gold a week and grant each of you your own room, how does that sound?"

Yalda marched towards him, "My lord, you can't seriously–"

Salaris' head turned slowly, his eyes alight like burning hot coals. "I can't? I can't what, Yalda?"

A sudden paleness crossed the captain of the guard's face, "My lord, I meant no offence..." her voice pleaded, but her master's face showed no signs of softening.

"Yalda, I don't care what you meant." Salaris' eyes narrowed, "I am the Master of Blades and I have wiped the vile stain of the press houses from Luthil's streets. Under my watch the people of this city and the Fereli have been liberated from slander and the universities have been humbled and brought to heel. There will be no offence because there will be no dissent." He scanned her form dismissively, from head to toe. "I have done all this. Me!"

He paused for a moment, allowing his face to relax a little. "You are a guard, Yalda. So guard me, I require nothing more from you than that and neither does the city."

Rillo avoided eye contact with either of them as Salaris spoke, but he noted the evident smirk that now rested upon the lips of Lady Aayla.

"To find that the crime of wanton free speech resides in one of your very own guards! What a terrible shame, Salaris," mocked the noblewoman.

He shrugged off the remark, turning to face Rillo. "She knows her place, as will everyone in this city, soon enough," he replied. "Now then, my man. If you and your friend want to join my household guard you will both be serving the city in the greatest cause that it has ever pursued, and for a generous sum of money. What do you say?" asked Salaris, casting a fleeting eye across to Aayla as he did so.

Rillo bowed his head slightly, every fibre of his being crying out in protest as he did so.

"We would be honoured, my lord," he answered with gritted teeth, only drawing comfort from the look of shock written across Yalda's face.

"Capital! An excellent decision," beamed Salaris, looking victoriously over at Aayla, who bobbed her head in mock submission.

"So be it, I can see that there's no accounting for taste," muttered Aayla, fiddling with an ornate bracelet that hung at her wrist.

"Oh no need to be a sore loser, my dear. What say we have another game of cards? You're always up for a bet."

Aayla shook her head. "Not this time I think, you have nothing worth losing that I want."

Salaris chuckled, stepping forward and pointing over to a side door at the far end of the room. "Ah, there you are wrong. It just so happens that I've come into a small patch of land in Abys, right next to your territory, I believe. The previous owner was found to be printing his own papers and news pamphlets, and not the complimentary sort either. The idiot got himself arrested and locked up in one of Nihilo's foundries, and his estate just so happened to fall into my hands. I have the cards ready in the next room."

The one eye that was not hidden behind Aayla's mask widened with interest. "Well, in that case, how could I refuse? Let's play one hand." She turned upon her heel, winking over at Aequo.

"Excellent. Yalda, show these two to their rooms and see to it that they're properly equipped. It's no use having guards if they don't carry any weapons!" he laughed, following eagerly after Lady Aayla, flanked by two of his guards.

Yalda glared angrily down at Rillo and Aequo, but her gaze did not last long.

"Avris!" she snapped. One of the guards to her right nodded his head, and stepped forward. "Get these two to the stores and see that they get the right clothes and a sword. No guns, not for the moment. They won't be needing those," she rasped with bitter breath.

Avris motioned for the pair to follow him, leading them to one of the doors that stood behind Salaris' throne.

"Rillo!" spat Yalda as he and Aequo walked away. "If you try anything, if I think that you're stepping out of line, even by the width of a hair, I'll be the first one to put a bullet in your head. Do you understand?"

He came to a stop, and looked casually back. "Completely," he smiled, before turning his back on her once more.

10

Vengeance

S he pulled the trigger.

Noise exploded across the room, bouncing from every wall and filling every space. There was no escaping it. It rang within her ears as a low throbbing beat. She could feel the vibrations shooting along her arm as her wrist absorbed the recoil of the smoking gun.

Lyra had not been quite sure what to expect. She had never held a weapon like this, and she was certain that even amongst the great artifice troves of old Abys there was no gun such as this. Her father's weapon was a thing of beauty. The pistol's design had gentle curves, a polished barrel, and elegantly rotating bullet chambers. However, on hearing the weapon fire – it suddenly resonated with a deep and terrifying brutality.

She fired again.

Noise – fierce and terrible, carved an almighty scar through the otherwise silent void of the room. The steel breastplate that sat just under her first target tore apart as the bullet left a hole the size of a man's fist. Lyra had never seen armour sundered to ruin with such ease, even by the finest flintlock pistol. But it was not the force of the weapon that astounded her; it was the disturbing speed at which it could fire over and over again.

She held it in her hands for a few moments, taking in every facet, and watching the light dance across its edges. It was made entirely of metal, and according to Virgil much of it had been magically imbued.

It was truly beautiful.

Virgil had so far refused to tell her what magical powers it possessed, stating that it was important that she simply learned to fire the thing correctly before worrying about what else it might be able to do. This had annoyed her at first, as more and more stories about the many wrongs which were now taking place at Abys-Luthil reached her ears every passing week. She had tried to discuss these with her father, but he was growing more withdrawn by the day, forever returning to his books.

They had taken him from her, just like they had the rest of her family, her mentor Castel, poor Tom, and her home.

And yet, a remnant remained. Lyra might no longer be able to speak to her father and share his council as she done in times prior, but she could still revel in his genius. A genius which now, more than ever, spurred her onward.

One of the few things that could quieten the silent screams which still wracked her heart was the book. Its very pages had screams aplenty, enough to share, and as Lyra turned every blood-soaked and torturous page, she saw the faces of those who had slain her family writhing amongst the barbed blades and molten lakes of blood that were littered across its prose. She saw other faces as well, their features contorted with pain, eyes wide with horror. The two men that she had slain in her very own home looked out at her in every moment of sleep that Lyra's frayed mind could steal. She saw them in the ruin of a fiery landscape, a sweeping tundra of ash and lava pits.

They called out to her, seeking refuge and deliverance from their torment. At first she had felt a terrible stab of guilt. There were nights in the rare hours that sleep took her, when Lyra desperately tried to rescue them from the flames, unable to look into their eyes for more than a moment.

Then came his scream. It was the same every time, eager, desperate and fearful. She heard it in her dreams, in the boiling of kettle upon the stove, and in the crowing of the birds outside.

Even as the haunting sound came to her again she fired the pistol once more, rending the target from its mount and sending it crashing across the floor.

The guilt began to die away, the mercy faded, and as Lyra slept and the nightmares descended she found herself pushing the faces of the two slain men back into the flames. Their pleas now fell on deaf ears, and even in this world of lava and ash Lyra could feel her whole body tense as her fingers forced the city guard and Fereli warrior wailing down onto iron spikes.

Lyra lost count of the days as she continued to train, becoming accustomed to the crack of pistol fire, and feeling her muscles quiver and ache after hours of close combat training with Alina.

After yet another troubled night's sleep in one of the guest rooms of Virgil's safe house back in the sandstone streets of Luthil, she made her way downstairs.

Today was the day. She would wait no longer.

"Good morning," said Virgil, placing a book that he had been reading to one side and gesturing towards a pot of coffee that sat on the far end of the table.

"Morning," Lyra replied quickly, taking a seat at the table and turning her attention to the drink in front of her.

Almost a minute passed before she spoke up. "Where is Kat?"

Virgil smiled reassuringly, in the hope that some reflection of warmth and familiarity might also be seen in Lyra, but he was to be disappointed.

"I sent her into the market around the corner to pick up some honey cakes. It's best that you don't face today on an empty stomach, and they are such a treat," he answered, his hopeful smile persisting.

Lyra frowned, placing her cup down on the table just a little too firmly. "Well, she'll need to be back soon. We don't have time to waste."

"She'll be back shortly, Lyra," he answered, the smile dropping slowly from his lips.

Another silence passed between them, and for a brief time, Virgil endured it.

"You still want to go ahead with this?"

Lyra looked up, grabbing her coffee, "Yes," she snapped, taking another sip.

"This will be dangerous. Salaris Bremmer might be an arrogant fool, but his household guard are not to be trifled with. They will not be so easily overcome as the rabble you have faced before."

She stared back up at him, biting her lip, "Is Lord Salaris Bremmer the Master of Blades and in charge of the city guard?"

Virgil sighed, "He is."

"The same city guard that burned my home and killed my family?"

"Yes."

"Is he a member of Nihilo's Council of Five?"

"Yes, but Lyra…"

Her stare hardened, "But, what?"

Virgil sat silent for a moment, thinking of the words that he had rehearsed a hundred times in his head since he had woken up that morning, but before he could speak Lyra's voice rose again.

"I'm surprised that you're suddenly so sheepish about violence, Virgil. Father always spoke very highly of your combat skills when you served together all those years ago. And let's be honest, you've hardly led a peaceful life since."

Virgil closed his eyes, shaking his head. "Those were different times and that was a very different fight. There were more than few times when your father nearly lost his life. To go to war is to open oneself up to a great darkness, a darkness that I've seen consume more than a few men."

"In that case it's fortunate that I'm not a man," and with a sharp collision of metal and wood, Lyra slammed the revolver onto the table. "There's plenty of darkness, right here, forged by your own hand. I've heard plenty of rumours of your past, but even if I hadn't…" she looked down at the gun, "it's clear that if there is a darkness in war, then it still resides within you."

Virgil made to speak, but suddenly stopped, leaning back into his chair.

"Do you know what my first commission as an artificer was? It was a toy boat. A little scrap of a thing," Virgil muttered, laughing grimly to himself. "A merchant had a son who loved this toy boat more than anything, and he wanted the sails to move as if it was being propelled by the wind. It was such a small, precious thing. I was an apprentice at that time, younger than you are now. I had seen the great artificers of my day forging magical cannons that could bring ruin to city walls, and arcane armour that no normal blade could penetrate. I was young and hopeful, eager to prove myself. You'd be surprised by the great variety of things that people wished to be warded by an artificer. Even a few bridges and carriages had been enhanced by some of my colleagues." Virgil's eyes seemed to drift into the depths of his memory before slowly wandering back to the present.

"I was wilful and arrogant, and the last thing I wanted to do was work on children's toys when the other apprentices were assisting with much larger projects. But I was left with no choice, so I did what any other apprentice did in my situation; I grumbled, and got on with it. It was supposed to be one day's work... It took me a whole week. My master was less than impressed, and I spent the next fortnight sharpening pistol flints because of that. But you should have seen this little ship, Lyra. Not only did the sails move, but the little wooden sailors would sing sea shanties, and the cannons along its bow would fire tiny plumes of smoke. It was more of a sea-worthy vessel than most of those which are now moored beside old Abys," said Virgil, taking a sip of coffee.

"I can still remember the moment when the merchant and his son came to collect this toy, and the look of joy on the boy's face. Not that this reception dampened my master's irritation with me, even after we got our gold for the commission and the merchant took his son back up north. But soon, I was ordered to start building weapons along with every other apprentice. So I did what I was paid to do, day after day, until three weeks later when the master walked into the forge and told us that the northern provinces had been wiped out by the enemy. Burned to the ground, all of them gone. We started working day and night after that, only taking what little sleep we needed..." Virgil looked at her intently. "...Anger and lack of sleep can do funny things to a person, Lyra. It was not long before we stopped working on rifles and moved onto bigger commissions, great and terrible weapons. Being an artificer is ultimately about producing art, and there was art in this work, both beautiful and horrific. We knew what we were doing ...what we were making."

Virgil placed his cup to one side and began slowly massaging his hands, looking down at his calloused fingers.

"I'd never seen such weapons before, let alone made them. By the end of the first month, each apprentice had their own memory codex, some of which hadn't even been fully translated. It was madness. But our masters were desperate, and whenever we became particularly nervous about what we were making, fresh stories of enemy atrocities made it to our ears. The anger boiled within us once more and we carried on."

He paused, once again meeting her gaze.

"I've seen darkness, Lyra, I've made darkness. I never fought in that war, I never went to the front, but I know what our weapons did, and all these years later, I know what happened. It's no accident that in all her time with me, Kat has only ever forged one weapon, and even that's only a short sword. What has happened to you, to Maellon, is beyond words, I know that. I too mourn the loss of your family, I too feel angry. I've said that I'll walk beside you in whatever happens next, and I will, you have my word. But Lyra..."

Virgil's eyes settled on the revolver.

"I would with all my heart that you would turn away from this. That you would leave this city, and make a new life for yourself somewhere else. The world is not so very small that you cannot begin anew. Your family have friends in Aurel and Dargestan; your father's name alone can get refuge in any of those nations. If the only reason for staying in Abys-Luthil is revenge, then I beg you to turn back. Killing Bremmer, Nihilo or any number of them, will not bring your family back," urged Virgil.

Lyra offered no immediate reply. She picked up the gun and held it in her hands, clicking the small lever that held the rotating wheel at its centre, and slowly spinning it with her finger.

"It's strange that darkness scares you so. It never stopped you forging weapons, did it?" she returned. "You could have spent your career enchanting buildings, ships and armour, and yet I've seen you forge many a gun. I wonder why that is?"

Virgil felt his face harden and sat unmoved, as Lyra leaned across the table.

"You are Virgil the Artificer, the greatest in the city according to many. So one has to wonder. In all that darkness, in that great industry of death which you speak of with such regret, did you find something of yourself in that void? Even all those years ago, were you good at it, Virgil?"

They looked at each other, their eyes fixed.

"I have protected your family for many years, Lyra. I will continue to do so, even now." His words were slow and weighted down with a firm assurance.

Lyra placed the revolver back down on the table. Two voices now competed in her head; she had never spoken to Virgil like this before. A faint echo of heart willed that she would dampen her fire and apologise for her sharp words, so that she might be able to find some support in one of the few important people left in her life.

But there was also another voice. This voice bubbled and ran thick and fast with blood and flame. It spoke to her from the pages of her father's book, and from the frayed edges of her nightmares, and it would not allow even Virgil to stand in its way.

Silence hung in the air, broken suddenly by the sound of a door being thrust open two rooms away. Kat's eager voice could be heard advancing through Virgil's home.

"They were out of honey, Virgil, but this one has plenty of icing so I thought it would do!"

Kat strode into the room, holding a large greasy bag full of cakes and smiling over to Lyra.

"Good morning, Ly," she uttered eagerly, until her voice died away, as she sensed the tension in the room.

"I got one for everyone," she muttered, moving slowly over towards the table.

"Good," answered Lyra, her gaze fixed upon Virgil. "We'll eat quickly, I want to be at the Bremmer estate by noon," as she placed the revolver back into its holster.

"This begins today."

The sun sat burning at its zenith, but the narrow alley in which Lyra and Kat now found themselves was almost bereft of light.

Virgil stood a few feet in front of them, his form outlined by the few thin trickles of light that seeped between the overhanging balconies and rooftops above them.

He spoke to unseen figures, who were still obscured by the alley's many shadows. "I am here as I said I would be, and I have the package."

Virgil pulled a small pouch from his belt. It was roughly the size of a man's hand, creased and worn with age. The artificer held it firmly, and it was clear to Lyra's eyes that despite its small size, the package weighed a great deal.

A voice rasped hastily from the shadows. "Hail Virgil! Master of the arcane, artist of forge and flame. What would you will of us today?"

Lyra felt a cold shiver run down her spine, noting Kat's sharp intake of breath as she too heard the voice. It was impossible to tell how many figures stood in the darkness that lay on the other side of Virgil. Lyra herself could only barely discern the outlines of three forms standing amongst the blackness.

But that was not what shook her. It was the eyes. A pair of bright amber eyes peered out from the unseen depths, sparkling with malice and intent.

Virgil however, paid their menace no heed. "You know why I am here."

"Indeed, we do," sneered the hostile voice once more. "But your status is not what it once was... artificer. The city moves and shifts in the wake of the High Magister's ambitions. Your influence and authority are in question, Virgil."

"I am not here to play your games and neither do I care to hear your idle rumours. Nihilo's ambition will be his downfall."

A wide and jagged smile emerged from the darkness, larger and lacking the symmetry that Lyra usually associated with human faces.

"Oh, you think that Nihilo's ambitions are for himself? No, the High Magister has sensed the same great movement that we have. The return of Magic. Real Magic, not the vain counterfeits of so many of the artifice forges. Nihilo has been warned of its descent from the northern wastes. The sins of Luthanril follow you," spoke the cruel voice, its eyes now flanked by half a dozen others, and for just the very briefest of moments, Lyra could have sworn that she saw a glimpse of dark crimson skin, resting just above the broken, yellow sneer.

"I have little use for your words, and neither do I recall requesting them. I have what I said I would bring; in return you will grant us passage so that we may approach the home of Lord Bremmer undetected," answered Virgil, drawing his one free hand to his back, which Lyra could clearly see was shaking, ever so slightly.

The sneer now stretched impossibly wide. Lyra heard Kat gasp and quickly went to grab her hand, squeezing it reassuringly, and stopping her from taking a step back.

"So you request entrance of Dis, do you?" rasped the figure, its lips and teeth moving with unnatural speed. Suddenly Lyra felt Kat's fingers grip tightly around her own, each of them now locked in a tight embrace of their hands, fuelled by fear of the thought of the legend that was Dis.

Abys-Luthil was a city divided in more ways than one. It had many different districts, quarters, languages, classes, and powers dwelling within its borders. But beyond the darkness of the most sinister of the guilds and even the most corrupt of magisters, lingered the depths of Dis.

It began as a legend of Old Abysuss. Dis was the darkest of cities, and the bleakest of homes that resided amongst the labyrinths of Abys' waterways and market squares. Legend had it that even after the fall of Abysuss and the establishment of Luthil, Dis spread further and further across the city, soon inhabiting both sides in equal measure.

Dis was not a place that a person could simply go to visit, but it was present everywhere. It was the darkness of every alley, the ignored shadows of every street, and the forgotten depths that were sunk under every waterway bridge.

Many within Abys-Luthil did not believe that Dis existed, dismissing it as an idle fairy story. But Lyra knew that the tales of Dis were not to be so easily dismissed; she had heard too many stories from Virgil for that. However, even if she had not, Kat could recall more than one incident from her childhood when the shadows and unknown denizens of Dis moved amongst the Water District.

Virgil took another step forward, his words less steady than they had been before.

"You are required to permit my entrance, by ancient decree," he answered, his hand still shaking behind his back, but now sparking with a fluttering blue flame. Lyra felt the hair along her arm stand on end and her ears detected a deep, hollow resonance punctuating Virgil's words. She did not know exactly what was happening, but here she thought, in some way, there was a meeting of worlds.

The sinister sneer remained, suspended amongst the darkness.

"You may not bring a human with you to walk this path so freely, that is not something that we care to abide," came the rasping voice, and as it spoke, six long and crooked arms protruded from the shadows, all of them covered in dark robes.

They each pointed squarely at Kat.

"I care not what you would permit or what you wouldn't. You will give us all entry or suffer the wrath of a power far greater than mine," growled Virgil, anger overcoming his nerves.

Lyra shook herself from Kat's grip and stood before her friend, staring into the darkness.

The grin cocked to one side ever so slightly and the darkness stared back.

"My friend and I are both human," said Lyra in as firm a tone as she could muster, looking over to Virgil, "we all are, and we will move forward together or not at all."

Laughter, great and terrible, answered Lyra's bold address. More and more crooked sneers sprang from the darkness and suddenly, eyes blazing like torches looked out hungrily towards her. However, the smaller amber eyes looked back over to Virgil, and a lower frame of yellowed teeth remained unmoved, until the creature spoke again.

"Oh what webs you weave, Virgil. To continue so great a deception for so long. One day you will indeed be fit to join our ranks."

The artificer rolled his shoulders back and his hands tensed. Without warning he thrust his small parcel into one of the outstretched hands, watching its unnaturally long fingers curl around the precious metal and pull it back into the blackness.

"Be silent, snake! You will allow our passage through the paths of Dis or I shall call upon that mighty force, which you know could disperse your shadows with all the ease of a great wind blowing chaff from the cornfield. Now, stand aside!" snarled Virgil, his form now leaning into the depths.

The laughter stopped and deafening silence took the scene. A hundred eyes now illuminated the alleyway and Lyra slowly brought her hand to rest upon her holstered revolver. All eyes remained locked on Virgil, except the twinkling spheres of amber that now settled upon Lyra.

"She is truly like you, Virgil."

The artificer now stepped directly into the darkness, his form partially obscured, his face leaning down towards the menacing eyes.

"I have given you my warning; there shall not be a second."

One by one the eyes slowly disappeared, falling back into whatever horrid depths they had arisen from.

But the amber glare remained. "We do not require it. You may walk the paths of Dis with the human, and not one of us shall harm you on your journey to the house of Bremmer. But we will speak again, Virgil. We have a home prepared for you. You will join us one day."

The voice faded and the eyes retreated into the far end of the unseen alley. Lyra and Kat stepped forward but could not quite will themselves to enter the shadows in which Virgil was now half submerged.

"What was that thing? Why was it calling me the human?" exclaimed Kat, clearly shaken.

Virgil turned slightly upon his heel until half of his face was illuminated by what little light the opening of the alley could offer.

"Dis is the house of lies and the home of deceits. Don't listen to those things, Kat. Stay focused. This is the only way that I can get you to Bremmer's house without Lyra being recognised. Keep your mind fixed on that end, and stay in step with me."

A thousand questions swam across Lyra's mind, racing alongside her fears and the terrors of pained faces that kept her up at night. She desperately wanted to understand what had just transpired, and yet she found herself unable to give voice to the questions which even now bubbled up to her lips. It was not fear that stilled her tongue, but the tantalising presence of vengeance. It had now been months since that terrible day, and now she was so close to weakening Nihilo's regime, one dead magister at a time. She had pondered the idea of simply attacking Nihilo directly, but his home was well guarded, and besides, she did not want this to be a quick affair. She wanted him to know that she was coming for him.

"Are you sure that you wish to do this?" asked the master artificer, now half enveloped by the shadows.

Lyra barely offered him the slightest nod, before she stepped into the darkness.

Lyra eased herself from the window ledge and landed silently on the carpeted floor below. The room was well lit, and by glancing quickly around she could tell that it was some kind of meeting room.

She took a few steps forward, carefully moving around the expensive furniture, watching the shadows that lay across the room become momentarily disturbed as Kat too climbed through the window. Their approach to the house had not been observed, at least not by any human eye, of that Lyra was certain.

Even only a few moments after leaving that darkness, Lyra could barely remember their journey to Salaris Bremmer's house. She had been walking through city streets, that much at least she could call to mind. But they were unlike any streets that she had ever walked before. Each step had felt as if she was making a descent into a world both ancient and harrowing. In the brief silence that marked her entrance into the house, Lyra suddenly thought about how close a likeness there was between the paths of Dis and the pages of her father's book. The fire and horror that she had witnessed in her brief journey through Dis was present in every page of *The Crimson Script.*

Another question, for another day.

"I can hear someone," whispered Kat, holding her rifle in both hands. It was an elegant weapon, freshly forged and bearing similar traits to that of

Lyra's revolver. It was made of delicately engraved wood and resting just in front of the trigger was the same style of rotating wheel that defined Lyra's own pistol. If Kat could get herself to a high enough vantage point, there would be few guards who would be able to withstand her fire.

Lyra crept slowly towards the door and leaned against the wall beside it. Kat did the same, and the two of them listened intently. This fight would be up to the pair of them. Virgil had seen them safely to the house and then retreated back into the paths of Dis to return once again to his hidden safe house. Deep within her heart Lyra wished desperately that he was standing beside them now, but she knew that this could not be. They could not risk Virgil being spotted in the coming battle, even whilst wearing a mask. His safe house was now their base of operations, and the only shelter that Lyra could find once she sneaked back into the city. If Virgil's secret shelter was compromised in any way then there would be nowhere from within Abys-Luthil from which Lyra could launch her assault on Nihilo's regime. Even Alina, one of the fiercest warriors that Lyra had ever seen, could not join them, since she was needed to protect what remained of Lyra's father.

This was down to her and Kat alone.

Lyra continued to listen, discerning two voices on the other side of the door, most likely two guards who were taking a break from their patrol.

She drew the Fereli dagger that she kept sheathed at her waist, and motioned for Kat to step back. They both retreated from the door until Lyra raised her hand and curled it into a fist, before opening it again and dragging it in a slashing motion across her arm.

Kat nodded and drew her short sword, pulling herself into the empty space next to which the door would open. Lyra stepped into cover behind a bookcase, and readied her blade. Then she gently drew a large book from the shelves, and threw it across the room with a great crash.

"What was that?" came one of the voices outside, louder this time. The pair heard a muffled response before the door was swiftly thrust open. Two guards stepped inside, wearing the faded yellow robes and silver armour that were the hallmarks of the Bremmer household guard.

Lyra stilled her breath to the suppression of even the merest whisper. The female guard was tall and saw the open window, heading towards it with one hand placed upon her sword. The other was a man of average height, stocky and broad across the shoulders. He was looking down towards the half-opened book that lay across the floor on top of pieces of shattered glass.

"What the–" began the male guard, bending down, his words suddenly torn from his lips by the slamming of the door that he had just entered. He spun around just in time to see Kat place all her weight upon the door and spring herself from the varnished wood, leaping across the small room and tackling him to the ground.

Before his fellow guard could rush to his aid, she felt a sudden, piercing pain tear across her arm, and she fell to the ground, an unexpected weight throwing her down to the carpet.

Lyra stabbed again and again with the cruel blade, feeling the warm blood of the guardswoman wash across her hand, as she used her body's momentum to thrust it into her leg. Her other hand desperately tried to curl around the woman's mouth as she stabbed once more, tearing at the leg's hamstrings, just as Alina had taught her to.

The guardswoman's howl of pain was half muffled by Lyra's fingers, as she wrenched the blade free, lifting herself up to her knees, and rammed the dagger into the woman's throat, just above the collarbone. Lyra removed the blade and shut her eyes, protecting them from the sudden spurt of blood that now shot across her mask.

The blood flowed and the muffled howling ceased, the armoured figure lying still upon the floor, save for the spread of crimson that now washed across the carpet.

"Are you ok?" came a familiar voice.

Lyra looked over to Kat, gazing at an almost mirror image of herself, standing over the body of a dead guard, covered in blood.

"I'm fine. You?" Lyra asked, wiping the blade on her sleeve and moving quickly towards the door.

"Yeah, yeah. I'm ok," answered Kat.

Lyra glanced back to the body of the dead guardswoman, whose face now stood alongside the two that she had slain the day that they had attacked her home. But this time, no sickness rose to the base of her stomach, and no sudden wash of guilt settled upon her mind. All she saw lying on the floor was dead weight, nothing more.

"We should head down this corridor, and if Virgil's intelligence is correct, then Bremmer will be viewing a selection of art in his main audience chamber. He'll have some guards with him, but the further we head into the house, the less security there will be. They won't be expecting an attack from the inside."

Silence followed her words.

"Kat?"

Lyra turned to see her friend kneeling over one of the dead guards. She was holding a small, finely crafted gauntlet, retrieved from the depths of her cloak.

"What are you doing?" hissed Lyra.

Kat paid her no heed, placing the fingertips of the gauntlet into the pool of blood at her feet. Lyra watched, as with slow and uneasy speed, small veins of blood rose from the pool and snaked along the gauntlet, filling small channels lined by unpolished golden armour.

"Kat, what is that?"

Her friend looked up, holding the gauntlet in both hands, and offered it to Lyra.

"A gift. Something that I have been working on for you. Try it on."

Lyra cast a nervous eye at the closed door before gently taking the gauntlet, and fitting it around her left hand. Even as she placed the silky glove-like folds of the gauntlet upon her fingers, pulling the small armoured plates over the top, she felt the armour move and shift with arcane energy. She saw as thin tendrils of blood coiled through the device, before finally seeping through the leather that kept the metal in place and into the silk beneath. On seeing the blood fade, Lyra felt the gauntlet tighten, and for the briefest of seconds she could have sworn that she tasted copper in her mouth. A newly-found energy coursed through her body, furious in its pace, but far from fleeting. Her pupils opened wide and her hands shook with the sudden shock to her senses.

"What is this, Kat?" she asked, her voice now tempered more by command than it was curiosity.

"It will help us, Ly. It will keep you safe. I made it only to keep you safe," answered Kat, suddenly not able to meet Lyra's gaze.

Lyra curled the gauntlet into a fist. Bright and violent sparks of orange light erupted from between her armoured fingers, crackling like flame. She flicked her wrist slightly to one side and without warning a large blue shield burst into existence, emitting from around the gauntlet. Its thin translucent surface moved and shifted with radiant energy, and Lyra could feel its pulsing beat emanating like a second heart across her body.

The energy swam through her, and Lyra looked down at the bodies on the floor.

They deserved to die.

"Kat, it's...it's beautiful," Lyra muttered as if in a trance, flicking her wrist once more and deactivating the shield.

"I could almost believe that Virgil himself could not have crafted something so beautiful," said Lyra, all thoughts of the many guards which patrolled the house gone, as she twisted her hand to watch the light dance across the armour's surface.

Kat stood still, her head cast down to the ground. "Virgil would not have crafted this, he would not have done what I have done."

Out of a place she knew not where, a sudden, quiet voice rang across Lyra's mind.

"The blood..." she muttered, as if briefly stirring from a daze. "It absorbed... it drank the blood. Did you make this from the codex that I found?"

Kat shook her head.

"No. That codex was of use. It detailed the manner by which arcane shielding could be imbued within armour, but it was hard to maintain for more than a few moments. To work, the magic required energy...tremendous energy. It was insatiable."

The apprentice artificer looked up.

"Virgil said that it was worthy of study but that I should abandon the project, resort to more traditional means of shielding. And I did, until the attack, until Nihilo tore everything down. It was chaos in the city for weeks on end. Books were being burnt for no good reason, even books like a memory codex. A friend of mine rescued one from the halls of the Great Library and gave it to me for safekeeping. I started to read it. It was an ancient tome and took a long time to decipher, but it spoke of tremendous power and... an alternate supply of energy. It terrified me, but it was so...beautiful," said Kat, looking across to the gauntlet.

"Virgil was so busy crafting your new gun, day and night, that at first I didn't have the chance to show the codex to him, and after reading it for a few days, I didn't want to," she rasped, shaking her head as if in conflict with herself. "The weapons and armour designed by the codex were powered by blood. Even a single drop could power it for a whole day. But it soon grew tired of mine," said Kat, gesturing to a small wrap of cotton that was tied around her thumb.

"The words of the codex said that in order for it to function properly... it had to be powered by blood shed in anger. I almost didn't give it to you. Lyra, I was so close to just tossing it back into the forge. But after just walking through Dis, everything became so clouded, and throwing it away just seemed wrong. The creatures asked me to give it to them."

Lyra breathed deep. "Kat, I walked that path beside you, no one spoke to us in Dis."

Kat moved towards the door, listening for a moment, and thrust her sword back into its sheath. "Yes they did, Lyra. They spoke to me many times. They wanted the gauntlet, they wanted it desperately. But I kept it."

Kat smiled the warmest smile that she could muster, looking intently into her friend's eyes. "I kept it for your family. I kept it for you."

Lyra found herself able to smile back, even amidst the blood and the fear.

"I could ask for no greater friend, and I promise you, that I will use this gauntlet on anyone who dares step in our way."

Kat sighed, "Virgil does not know. He does not know how the armour is powered. Ly, if he was to find out..."

"Then we won't tell him. That man has more than enough secrets, and I intend on keeping this one between us," replied Lyra, stepping towards the door. She placed her free hand gently on Kat's shoulder.

"They brought fire and death to our home, to our city. So let's show them a flame which they will never forget."

11

Blood's Debt

The first thing that Rillo heard was the screams.

At first, they came only as a whisper, creeping across the corridors of Bremmer's great house so quietly that they might be mistaken for the bustle of the crowd passing on the street outside.

Then they came again, becoming louder and more shrill with each passing moment.

"What was that?" snapped Salaris Bremmer, removing his hand from the magnifying glass and taking a step back from the sculpture. The nervous artist standing beside him stepped quickly to one side, his face contorting with confusion as the sharp crack of a gunshot echoed through the house.

For a moment everyone in the audience chamber stood still, until Yalda stepped forward from beside her lord's throne and gestured to a few of the guards standing beside Rillo.

"You two! Go and see what that noise is!" barked the captain of the Bremmer household guard. "Thalos and Riven, make your way to the back of the house, now! If there is a clear exit to the carriages you are to run back here and tell me immediately. I have no intention of retreating into an ambush."

The guards followed her orders without delay, running to their opposing objectives even as another gunshot roared across the corridors.

Rillo looked over to Aequo, whose hands were instinctively reaching for a pistol that was not there.

"Yalda, give us some guns! Now!"

The guard captain curled her lips in response, her snarl leering down at Rillo who stood at the base of the steps that led up to Salaris' throne. "Give you two guns? I think not" She leaned forward, her half-mask resting firmly across her face. "Your time has not yet come, Rillo. You will do what you are paid and ordered to do, with the swords that you have been given."

Another shot rang out, closer now, but it was not like any gunshot that Rillo had ever heard before. Desperate cries followed the weapon's shrill utterance, and the battle drew nearer.

Lord Bremmer began to withdraw beside his throne. "Yalda, what is happening out there!?" he stammered, his voice almost swallowed by fear.

The guard captain stepped forward and walked across the room, taking four armed guards with her. She pointed at Rillo and Aequo. "You two, stay with Lord Bremmer. I've had enough of–"

Suddenly a body tumbled down from the balcony that hung over most of the room. It was wearing the same faded yellow of all the other Bremmer guards, and uttered no scream. Its crumpled form slammed down upon the marble floor, a large gunshot wound having already removed a large chunk of its head.

A figure ran between the columns that lined the balcony. It cast only a fleeting presence between the towers of stone, but with its passing shadow came the deep roar of a rifle that was alien even to a man as experienced with the ways of war as Rillo. He watched as another guard dropped to the ground, blown back by the force of whatever mighty weapon was being wielded up there. Just as he caught a glimpse of the assailant, another figure moved with terrifying speed under the balcony, advancing through the very room in which Rillo and Aequo now stood.

"Open fire!"

Yalda drew her pistol and took a shot at the running apparition. Her shot flew at blinding speed across the room, and then the artifice runes upon her pistol began to flare with power and soon, hot, searing streams of flame followed the bullet's path. The wide and aged columns which upheld the balcony were now wreathed in a flame that illuminated the vast audience chamber with a bright red light. The very stone itself appeared to crack and blacken with the heat of the unnatural fire, and even from this distance, Rillo could feel his eyes wince from the bright light which now shone from Yalda's pistol.

As Rillo forced his eyes open, he saw an impossible sight. Running into the scorching inferno he saw an armed woman, her hand raised, her upper body cloaked with a translucent blue shield. The flames spat and smoked, but she paid them no heed, keeping her armoured gauntlet raised, and using the blue ward which emitted from it to force her way through the flames like they were nothing but wheat in a field.

More shots rang out as Rillo ran forward with Aequo to find some cover from the shooter in the balcony, but no sooner did he take a few steps forward than his body became ridden with a sudden pain.

The advancing attacker, her arcane shield still aloft, launched her free arm forward and from her free hand flew two silver spheres. Rillo saw the shock grenades, a weapon he had not seen outside the armouries of the Vox Militant, roll across the floor, but was too late to avoid them. He felt cords of fierce and blinding pain course through his body, as the shock enveloped him, and he watched as all the other guards around him fell to the ground.

Rillo's sight was obscured by the thick tendrils of burning pain that now wrapped around his head, but even as he lay upon the floor, he saw the flames of Yalda's pistol dissipate, the blue shield lower, and a strange gun fire amidst the smoke.

The guard to Yalda's right fell lifeless to the ground in a shower of blood, his lower jaw and throat left exposed by a terrible gaping wound. Even as the brutality of this moment settled in Rillo's mind, the gunwoman's aim shifted and without a moment's delay another corpse was made, hollowed out by a gaping, fleshly maw that now sat where the man's heart used to be.

Seeing her people slain on all sides, Yalda forced herself to her feet, pulling a shining blue blade from its scabbard. Yet, even this great feat of endurance could not halt the wrath of the warrior, who now launched herself upon the guard captain. Yalda's short sword was swatted aside by a mere flick of the attacker's gauntlet, before she kicked at Yalda's knee, grappled her across the chest, and used her own weight to bring the guard captain crashing down onto the ground.

Yalda's half-mask skittered across the floor, and her voice was barely audible as Rillo and Aequo brought themselves shakily to their feet.

"W—who, are you?"

Rillo was too far away to reach Yalda in time. All he could do was walk as fast as his wobbling legs would allow and watch as the attacker, now leaning with all her weight upon Yalda's chest, pulled down her own mask.

"I am the daughter of Maellon and Beatrice, and I am the ruin of Nihilo's regime," the young woman spat, leaning forward and placing her pistol between Yalda's eyes.

"I am Lyra Alpheri!"

Blood burst across the ornate marble floor, as with the sickening crack of bone and the blast of firing powder, Lyra pulled the trigger. One of the remaining guards shakily readied their sword to strike Lyra, but a crack of rifle fire was heard from the balcony above and he collapsed, now forever unmoving. Before Rillo could look up, he saw Lady Alpheri's pistol point at Aequo, who had just retrieved his sword, and before he knew what he was doing, he charged.

"Lyra, watch out!" came the voice from the balcony, just as Rillo's hand lifted Lyra's gun. A wasted shot echoed through the room, Aequo dived for cover under the balcony columns, and Rillo attempted to land a blow on Lyra's exposed face. However, before his fist could make the connection, Lyra dived forward. She used Rillo's own weight against him, pulling her leg behind the back of his knee and grappling him down to the floor.

They exchanged blow after desperate blow, in a furious battle of elbows and fists. Try as she might, Lyra could not bring her pistol up to bear, as Rillo swatted it away again and again, hammering his fist into her ribs.

"Wait!" Rillo cried, but to no avail, as Lyra continued her furious assault, slamming into his jaw with an open palmed strike.

"Wait, damn you!" he bellowed, using every ounce of the remaining strength in his legs to launch himself forward and pin his body across hers.

"Look at me! I know the daughter of Maellon Alpheri will recognise me! I'm Rillo, captain of the Vox Militant!"

Lyra snarled, butting her head against his and taking advantage of the moment to roll him over and force her elbow down across his throat.

"The Vox Militant are gone! The cowards surrendered without a fight, so even if you were Captain Rillo, you'd still deserve to die alongside the rest of these scum!"

Lyra leaned down harder, feeling Rillo's neck strain against the pressure of her arm, and allowed small sparks of energy that emitted from her gauntlet to wrap around his arm, keeping it at bay. Then without warning, a hand gripped across her throat, and Lyra was pulled sharply backwards and sent rolling across the floor.

Spluttering, Rillo looked up to see the advancing form of Aequo now bearing down upon Lyra. Aequo was almost in a position to launch another blow, before Lyra kicked out with her legs, and sent him sprawling backwards. In one fluid motion, Lyra launched herself back to her feet, and with one solid smack of her glowing gauntlet, Aequo was knocked firmly to one side.

Rillo raised his open hands as he slowly made to stand. "Just listen to me for a moment! I know your father!"

Lyra cocked her pistol. "I saw you order the Vox Militant to point their weapons at my father at the last forum! Weapons which you so easily laid aside for Nihilo's rise to power!"

"Only because those idiots drew weapons on the crowd!" protested Rillo, pointing at the bodies of the slain.

Lyra raised her gun. "You look a lot like one of those idiots to me, and a dead one at that," she snapped, stepping forward.

"I am here to spy on Bremmer! To learn the strength and weaknesses of Nihilo's forces. I heard of what he did to your family. He took everything from me too!"

Lyra took another step forward, her eyes narrowed. "You know nothing about my family," she hissed, her words pointed and bitter.

Rillo breathed deeply, standing his ground. "I know enough of violence and war to know what happened and why. If revenge is what you want, then my friend and I can help you," he replied, gesturing over to Aequo.

A vicious snarl crossed the noblewoman's lips. "What they did to my family was not war."

He met her gaze. "If this isn't war, then what are you doing here?" he asked, leaning forward. "I have information on the Fereli, the Council of Five, weapons suppliers and Nihilo, that I will surrender to you without pause, if you would but lower your gun."

Lyra thoughtfully cocked her head to one side, grinding her teeth. "Very well," she muttered, and even as her words reached Rillo's ears, a blinding flash crossed his vision, and a blow from Lyra's gauntlet knocked him unconscious.

She turned around to see that somehow, Kat had made her way to the ground floor, her rifle smoking from a fresh shot. On the other side of the room, crawling away from a large throne that was seated under the massive skull of a great sea beast, was Salaris Bremmer. As she walked forward, Lyra heard the desperate utterances that even now were spilling from the magister's lips.

"No – no," he cried weakly, blood pouring from his left thigh.

"Where do you think you're going? I wish to have a special audience with you, Lord Bremmer!" yelled Lyra across the room.

"No, no – no," moaned Bremmer, desperately crawling across the floor.

"Please don't deprive us of your presence!" she mocked, taking a stand beside Kat and noting the wound that now hindered the magister. "Good shot, that."

"Thanks, though I was aiming for his knee," answered Kat, reloading the rifle's rotating bullet wheel.

"Well, best make use of the target practice while we have it," replied Lyra, in a manner so relaxed that it sent a shiver up Kat's spine. "Shoot his other knee."

Confusion crossed Kat's sweating face. "What?"

"We can't have him escaping. Shoot his other knee," Lyra answered, almost smiling as she did so. The fire burned in her heart, the tortured faces still ran across her mind, but in these few moments the desperate cries of her dying cousin faded behind the agonized moaning of Salaris Bremmer.

Kat watched as the wounded magister crawled desperately across the floor, his speed slowing with every passing moment and still hopelessly far from the nearest exit. It was a pitiful sight.

"Lyra, he's not going anywhere. Just put a bullet in his brain and be done with it. There'll be more guards coming soon."

Her childhood friend slowly shook her head. "The guards will be a few minutes yet. We have him all to ourselves." Her wide and bloodshot eyes met Kat's. "We have many more magisters to kill, and Castel always taught me that training was the most important part of combat. So, let's train."

Lyra quickly placed more bullets into her revolver, and raised it until her eye looked evenly along the barrel. She slowly exhaled and fired.

"Ahhh!"

Salaris screamed, his agonising wails bouncing from the walls, as Lyra's shot tore through his right foot.

She sighed, lowering her weapon. "You always were a better shot than me."

"Lyra! What is this? Just go over there and–"

Lyra's breathing became heavier as Kat stalled, her free hand curling into a fist. "Kat! Just put a bullet in his knee! Remember who he is! Remember what he has done!"

Kat looked across at her friend, almost in disbelief. "I remember, Lyra, believe me! But we came here to kill him, to weaken Nihilo's hold on this city. Not, – not to do this."

Kat's voice slowly faded as Lyra leaned forward. The face of the woman that Kat had known for most of her life was almost unrecognisable, practically animalistic in its intensity.

"Don't you pity him, Kat! Don't you dare! All this blood, all this pain. It is because of people like him. People are dying in the streets because of him," Lyra spat, as her eyes suddenly twinkled with cruel intent. "Hundreds are starving because of people like him."

And just like that, Katerina Darrow could hear the sound of her own breathing, as a myriad of suppressed images from her childhood rose from the depths of her mind.

She gave Lyra no reply other than a look of hurt and anger, the like of which she had never before offered to her friend.

In one single, precise moment of instinctive marksmanship, Kat raised her rifle and squeezed the trigger.

Lyra slowly exhaled as she heard Salaris Bremmer's knee explode, covering the ground around his leg in gore. He watched her approach through a weeping veil of glistening tears.

"Master of Blades, never was there a title more fitting for a man such as you," said Lyra, still walking forward.

"Nihilo – ordered me to send the City Watch, ahh! He said I had no - no choice! Your family, I'm so – so sorry," wailed Salaris, beating his fist on the ground as the pain in his legs overwhelmed him.

The advancing noblewoman snarled, tapping the barrel of her pistol lightly against her lips. "Sssh, ssh, Magister. There's no need for words. I didn't come to speak with you, I only wanted to watch."

Two shots rang out across the room as Lyra fired at the large supporting hooks which held aloft the monstrous head of the great sea beast looming over the magister and his throne.

Salaris tried to scream, but even if his tongue had not been rendered numb by the pain of his wounds, nothing could be heard above the collapsing towers of bone. A huge, leering grin formed across the sea beast's contorted jaw as jagged teeth, the size of horses, consumed the magister. The creature's jaw shattered into a thousand pieces, causing both Kat and Lyra to recoil backwards as they saw a giant fang cleave through Salaris' chest.

"The guard over there, the one that's still breathing, cut his armour free and grab him. I'll get the other one. We're taking them back through Dis," said Lyra, as the deafening sounds of the collapsing skull faded away.

"What do we want with two guards?"

"They claim to be Vox Militant and have information on Nihilo's strengths and weaknesses. If that's true, then we might be able to end this fight quickly."

Kat gritted her teeth. "And that's what you want, is it? To end this quickly? Because a minute ago it seemed to me like you were trying to drag it out."

"What are you trying to say?"

Kat looked Lyra in the eye. "I'm not trying to say anything. I just want to know that the next time we do this, we're here to kill these monsters, not turn into them."

A sudden quiet settled upon Lyra's mind, Kat's words cutting swiftly through the anger and the pain. Shame began to creep through the frayed edges of her consciousness, and Lyra felt that if she did not speak soon, it might overwhelm her.

Had she really just smiled as she sent the magister to his death?

"I couldn't do this without you, Kat. Without you... well, without you I don't know where I would be. I need you. I just...they have to pay, Kat. All of them, they have to pay."

Kat considered speaking more, but heard steps approaching the large audience chamber. She once again raised her rifle and downed another foe. However, this one continued to move, long after the sound of the blasting powder faded away. Without warning, Lyra's gauntlet flared with renewed energy. Kat eyed the piece of armour suspiciously, her thoughts made uncertain by the sight of an artifice that she herself had created.

"Leave him to me. Grab one of those guards and make for the window we came in by," said Lyra, as she went to stand over the bleeding man.

Fresh screams soon filled their ears, fuelled by the gentle pressure that Lyra was applying upon the bleeding guard's shoulder with the barrel of her revolver.

"You're going to send a message to Nihilo for me," Lyra growled, watching the blood seep across the man's arm, her mind's vision once again filled with fire and smoke. The man made to speak, but was soon silenced with a pained spasm as the cruel grip of Lyra's gauntlet latched around his throat, sparking with bursts of energy.

He looked down in horror, seeing that the blood no longer poured down his arm but instead curled, in snakelike tendrils, up across his shoulder and into the gauntlet.

"You don't need to speak, I only require that you listen. You will run along to Nihilo and what remains of the Council of Five, you will tell them what happened here. You will tell them that Salaris Bremmer died slowly, in agony, crawling away only to be crushed by the weight of his own pride. You will tell them that I, Lyra Alpheri, the daughter of Maellon, did this."

She leaned forward, watching the agony bring torture to the man's eyes. "Tell them I'm coming for them!"

12

Bound Together

The cords felt uncomfortable around Aequo's wrists. He'd certainly been in tighter binds, but he had to admit to himself, whichever of the gunwomen had tied him to this chair had done a pretty decent job of it.

"So," he began, casting a lazy glance over at Rillo.

"I've always known that officers can't fight worth a damn. But if I didn't know any better, I'd say that she slapped you about like a new recruit who's several pints into his night."

"Shut up, Aequo."

"I mean just look at your eye," the former sergeant continued. "It looks like a butcher's chopping board. I've seen punching bags in better condition."

Rillo breathed out slowly and gave his binds another tug , but to no avail.

"It was like watching a raging bull stampede all over a... over a kitten. It was a crying shame to see!" Aequo chuckled, filling the small storage room with his mocking voice.

"Oh yeah? From what I remember, she knocked you out in one swing! So that's big talk coming from a man who goes down after a single punch."

"It was a magic gauntlet! What am I supposed to do against that?"

"Well what do you think she was hitting me with?! A cotton knuckle-duster?!" replied Rillo.

"She didn't seem to need it from where I was standing."

Rillo rolled his eyes. "So now that we're not being overseen by your friends in the guild, you're getting nervous? Worried that you're going to be rendered mute by the flick of her finger again?"

"Hey, I can handle myself just fine," muttered Aequo.

"Oh, clearly," answered Rillo, glancing dramatically around the room.

Silence filled the void left by their speech, and for a few moments the two of them could hear the sound of hammer strikes echoing across whatever building they were now inside.

"To be fair, this isn't as bad as that one time in Havenvale," said Aequo.

"Oh yes," reminisced Rillo, his irritation dampened by the remembrance of that fateful week. "It's certainly cooler here than it was in that dungeon."

"Less spikes, too. What was the name of that jailor again? Was it Bunsten? Britso?"

"Braksen," Rillo answered. "Whatever happened to him? We left in quite a hurry."

Aequo rolled his right ankle from side to side, trying to get the blood flowing again. "You know that fire pit he used to tie us over during the interrogations?"

"Yes, I remember that bit."

"Well, I threw him into it."

"Really?" asked Rillo, trying to recall the events of their escape. "He was a big lad if I can remember."

"Can't say that I really noticed, not when I pushed him into the coals. Told him not to play with fire."

Rillo turned and looked at his friend with an expression of disappointment that dwarfed even the perilous nature of their current surroundings.

"Tell me you didn't actually say that?"

"It was a good line. He didn't appreciate it much, but still, it was a good line."

"Don't play with fire," said Rillo in imitation of Aequo's Abyssus accent, before chuckling to himself.

"Hey, just because you're not as witty as me, there's no need to be petty."

"Yes, Aequo, because it would really lower the mood of tonight if one of us was petty. It would really put a dampener on things. Spoil the whole evening."

Before Aequo could reply, the door slowly eased open, and one of the women who had shot their way through Bremmer's estate stepped inside. She appeared to be chewing on some sort of honey cake.

"Lyra! They're awake," she shouted down the corridor, her words briefly muffled as she took another bite of the sweet treat.

Aequo leaned back into his chair. "Afternoon, miss," he began in a tone that Rillo knew all too well. "I don't suppose you have any of those cakes going spare? Or maybe some tea? Or hey, what about a coffee? If not, don't worry about it, don't be embarrassed. I'll settle for a beer, any beer."

The woman's eyes narrowed as she took another bite of cake. "I'd hurry up, Lyra, they may not be conscious for long!"

An awkward silence attempted to settle upon the scene, but as usual, Aequo barged it out of the way.

"So, just to be clear... that's a no to the beer?"

Before the woman could respond, the sound of approaching footsteps came from down the corridor. They watched as Lady Lyra Alpheri entered the room.

"Ah! The management! Excellent, so what does a man have to do to get a drink around here?"

Lyra's eyes stared like hot coals down at Aequo. "A man has to be alive to enjoy a drink, and unless you help me, that possibility is looking unlikely."

A grin slowly formed across Aequo's lips as he turned to Rillo. "I'm not sure, but I think that was a no."

The noblewoman stepped towards the chair. "Did I hit you so hard that you still have a concussion? Or do you just want to die?"

The grin receded at a perilously slow speed from Aequo's face, and he looked straight at Lyra, his teeth resting just over his bottom lip.

Rillo watched as Lady Alpheri's face paled ever so slightly.

"You think you're scary, do you?" the former sergeant hissed back at her. Both women looked slightly taken aback by his sudden change in demeanour, and Rillo knew exactly why.

In Aequo, Rillo had always thought that he had several friends. Put the man in a uniform, and he was as stable as a gatehouse, a by-the-book, hard-nosed sergeant, cool and steady. Walk him into a tavern and you were never quite sure what was going to happen first, a bar-room brawl, or finding him sweet-talking the staff into a few free drinks. Either way, Rillo usually found himself carrying Aequo home. If you were in trouble, real trouble, there were few more willing ears to listen to your woes than Aequo, regardless of your rank or social standing. However, when crossed, the man was a wolf amongst sheep. Rillo had seen bears with less convincing snarls and cries for blood than Aequo when his anger got the better of him. Underestimating Aequo was generally a bad idea, and angering him an even worse one. Rillo had done it when the two had met during the war in that cursed forest all those years ago, and the Fereli had done it at around the same time, and they had ended up losing the war. Rillo would never have made the argument that the Fereli had lost the war solely because they had enraged Aequo, but he suspected that they would have fared significantly better if they hadn't.

"Look at me!" shouted Aequo, straining forward in his seat, veins bulging across his neck. The woman whose name Rillo did not know jumped back, but Lyra just stood there, staring him down.

"If you think for one moment that you're going to intimidate me, then you clearly don't realise that when you were still slurping milk from mummy's silver spoon, I was busy opening up Fereli throats with bayonets, knives and my bare bloody hands!"

The chair creaked audibly against his tense arms.

"If you want to smack me about with those magic mittens of yours, then go right ahead! Or if you want a proper fight, untie these binds, put the toys aside, and I will knock seven kinds of sense into the lot of you!"

The chair creaked again, louder this time. One might have been forgiven for thinking that its wooden frame was beginning to crack.

Lyra's eyes gently scanned across Aequo's face, noting his words and his features.

"So what, are you the angriest man in Abys or something?" she said, leaning forward.

"Abys? No, your ladyship, not Abys, try the whole bloody world! Threaten to kill me again, and I will rend you limb from limb!"

How long had it been since Aequo had had a drink?

Rillo couldn't quite remember. He watched as Lyra kept the steaming man's gaze. All told, Rillo was rather impressed. He'd seen more than a few men and women, crumple under Aequo's barrage, though never when he himself was in plain sight. It didn't do to talk the troops down like that in front of officers. Only the sudden change of complexion in Lady Alpheri's face and the slight quivering of one of her hands, gave her suppressed fear away. Rillo had always been good at noting details like that.

But now was not the time to be spectator.

"I think what my associate is trying to say, Lady Alpheri, is that there might be more constructive channels of conversation for us to pursue, rather than resorting to threats," said Rillo.

"Limb from limb!"

"Yes, quite," continued Rillo, before Aequo cut him off again.

"Oh, spare me the Luthan pleasantries!" Aequo's eyes turned to the other woman in the room. "Hey you! Water District!"

"Aequo!" snapped Rillo.

"You get to say it if you're from there, all right!?"

Lyra's posture stiffened. "Ignore him, Kat."

The chair creaked, with a violent wrench of the wood. "Oi! You, tea and crumpets, shut it!" Aequo barked at Lyra before turning to Kat again. "You don't want to be following these nobles around too closely. They're insane, the lot of them, take it from me!"

"It was your idea to start working for the guilds, you idiot!" Rillo pointed out.

Aequo rolled his eyes. "I'll get to you in a minute!" he spat, his gaze spinning from Rillo to feast on other victims.

"So what's it going to be, eh?" his gaze now locked on Lyra. "I can see that you're scraping for a fight! Well, either we get at it, or you can let us walk out that door!"

"Or we could just shoot you." Lyra pulled out her revolver and placed her thumb gently on the back of the firing hammer.

"You're not going to shoot us."

All eyes now looked over at Rillo.

"And why not?" asked Lyra.

"You're not going to shoot us, because you need the information that we have on Nihilo and the Council. Without that, your little assassination run or whatever this is, will not get you very far."

The noblewoman's face was cool and collected, and yet there was something in those eyes of hers that willed Rillo to avert his gaze.

"Tell us, don't tell us. The choice is yours. I will kill Nihilo no matter what information you do or don't have. However, I do have one question. I can't help but wonder, what brings a former officer of the Vox Militant so low, that he finds himself working as a noble usurper's lackey? Do tell me..." Lyra knelt down in front of him. "How did that feel? I'm curious."

A crack in the wood tore across Aequo's chair as his arms pulled once more at his binds.

Rillo leaned forward, his nose hovering mere inches from Lyra's face.

"You really want to know how it felt?" His jaw clenched, and his face bent low. "Then do what my friend says. Cut us free from these binds, and I'll show you."

"No one is fighting anyone!" came a familiar voice from the corridor.

The audible chewing of a honey cake made its way through the doorway as a figure stepped inside.

"Ah! Speaking of tyrants with blood on their hands! How are you, Virgil? Still selling guns for a living?" spat Aequo.

Virgil took another hearty bite of his cake before responding. "Good to see you, Aequo. As a matter of fact, yes I am, though business has been disrupted lately. I've not had a sizable order since... well, since the Vox Militant, actually. How about you, Aequo? Still shooting people for a living?"

"Eh, like you say, business has been a bit off and on recently, but at the moment, there are a few people that I'd gladly shoot for free," he answered, with a snort of derision.

Virgil smiled, "Good to know. Ah, Captain Rillo, it's good to see you alive."

"Virgil," replied Rillo with a simple nod of his head. "As you are no doubt aware, I am no longer a captain. But I must say, it is good to see you too."

The artificer's smile broadened warmly as he briefly bowed his own head in acknowledgment. Rillo had always liked Virgil, although it was not as if he and the artificer were especially close. Getting to know Virgil was like trying to make friends with the sun. It was there, in plain sight, but the closer you looked at it, the harder it was to see, and the easier it was to get burned. There were plenty of rumours surrounding Virgil, but none of them were off putting enough to stop Rillo from ordering plenty of artifice weapons from him on behalf of the Vox Militant. Nevertheless, there were a few stories, just a few, that hovered around the mysterious Virgil, and these had more than once kept Rillo up at night.

Virgil brushed a few crumbs away with his fingers.

"While it is true that the Vox Militant has been disbanded, for many people in this city, you are still a captain."

Rillo met the older man's gaze, pondering on where he had heard those words before.

"Untie them," said the artificer, glancing over at Lyra.

"What if they try to escape?"

"Then they are free to go. I have no interest in keeping anyone a prisoner in my home. But somehow, I do not think that they will leave just yet."

"And if they attack us?" asked Lyra, walking over to Aequo.

Virgil looked back over at the two men.

"I do not think that would be wise."

With no more words, both Aequo and Rillo had their bonds cut, and they were escorted deeper into the house. They soon found themselves in a large sitting room, which was decorated with oak furniture and a lavish crimson rug. Rillo felt the gentle heat emanating from the fireplace, and took a seat in a leather chair as Aequo did the same.

"So what were two former members of the Vox Militant doing, acting as bodyguards for Salaris Bremmer?" inquired Lyra, leaning back near the fireplace, and glancing sceptically over at Kat.

Rillo ran his fingers through his hair and leaned back into his seat. He proceeded to tell them the whole story of their offer from Karrick's Pale Star Guild, and the terms of their employment within Bremmer's household guard. The only detail he withheld was the name of Dr Schumon. They did not need to know that.

"So you also wish for Nihilo's downfall?" asked Kat.

Rillo shifted uneasily in his chair, feeling a dull ache of pain where Lyra had struck him solidly in the ribs.

"The man is a tyrant. For me that is enough. I don't care what philosophy he uses to mask his rise to power. I've seen enough of his "security" around the city to know that rather than protect, all they do is rob people of their voices. Four factory workers were shot last week because they sought to quicken the production line in their workplace. Something about changing some machinery, and moving different members of staff to other workstations, not that it matters. Their comments were seen as critical and deemed hateful, and they were executed that same day."

Rillo's hands tightened around the arms of his chair.

"A tailor's home was burned to the ground because he dared suggest that Abyssus tailoring was superior to that of the Luthans. Unless something's done, he'll spend years working in a foundry or worse, and he is only one of many other such unfortunates."

Rillo's eyes traced the flames which rolled across the fireplace's burning logs, then settled upon Lyra.

"I'm sorry about what happened to your family, truly I am. They did not deserve that, and I can understand why you want revenge, why you want to burn it all down. But there are others, so many others who are suffering because of what Nihilo has done, because of what he is doing."

A terrible wave of shame and remorse forced Rillo's eyes to close for a moment. He knew these feelings well, but never before had they assaulted him with such force. Except for once, but that was all over now.

"It was my–" his eye caught Aequo's, sensing that the latter's demeanour matched his own. "It was our duty to protect those people. We failed, and we can't change that. But I promise you, even if you were not here, even if your family had not been so horribly wronged, we would still be using whatever we could to fight back. So listen to us, don't listen to us, I don't care either way. But we will bring Nihilo down, with or without your help."

The room fell silent, in the wake of Rillo's words, except for the occasional scrape as Virgil readjusted the logs in the fire with his poker.

"After killing Bremmer, what was your next move?" asked Aequo, his temper now cooled.

Virgil and Kat looked to Lyra.

"We're moving our way through the Council of Five. The next time an opportunity presents itself we attack the Council again, and weaken Nihilo's hold on the city, magister by magister."

Rillo rubbed his eyes, suddenly feeling more tired than he had been in a long time.

"If you were anyone else, I would say that that plan was insane and doomed to fail. No offence."

Lyra offered a curt smile.

Rillo continued. "But with a few artifice weapons from Virgil, you might just survive."

Aequo rolled his head from side to side with a few audible clicks from his neck, and slowly exhaled. "Not that there's much chance of that now, now that they know that you're coming. Well, at least they don't know that it's you. That might give you a bit of an edge."

On hearing this, Kat coughed loudly, giving Lyra a meaningful look.

"Yeah, about that..."

An unhappy voice arose from the other side of the fireplace, with poker in hand. "What about that, Lyra?"

Lyra attempted to idly play with a stray thread hanging from her sleeve. "I may have left one of the guards alive and told him who I was..."

She saw Virgil's knuckles whiten around the handle of the poker, before his hand slowly relaxed and he placed it to one side.

"Why did you do that?"

On hearing this, the pages of her father's book swam across Lyra's mind. Their fiery prose justified her every action with each sulphurous sentence. She had been compelled to do what was needed; justice demanded nothing less. There were moments, small, quiet moments when Lyra wished for nothing more than to walk the Noctus Bridge with Kat, planning their next trip to the theatre or talking about Kat's latest artifice project. She missed those conversations. Those times seemed so small and delicate now, having been swept away by the monstrous shadow that was the attack on her family's home. Last night she had wondered about the business trip that her father had planned for her in Aurel, and what her life might have been if her visit to the Aureli embassy had gone ahead.

As her mind flirted with these hopeless possibilities, she heard the screams.

Only reading the pages of the book would calm them. In it she had read of a place, deep, terrible and dark, where those guilty of the offence of pride were compelled to bear the weight of a great boulder upon their backs as punishment for this transgression. The boulder would contort their forms, snapping their bones with its weight until it eventually crushed them. No reprieve was offered to the guilty, as their bodies were raised anew each day only to be crushed once more.

Salaris was a man famous for his pride, and so she had deformed the wretched husk of his body and crushed him under the weight of his own grand trophy.

For this, she felt no remorse, and there was no reprieve.

"I want him to know that I am coming for him, Virgil. I want Nihilo to know that even in the hours when he lays his head to rest, I am plotting his end."

"I will not let you do this only to get yourself killed in the process."

Lyra felt her blood rise with the thought of launching an attack on another member of the Council. The gauntlet, which even now she wore upon her hand, throbbed with light touches of energy.

She stepped towards him, her body now illuminated by the light of the fireplace.

"Virgil, your artifice, your revolver, it functioned without flaw. It was perfect. They fled from the weapon that you made, Virgil! No one but you could have done that. What you have made for me, what Kat has made for me..." said Lyra, twisting the gauntlet around against the light of the nearby flame, "they're things of beauty."

"Lyra..."

"Nathan, Virgil. We're doing this for him and for my aunt and uncle, and we can only fight because of you. Nihilo will not be destroyed without your artifices. Every time that a servant of this terrible regime falls, it is your work, Virgil! Nihilo won't fear me, he'll fear the weapons that I wield. Only you can bring an end to the city's suffering, and if we have to warn Nihilo of our coming so that his ranks may be tortured by fear, then so be it."

Virgil looked at Lyra with wearied eyes in a rare moment of frailty. Rillo perceived a lingering sadness that furrowed the artificer's brow and weighed down his eyes. But there was something else also, something that for a moment seemed to hollow Virgil's cheeks.

Guilt.

"I never meant for you to enter this world, either of you," he said, looking at the two women, "my world."

"Well, it looks they're hard in it now, like it or not. Now, you ladies started something today that will trouble Nihilo's sleep for a fair while. Question is, what do you plan on doing next?" asked Aequo bluntly.

"That depends. What information do you have for us?" asked Kat.

Aequo nodded to Rillo and the former officer leaned forward.

"We don't have any information on weapon stores or Fereli movements that we've not already given to the Pale Star Guild. From what we hear, they have their own plans to deal with those. But we did hear about an outdoor ball that Lady Aayla, the Master of Coin, is holding tomorrow night," said Rillo.

"After today's events we can be sure that she'll cancel that," muttered Kat.

"I would not be so sure," said Rillo. "One of the things that unites the

Council members is arrogance. Even with the loss of Bremmer, they'll want to show that they're in command. Besides, there will be plenty of foreign dignitaries at this ball that pour a lot of merchandise through Aayla's docks. She'd be reluctant to disappoint them."

"Even if that is the case, we can expect to meet plenty of security," sighed Lyra.

The room fell silent as everyone acknowledged the truth of Lyra's words and the greater challenge that they now faced.

Rillo looked slowly over at Aequo, cocking his head to one side. "There might be a way that we can enter the ball unnoticed. We know some people...
"

"Rillo, no."

"Aequo, the Guild uses these men all the time. They'll be able to get us in unseen."

"Well maybe they can, but I've heard about them. They'd hardly be my first port of call for help."

Rillo's eyes narrowed.

"Who are these contacts of yours?" inquired Lyra, observing Aequo's soured expression.

"A few friends of the Pale Star Guild, nothing more than that. They're located in old Luthil. If we meet them at the right time tomorrow, we might be able to get an edge on assaulting Aayla's ball."

Lyra looked thoroughly unimpressed and more than a bit sceptical, but nonetheless she looked over at Kat, who simply shrugged. She appeared to be out of options.

"Very well, if that's the way you want to play it then we'll meet your contacts. But if I get the feeling, even for a second, that you're about to betray us, then Aayla's extra Fereli help will be the least of your problems."

Aequo's troubled scowl gently eased into a malicious grin. "Whatever you say, your ladyship."

An uneasy silence settled upon the room and Aequo eased back into his chair once more. It had been a long day, but it was slowly getting better. It just needed that final touch.

"At the risk of sounding repetitive, could I get a beer? Just the one? Being in such refined company makes me nervous, and a touch of ale would steady my nerves."

Virgil grinned despite himself. "I'm sure I can find you something, and if either of you are to be of any use tomorrow, you're going to need some weapons. If you'll kindly follow me, I'll take you to both beers and swords."

Aequo rose sharply to his feet, rubbing his hands. "Virgil, I've always said it, you're a fine man, a fine man indeed."

"I think not," interrupted Rillo, making to follow Virgil. "Right now, I don't want you holding both a beer and a sword. Rest up here for a bit and I'll fetch you back a drink."

Too tired to force the point, Aequo fell back into his seat, playing with the teaspoon that he had left upon its arm.

Lyra also turned to the door, "I'm off to make some tea, you want anything?" she asked, looking back over her shoulder at Kat.

"You know, right now, a beer sounds pretty good."

"Very well," replied Lyra, an eyebrow raised as she left the room.

Kat slowly dropped into a chair next to Aequo, reaching out one hand towards the warmth of the fire. The promise of the incoming beer and a comfortable chair calmed Aequo's mind considerably.

"Not a bad place this."

Kat reached her other hand out towards the fire. "There are certainly worse places to be, that's for sure."

Aequo leaned upon the arm of his chair, peering at a few books that sat on a nearby shelf. Kat's Abyssus accent had been somewhat tamed by years of living in Luthil, but remnants of it remained in every other word that she spoke. Aequo had spent enough time in Abys to recognise that accent anywhere, no matter how far removed by time or distance. There was a harshness to some of Kat's vowels that spoke to him of the narrow waterways and sunken shadows of the Water District. She was not only from Abys, she was from the part of Abys that even the poorest citizen tried to avoid.

"How did you end up here?"

Kat's gaze remained fixed on the fire. "Virgil is a very kind man. He and

Lord Alpheri took me in after the last famine."

"That was a dark year," said Aequo, observing the skin which even now clung tight upon Kat's arms and fingers. There were some hurts that no amount of food or recovery could heal, he knew that well enough.

"It's a dark place," Kat turned and now it was she that examined Aequo. "Those of us that manage to get out of it are the lucky ones."

"You're not wrong there."

"So, what about you? How did you get out?"

Aequo chuckled grimly to himself. "It's funny, to escape the horrors of my own home I had to jump headfirst into a war that was far worse than I ever could have imagined, only for the hope of finding something better. I did what I had to do to avoid the gangs, I joined the army."

"That's where you met your friend?"

"Rillo? Yeah, that's where we met. I've done my best to keep him alive, not an easy job that."

Kat smiled, "Looking out for nobles never is."

Aequo leaned forward. "Any fool can see that she wants revenge, but what's her endgame in all this? What is she going to do if she actually kills Nihilo?"

Kat sat still for a moment, the grip of uncertainty knotted at the base of her stomach. "I don't know," she replied simply. There was no concealing the look in her eyes; it was more than the unknown, it was fear.

"A word to the wise," muttered Aequo in a low voice, his words partially obscured by the crackle of the fire. "What happened to your friend was a terrible thing and no mistake. But you and I both know that terrible things happen every day, they're just not always within sight. Now I'm willing to bet that you've seen a few things that you'd rather forget, same as me." A heavy Abyssus accent now ran thick and fast through his words. "But I'm also willing to bet that until that day when the city guard knocked on her door, your friend hadn't seen anything like that, not really, nothing that had threatened her world so completely."

He sighed, "Back in the District, when I barely knew which end of a rifle to hold, a murder in my street, in my building, was just... well, it was just life. I learned to sleep standing up when I had no home to go to, just so that I could find a space outside, in the street, to get shelter from the rain. We've lived with that, you and I, and like it or not, it shapes who you are. It leaves a mark."

He pointed to the doorway through which the others had left. "They didn't grow up with that life, they weren't shaped by it, prepared by it. It not their fault, of course, same as it isn't ours, it's just how the pieces have fallen into place. But when life hits hard, really hard and they're not ready for it, it can affect them in strange ways."

Kat tore her eyes away from him and stared back into the fire. "Thanks, I'll bear that in mind."

Aequo left her to her thoughts, laying his head against the back of his chair and enjoying a few moments of comfort. Years in the army had trained him to relax even after the deadliest of situations, and this was far from his worst day.

Where was Rillo with that beer?

"So what about yours, what's wrong with him?"

Aequo clicked his neck and slowly slipped further back into his seat.

"Honestly, at this point, I'm not even sure that Rillo knows."

13

Curious Friends

I t was a small shop.

Lyra had often visited Tyrl Street as a university student, and had walked past Luder and Zwing's Mercantile Store many times when frequenting her favourite coffee house. Even now she could see numerous lecturers in their academic gowns, walking between the tightly-packed buildings that housed several university colleges.

A host of memories marched in step along the cobblestones beside her, the thought of them bringing a momentary smile to her lips. Lyra had learnt many lessons here. She knew very well that she could not remember them all, but they had each left their mark on her. She looked across the street to see a small group of students talking with excitement about their favourite book. A few of them spoke with accents that were not native to Abys-Luthil, and one of them wore the clothing of a student member of a university sports club. Lyra could not help but listen to their conversation, slowing her pace. Their discussion was eager and passionate, occasionally tempered by some wise and well-considered words by a more experienced member of the group.

A small, quiet voice stirred in Lyra's mind. She envied these students the moment that they now shared, well remembering similar conversations that she herself had been a part of. Those conversations haunted her, though not as one might expect to be haunted by a spectre. Visions of her former self lingered at the back of her mind, surrounded by these sandstone walls and ancient college crests; small silhouettes of potential that she feared she had never fully realised. Those years had been amongst her happiest, and yet, as she had never been a particularly gifted academic, Lyra had always felt that within these walls she was more of a long-term guest rather than a member. She could never have claimed to have advanced the research of her chosen field of study, or written a paper that had warranted much note beyond a kind word from her tutor. But she had shared moments, small, fragile and precious moments, in which even a few words of conversation or debate had slowly, inch by inch, changed the person that she had once been.

She watched as a pair of city guards followed by half a dozen Fereli made their way down the street, occasionally inspecting the books that the students carried in their arms and satchels. The group that she had been observing quickly submerged their precious tomes into bags or within the tight embrace of their jackets. Their discussion stopped as they now made their way hurriedly through Tyrl Street.

Sadness mingled with anger as Lyra looked on, her heart disturbed by the sudden loss of conversation. The absence of a free street in which to talk broke the moment like a great shattering of glass, as the students now cast their faces to the ground.

Lyra shrugged her shoulders and flexed her fingers, staring directly at the city guards.

"Not now, not now!" hissed Kat, pulling Lyra gently back towards the shop to which they had been heading.

Rillo glanced back at them. "Is there a problem?"

"Problem? No, no problem" replied Kat, keeping a firm hand on her friend, until the guards and the Fereli were out of view.

Rillo nodded to Aequo who slowly strolled up to the door of Luder and Zwing's, before giving the all clear.

"This is the place," said Rillo, leading the two women and Virgil to the front door.

"Now, Luder and Zwing are an odd pair. But don't pay them any attention and let me do the talking. They used to run a small printing press before Nihilo took over the city, and rumour has it that they still keep the machine in their back room. They're providing some of the wine for Lady Aayla's ball this evening, and they also have the uniforms of the serving staff who are working at the event. If you want to get close to another high-profile magister, this is the best way to do it," whispered Rillo, just before leading them through the front door.

A small bell chimed as the group entered.

The room was like many in this part of Luthil, oak-panelled and musty with the smell of old books. Lyra saw a vast row of shelves from which a few manuscripts had been recently removed, but these spaces were now filled with an assortment of expensive stationery and the type of household oddities that lined more than a few rooms of the nearby colleges.

"For the last time, that wine is not real!"

"What a ridiculous man you are! Of course it's real! Do I need to write out exactly what he said for you?"

A pair of raised voices preceded the entrance of two men wearing long dark robes.

"Luder! Of course the wine isn't real! The merchant was speaking in metaphors! He referred to his ship as the "great light", but that doesn't mean that he sails around on a giant torch now, does it?" spat the man who Lyra assumed was Zwing. He was shorter than Luder and certainly thinner around the waist, with wispy locks of grey hair curling over his temple. But his eyes were bright blue, alive, and fierce with a sense of certainty.

"Ah, gentlemen," began Rillo, only to find that his voice was being overrun by the enraged debate now taking place on the other side of the shop counter.

"Metaphors!? He said it simply, as plain as day. It's real wine! Not everyone speaks in riddles like you, Zwing! Look, there's some cold sausages in the pantry. Go and have lunch while I get on with some real work. And when I say sausages, I mean real sausages! It's not a code, not a metaphor for banana cake, they're actual sausages," snapped Luder.

Zwing shook his fists in frustration. "Oh, you really are an insufferable man! Go back to your tavern and your beer, I can finish the rest of the order without you. The "wine" you brought us is no more than flavoured water, so that's the crate in which it will be packed, end of discussion!"

Luder scowled, and with one swipe of his meaty hand, he grabbed a piece of chalk and began to write furiously upon the surface of the counter.

"The. Wine. Is. Real."

Zwing rolled his eyes and waved his hands in a moment of exasperation.

"Really?! You're writing on the counter now? You're worse than Hus!"

"Gentlemen!"

The two men looked up, staring indignantly at Rillo.

"What do you want?" they replied, almost in unison.

Aequo couldn't contain an amused grin, as Rillo sighed and spoke again.

"I'm here to pick up an order."

"What order?" asked Zwing, wetting the tip of his thumb and rubbing the chalk letters away.

"An order set aside for Dr Schumon."

The rubbing stopped, and a disturbingly sober expression crossed Luder and Zwing's faces.

"Dr Schumon? We weren't expecting that particular delivery to be collected until this evening," replied Luder.

"Plans have changed. We'll be collecting it now."

Zwing slowly leaned across the counter, noting that no one else had entered the shop.

"Are they finally going to do something then? Are they going to make a move?"

Suddenly Aequo's hands landed heavily upon the counter, and he edged uncomfortably close to Zwing's face.

"Exactly who do you mean by "they"? Speak up. How many questions do you have for us about the work we do for Schumon, eh? Best get them out now, because later you might not be able to."

Despite the clear look of surprise on Zwing's face, Lyra was impressed to see that he did not recoil away from Aequo's outburst.

"No explanation necessary. If you've got the coin, then we have your delivery." Zwing examined the small group carefully and watched as Virgil attempted to hide his face behind a large leather-bound volume.

"Virgil?"

The artificer slowly lowered the book and smiled meekly over at Zwing.

"Virgil! It's good to see you. We have the bound editions of your latest work ready for sale!"

Kat and Lyra spun on their heels. "You know these men, Virgil?" asked Lyra.

"And you write books?" said Kat, with a look that was not dissimilar to that of a cat who had just discovered where all of the smoked salmon was kept.

He stepped forward. "Yes. Hello Zwing, we needn't discuss that right-"

However, without pause, Zwing reached into a shelf under the counter and pulled out several freshly-bound poetry books. The two women grabbed them with shameless abandon.

Lyra flicked hurriedly through several pages whilst Kat glanced down at the cover.

"The Aenei-" she began to say before Virgil snatched the book from her hands.

"That's enough of that," he said quickly but was unable to remove Lyra's book before she placed two silver coins in Zwing's hands.

"We'll take two."

"Lyra, there's no need to be looking at those!"

"Ly, what's it about?" asked Kat eagerly.

"I'm not sure," she replied, her eyes firmly locked down on one particular page as she pulled away from Virgil's grasp. "It looks like poetry. It's some sort of origin story."

Aequo sidled up next to the artificer, looking down at the book held firmly in his grasp.

"So here I was thinking that you were this cold-hearted killer, Virgil. And now we learn that you're a delicate poet," said Aequo with a grin.

Before Virgil could offer any sort of response, Zwing marched over to the pair and stared straight at the former sergeant. Zwing examined Aequo from head to toe, looking at him with all the interest that one might apply to seeing an unusually large dog.

"Ex-army, what regiment?" Zwing asked simply.

"Twenty-Eighth Rifles," answered Aequo, drawing himself up to his full height.

A momentary pique of interest raised Zwing's brow. "The Twenty-Eighth?" He looked across at Rillo. "The stories say that very few of the Twenty-Eighth survived the retreat from Dargestan. You two are a rare breed," the shop owner responded thoughtfully.

"Rare, dangerous, in a hurry, take your pick. But either way we'll be needing that order."

Zwing's hand slowly brushed the surface of the shop counter, and Lyra looked at its aged surface and the vast plethora of treasures that littered the shelves of the small shop. She wondered what exotic contents might have travelled from shores far across the sea to be sold across that very counter. It amused her slightly that such a small space could contain such vast and well-travelled goods.

Her thoughts returned once more to the Aureli Embassy and the future which her father had once been guiding her towards. A future in which she would travel and see sights that Virgil and her father had so often spoken of, sights of which she had once dreamed and upon which she had built such vast stories for Nathan to listen to as he fell asleep by the fireplace. Stories of a world which now, he would never grow up to see.

Even as her newly-found compatriots from the Vox Militant continued to make demands upon the unflustered shopkeepers, she felt a small tear well up in the corner of her eye.

Not now, not here.

Lyra gritted her teeth and clenched her fists, feeling the warm embrace of the gauntlet that Kat had fashioned for her. Even now, the blood which it had harvested from the attack on Bremmer's household ran magical cords of energy through its seams. A horizon of fire and blood filled Lyra's mind's eye, the tear failed to fall upon her cheek, and she turned to see Zwing ushering the group through to the back room of the shop.

"I can see that we're dealing with dangerous men," muttered Zwing with a sideways glance at Luder, whose expression mirrored his own.

"We might not have the killer reputation of the poet over here, but we can get the job done," snapped Aequo, gesturing over to Virgil, having noted the obvious sarcasm in Zwing's voice.

The shopkeeper suddenly turned upon his heel, the meagre light that trickled into the storage room illuminating his sunken cheeks.

"You are not the first soldiers to step into this establishment, and hopefully, when Nihilo is one day brought to heel, you shall not be the last. I'm sure that you have fought many battles and survived many blades. But if the tale of my years has taught me anything, it is that poets are far more dangerous than soldiers."

Behind Zwing, Luder continued to descend into the depths of the storage room. This cluttered space seemed far larger than the shop front, and Luder could be heard grunting as he stepped over carefully stacked boxes and edged around the frame of a loosely covered printing press.

Aequo nonetheless kept his eyes fixed on Zwing. "I enjoy a good read as much as the next man, but I have yet to see a book that will tear through a man like a rifle shot. Pretty pages have their uses when a country is at peace, but in war, blade and shot are what really count."

The older man smiled in response, stepping backwards as the rest of the party made their way into the room.

"With your blade, master soldier, you may kill several men in a single battle, but that same day, the words of the poet will send thousands of young men into the fray. It is the poet who, through art or deception, though if you ask me they are much the same thing, speaks of war as a thing of glory, honour and virtue. Through their words, the poets make death a noble thing, both to give and to receive. To kill the foe becomes the most revered of professions. They craft a silken prose which exonerates, rather than merely observes. You may impress a tavern with your tales of war, but a poet will rouse a generation with one page. Fear the word, master soldier, not the shot."

Lyra could not help but smile on hearing these words, not because listening to them brought her any joy, but because she had not heard anyone speak like that for a long time. It reminded her of a university lecture, one of the few that had really grabbed her attention. Hardly anyone spoke in the way that Zwing just had. His words had not been practical, and they had no immediate application, but they spoke of something higher than the moment offered, and that was special.

The sound of Luder's rougher voice broke the silence that followed. "There at least he is correct." The larger man came back into view carrying two large bags. "No matter what we, the Pale Star Guild, or you plan to do, there is no greater power than the word."

Luder handed Rillo both bags, his eyes resting momentarily on Virgil. "Especially a word that cannot be shaken." The artificer nodded slowly but offered no reply. Luder descended once more into the depths of the room as Zwing gave the bags in Rillo's hands a light tap.

"These are the requested uniforms for Lady Aayla's ball. Her ladyship is very particular about what her serving people wear, so these clothes have been made especially for tonight. Once you wear them you should be able to slip in unnoticed, as I can only assume is your intent. My colleague is collecting some wine, some real wine, which the magister has requested for the event. It is a rare vintage and it should complete your disguise."

Zwing's words hung expectantly in the air. Rillo looked at Aequo and nodded, watching as his friend pulled out a small satchel that rustled with the sound of coin and handed it over to Zwing.

"Very well, it seems that for now our business is concluded. Your wine will be brought to you shortly." Zwing gave the party one last scan with his eyes, framed as he was by shelves filled with rare trinkets and the looming presence of the printing press behind him.

For the first time, his gaze fell upon Lyra.

"You are a curious group, to be sure. You never fail to surprise with the company that you keep, Virgil," said Zwing, his eyes not shifting from the young noblewoman.

"I do not desire to know exactly what it is that you plan to do, or to what end, but be assured that I wish you well."

Lyra smiled, seeing the kindly expression that now wrinkled the sides of

Zwing's pale cheeks.

"Thank you," she replied. "I have no doubt that with your help, we will be successful in our cause."

Zwing breathed deeply, the warmth unshaken from his face.

"I cannot say that I wish you success, because I do not know to what end you strive, my lady," answered Zwing with the lightest nod of his head, a light twinkle catching the corner of his eye. "I can only wish you well, hoping that before too long, you may seek an end which is worthy of you."

Lyra kept his gaze. "Even if now I desire a tyrant's end?"

Zwing nodded slowly. "A tyrant is simply one who wields power unjustly. They may be killed, deposed, and exiled, but rarely is their place left vacant. They are too often replaced by men and women of similar ambition, and thus the tyrant lives on. I believe that one day, you may kill a man, my lady, but I cannot know for certain at this time whether or not you will free this city from tyranny."

They left the shop in much the same manner as they had arrived, with caution, and keeping a watchful eye out for Fereli mercenaries and city guards. Rillo and Kat carried the clothes and wine they had collected, eager to return to Virgil's home so that they might prepare for the evening to come. Lyra was careful to keep looking towards the ground, with a half-mask concealing much of her face. Every few moments she would look over at Virgil to see the artificer glancing between the pages of the book which he had confiscated from Kat.

"You three go ahead, we'll catch you up."

The rest of the party looked back at Lyra.

"We don't have long until the beginning of Lady Aayla's ball, and we need to get a proper plan together," said Rillo.

"I know, but we've been away from the safe-house for a few hours, and there could be who knows how many of Nihilo's spies walking the streets. You go on, while Virgil and I pull back and check that you're not being followed."

Rillo looked at Aequo, who simply shrugged his shoulders. "It's not that bad an idea," spoke the sergeant.

Rillo sighed. "Fine, but don't be long."

"Want an extra pair of eyes?" asked Kat, taking her place beside Lyra.

"You best stay with them, make sure that they save the wine for the ball," answered Lyra, her voice low.

Kat grinned. "Good point, but don't be long. I'm not sure if I have the energy to come and rescue you two and take out a magister on the same day."

With no more delay, the three of them hurried on their way as Lyra and Virgil did their best to merge with the gentle tide of people and carts that bustled through the street.

"You know full well that we're not being followed," muttered Virgil, his attention momentarily distracted by the not-too-distant smell of the bakery just across the street.

"Yes."

"And you also know that Nihilo has no reason to be subtle. If he traced you back to my house it would already be in flames."

"Yes."

"Good, just making sure that we're on the same page," replied Virgil, stepping into the bakery and purchasing a few honey cakes, offering one to Lyra.

She took it gladly, lifting her mask slightly to get a larger bite of the delicious honeyed pastry.

"So what are we doing here?" he asked, already moving onto his second cake.

Lyra looked at the artificer for a few moments. Even to this day, after all these years, Lyra was not sure exactly how old Virgil was, and looking at him now it was hard to tell. Though perhaps a greater mystery than his age was his uncanny ability to consume honey cake after honey cake and yet never put on weight. She didn't like to say it, but Lyra was fairly certain that if anyone else that she knew managed to eat pastries like Virgil did, then even the mightiest bridge of old Abys would buckle under their weight.

"Who are you, Virgil?"

He paused mid-bite, wiping a fine trail of crumbs from his chin.

"What?" came his muffled question.

Lyra took a step closer towards him. "Who are you?" she repeated, her every syllable weighed down with sharp intent.

He looked back at her in the same manner that he had done when she was a child, not with condescension but with an unbridled sense of care.

"You know who I am, Lyra," he answered slowly.

The features of the noblewoman's face fell, her eyes hardening even as she willed them not to.

She shook her head for a few moments before words touched her lips. "I thought I did, once, but now... now I am not so sure."

To these words, Virgil did not reply. He broke her gaze, observing a cobblestone at his feet, until Lyra's voice rose again.

"When they attacked my house I lost everything, everything except you and Kat."

"You still have your father."

On hearing this, such a look crossed Lyra's face that Virgil could barely will himself to look at her.

"I have what little is left of my father, Virgil. He is not who he once was. When I speak to him, I can barely recognise his voice."

"You don't mean that."

Lyra felt her fist clench once more. "Oh I do, Virgil, I really do." Lyra relaxed her hand, running her fingers through her hair.

Her voice began to shake but whether it was through anger or sorrow Virgil could not tell.

"My life and my family were burned away in moments, and as I begin to take my revenge for what Nihilo has done to me, I find that you, one of the few constants in my life, are not the man that I thought you were."

"Lyra, I have been standing beside your family for years – "

She leaned closer, taking a step towards a side alley, away from the bustling crowd.

"How many years, Virgil?"

The artificer breathed in deeply but found that he could not reply.

"How many years have you been standing beside my family? That story you told me, the one when you were an apprentice and made a toy boat for that merchant's boy, after which you helped craft terrible weapons for a time of war. When was that exactly?"

"Lyra —"

"Because I know it wasn't the last war or the one before that when you served in the cavalry with my father. The war before that was many years ago, and I remember enough of my lessons to know that very few artifice weapons beyond rifles and armour were used to win that fight. So what war were you talking about, Virgil?"

"Lyra, these are not questions which are going to help you right now."

She leaned forward still further, her voice accusatory in its tone. "How old are you, exactly?"

Virgil's face hardened. "This is not a path that you want to walk down with me, Lyra."

"Why not? Kat and I have already travelled the paths of Dis with you, and I doubt that this path could be much darker. Those creatures, those things that spoke to us out of the darkness, they claimed to know you." Her words slowed their pace as the broken memories of the path of Dis shook her speech further still.

"What were they, Virgil?" Lyra asked, and for the first time in months, fear rather than anger fuelled her voice.

The artificer placed a gentle hand on her shoulder. "You know that I work with magic, Lyra. I hope that I have not failed you so completely that you have forgotten what I have taught you. That once, many years ago, magic was a greater force than it is now, even before the times of Luthanril or that of Abyssus."

"Can it be possible that your memory stretches back that far?" she asked, pulling away from his grasp.

"My memory, I'm afraid, is not what it once was. But in the times when the magic of the first age still rolled across lands far from here, creatures fair and foul walked even this very ground in untold numbers. It is right that we speak of paths, for we live in a world where each person is said to walk their own, but in truth there is only one. One must either stick close to it, or stray away from it. As the creatures which now guard Dis once did, such is their fate."

"But they said that one day, you would join them," said Lyra, though this time, with more concern than fear.

The shadows that sat under Virgil's eyes deepened. "Yes, they did. However, that is not their decision to make. My past holds many stories, Lyra, but at the end it will not be their judgement that I sit under. I have yet some good to do, what that is worth I cannot say, but there it is."

"You speak to me in riddles and I have had enough of those from you and my father," Lyra's eyes winced shut as she recalled more claims from the denizens of Abys. "They said that you weren't human, that neither you nor I were human. What did they mean?"

Virgil drew her further into the alley, keeping a careful eye on the passing crowd.

"Lyra, nothing good comes from Dis. I should never have led you and Kat into that place. All that you heard were words from hateful creatures, trying to do you harm."

"They said that Kat was human and that you and I −"

"They said many things, but what they did not say is that I have been looking after your family long before your father met your mother, and I'll be watching out for you and Katerina for many years to come."

Suddenly, Lyra's thoughts came to a stop. The horrors of Dis washed away from her mind and for a moment all she could see was the painting of her mother that had once hung in her home before it had been consumed by flame. Guilt filled her mind with the thought that she had barely thought about her mother for months. She closed her eyes again to try and picture her face, but now her figure seemed obscured, hidden by a fog. The terrible realisation dawned upon Lyra that she no longer had a painting to turn to. All that remained was memory, and even now that was beginning to wane.

Will I forget her face?

Anger burned across her once more, forcing back the pain that this question brought her. She needed to read more of her father's book today. She needed to know how to punish Lady Aayla.

"Lyra."

She looked up.

"I know what you've lost, but I also know what you have. Katerina and I will stand right beside you, no matter what."

She opened her eyes to see Virgil looking back at her, and on sight of the rugged compassion of his face she felt the fires of her rage shrink ever so slightly.

"There's a big world out there, Lyra, and once all this is over, at that time, much more will be revealed to you."

A faint rustling sound disturbed the poignancy of the artificer's words, as Virgil lifted the small brown bag in his hand.

"Tonight, you'll have time for revenge aplenty, but for now, have a cake."

14

Vanity's Toll

The sound of fireworks reverberated across the wooden boards on which Lyra now stood. Flares of colour and the dancing light of wondrous spectacle filled the air.

"There's no time to take in the sights. Get moving!" hissed Rillo from behind her. He was wearing the same brightly-coloured array of robes that she was, fashioned from silks that were awash with purple and silver trim.

Another rocket shot into the air above, illuminating those below in a dazzling shower of green light that shone from the night's sky.

"Any eyes on the magister?"

Lyra looked back at Aequo and shook her head. "No, she'll be closer to the docks, greeting those much-admired guests of hers."

Kat was nowhere to be seen. Her rifle was far too large to be smuggled inside the small wine crates that the rest of the group were carrying, so she had hidden it at the bottom of a long firework box and was even now making her way over to the elevated platform of the firework station.

"Well, no matter what the magister does or doesn't do, we stick to the plan," muttered Rillo, slowly edging himself around a table laden with food.

"And if the plan doesn't work? If she doesn't move where we need her to move?" replied Lyra, keeping a wary eye on some nearby serving staff.

"Then we keep with the plan. We fall back and we wait for another day," snapped Rillo, looking across the square to see at least a dozen city guards idly making their way through the crowd of revellers.

Lyra felt her jaw clench. "Another day."

The plan, what little of it there was, centred around what had become a common custom in noble balls. These events were famed for their choice foods and exotic entertainment. Not to mention the pageantry and the intricate beauty of the costumes on display. Lady Aayla was famed for the extravagance of her household, and the balls which she hosted were no different. This night alone, she had dedicated a large amount of dock space and countless Abys market squares to hours of drinking, dancing, artistic displays, and most importantly, a few quietly-spoken words.

As Master of Coin, a crucial part of Lady Aayla's duty was to negotiate rates of pay, tax, requisitions, and asset management that kept the city coffers full. This involved speaking regularly to merchants, bankers, diplomats, and endless queues of local and foreign officials. This was taxing enough for any Master of Coin, but for a magister of Lady Aayla's ambition and corruption this particular aspect of her role was a joy. Money was such an obsession for her that it was rumoured amongst her waiting staff that were she to bleed, she would bleed pure gold. There were few trading nations that imported goods from Abys-Luthil over which Lady Aayla did not hold some sway. Her words dropped like sweet honey in the ears of any whom she felt could further increase the riches of her coffers. Newly-struck trade deals and freshly-collected taxes warranted yet more of the balls and rich silk gowns with which she flaunted her wealth, such wealth as was beyond the grasp of any other merchant in the city. This ambition had clearly only risen further still since her elevation to the Council of Five. No doubt, Nihilo was happy to turn a blind eye to Aayla's indulgences as long as his weapons factories received all the funding that they needed.

Much of the event was taking place on the wooden platforms that supported the city's docks. These were held aloft by thousands of wooden beams submerged in the rolling waters below, and connected by a series of large and ornately-decorated bridges. Any attack to be launched in these open areas was nothing short of suicide, or so Rillo had repeatedly emphasised as they had discussed their plans. Aequo and even Kat had seemed to agree with him, and any opposition that Lyra might have hoped to raise was soon quashed.

They did not understand, not really. They did not know her need, and the extent of her passion to rid this city, her city, of the filth that was Lady Aayla. The magister was as guilty as Nihilo, and just as responsible for the haunted screams which had filled the burning halls of her home and now haunted the void-like terror of her dreams.

Fortunately for their plans, part of the entertainment spilled out into the more cloistered spaces of Abys' market squares. These were tightly packed, with high walls and many windows, and luckily enough, some of these buildings backed onto the firework platform where Kat had smuggled her rifle, granting her the perfect shooting position. Rillo had made a convincing case that this was the best place to ambush Aayla and make their escape, once the deed was done.

Lyra had been forced to agree. Once their target made her way into these cobbled squares, they would launch their attack.

"You there! I say, you there! Come fill my drink!"

Lyra grunted and turned to face an almost impossibly large man, dressed in traditional Luthan attire, with a host of richly adorned rings encircling his fingers.

"Certainly, sir," she smiled, her lips visible under the slender curves of the golden mask which rested over her eyes and nose.

"Faster, girl! Faster! I cannot bear to breathe this sullied Abysuss air without a good glass of wine in my hand," spluttered the nobleman, as Lyra carefully filled his recently emptied glass.

A woman with tired eyes and long blonde hair stood awkwardly beside him. "Augustus! You really shouldn't speak in such a manner!"

The man who Lyra could only assume was her husband helped himself to a healthy gulp of red wine and waved a hand dismissively.

"I will say whatever I please! You're just as likely to catch the rot lung in Abys as you are to be robbed by the degenerates that spill out of those ships every day," said Augustus, gesturing over towards the nearby ships that stood towering over the docks.

At this, the woman's face grew steadily redder than the wine that they were both drinking. "My dear, you mustn't say such things! It's against the law now. You'll get yourself in trouble if you carry on so."

"I'll say whatever I please! I've got that right! I've jolly well paid enough for it. Nihilo may well be able to silence the surfs and those glorified paper merchants in the press houses, but you and I, my dear, we're different beasts altogether. We have the right to talk because we've earned it, we've paid for it. You can't silence coin!"

Lyra forced the smile to remain painted upon her face, bowed her head slightly, and descended further into the crowd. She had attended many of these occasions, and knew exactly what was required of the serving staff. Servants were only to be seen when requested; otherwise they were to blend in with the rest of the rented furniture. When she was younger, Lyra could barely remember seeing any servants at the balls and parties that she had attended with her father. She later realised that this was because those who served at the most prestigious of Abys-Luthil's social gatherings had been the very best. They had known when to blend in, and when to emerge from unseen corners.

Despite the anticipation of the kill to come, Lyra could not help but notice the plethora of different ornamental masks that were on display. Grinning faces, polished to mirror the likeness of pearl, looked out from every side.

Lyra looked around, and with a realisation that brought a chill to the very rhythm of her heartbeat she saw familiar masks and faces amongst the figures which indulged themselves in the corrosive pit that was Lady Aayla's wealth. Many masks bore small hints as to the identity of their wearers, whether though subtle patterns or through small sections of family crests that were worked into their designs. Without a keen eye and a good knowledge of Abys-Luthil's noble class, it was unlikely that any one mask could identify its wearer.

But now, for reasons that she could not explain, even to herself, Lyra recognised faces, so many faces, masked or otherwise, that she knew. These were people that she had shared dinner with and sat beside as her father had invited them into his home. They had applauded his speeches, nodded along to his words, and celebrated his guardianship of the people's rights. He had taught their sons and daughters, he had shared their views with the Council chambers, and night after night he had wracked his mind over an ink-stained desk in order to defend them, to defend their city. Not one of them had been beyond the council of his care or the ambition of his compassion, but here they were, dancing in the ashes of his ruin.

Even now, as her home lay in a grave of burnt wood and broken stone they feasted on the horror of Nihilo's victory, singing as wine poured like blood from the corners of their lips.

They disgusted her.

They would burn.

Lyra's hands squeezed the bottle she was holding so tightly that for a moment she feared it might burst. She could feel the weight of her revolver resting on her hip, flanked by a small row of bullets that were fitted into her belt, concealed by the robes of her serving uniform. A short sword was strapped across her back, and her prize Fereli dagger was concealed within her boot. Beside her pistol were two grenades that she had taken from Virgil's secret forge no more than two hours ago. Lyra had retrieved them secretly when the artificer was busy finding some artifice swords for Rillo and Aequo, who to Lyra's eyes had never looked happier than when they had caught sight of them. Virgil had forbidden her from taking the grenades, insisting that the area was too crowded and that they would incur too many innocent casualties.

Earlier, even on arrival at the ball, she had doubted her decision. Without Virgil, she would never have been able to venture back into the city, and without Virgil she never would have met Kat.

Was it right that she could so easily abuse his trust?

However, as Lyra now looked out across the sea of faces, she saw no innocents, only gluttons. They fed on the riches that Nihilo and Lady Aayla piled upon their plates, only to be served by the very people who had been robbed of their voice and consequently, their freedom. With every sip of wine they burned another press house, and with every morsel that they licked from their fingertips, they condemned another soul to work in the torment of Nihilo's weapon factories.

One did not have to swing a sword or fire a gun to be a murderer, this much she would soon teach them.

"You! More wine here!"

Lyra smiled and stepped forward.

Rillo picked up a fresh bottle of wine and headed once more into the riot of colour and dance that was the ball. Almost an hour had passed since they had arrived, and still no sign of the Master of Coin. Only a noblewoman of Lady Aayla's wealth and reputation could afford to be fashionably late to her own ball.

Careful not to step too far out of character, Rillo craned his neck around one particularly large pastry table to see that Aequo was still at his post, albeit helping himself to small sugared treats when he thought that no one else was looking. He made sure to make eye contact with him before descending closer towards the festivities around the docks, scowling as Aequo nodded back at him whilst wiping fine trails of icing from his fingers.

They were careful not to walk too close together, but kept a healthy distance apart, ready to watch each other's backs if anything went wrong.

Rillo served when requested before moving on as quickly as he could. He had attended many similar occasions in his role as the head of the Vox Militant, and knew many of the nobles that now cluttered the wooden platforms of the docks, and he could not risk being spotted.

Suddenly a drunken cheer arose from the crowd as a large ship, decorated with elaborate carvings of figures from the legendary history of Abys, approached the docks.

A galleon, the size of which dwarfed even the large troop carriers that Rillo had boarded during the war, slowly eased into view. Its enormous figurehead bore the frame of a woman holding a large trident pointed towards the sky, and wearing the skin of a great lion across her head and shoulders. The ship's sails obscured countless stars from the sight of those below, each seemingly the size of a city square. Cannons bristled along the vast swathe of varnished oak and copper plating that made up the body of the vessel.

Another salvo of fireworks raced into the sky, washing a vast kaleidoscope of colours over the large party of people on-board.

"Got to give it to her, the woman knows how to make an entrance."

He knew that voice anywhere.

"Just try to keep your fingers off the prawns."

Aequo grinned as he walked speedily past, joining the growing cluster of serving staff who were now preparing to greet the Master of Coin's arrival.

Rillo heard the blast of trumpets and the crescendo of thunderous applause as Lady Aayla was welcomed to her own party.

"My friends, my dearest friends."

Lady Aayla's voice rose unnaturally high above the competing sounds that swarmed across the crowd.

"My heart is warmed by your presence. Truly I am blessed to walk amongst each and every one of you."

Silence swiftly spread from group to group, as the music died away, the laughter faded, and all eyes were drawn to the lavish figure of the hostess. Aayla held a small copper ball before her lips, and it sparked with a sporadic green light.

A projection orb.

Rillo had seen many of these before, especially at the larger magister forums. He had even owned one himself as the captain of the Vox Militant, although that was long gone, and there was little chance that he would get his hands on another. Projection orbs were very expensive items, even by the standards of Abys-Luthil's elite.

Aayla raised a glass in the air. "You, my friends, are the forerunners of this city's freedom! A threat, unknown to the shores of this great state for a thousand years, builds its power in the far-flung reaches of the northern wastes."

Her voice flowed as freely as the wine, pouring effortlessly into the ears of all who watched. Even those who were sheltered within the squares beyond the docks could not escape the honeyed tone of her words. Nothing could amplify a voice quite like a projection orb, and there were very few artificers in the city who had the skill to create such tools.

"In the face of this imminent danger, you yourselves are the greatest hope that this city possesses!"

Aayla surveyed the scene before her, observing the many faces that looked out at her from between the swinging lanterns of crimson and gold that were criss-crossed above the platforms.

"Even in this time of mourning after the tragic murder of our dear friend, Salaris Bremmer, there is hope."

A disturbing note of sincerity underlined Aayla's words which pricked Rillo's ears.

"For the first time in living memory, this city is free from those who would wantonly speak hatred upon our streets. No more will the universities harbour those who seek to cause division amongst us! No more will they breed speakers of dissent who so viciously mocked the very government which now secures your freedom! Without your continued support, we would not be able to silence the bile which spills forth from those who protect the secret press houses. Without you, my friends, there is no freedom!"

Aayla raised her glass higher into the air to a chorus of applause and loud cheers from her audience. She took a sip of red wine, and Rillo watched as light from a nearby lantern danced across the rolling spheres of pearl rings that ran across her fingers.

"Those who oppose us will face the full wrath of this free city state! Many of you here will know of the traitorous plot of that false defender of the people, Maellon Alpheri."

Rillo drew his eyes away for a moment to look at the spot where he had last seen Lyra. She was beyond his sight, and a cold shiver ran down his spine. He slowly moved through the crowd in search of her.

"He sought to leave you defenceless against those who would have brought you harm! He conspired with foreign powers to bring famine and ruin to this city, and we have recently discovered new evidence of his many past crimes against the people of Abys-Luthil!"

Moment by moment, as each of Aayla's words raced through the air, Rillo quickened his pace. The sea of colours sparkling around him flooded his vision, and yet still he hunted for Lyra. She was far from where she was supposed to be.

"Now we learn that our dear friend Salaris Bremmer has been slain by the daughter of Maellon Alpheri. She seeks to continue her father's campaign of violence and ruin against this city!"

Rillo looked up to see Kat standing upon the fireworks' platform, staring into the crowd, scanning every face as he himself was doing, and yet there was no sign of Lyra.

"The survivors of her vicious attack on the Master of Blades have spoken to us of her savagery, and the cruelty with which she tortured and killed her victims. Such was the horrific nature of her terrible deeds that I cannot bring myself to utter them to your fair ears."

A murmur of shock ran through the crowd, filled with yet more rumours of Lyra's violence.

"But fear not, my friends. Your magisters are here for your service and protection." Aayla smiled, raising her projection orb high into the air before clicking her fingers.

Rillo cringed as the sharp note stung through the air, and was accompanied by a flurry of discarded cloaks and removed masks. Dozens of previously-disguised city guards and Fereli suddenly appeared from nowhere between the various groups of stunned nobles, who retreated further into their small groups. No sooner were their masks removed from their faces than the city guards stamped to attention, whilst the Fereli simply rolled their shoulders, leaning upon their large weapons.

"See, my friends, you are more protected than you know."

Armoured boots once again slammed upon wooden planks, the guards now providing a protected avenue of armour and swords down which Lady Aayla was now walking through the crowd.

"I realise the cost may be high, and I too lament the necessity of raising taxes. But ultimately, as you can see..." Aayla ran a finger across an armoured shoulder, "we will spend your money wisely. The High Magister and myself will protect you from threats within this city and against that which gathers in the north. We celebrate your partnership in this great enterprise!" A fresh glass of wine promptly appeared in the magister's hand, and she drank to the sound of cheers and applause from the jubilant crowd.

A familiar feeling settled at the base of Rillo's stomach. He knew it well, and his jaw clenched at the bitter taste of the rising dread that spread across his senses. It was the same feeling that he got before every battle, and now every fibre of his being was warning him that a fight was coming.

He could not allow that to happen. There were too many guards. Far too many. They would have to pull back and try another day.

He had to find Lyra.

"Oh! You clumsy oaf!"

Bottles of wine smashing to the ground followed by cries of protest rose to Rillo's ears.

"You stupid girl!" blustered an angry noble, berating a serving woman. The latter offered him a towel with which to dry himself as fine drops of red wine ran across his arm. He snatched at the cloth hastily, his fingers pulling at the straps of the servant's mask as he did so, tearing it from her face.

Lyra looked back at him, her eyes narrowed with hate, and the feigned servility of her disguise all but lost. Rillo quickened his pace, making his way over to her as fast as he could, but already he knew that it was too late. All eyes were now upon her, as the man protested further, until a few members of the crowd started to withdraw, recognising the face that was now plastered on so many wanted posters across the city.

Guards now stepped towards her, uncertain what to make of the sudden disturbance. Rillo willed Lyra to run. In this moment he felt that he would sacrifice anything to see her flee through the cover that the crowd provided.

But there she stood, her feet slightly apart, her hands hanging by her waist.

The guards advanced and Lyra remained, her hateful stare unshaken as the Master of Coin turned to witness the sudden commotion. Rillo thrust his hand into the body of his robe and wrapped his fingers around the handle of his pistol.

Lyra's body froze, her feet rooted to the spot.

Lady Aayla's gaze looked back out at her from across the platform, the music slowly fading as the lanterns swung idly in the air.

She saw the look of realisation dawn upon Aayla's face, as sudden suspicion formed into dreaded certainty. The magister's eyes twitched and she slowly lowered her wine glass from her lips.

The air grew silent, the music coming to a halt in a series of dissonant notes. The crowd parted as uneasy faces looked left and right for the cause of the merriment's sudden end, before all eyes quickly settled upon Lyra.

As the tread of approaching guards made its way across the floorboards, Lyra felt all of her senses attune to a singular point, as her world shrunk down to encompass nothing more than Lady Aayla. Her mind shut out the gasps of shock that ran through the crowd.

Fear soon stilled their words and the nervous hands of many guards now hovered over their weapons, as they waited for the order. But Aayla said nothing, her cold, hard stare content to challenge her would-be assassin.

Fire burned once more in Lyra's chest, and grew with every passing moment that their eyes remained fixed. Screams broke the silence of her mind, now as familiar to her as the feel of the passing breeze. Fires that swam around the tortured forms of the innocent and the guilty framed the magister, and arms charred and blackened by the flames reached out to her in desperate torment. A shrill cry rose above the others, cut off by the sudden fall of timber, and before Lyra could even track the fleeting movement of her hands, two of Lady Aayla's guards flew backwards under the roar of her gun.

Lyra dropped another guard with a swift shot from her revolver that tore his helmet to pieces. No sooner had she pulled back the weapon's firing hammer and another target was in her sights, shielding the fleeing Lady Aayla.

The next few moments were a haze of colour, screams and the violent blast of gunpowder. Lyra ducked and weaved herself through every assault of Aayla's protectors. With every volley of their guns she raised her gauntlet, deflecting shot after shot. Her legs danced around the frenzied strikes of Aayla's family guard, and her sword punished every missed blow with swift vengeance.

All was noise and blood, a deafening crescendo which played the beat for every one of Lyra's bloodied steps.

She heard the sharp crack of Kat's rifle firing down from the elevated fireworks platform. Even as her sword, its edge alive with blue cords of artifice-imbued energy, burst through the chest of another masked guard, a second fell behind him, his eyes rendered suddenly cold by the precision of Kat's shots.

Smoke coiled around the periphery of Lyra's vision, as the smoke grenades that Rillo had insisted on bringing obscured the fleeing figures of the terrified crowd. The rude blast of pistol shot lay in her wake, mingled with the eager cries of Rillo and Aequo, whom she heard battling with whatever number of guards had formed behind her.

The smoke swelled around her and yet Kat's shots still fired with deadly accuracy, her vision unimpeded thanks to the various optical enhancements that Virgil's artifices provided.

"Lyra!"

Rillo's cry was lost in the chaos that had shattered Lady Aayla's ball. The guards kept coming but still Lyra pressed forward. She performed a quick reload of her pistol, before hammering her elbow into the throat of a guardswoman who wielded a long rifle adorned with an elaborate bayonet. The woman spluttered and coughed, desperately attempting to shield herself from further blows with her rifle. Yet nothing would halt Lyra's assault. Her right foot hammered down upon the woman's knee, knocking her to the floor, before her sudden wail was silenced with a single pistol shot.

"Lyra!"

The cry came again, barely audible over the screams of the fleeing crowd and the blast of gunfire. Yet now was no time to stop; she had come too far, and the Master of Coin was soon to be within her reach. Guard after guard stood before her, and each fell in their turn like apparitions existing only briefly in the swirling shroud of blood. Even as Rillo's smoke grenades continued to obscure the scene, everything was bathed in a soft amber light as the lanterns swung high above the firefight.

An armoured fist flew out towards Lyra, only to be caught in the firm grip of her gauntlet. She squeezed, feeling rippling cords of energy wrap around her fingers. Lyra tightened her grasp, not yielding to the shouts of pain that now spilled from her assailant's mouth, and watched as their armour crumpled, breaking the bones beneath.

Suddenly the screaming guard was unceremoniously thrown aside, tossed into the water that flanked the still crowded platform. A large figure now loomed out of the smoke, carrying a great axe, the size of which nearly obscured the sight of the fleeing Lady Aayla. A heavily tattooed face leered out at her, decorated with the form of a raven whose wings spanned the full width of the Fereli's head. The beard that hung from his face bore many decorated tribal ringlets, and ran down across his barrelled chest. His eyes expressed a malice beyond that of any other of the magister's defenders, and within their sunken depths Lyra detected a note of sinister familiarity.

"The girl that got away."

The harsh and broken words of the Fereli chieftain came spitting at her as he advanced, and for a second it seemed to Lyra as if the man were walking through a sea of flame. No sooner were his words spoken than she recognised him: the Fereli warrior that had set her home ablaze and butchered Castel before her very eyes.

"No one to save you now," the chieftain snarled, rolling his shoulders and raising his axe.

Lyra cocked her revolver. "I'm not the one that needs saving."

She went to take her shot, one that she had rehearsed for many sleepless nights. However the chieftain's boot slammed into her abdomen with a furious speed.

Her back protested with pain, the air forced from her lungs. She barely managed to summon the energy to roll to one side, narrowly avoiding the chieftain's axe that bit into the wooden planks on which she had landed.

Jumping to her feet, Lyra lashed out with her gauntlet, striking the chieftain on the shoulder. The Fereli howled in pain as magical sparks scorched his flesh. Lyra raised her pistol once more, but fired harmlessly into the air, her body reeling from a solid punch from a tattooed fist that struck her hard upon the jaw.

With a savage tear the chieftain pulled his axe free and raised it over her again. She looked up at the terrible weapon, the fiery rubies encrusted upon it burning with magical energy. Lyra could feel the blood dripping from the corner of her lips and taste it on her tongue, even as she watched the weapon's terrible rise.

Suddenly a shot rang out, carving a hole through the smoke and sending a flurry of crimson across the chieftain's shoulder. He roared in pain, and looked around to see where the shot might have been fired from, before lifting his weapon forward with an anguished grunt and watching the rubies come alive with power.

Lyra felt the air grow hot as a sudden burst of flame launched from the axe, shooting across the wooden platforms and sending great balls of fire crashing into the fireworks platform.

"Kat! No!" Lyra screamed, rolling across the floor and forcing herself to her feet. Her voice was soon cut short by the explosion of light and colour that erupted from the platform, seeming to tear a hole through the night's sky. Burning embers rained all around, and for a moment it looked as if the very stars themselves had been plucked from the sky to fall upon them.

The Fereli grinned. "Lost another one," he growled, looking straight at Lyra.

Her muscles tensed, and her stance dropped low, the gauntlet crackling with power in one hand whilst the other wielded the captured Fereli dagger. No scream came forth from Lyra's lips, no great bout of rage, no harsh word. Her jaw clenched, her eyes narrowed, and she charged.

The air chased through her lungs, her breath fleeting and desperate like her steps. She stabbed and lunged, keeping as close to her enemy as possible, depriving him of the space he needed to swing his great axe. Several times she drew blood, striking at his arms and knees. His cries of pain sullied the air, but still he fought back. Her body was littered with bruises from a dozen strikes, each one protesting at the sudden movement of her limbs. Blood swam in her mouth and a blinding pain assaulted her right eye, barely avoiding further injury by repeated use of her gauntlet's shield.

Suddenly the chieftain's form moved to one side and the full force of his axe's handle knocked into her chest, throwing her to the floor.

"Your toys won't save you," he rasped, moving towards her.

The snarl which formed across Lyra's lips was framed in blood, with thick trails rolling down her bruised cheeks.

"This one just might."

Her thumb pressed hard upon the arcane runes that ran across the grenade in her hand. Her fingers released and she launched herself backwards with what little remained of her strength.

Everything went dark as Lyra's eyes blinked helplessly and a dull ringing sound rested upon her ears. She could feel the sharp sting of wooden splinters upon her fingertips, even as her back protested her every movement with swift waves of pain. The Fereli chieftain was nowhere to be seen, and all Lyra could now perceive was a thin veil of smoke and a host of shifting images beyond. Sound slowly crept through the ache of her ears, and soon screams and the roar of flames fought for her attention against the jostling currents of the waters below.

A voice cried out, sharp and shrill, with words that were tossed to and fro amongst the cries of the frightened and the wounded. Within a moment, small spheres of red light leapt out of the smoke, and the air was once again filled with the sound of wood torn asunder. Lyra launched herself to her feet, crying out in pain as her wounded limbs burned and bled with every step. Cannon fire now rained down around her, pouring from the fiery gun barrels that ran across the deck of Lady Aayla's grand galleon.

Fear hastened Lyra's steps, and she sprinted with agonising speed as the cannon balls destroyed the wooden platform on which she stood. But even as the hurtling spheres of death flew around her, familiar shapes stepped into her sight. Lyra's hands curled into fists as she discerned the fleeing figure of Lady Aayla racing across the docks with four guards at her heel.

A broken growl rose from the back of Lyra's throat, seeking to overcome the hooked claws of pain that tore at her wounds.

Her legs burned, but she ignored them.

Her arms wept fierce trails of crimson blood, which poured over the splinters that dug into her skin. But she ignored this.

Sweat poured down her face, flying from her lips with each rasping breath that tugged at her fatigued lungs. But she ignored this.

Her strained eyes, coloured red by burst blood vessels and the rigours of combat, narrowed upon the sight of her hated foe, acting bastions against a flood of tears that bore the memory of her fallen home. This Lyra embraced.

The grenade flew straight and true from her hand, landing atop the busy deck of the vast ship. Cannon crews reloaded their guns, and marksmen took position upon the quarterdeck to take aim upon the assailant below. Only one lowly officer thought to drag his eyes away from the burning abyss below, to see the small copper sphere roll across the deck, with every rune upon its polished surface blazing alight with orange flame.

Cannons tore from their mounts, issuing black smoke in their thunderous passage through the shifting air. Rigging twisted and snapped, contracting with sudden speed and leaving fleeting tendrils of blood in their wake as they tore through recoiling sailors. Whole cannon crews were swallowed by great blasts of firing powder, as the fire from the grenade set off a dozen explosions that rippled across the upper deck.

Two of the guards following Lady Aayla were pulverised by the sudden passage of a fractured cannon that landed upon them in a great red cloud. Lyra felt a wave of heat from the explosions that had all but decimated the upper deck wash across her cheek, even as she leapt over the remnants of the sundered cannon.

Lyra watched Aayla and her two remaining guards leap from the elevated platforms of the Abys docks to land upon the muddy bank below, hoping to board any nearby vessel. Lyra quickened her pace, angered to have lost sight of her quarry, even for a moment. She soon reached the end of the dock, and looked down to see Aayla and her guards flailing in the mud below, struggling to move with the weight of their finery and knee-high boots. One guard fell into the oozing mud, and her feet sank hopelessly into the shifting surface, which seemed unwilling to release her from its murky grasp. She was not afforded the chance to rise a second time as a sudden weight landed across her back and the tip of a silver and blue artifice sword erupted from her chest, pinning her forever into the mud.

Lyra rose, using the bleeding form of the guard at her feet to steady her movements, watching as her two remaining victims observed her advance. So hindered were they by the slippery nature of the bank, that the magister's final guard could barely draw his sword before Lyra had loaded a bullet into her revolver.

"No! Wait!" His arms flew wide in a desperate plea, but this did not stop the sound of Lyra's pistol from roaring across the scene. The guard's body fell and Lyra stepped forward, holstering her pistol.

"I didn't kill your family!" screamed Lady Aayla, her voice devoid of its usual coolness.

Lyra offered no reply but continued to walk forwards, feeling the energy of the gauntlet radiate lightly across her arm.

"It was Nihilo. It was Nihilo! He and the Fereli! Those barbarians wanted a prize, a trophy, a symbol of their new place in this city. I didn't order the attack!"

Lyra felt her hands clench as the rest of her body became numb. Lady Aayla fell to the ground once more, the mud creeping up her legs. The vibrant colours of her robe became muted in a sea of browns and greens, and her long cloak was torn, its many pearls lining the path down which Lyra now trod. The rubies that sat upon the rings on her hands fell into the dirt, soon lost within its unyielding depths.

"Please, please! I can help you! You want to get to Nihilo? Fine! I can bankroll your rebellion, restore your family's wealth, restore your family's name!"

Lyra ceased her eager steps. Behind her came another explosion from the galleon, showering the bank in flaming wood and torn canvas sail.

She saw the briefest flicker of hope settle upon Lady Aayla's face.

"Yes, yes! I will help you restore your family's honour. All of my vast wealth will be at your disposal, my lady," she spluttered with a sharp nod of her head. "Nihilo will be made to pay for what he did to you. My coin will help you buy every mercenary in the land! You will be restored to your rightful place! Your family will be celebrated, and the Alpheri name will be written in gold across every city street!"

Lyra's face contorted in a snarl as she knelt down next to Aayla. Flames ran across the periphery of her vision, and from within them she could hear the childlike screams.

"My family will not be honoured!" shouted Lyra, the armoured fist of her gauntlet slamming into the magister's face.

"My family will not be celebrated!" came her cry as her fist struck again.

"My family are dead!"

Lady Aayla's jaw broke under the frantic force of the third blow, and Lyra began to hear her choke and splutter as the magister's mouth filled with blood.

"The Alpheri name will be written across every street. But not in gold!"

The gauntlet wrapped across Aayla's face, her broken mouth screaming in twisted agony as the artifice armour drew swift channels of blood from every wound across her face. Lyra felt the power surge through her arm, drawn from the gauntlet, and washing across her body and mind. She closed her eyes, feeling the magical energy move through her veins. However even as her eyelids closed, it was not darkness that she saw. Her unveiled gaze looked out across a sea of sulphur and flame, pocketed by terrible and torturous islands. Men and women sank into the fiery earth, bearing a burden too great for their backs to hold, only to be birthed again to repeat their fruitless toil. Others ran from pursuing beasts amidst trees that produced branches as sharp as knives with leaves like razors, drawing blood at every touch.

In this vision, foul creatures presided over the macabre display, watching their doomed charges with a sinister gaze. However, as Lyra looked down upon all this, with no expression of pain shielded from her sight, she saw that one by one, the presiding creatures, with cruel instruments of torture in their hands, stared back. Soon, a thousand eyes peered out at her from a sea of countless horrors, and the creatures smiled. They cocked their heads to one side as if to hear the screams of Lyra's victim, and with crooked fingers, their nails painted black by countless specks of dried blood, they drew the name Alpheri in the ground at their feet.

Horror ran cold through Lyra's veins, but her gauntlet remained like a vice over Lady Aayla's face. She looked into the abyss and it stared back at her, her name engraved within its very centre. She felt the darkness draw closer, the anger that boiled in her heart fuelling its advance across her very being.

Suddenly, a fierce blue light rolled across her vision, and the darkness of her mind's eye was swept away. A modest fire appeared in front of her. Lyra found herself in a small cave, and as the flames from the fire danced in front of her, she saw wondrous shadows cast along its walls. She saw the shadows take forms familiar to her, people who embraced and greeted one another in love. No sooner did she have a chance to look upon these than a blue robed figure stepped out from a dark corner.

"Lyra."

She rose, and looked back at the robed man, his face obscured by a deep hood.

"Lyra," he spoke out again, his voice firm but gentle. She stepped towards him, moving past the fire. As she did so, the shadows upon the wall changed, collapsing in upon themselves and falling away as the fire was suddenly snuffed out.

"Lyra."

She blinked, finding herself back at the Abys docks, the vision she had seen removed from her sight.

Kat was standing a few feet away, her boots caked in mud and her face sweaty and bruised on one side.

"Lyra, are you ok?"

Lyra froze. She looked down at Lady Aayla's body to see her face drained of all life, locked in a torturous expression. Her eyes bulged, her cheeks were hollow, and not a trace of blood could be seen upon her.

"A cave. I was in a cave..."

"A cave? What cave? What are you talking about?"

"You didn't see it?" Lyra could feel her legs shake, her eyes darting wildly around her. "There was a man...I don't... I don't understand."

Kat held her rifle in one hand as she placed her other hand gently upon Lyra's shoulder.

"There's no cave, Ly, no man. We need to go, it's not safe here."

Lyra's eyes once again rested on the corpse of Aayla. Even amongst all of the death, the fire and the blood, small traces of finery could still be found resting on the magister's fingers and clothes. What had been a large square of canvas sail lay beside the body, its fire all but extinguised. The mud had dirtied it, and the fire had eaten away at its edges, blackening and fraying its already coarse texture. It was an ugly remnant of something previously majestic, and as Lyra's thoughts drifted back to the pages of the Crimson Script she picked it up, and laid it across her victim's body, leaving the head exposed. Lady Aayla was now a picture of ruin, her many vanities snuffed out by the charred remnants of her ambitions.

"What's that?" asked Kat, the curiosity in her voice barely able to mask her clear concern.

Lyra looked down to see something poking out from the corners of the burned canvas.

"It's a book, some kind of journal," answered Lyra, examining the leather-bound tome, noting the various loose pages that spilled from its edges. She brushed the mud from its worn green surface and read a page heading.

"It contains some recordings of meetings in the Grand Magisters' Chambers, special edicts of the Council of Five."

"A strange book for Lady Aayla to be carrying around. This is a clerk's tome," muttered Kat.

Lyra nodded, handing the book over. "You have it, Kat. It may have some useful information for us, but I cannot will myself to read it." She looked down at the horrid figure. "I cannot bring myself to see her as anything other than a corpse."

She sighed, feeling the satisfying movement of air passing between her lips. Pain echoed across the bruised chambers of her body. Her bones ached and her muscles protested with every movement, and yet even now she felt the steady flow of power emanating from her gauntlet. The fires around her had died away, one by one, slowly consumed by the mud. She could feel her friend's eyes upon her. Lyra knew of Kat's concern, her fear, her worry. The joyful memories and companionship that she and Kat had shared together were beyond number. She could not even call to mind all the times that Kat had seen her cry, or patiently listened to her as she imagined out loud what sort of woman her mother had been. In turn, Lyra had heard of the shadows of Kat's childhood, and smiled upon hearing her many plans for the future. There had never been a barrier between them, and yet, even in this moment, Lyra had never felt further from her.

Kat took the book, silently observing her friend, her eyes wide and troubled.

"Thank you," Lyra looked down at her feet. "For covering me, earlier. I never would have made it this far without you."

Kat smiled. "I'm in this for the long haul, Ly. Same as always."

A brief look of contentment fell upon Lyra's face.

"Hey, idiots!"

The pair looked up to see Aequo's face glaring down at them from the balcony of the docks above.

"Whilst I hate to disturb your chat time, there's still a lot of rather angry ladies and gents up here! Either you get up here now, or you'd best start swimming!" His words were framed by the sound of clashing steel and the sharp crack of rifle fire.

"Back to the forge," and Lyra began her uneasy tread across the mud.

Kat followed, giving a cursory glance to the ruin of their surroundings. "Yeah, only that the forge, hidden as it might be, may not be the safest place right now. I doubt Virgil's going to be happy about all this."

"It's fine. We'll grab some cinnamon rolls on the way back. He's far less intimidating when his lips are covered in icing."

"Where are we going to get cakes at this time of night?"

"I know a guy."

"You're telling me that you know a moonlighting, all hours, cinnamon roll baker?"

"Yeah, like I said, I know a guy." Lyra's feet steadied as she made it onto the steps leading to the upper dock platform, her pace hastening as Aequo's voice once again rose angrily through the air.

"I swear, if you two don't get yourselves up here right now, I'll shoot you myself! Magic mittens or not!"

267

15

Aftermath

he tavern was quiet, and for this Rillo was very thankful.

"You look like you need a drink."

"Coffee."

Marion scowled. "It's midnight."

"Coffee. Please."

The wooden legs of the chair protested as Rillo almost collapsed upon it, his elbows leaning heavily upon the table. He heard Aequo take the seat beside him, his head held in his hands.

"I assume that it won't be two coffees?" said Marion, glancing over her shoulder whilst grinding some beans.

"Beer," muttered Aequo, dragging his fingers across his fatigued features. "Just beer."

A few silent minutes passed. The water grew hot, the coffee was prepared, and Aequo's beer was poured generously into a large tankard.

"Looks like you two have had quite a night." Marion leaned against the bar, her eyebrows raised with suspicious curiosity. Rillo and Aequo offered no immediate reply. Their robes were torn, stained with blood, and badly singed. Rillo took a satisfying sip of coffee and breathed a heavy sigh, wrapping his bruised hands around the warm cup.

"Must have been some party," continued Marion, refilling Aequo's already emptied tankard and noting what remained of their multi-coloured robes.

"It certainly went off with a bang," replied Aequo, before taking another hearty gulp.

Marion's eyes narrowed. "Yes, I've never heard fireworks quite like that before." She turned back to the bar, cleaning up the remnants of what had been a very busy day.

"This isn't going to work."

Rillo turned to face his friend. "What do you mean?"

"You know exactly what I mean," answered Aequo in a quieter tone than usual. "She's going to get us killed, and much as I enjoy watching magisters' families murder each other, I have no intention of dying for any of them."

"We're not doing this for the Alpheris. I'm not fighting for Lyra. This is about the city, that's all."

"The city, right. But how much of the city do you think will still be standing by the time she's done?"

"What?"

Aequo replied by holding up his finger, bringing the conversation to a sudden pause whilst he finished his drink. "Just look at the company she keeps."

"I of all people can't judge Lyra based on the quality of her friends," answered Rillo with a smirk.

"You grin all you want, you'd be grinning from a grave in Dargestan if it wasn't for me," said Aequo, pointing vigorously down to his empty tankard until Marion refilled it.

Sated by the presence of more beer, he continued. "Her best friend is a woman with more than enough reason to hate this city, and is currently being trained in artifice magic by Virgil, of all people. A man who has left more than his fair share of bodies in his wake and..." Aequo leaned in closer, "If the rumours are true, those bodies could be in the many thousands."

Rillo leaned back, hoping to obscure the smell of beer now pouring from Aequo's breath by taking another sip of coffee.

"I've heard the stories. A few of them could well be true, but most are far too fanciful to be real. But..."

"But?"

"It is true that Virgil is not a man to be taken lightly."

"And then there's her father," Aequo snorted.

"Maellon."

"Yes, bloody Maellon. There's no doubting the crimes he's committed."

"So you're saying that Lyra is going to turn into her father?"

Aequo shook his head. "Not at all, at least the girl's got the guts to do her own killing."

"She's certainly no pacifist," mumbled Rillo, feeling a migraine already forming behind his eyes at the mere thought of the night's events.

"What I'm wondering is, what's her end goal in all of this?"

Rillo's eyes narrowed. "She wants the same as us. Nihilo's head impaled on a spike. A big one."

"Right, and as beautiful as that wondrous image is, what then? What does the young noble girl, with the grand Alpheri name, who's just toppled a tyrant, do then?"

Rillo lowered the coffee cup slowly from his lips, noting every one of his friend's words.

"She'll be armed with whatever terrible weapons Virgil dreams up, and she'll have a host of thankful citizens cheering her name. What does the resourceful and clever Lyra Alpheri do next? Because I don't know about you, but somehow, I don't think she'll just step away from Nihilo's body, and walk sweetly into the sunset."

"Tyranny gives way to tyranny," Rillo recited, almost to himself.

The scene grew strangely quiet for a few moments, broken only by the sound of Marion stacking some glasses on the other side of the bar.

"I'm not risking my life simply to replace one crazed magister with the daughter of another," said Aequo. Rillo nodded slowly, unable to offer any reply. His mind was too busy with a hundred thoughts and fears, each fighting desperately for his attention.

Aequo leaned in closer still, casting a wary eye over towards Marion. "I've been speaking to some of our old friends from the Vox Militant."

On hearing this, Rillo's mind suddenly jumped to a halt. "Friends from the Vox?" Memories of his cherished order warmed his heart, even bringing the faintest of smiles to his lips. He had thought about getting in contact with some of the others after they had been disbanded. But as of yet, he could not bring himself to do it. The shame of having failed them, of having allowed Nihilo to take control of the city from under his very nose, still plagued him.

"I've been having the occasional chat with some of them, yes."

"Them? I'm surprised most of them haven't left the city."

Aequo scowled with even greater intensity than normal, and Rillo could tell that this wasn't because of the beer. "This is their home. Many of them have shed blood defending those streets outside. They're not going to just get up and leave."

"Point taken, Sergeant, continue."

Aequo muttered curses into his half-full tankard. "They're still in the city, Rillo, and they're not happy about what Nihilo and his cronies have been doing to their home. Now most of them have been able to get hold of some weapons, even some artifice devices. A few have already led some raids on more than one Fereli patrol. You know that city guard house that was burned to the ground last week?"

"The one by the spice market on Corlia Way?"

"That's the one. Well, it was the handy work of Corporal Reynes and his old squad from the northern gatehouse."

"What, mad Corporal Reynes? He organised an assault on a guard house with only a handful of Vox?" replied Rillo with genuine surprise.

"Yes, from what I hear. Apparently, none of the guards outside or inside the building survived."

"I'm not surprised."

"Also, he's not mad, technically."

Rillo placed his cup gently upon the table. "Aequo, present company excluded, Corporal Reynes is quite possibly one of the maddest and most volatile soldiers that I have ever commanded. The only reason that I didn't fire him after that incident with the saffron merchant last year is because even some of the guilds are scared of him."

"Oh, that whole thing was blown way out of proportion."

Rillo gave Aequo a sideways glance. "He bit a man's ear off."

"Ah yes, but as Reynes himself pointed out, he had the courtesy to spit it back out again."

A small voice suddenly spoke up from the corner of the room. "You shouldn't spit at people." Mia shuffled sleepily forward, wiping the corners of her eyes.

"Young lady, what are you doing out of bed at this time of night?" snapped Marion, throwing her bar cloth over her shoulder.

"I stayed up to finish my writing, so that Mr Rillo could mark it for me. Also, we need to buy some more candles."

Marion rolled her eyes and placed another coffee in front of Rillo.

"I didn't ask for a second."

The tavern owner smiled. "No, but you've got some work to be doing. Consider this an advance of your fee."

"I'm literally covered in blood."

"Yeah, life's just a vale of tears, isn't it?" replied Marion with a wink and healthy dose of sarcasm. "Mia, give this fine gentleman your homework and then get back to your room. You've got some work of your own to be getting on with tomorrow."

The young girl shambled over, placing a pile of loose papers before Rillo, whilst at the same time giving Aequo a wide berth.

"I did everything. Some of the words got mixed together, but they are still the right words, so I did get them right."

Rillo sighed. "I'll look at them now, Mia," he said, looking down to see that Mia had already taken the liberty of drawing a smiley face on every page.

"Thank you," she answered with a strained smile, before turning to face Aequo.

"You smell of beer."

"It's a tavern," he answered bluntly.

"Yes, but you really smell of beer. Like, a lot."

This continued until Marion led Mia up to bed, leaving a spotless bar in her wake.

"Are you really going to read all of that tonight?"

"Not sure that I was left with much of an option," replied Rillo, taking what was at this point an essential sip of coffee.

"You're insane," scoffed Aequo, drinking the last remnants of his beer.

"Not as insane as Corporal Reynes."

Aequo rose unsteadily to his feet. "Maybe not, but that reminds me. As I was saying before I was rudely interrupted by that scribbling urchin."

"Her name's Mia, you drunken oaf."

"Whatever. Anyway, I've been talking to some of the guys and girls from the Vox, and they think that when Nihilo eventually gets what's coming to him, you should take charge of the city. Until, you know, we can elect some more magisters or something."

Rillo didn't even look up from the table. "Go to bed, Aequo."

"No, wait. I'm serious! And so are they. With Nihilo gone, there'll be a power vacchum? vacumon? Ah, wait..."

"A power vacuum."

"Yes, exactly! He'll be dead, but the city will be in chaos! Every gang and guild in the city will be trying their luck to take charge. Not to mention the snivelling magisters." Aequo's hands suddenly landed upon the table as he edged closer towards his former commander.

"But to stop that from happening, the Vox Militant could take charge. You could take charge! You'll have enough soldiers and the support of more than few merchants. Just think about it Rillo! Just give it some thought, ey? You could keep this place stable and safe for a bit, with the whole of the Vox behind you. And you know, if you wanted to try out democracy for a bit, then fine. It didn't work out so well last time, but whatever. You could install... I mean, lead the votes for some new magisters. People who would lead this city well, and it would all be down to you."

This time Rillo looked up. For a moment he didn't say anything, and much to his own surprise, he briefly pondered Aequo's words.

"One thing's for certain, and it's that Nihilo is not going to be deposed this evening. We've had a long day. Get some sleep. We'll plan tomorrow."

16

Sins of the Father

The forge stood quiet and cold, with every tool resting in its proper place. Hundreds of small hooks, flanked by vast towering shelves, bore the weight of Virgil's many magical instruments. Many of them resembled traditional forge tools that would not look out of place in the workshop of a blacksmith, whilst others grew stranger and more elaborate, twisting into unfamiliar shapes, and bearing great runes of power upon their shining surfaces.

Lyra walked over towards one of the great shelves of books, which varied tremendously in size and colour. One codex was bound with well-worn leather, and scuffed with age and use, whereas another was covered in small sheets of metal, and held together with finely-grafted wire. Some bore large runes upon their spines, whilst others were devoid of markings, and simply glowed with the pale light of whatever colour their pages had been written in.

A curious thought came to Lyra's mind, and she raised a finger from her armoured gauntlet to touch the surface of one of the many instruments. But before contact was even made, a long series of winding orange runes appeared along the surface of a small hammer, which began to shake. Her finger paused, and before she was even able to withdraw it, a small blue spark flew from the hammer's surface, landing harmlessly upon her gauntlet.

"Katerina's skills as an artificer have grown indeed. That is quite the artifice that she has made for you."

Lyra turned to see that Virgil had entered the forge, carrying several memory codices in his hands.

"You have seen it many times and yet you are only commenting upon it now. Why?"

Virgil placed his books upon a small table in the corner of the forge, next to a battered old chair.

"If I am to truly train Katerina to be an artificer, then I must show that I can trust her. If she continues with the same dedication and passion that she has so far, then one day she will be able to forge some truly powerful artifices. I have to trust that when this happens, she will do so with wisdom."

Virgil pulled another small table over to the chair. It bore upon it a large number of magnifying glasses, each of varying size and colour. He lifted the codex from the top of the pile that he had assembled and began reading it, using a range of different magnifying glasses to do so.

Several days had passed since the assassination of Lady Aayla. Virgil's temper had cooled in the way that Lyra had known that it would. However, most of his weapons were now locked away in vaults that not even Kat could access. Lyra was allowed to keep her sword and pistol, but all the forge's grenades were locked securely away. The city, however, had not escaped as freely as Lyra had. Fereli and city guard patrols had increased, and more and more illegal press house had been purged. One of the city's two universities had been closed, whilst the other was now under the direct control of the High Magister's office. It had come to Lyra's ears that Nihilo's chamberlain, Silo Rees, as a former alumnus, had been appointed the head of a new Education Committee, which was in charge of the running of the university as well as silencing any unregistered schools. Even the Tomaso Aquin, the city's great library tower that rose so majestically above the skyline, was now closed to the public.

She had left the city for a few days to see her father. She missed him terribly, but going to see him was harder than she could have expected. He was now such a quiet man, so withdrawn into himself, and contenting himself with reading his books and walking around the farm in which he sheltered. They talked, but it was not the same. She could tell that despite his words of peace and letting go of the past, there was still a rage of grief inside him that was not yet ready to let go. Much to his own surprise, he found that he penned more pages of the *Crimson Script* daily. In the hours that Maellon slept, Lyra found herself pouring over these pages, devouring every image of torment that she had time to read. In each chapter she found new struggles being endured by those who had sided with Nihilo and betrayed her family. Her mind wandered from each horrid judgement, as she wondered how she might bring such a hammer blow against those who now ruled the city. And yet, try as she might, she found that her thoughts lost their focus. She could not see the pits of fire or hear the screams of the damned as clearly as she once had. A mysterious figure interrupted her visions, clouding her thoughts. His long blue robe cut off her sight from the flames, and a swift wave of his hand brushed aside images of unending torture. Many times had she chased after him in her dreams, and each and every time, he had eluded her.

She asked her father what this could mean, but he would not say, simply smiling at her and asking that she share one more pot of coffee with him before she had to leave. Alina and her two remaining guards protected him well, and for that at least Lyra could be thankful. But for Lyra, there was work to be done. Her revenge could not be limited to the pages of a book.

Lyra looked over at Virgil, who sat happily, reading a codex, whilst the glass of the magnifying lenses warped his eyes to comical proportions. She began to walk over to him, and was content to sit beside him for a while, until the door of the forge suddenly flew open.

"Kat? What's the matter? Are you all right?" asked Lyra, swiftly withdrawing her hand from the grip of her revolver.

Katerina Darrow stood in the open doorway, staring at Lyra and Virgil with a hitherto unseen intensity, with drops of rainwater dripping from her hair. For a few moments she just stood there, her bitter gaze looking over at Lyra before coming to rest finally upon Virgil.

"Kat? Kat, come on, speak to me. What's wrong?"

But she offered Lyra no reply, instead taking a few hasty steps towards them. She was wearing her heavy coat, with her rifle slung over her right shoulder, whilst the other bore a large travel bag, filled to the brim. However, the thing most notable in her possession was the journal of Lady Aayla, which was fixed, unmoving, within her grasp.

"Tell me that it isn't true," rasped Kat, her eyes locked on Virgil.

"Kat, what are you talking about? Why are you dressed like that?" asked the artificer earnestly, rising from his seat.

"Tell me that it's all a lie," she said, her words laden with both sorrow and anger. Lyra went forward to comfort her friend for a grief she knew not what, but before she could, Kat's arm flew forward holding the journal in front of the shocked pair. Before Lyra had the chance to read the title, she heard the sound of Virgil's flat, horrified voice.

"Oh. I see."

Lyra leaned closer, reading the title. *The Master of Stores' Records on the "Great Autumn Famine."* She turned to face Virgil for some hope of understanding, but she saw only that his face had gone a ghostly pale, his eyes watering as in a great sea of distress.

"*The Great Autumn Famine*," Lyra repeated slowly, until realisation dawned. It hit her like a brick wall, but did nothing to rid her of her confusion as to why Kat was staring at Virgil like that. That famine, notorious as it was, had lasted for many months, killing thousands of Abys-Luthil's most vulnerable citizens, especially in old Abys. But more than that, it was the famine in which Kat's parents had starved to death, as they gave what little food they had to their young daughter. The reasons behind the famine were disputed. Abys-Luthil had just come out of the other side of one of its many wars which had ravaged the countryside, and to top it all off, a terrible flood had washed away many farms. It was a tragedy, but one in which there seemed to be no obvious culprit other than that of horrid circumstance.

And yet, Virgil now looked so pale.

"Katerina, listen to me. You don't understand –"

A snarl formed across Kat's lips. "What!? What don't I understand? That I've been lied to all of these years? That for every single day that I've lived under your charity, it was because Maellon Alpheri was responsible for killing my parents!"

A cold shiver ran down Lyra's spine. She suddenly felt her hands tremble as if shaken by the wind. "What? Kat! What are you talking about?"

The rain-water continued to roll from Kat's hair, pooling across the wrinkles of her brow, now furrowed by a deep hatred. "Tell me it's a lie!" she shouted, before her hand suddenly pointed towards Lyra. "Tell her that it's all a lie! Tell her that her father isn't a murderer with the blood of thousands on his hands!"

Lyra felt her hands steady, her heart racing just a little bit faster. She wanted to shout back and hug her friend at the same time, but she could not will herself to move or think of the words to say. She waited for Virgil, looking to him in the hope that he could dismiss Kat's words.

"Katerina, whatever you've read in that book... it was a different time. The city was different. Maellon had to make some terrible decisions. You have to trust me −"

"Trust you!? How can I? For years you walked with me to Mrs Magorin's! You heard me talk about my parents, my home, over and over again. You stepped into those streets with me, those same streets which Maellon robbed of food, for months!"

Lyra's right hand curled instinctively into a fist. "Kat, my father was not even the Master of Stores during the famine. He only took that position afterwards. He was the one who led the relief effort when food entered the city!"

Her friend's lips curled in bitter mockery. "That's what they told us, Lyra. But it was all lies, all of it." She pulled out the loose page, handing it to Lyra.

"These records show that the real Master of Stores died from a war injury one week into the famine. Maellon, as his next in line, took over, and presided over the whole thing!"

Lyra's eyes poured over the page, and also over the following ones that Kat then thrust in her hands, each bearing the official seal of the Master of

Stores' office.

Forgeries, they must be forgeries!

But Lyra knew in her heart that this was not the case. She had seen more than a few forgeries in Abys-Luthil's black market, and none of them looked anything like this. A small stab of horror struck her each time that she saw her father's signature at the bottom of page.

On reading one line, she felt as if her heart had almost come to a complete stop, "*The offer of food relief from the kingdom of Aurel has been rejected by acting Master of Stores, His Excellency, Lord Maellon Alpheri. All offers of food, or any other forms of support from the Aureli, are hereby to be rejected.*"

"Keep going," rasped Kat.

"*The purchase of food stores from any other nation is hereby prohibited. Any merchant or private citizen found doing so is to be detained on charges of treason against the city of Abys-Luthil.*"

Lyra turned towards the silent artificer. "Virgil?"

He looked at the ground at Kat's feet, his eyes wincing with pained memory. "You must understand, both of you, that the city had just finished a war with Dargestan. The floods had washed away most of the crops, and suddenly the city had to feed not only all of its hungry civilians, but also, all of the returning soldiers. The war had already forced rationing upon us, and by the time the famine came, many had already endured several months of hunger."

He met Kat's gaze to see that her temper had not cooled. "Maellon and I had been serving at the front, and we returned to find the city almost on the verge of collapse. The city's coffers were almost empty, and food was already running low. Maellon quickly took up his seat in the magister's chambers, but by then it was already too late."

"No!" yelled Kat. "No! It wasn't, stop lying! These records clearly say that many kingdoms as well as the Aureli were offering us food, and lots of it! Enough for everyone! But Maellon turned them down and watched the Water District starve!"

Virgil slowly shook his head. "It was not like that, Kat. The Aureli Kingdom was a different place back then, as were many others. Yes, they were willing to trade us food, but for every shipment of bread they offered, they demanded that we supply them with artifice weapons and ships. Had we agreed to what they wanted, then Abys-Luthil would have lost half its fleet, let alone most of its armouries. We would have been defenceless, and the Aureli would have been unstoppable. We were not ready for another war."

Kat paced furiously in front of her mentor. "No! That's not true!" She came to a halt, glaring intensely at Virgil. "People in the Water District starved whilst the nobles of Abys and Luthil continued to eat like kings!"

"That's not true..." began Virgil.

"Then why the shame? Why the lies? Why have I only found out now?" snapped Kat. "Could it possibly be because, when my parents were starving, when I cried at night for lack of food, we were told that it would soon be over? I don't remember many conversations with my parents, but I remember the hope that they had. The promise that they heard every day from the magisters, from the Vox, from Maellon, that everything was being done to get us food. They believed that, Virgil, they really did!"

She looked towards Lyra. "I remember my mother. I remember her holding me close, telling me of the coming promise of food, reminding me of how everyone in the city was going through this together and how it would soon pass... How many magister's families died in that famine, Virgil? How many noble parents watched their children starve before their very eyes?"

"Katerina..."

"None! Not one! Maellon rejected the Aureli's deal to protect the power of the magisters! He was looking out for himself, just like the rest of them!"

She took another step towards Virgil. "How did you do it, Virgil, ey? How did you ever step foot into Abys after that? How could you have looked Mrs Magorin in the eye?"

A singular tear rolled down the artificer's cheek. "The same way that I looked you in the eye, every single day. Because I had hope. Hope that this city could change. Hope that you would have a bright and wonderful future ahead of you. Hope that I could be something different," he looked down, "one day."

For a moment the scene grew quiet, but the fire in Kat's eyes still burned.

"Well, my parents have no hope, because they're dead, and Maellon murdered them. He's no better than Nihilo," spat Kat.

The fingers of Lyra's armoured gauntlet twitched. "Kat, I know you're upset, but–"

"But what? What do you think you know, Lyra? Because I'll tell you what I know. You're certainly your father's daughter. I've watched you kill and torture your way through Nihilo's cronies these past few months. Tell me, how many of those people that you've killed do you think had a real choice in whether or not they served Nihilo? Or are they just more bodies of poor people to be piled over the pride of the Alpheri family?"

Lyra's back straightened, and her arms tensed. "Careful, Kat."

Kat leaned closer. "Or what, Lyra?"

"Lyra," said Virgil, "I think it would be best if Kat and I had some time alone."

Kat stepped forward. "There's only a few words that I have left for you," she replied, starting to push Lyra out of the way. But Lyra stood firm, her arm now blocking Kat's advance upon Virgil.

"Step aside," Kat growled, allowing a brief pause to hang in the air, "... Alpheri."

"You need to walk away," said Lyra, her own words hardening.

"Make me. Or do you and that murderer of a father of yours have enough Abyssus blood on your hands?"

The room suddenly erupted in a savage clash of blue and orange light. In truth, Lyra could not tell which of them had decided to strike the first blow, but as the ethereal shield of her gauntlet was struck by the steel and wooden stock of Kat's rifle, magical sparks flew across her field of vision. Without even thinking, Lyra lifted her right foot backwards, kicking Virgil in the stomach and sending him reeling backwards, clear of the fight.

Lyra and Kat traded blow after blow, the bright blue shield of the gauntlet rippling with magical energy at every blow. Cords of white light wrapped around her fingers with each attack she made, only to be blocked in turn by parries from Kat's rifle. The elegant artifice gun shone with the power of many bright orange runes that lay upon its barrel.

Kat went to strike again, but Lyra spun on her heel, catching the seemingly intangible blade of Kat's bayonet in the grip of her armoured fist. Her hand was soon wreathed in flame, her gauntlet's armoured plates glowing red from the terrible heat, as she attempted to pull the weapon from Kat's grasp. Only the magical properties of the armour kept her hand from burning, still fed by the terrible flow of blood that she had drained from Lady Aayla.

The gauntlet burned, and the horrors of Lyra's many visions swam across her fractured mind. Instinct gave way to anger, and Lyra's free fist connected with Kat's jaw, sending her reeling backwards, her rifle torn from her grasp. Lyra advanced, but already Kat was on her feet, and she tackled Lyra to the ground with a sudden burst of speed. Elbows and fists hammered away at whatever targets they could find, and soon, with a swift strike of her knee, Lyra found herself on top. Her gauntlet rose high in the air, radiating blue light and ready to fall upon Kat's exposed face.

But it did not descend. It simply hung there for a few moments, threatening doom, as Lyra's face contorted with conflict and confusion. She looked down at Kat, and her mind became clouded in the midst of the great war that raged within her. Anger, power, and hatred flowed from the gauntlet, which even now sparked with energy, but she could not bring her fist to fall.

"Kat–"

Lyra suddenly lurched backwards. A bright cord, shining like the sun, was now wrapped around her chest, and she tumbled across the floor. Winded by the sudden motion, Lyra coughed and spluttered, gasping for air and unable to move as the cord kept its grip upon her. She watched as Virgil released the other end of the cord, and stepped forward to face Kat, who had already grasped her rifle again.

He said nothing, simply looking at her, even as the rifle barrel was pointed firmly at his chest.

The weapon began to shake as Kat's hands trembled, tears pooling in the corner of her eyes.

"I am sorry, Katerina, for everything. And whatever you choose to do, know that I'll never turn my back on you. I'll always be there."

Tears rolled down Kat's cheeks, dripping down from her chin. The rifle slowly lowered, "I'm not here to kill anyone. I'm not you."

Tears gave way to tears as Virgil slowly nodded. "I know. You are a far better person than I could ever hope to be."

Lyra tore at her restraints, desperate to get free, her words still eluding her as she clawed back her breath.

Kat wiped one final tear from her cheek, cast her eyes to the ground, and walked out of the forge, disappearing into the rainswept night beyond.

Virgil sighed and laid a single finger upon the rope binding Lyra. H watched its light fade, its cords loosen. Before he could utter a word, Lyra was on her feet, running over to the door.

"Kat! Kat!"

No reply came. The wind howled and the rain washed over the cobble-stones, but there was no sign of Kat.

"Lyra..."

"Kat! Kat!"

"Lyra. She's gone."

Lyra stepped out into the cold night air, feeling fine drops of rainwater wash against her cheek. Suddenly the world seemed very small. The street outside the forge felt vast and unending, and the buildings which flanked it towered up to unfathomable heights. The darkness that lay in every corner seemed to grow, swallowing up any source of light. Lyra's world suddenly shrank down to the singular space in which she stood.

She had never felt so alone. She had never been so scared.

Her hands began to shake and her mind grew faint. The anger that had kept a constant vigil over her heart ever since the attack on her home slowly died, fading and spluttering out of existence.

"Kat."

Lyra wandered back into the forge, her legs shaky and only just bearing her wearied frame. The light went out, and the vast walls of bitterness behind her eyes fell to pieces. She tore the gauntlet from her arm and dropped it at her feet. As soon as the artifice hit the floor, Lyra felt as if a crutch had been ripped out of her grasp. A thousand suppressed aches surfaced across her body, and fleeting images of recent horrors ran through the fractured walls of her consciousness.

"Why didn't you tell us? Why didn't my father tell me?"

Virgil looked down at the gauntlet, a single tear falling from his chin. "How could we? Even if we could have brought ourselves to speak about it, what would we have said?"

"So you lied to her, for all these years?"

He shook his head in response, absently picking up the artifice and placing it on a nearby workbench. "When it was finally safe to ship food back into the city, the first thing that Maellon did was to buy up as much of it as he could and lead a relief effort into the Water District. We saved the few that we could, including Kat. But your father could never go back. Not after having seen what we had seen."

Virgil went to speak again, but as he looked harder at the gauntlet before him, his body froze. His fingers hovered carefully above the armour's metal plates, slowly tracing the dormant veins of magical energy that ran all the way to the fingertips. Virgil mumbled something to himself, before retrieving two tools from the wall, and with a sudden hammer blow, he drove a fine silver spike directly between two of the plates.

"What are you doing?" asked Lyra in shock.

He ignored her, and hammered another spike into the gauntlet, before activating a single rune upon each spike. No sooner did the small orange symbols burn furiously into existence than a high-pitch screech quickly filled the room. Lyra covered her ears, desperately trying to block out the noise, and yet try as she might, the sound only grew. The wailing voice howling out from the very essence of the gauntlet shrieked with such intensity that Lyra saw two glasses resting on a nearby table shake and crack. Holding a much larger hammer this time, which itself seemed to consist entirely of an enchanting blue flame, Virgil struck the burning runes. For a second the howling grew further still, and the entire forge was bathed in a soft red light. However, it swiftly faded, rendering the room quiet and still once more.

"What was that?" shouted Lyra, gently massaging her protesting ears.

With a flick of his wrist, Virgil extinguished the hammer's flames, and carefully placed it back on the wall. "That, Lyra, was my past coming back to haunt me. Yet again."

He turned to face her. "What did Kat tell you about this gauntlet?"

Lyra watched as the runes still protruding from the artifice slowly faded away. "She said that she made it for me. But she nearly threw it away. She seemed nervous of it, scared almost. She said that you would never have forged anything like it..."

The master artificer sighed, and pulled the silver spikes from the gauntlet. "Well, she was wrong about that. I know this artifice design well."

Lyra shook her head, as grief mingled with confusion. "What? No, no. Kat said that it was powered by an ancient design, from a book from the Great Library. It... it was powered by blood, Virgil. Even wearing it, I could feel something ancient, something... dark, staring back at me."

"Why didn't you tell me about the blood, Lyra?"

She met his gaze. "I needed to kill the magisters. I couldn't do it without artifices... without Kat. I knew that you wouldn't let me use it if you discovered how it was powered."

Lyra thought about defending herself, about explaining that even a weapon of such dark power could be used for good.

The magisters had to pay. It didn't matter how this was done, the cost would be worth it.

And yet, even as this thought raced through her mind, a feeling of terrible shame fell upon Lyra. She stared at the gauntlet, and watched fine tendrils of steam rise from the points where the silver spikes had been inserted. When she had worn it, the gauntlet had felt like more than just a tool, more than just a weapon. It a been a thing of beauty, but now it just lay there, its power torn out and its uses expended. The shame welled and built up within her, as she realised that even a few hours ago, she would have been horribly close to thinking the same thing of the now departed Kat.

Was the sum of this evening just that she had lost two tools? Two weapons of war, by which she had hoped to tear down all that Nihilo had built?

These thoughts sickened her, and what felt like a hundred moments suddenly swamped her mind's eye, each reminding her of a word or a thought that she would now give anything to retract. It was like waking up from a thousand nightmares that were not her own, but ones in which, every time, it had been her playing the demon.

She waited for the harsh words, and the shock that would undoubtedly come as Virgil learned of all the blood that Lyra had harvested to fuel her dark weapon. But no words of rebuke reached her ears. No condemnation of her dark deeds spilled from Virgil's lips. Maybe this room could bear no more sudden revelations. Lyra was not sure that she could.

"I designed it, Lyra. The shield, the power drawn from blood shed in anger. All of it."

"No, no. She got it from this ancient book – "

"I wrote the damn book, Lyra! I wrote a whole library of books, each drenched in blood!" shouted Virgil with more anger than Lyra had ever heard.

"I have drowned cities in blood! Luthanril! Abyssus! And now..."

Lyra needed to hear no more words to know that Virgil's rage was not directed at her.

"Your family, Kat, this city... everyone I know is paying for it!"

"Virgil, I – I don't understand."

"Beatrice warned me that this would happen, all those years ago."

The mention of her mother's name, a name so rarely spoken, added yet more confusion to suffocate Lyra's already pained thoughts. Her lips trembled, as a feeling of complete helplessness overwhelmed her. Everything was now gone, every source of power, every hope of comfort, and every ounce of strength had been taken from her. There was nowhere to turn.

Finally, her knees began to buckle, and Lyra fell to the floor, her strength sapped away by many layers of grief. But even as she fell, Virgil was there to catch her, holding her in his arms.

Her fingers dug tightly upon Virgil's sleeves, and she wept.

"I'm here, Lyra, I'm here, my girl. It's going to be ok. We're going to visit somewhere that I should have had the courage to take you to a long time ago."

17

Wisdom

L yra held the small honey cake in her hand, and watched the sunlight dance across its glazed surface.

"Thank you."

Virgil smiled back, taking one last bite of his own cake before looking over towards the cave.

"Where are we?" asked Lyra, looking around at the trees which surrounded the small clearing in which they stood. She remembered collapsing in the forge, and feeling Virgil's arms catch her just before she hit the ground. After that, everything had gone dark, and the next thing that she remembered was waking up in a large field with a warm cloak wrapped tightly around her, and a travel pack resting next to her head.

"This, Lyra, is Elysium."

Lyra almost choked on her cake. "Elysium? The capital of Old Luthanril?" She looked around once more, seeing only rocks, trees, and the entrance to a small cave. This could hardly be the legendary city of Elysium, from which the Luthan Empire had mustered a vast army of soldiers and sorcerers. Elysium was supposed to be a city of culture, learning, and countless magical marvels. However, all that Lyra could see at this moment was dirt and tree bark.

"Elysium was truly a great city, but it was a name that the rulers of Luthanril took from an old legend of their people. In ancient times, before even the first stone had been laid in what would become the capital city of the Luthanril empire, Elysium was a place of hope and refuge for people of every nation and tongue. It promised the gifts of wisdom, peace, and final victory to all that had pursued good in their lives. The rulers of Luthanril sought to take advantage of what had become little more than a myth. But what they failed to realise was that Elysium was anything other than mere myth, and that those who had used the power of the world for their own selfish ambition would not be granted access here when the darkest of times came."

Lyra looked at the cave, hearing the wind rush through the trees and the sounds of birds flying across the vast blue skies, which rose above the endless fields behind them. She breathed in, and tasted the cool crisp air, whilst watching for any sign of movement from the cave's depths. Everything seemed so still, so peaceful. She looked down towards the pistol that hung at her hip, suddenly feeling guilty at the thought of bringing an instrument of violence into such a serene place. She watched as a deer walked through the undergrowth beneath the great canopy of trees. The animal met her gaze, not fearing to tread closer as it went to inspect some grass by her feet. Far from feeling nervous or shocked by this, Lyra was surprised to note that in this moment, she felt very little at all.

She breathed easily, noting how green the leaves of the trees were and how pleasant the sun's warmth felt on the back of her neck. A sudden but steady smile spread across her lips as she looked at a bird perched upon a nearby branch. It stretched out its wings and began cleaning them with its beak, and for a few moments, Lyra's mind revelled in the simple joy of looking at such a beautiful creature.

And yet far-flung images of pained faces and spilled blood lingered, even underneath this simple joy.

"I shouldn't be here, Virgil. I cannot walk in this place."

The artificer sighed and placed a hand upon her shoulder. "Lyra, if a man such as I is able to tread this land, then so are you, and if there are memories and deeds which haunt us, even here, then you and I shall draw strength from walking this path together."

He pointed to the entrance of the cave. "Let us go in."

Lyra stepped forwards, casting an eye up to the swaying branches and the clear sky above as she approached. She came to a stop upon reaching its entrance, and leant forwards to hear the small crackle of a gentle fire within.

"You must go first," said Virgil, "but I will be right behind you."

Lyra nodded, wishing for a moment that Kat was with her, and stepped inside. The cave was dark, save for the meagre light projected from a small fire at its centre, which was surrounded by a series of modest stones. Shadows danced across the walls, casting fleeting images that appeared to dart between the fire and the darkness. She trod around the spluttering flames, making her way over to the other side of the fire, and observed the cave's largest wall, upon which the firelight was particularly enchanting.

Virgil followed suit, taking a stand beside her, but Lyra barely noticed him, so fixed were her eyes upon the shifting shapes projected by the light of the flames.

"Virgil, look!" uttered Lyra, almost breathless at the sight of the image before her. To her mind the shadows had conjured the shape of a man that could be none other than her father. Flashes of light and the creep of the shadows bestowed a gentle disposition upon her father's face. He was looking down upon a small crib, his arms lovingly wrapped around the figure of a smiling woman. Lyra's heart almost came to a stop as her father kissed his wife, her mother, Beatrice, upon the cheek, and the pair of them looked down at Lyra's infant form.

Her mother looked so happy, so full of joy, that even this projection of shadow and flame brought a tingle to Lyra's fingertips and a tear to her eye. She looked on, content to do so until the grass beyond the cave withered and the sky faded away.

Soon the shadows twisted and turned, and adopted the shapes of two young girls running across cobbled stones, laughing and smiling as they went.

"Kat."

Scene after scene formed before her very eyes, from the duo's first sword training session with Castel to the time that Kat had stayed up all night with Lyra as she revised for her university exams. A lifetime passed by in a moment, and still Lyra could not look away. Even as Kat slowly retreated into the deep corners of the cave, Lyra could not avert her gaze, as the whole city of Abys-Luthil was suddenly projected before her. The streets of Luthil teemed with the advance of industry and the works of the printing press, and scholars filled aged halls with debates of law and philosophy. The exotic trading squares of Abys swelled with spices, silks, and other wondrous goods, each calling to passers-by with their promise of luxury and hint of adventure. It was every part the city that her father had once dreamed that it could be, and it was truly a marvel.

Then without warning, the shadows crept in once more and the flames shifted, transforming Abys-Luthil into a ruined shell of its former self. Its buildings became empty husks, and its great dockyards were ravaged by both water and flame. No silks coloured the streets, and no great tome lay open within its libraries, for all was ruin and death.

Lyra's heart sank as the ashes of her home came together, spinning in many elaborate circles until they formed the body of a young boy. He ran towards her, reaching out his hand, and willing her to take it.

"Nathan."

Lyra stretched out her arm to hold his hand in hers, barely registering the shock as her fingers scraped against the cold surface of the cave wall.

"Those are but shadows. To see the truth, you will need to walk far from here and embrace the light," spoke a voice behind her.

Lyra turned to look at the man standing on the other side of the fire, and to her surprise she realised that she had laid eyes upon him before.

"You? Who are you?"

The stranger, clad in a dark blue robe, bearing a short grey beard, smiled, and gestured to three small seats that had suddenly materialised around the fire.

"Who I am or what I claim to be is of very little consequence. It is who you are and who you believe yourself to be, young Lyra, that is of real consequence here."

Lyra took a seat, observing the kindly expression on the old man's face as he turned his attention to Virgil.

"It is good to see you again, old friend."

Virgil bowed his head. "You as well," he answered with more reverence than Lyra would have expected.

"I have seen you before! On the docks at Lady Aayla's ball, and in my dreams since," she said.

The stranger adjusted his robes, the light of the fire dancing across its many folds. "If I am not mistaken, you have seen many shadows in your visions of late. It appears that you walk a dark path."

"I have been left with no choice. Everything was taken from me. Something had to be done."

The fire crackled with a small spurt of flame and the stranger smiled. "Ah yes, choice. Tell me, Lyra, after all that has happened in recent months, do you really believe that you have had no choice other than to do what you have done?"

Lyra scowled, looking to Virgil for support, but found his expression uncharacteristically stoic. "Nihilo and his Council burned my home to the ground and slaughtered my family."

"I was under the impression that your father is still very much alive?"

Lyra felt a stab of sadness strike her heart even as she thought of her reply. "He's not, not really, not like he was."

"I see," said the stranger. "So because of all that has befallen you, you felt as though you had no other option than to kill those who had wronged you?"

Lyra leaned forward. "I couldn't just run away, living my life in exile whilst Nihilo brought Abys-Luthil to ruin. It wouldn't have been right."

The smile on the stranger's face broadened, but not with malice or conceit. Despite her fears, Lyra saw only kindness in the man's eyes.

"It wouldn't have been right," he repeated. "You think that killing Nihilo and his accomplices is the right thing to do?"

"Yes," replied Lyra, after a brief pause.

The stranger's gaze flashed across to Virgil for the briefest of moments before he looked back at Lyra.

"Lady Alpheri, I have been alive for a very long time, and in those many years I have never encountered greater strife than when men and women have tried to do what they deemed to be right." The dark corners of the cave seemed to grow in size, dwarfing the little fire at its centre, and hindered only by the sudden brightness of the light that marked the cave's entrance.

"Right and wrong. Good and evil. For too long have people recklessly laid claim to these words simply to defend their own desires," said the stranger.

"What exactly are you trying to say?" asked Lyra, her voice less reserved than before.

"I mean, Lady Alpheri, that in your slaughter of Salaris Bremmer and Aayla Farris, as well as so many of their servants, did you really believe that you were doing a good thing?"

The last few shreds of tranquillity in Lyra's mind faded away.

"Who are you?" she demanded of the man, before turning to Virgil, "and why am I here? I didn't ask to be brought here, and I don't have to defend myself to some hermit sitting in a cave!"

"So your actions require no defence?" asked the stranger, still smiling, his voice low and his words calm.

Lyra scowled in irritation. "No, I did what I had to do!"

"And there stands the great lie of this age. The truth, Lyra, is that there is absolutely nothing in your world that you have to do. There is no outside force that can compel you to act against your will."

"Something had to be done!"

The smile in the stranger's expression remained gentle, all except for a sudden focusing of the eyes. "Those words have defended a thousand dark deeds. You really believe that they did not pass through Nihilo's mind before he ordered the attack on your family? You really believe that in his mind and in those of many others that you are not the villain of this piece rather than him?"

"I do not kill innocent people."

The stranger's eyes narrowed further. "Another relative term. As much devoid of meaning as right and wrong. Lady Alpheri, the time has come for you to understand that in all probability Nihilo believes that he is doing the right thing for Abys-Luthil and its citizens. Very few people have the wisdom to observe that they are the villain of their own story."

A brief silence descended on the scene, all save for the noise of the fire. She thought of the rebuke that she desperately wanted to shout back at the stranger, and she even considered storming from the cave and walking back out into the light outside. However, something quenched her words and halted her steps. There was something in the stranger's voice, in the quiet but commanding aura of his words that kept her seated. It almost sounded familiar.

"So you're telling me that there's no right and wrong, just opinion? If so, then why are you even talking to me? If good and evil are just relative, then I have done nothing wrong and there is no hope for me to look forward to," muttered Lyra, wondering about what little reason there was now to return to Abys-Luthil.

"Lyra," the stranger began, one hand clasped upon his robe. "I am not here to take hope from you. You have been brought to this place so that you may have a greater hope than you ever dared to dream."

"I don't understand."

"Few do. The shadows that you saw cast upon that wall took the forms of your family and loved ones. But as you know, those were just shadows cast by the light of this fire, they were not real. And yet if I were to ask you who Katerina and Nathan really were, I expect that you would be able to tell me wonderful things about their character and personalities. Am I wrong?"

Lyra simply shook her head.

"But for Nihilo they were and are something different. Regardless of their age and accomplishments both Nathan and your friend Katerina were obstacles to a greater goal. In his mind, warped as you may believe it to be, they were obstacles to the good that he wishes to achieve and to him they are an evil."

The stranger leaned forward, the firelight casting shadows across his aged face. "To make the people that we love valuable, I mean truly valuable, their worth must come from something other than our feelings for them." The dark corners of the cave seemed to grow once again, but even as the darkness spread, the light from the cave entrance grew brighter.

"Our friends and families are more than our hopes of what they will someday become. They are people, whole and wonderful in themselves, regardless of our love or our hate. But this truth is found only in accepting that there is a greater force moving in the world than our feelings or our desires."

Lyra felt the heat of fire washed gently over her hands as she listened to the stranger's words.

"You think that I should abandon my fight against Nihilo?"

"I am not saying that you should give up the fight, Lyra," he answered. "But I would have you fight for something more than revenge. If you really believe that goodness exists, and if love and good are as real as the ground beneath our feet and the trees beyond this cave, then fight for that, regardless of how you are tempted to feel."

"But if I don't act on my feelings, then how do I know what the right thing to do is?" Lyra asked with genuine bemusement.

On hearing this the stranger clapped his hands together. "That, Lyra, is the most important question of all! You know that goodness exists because you can feel it, right there," he exclaimed, pointing to his chest.

"But like the shadows on the wall, much of what we see in life is only the merest glimpse of a far greater truth. Courage, real courage, is found in holding on to the good, whilst admitting that we are not its source. It is by no plan of his own that Virgil was led to bring you to me here today, and it was no lucky happenstance that forged such a great friendship between you and Katerina, which even now is far from broken. There is a far greater plan at work than any of us here can fully explain, but its goodness is as real and as tangible to each of us as the very rock of this very cave. All we have to do to see it is simply step into the light and look."

Suddenly a great wind roared through the cave, carrying with it a dazzling light that cast out every shadow that encircled the firelight. Lyra looked around, and found herself standing once more under the towering branches of the great trees that stood between the vast, unending fields and the very cave in which they had been sitting.

"Our time together must soon draw to a close, but I am glad that as you continue to walk this path, you will not be alone. Your family walk with you," said the stranger, as he, Lyra and Virgil stood in the open space.

Lyra smiled. A hundred questions raced through her head, but without the frantic rage that had taken hold of her mind over the past months. She felt both calm and alive with curiosity at the same time, and her thoughts drifted like the easy breeze which cut across the swaying fields beyond.

"If only that were true and my father could be here with me. I'm sure that he could think of many things to say."

"I was not speaking of your father," said the stranger, looking over to Virgil with an accusatory look.

The artificer sighed, and glanced once more across the fields before he turned to Lyra.

"Lyra, when we first entered Dis, the three of us. Do you remember how the creatures there spoke of Katerina as human but would not say the same of us?"

"Yes..."

"That is because neither you or I are fully human, Lyra. We have a lineage that comes from Elysium itself. This place was my home once, and many years before even Luthanril came into being, here I was," said Virgil, continuing even as the shock widened Lyra's eyes. "But I was not alone here; I too had a family. I had a sister: her name was Beatrice, and she was very precious to me."

The wind finally settled over the fields, rustling its grain no more.

"When my sister passed from the world, I was shaken to my core, like your father. Despite all of Maellon's faults, I believed him to be a man worthy of her, well as much as any one man could be. So when Beatrice told me that she had fallen in love with a mortal, I did all that I could to support her and her new family – which swiftly became mine also."

Lyra looked back at her uncle. "All this time..."

"Yes, Lyra, I can't imagine how difficult this is to take in, especially now.

But I can no longer hide it from you."

"Did my father know? Why didn't you tell me this before, why all the secrecy?"

Virgil's eyes turned to the cave. "You know already, Lyra, that beyond Abys-Luthil lies a vast world, far greater and wider than you have yet seen. But further still, there reside other planes of reality, like Dis and Elysium, all encircling the same truth of good and evil, that, knowingly or unknowingly, we all live by, and by which we will all be judged."

He smiled. "You, Beatrice, Maellon...Katerina. You all mean a great deal to me. Which makes what I know to be true all the harder to share with you. You have heard the rumours of the war building to the north of Abys-Luthil?"

"Uh, yes − I think so, something about the tribes in Luthanril gathering together," replied Lyra, struggling to keep track of her many questions.

"Luthanril was a kingdom brought low because of the arrogance and greed with which it wielded the magic of the world. I know this... because I was the kingdom's chief artificer."

"But Luthanril was destroyed −"

"Two thousand years ago, yes. Such a story is indeed long in the telling, and we have not the time for it now. All that you must know is that even with the kingdom's destruction, the wrongs of Luthanril still haunt me, and before too long there will be a reckoning. The blood that I and many others have spilled did not cease with Luthanril's downfall, and soon the world will be so weighed down with blood that the powers of Dis will be opened upon it. It has already begun in the ruins of my former home, and it will spread. Nihilo knows this. I know not how, but he has been informed of the coming danger, and it is that and that alone which has granted him the boldness to take over the city. War is coming from the north and Nihilo readies the city for it."

"Don't try to tell me that Nihilo is the good guy in all of this, Virgil," said Lyra.

The stranger stepped forward. "No one here is trying to justify Nihilo's plans or deeds. But even in his madness there is some purpose."

Virgil nodded. "Nihilo silences the people's voice to bring order, which makes them easier to control. He may be doing it, through some twisted plan of his own, to stifle the bitter talk and conflict within the city. He may even be seeking to make it a safe space, however he defines it. But now, those within the city who could once make their objections with words, spoken or written, find their voice taken from them, so violence becomes their only recourse. He must be stopped."

The stranger's expression hardened, and his jaw clenched. "Knowing as you do what has escaped Dis and what descends from the north, you still think shedding more blood by toppling Nihilo is the right thing to do?"

"With Nihilo at its head, Abys-Luthil will become a bastion for Dis like no other. His tyranny will spread to every street and every home. The war has already reached the city, and the only question for us is do we act now, or wait until it is too late," answered Virgil.

A sigh escaped the stranger's lips. "It's been two thousand years, Virgil, and I still feel like we are having the same discussion."

Lyra's voice cut off the artificer's response. "Who are "we", exactly? You say that you're not human and that neither am I. So what am I, really? Half human, half what else?"

"Ah, yes." Virgil's eyes suddenly shimmered with an unnatural blue light, which flashed across his pupils for just a few seconds before vanishing as quickly as it had come.

"What was that?" demanded Lyra, inspecting Virgil's eyes from a distance.

"We are known as the Watchers, Lyra. Our people were brought into being when humanity was first granted the gift of speech. With communication and an ability to share teaching about the power of the world, humans soon gained an understanding of magic. Our people, having begun our own journey on a very different plane, were shepherded here to guide humanity in the ways of magic."

The look of sorrow in Virgil's eyes brought a pause to his speech. "Not all of us were the guides that we were meant to be, and with each and every one of our failures, humanity turned further and further away from the goodness for which they were intended. We were supposed to guide them with our words, but the allure of magic's power grew too great, and soon we were using our words to subjugate rather than to inspire. Many of our kind fled to Dis when the light became too much for them to bear."

The stranger stepped forward. "But some of us are still able to seek the light, even if it is not always the easiest path to tread," he said, with the same blue light flickering across his eyes.

Lyra held her head in her hands for a few moments, before running it slowly through her long hair. "Ok – ok. So, if you, I mean I, or rather we – ugh! Whatever! If my mother was immortal, a Watcher? Then... how did she die?"

The light in Virgil's eyes rose once more. "Your mother was one of the finest of our people. She guided humanity like no other, and she was a far greater Watcher than I could ever hope to be. Beatrice could wield magic in a way that few artificers, human or Watcher, could dream of. She was an inspiration, and she held back the forces of Dis with all the strength that she possessed. And then she met Maellon, and not long after, she was pregnant with you."

Virgil's speech slowed, pausing for a catch in his throat. "She was so happy. I'll never forget the day that she told me that I would be an uncle. But in the end, bearing a half-human child and using her power to fight the powers of Dis at the same time, proved too much for her. You were born, and Beatrice was taken from the world. After that, well, I could not bring myself to leave you or Maellon, so I decided to remain within Abys-Luthil."

The smallest spark of hope kindled within Lyra. "You said that she's not in the world anymore, so, is she here, in Elysium?"

"I'm afraid, Lyra, that for now, your mother is beyond either of our reach," answered Virgil. "Elysium is itself a wide and varied land. There are paths that you and I may walk here, and others, that for now, are obscured from our sight."

"But one day, will I be able to see her? If she's still here, can I find her? Can those paths be opened?"

Virgil smiled. "Yes, one day, dear niece, you will walk and talk with her. As I too hope to." He placed a hand gently upon her shoulder as the wind began to stir. "But not yet."

18

The Ultimate Price

Lyra knew that change was inevitable. That's just the way things were. However, she could never have imagined the way in which her world was to be turned upon its head. No expectation of change could have readied her for the paths of Dis, the fields of Elysium, or her mother's true identity.

"I'll make us some tea," said Virgil, stepping out of the secret forge.

"Thanks," replied Lyra.

She could not say that she was happy. But the anger that had been burning within her for what felt like an eternity had been tempered. It was still there; she could not will herself to release it just yet. However, now there was something else, something more: a focus, a singular point of need that even within herself, she did not fully understand.

Virgil soon returned with the tea.

She remembered the stranger's words about the nature of the Watchers, how they freely crossed into the plane of the mortal world from their home in Elysium. The ever-present reality of Dis spoke to her also, and for a moment, her thoughts lingered upon the truth that many Watchers who had fallen from grace now resided in Dis. That had been their choice, and it was their judgement.

When the end came, where would she be allowed to rest?

She and Virgil waited, anticipating the arrival that they knew would soon come. Rillo and Aequo, though far from happy with the events that had taken place at Lady Aayla's ball, still wished to pursue Nihilo's destruction.

Soon enough, three knocks struck the forge door, though Lyra noted that they were a touch lighter than normal, lacking Aequo's usual impatience.

She stood back, and placed her hand lightly on top of her revolver as Virgil pulled the door slowly open.

"Lyra, it is good to see you again!"

Lyra's hand swiftly fell away from her gun. "Dr Schumon? You as well. What are you doing here?"

The academic observed the steam still rising from the nearby teapot. "Ooh, Virgil, yes please, I would love a cup," she said playfully. Virgil rolled his eyes and went to pour some more tea.

"Wait," began Lyra. "How do you two know each other – no, actually I'm not even surprised at this point."

Dr Schumon laughed. "You always were an observant student, Lyra. The greater question would be who doesn't Virgil know? But I've always found him to be rather cagey on the subject, haven't I, Virgil?"

He placed the cup before her, adding two cubes of sugar to the rim of her saucer.

"Ah, you remembered how I take my tea, you're too kind," said Schumon.

"What can I say? We've known each other a long time," muttered the artificer before attending to his own drink.

Her smile broadened. "That we have, Virgil, that we have."

"So," Virgil raised an accusatory eyebrow, "how is the guild?"

"Oh fine, fine. Actually, it's easier to manage than most academic departments. There's far less backstabbing for one thing."

This time Virgil grinned. "Why would you stab someone in the back when you can go straight for the throat?"

"Exactly," nodded Schumon, "The people are certainly more... up front. And, given the current state of the city, my guild now owns considerably more books than either of the universities."

"Hold on," said Lyra. "Something tells me that I shouldn't even ask, but are you really a member of a guild, Dr Schumon?"

"Why yes, Lyra, there's no harm in you knowing now. I am a member of the Pale Star Guild."

Not long ago, Lyra would have leapt out of her chair in shock, barely able to contain her surprise. However, as her brain tried to process the words that her one-time history lecturer was saying, it faltered and simply stored this news with the rest of the recent revelations that she still had yet to process.

She sighed and drank some more tea.

"Tell her the truth, Karris," said Virgil with a scowl.

Dr Schumon responded with a playful look. "Ok, I may have significantly more influence in the guild than the average member."

"Karris," came the low growl from the other side of Virgil's tea cup.

"Very well," she took another sip of tea. "You have heard of Karrick, our brutal guild's infamous leader, I trust?"

Lyra nodded.

"Well," said Dr Schumon, throwing her arms dramatically outward, "ta-da!"

"Nooo," muttered Lyra, almost to herself.

"I'm afraid so," replied Karris Schumon.

"But – but, I've fought with your guild. Kat and I, we both fought and stole from your guild!"

"Yes," said Karris, now glaring back at Virgil, "dear Virgil neglected to inform me of you various... heists. But I must admit, I am rather glad that you didn't kill any of my members, thank you for that."

"So, how do you – "

"How do I keep up the myth of Karrick? It really isn't as hard as one might suppose. Create the odd rumour here, the occasional story of brutality there, not to mention a few well-paid henchmen, and Karrick can keep running his guild with supposed brutal efficiency for many years to come."

"You really don't have to act quite so pleased with yourself," snapped Virgil.

"I don't have to do anything, Virgil. That's one of the bonuses of being the head of a guild."

Lyra suddenly lurched forward in her seat. "You recruited Rillo and Aequo!"

Karris nodded. "I did indeed. It seems that the five of you have done quite well together. I certainly didn't expect Aayla to die quite so promptly. Speaking of which, where is Katerina?"

An uneasy silence settled upon the room and Virgil gave Dr Schumon a knowing look.

"Ah," she stared back at him with what looked like genuine sympathy. "I am sorry, Virgil. Really, I am. You've done well to look after her for so long, you and the Alpheris. But you and I both knew that she was going to find out sooner or later." Karris paused, carefully considering her next words. "Might I assume that other revelations have recently... come to light?"

"You may."

"Excellent," said Dr Schumon, now looking over at Lyra, her eyes suddenly alive with a pale blue light. "I was beginning to wonder whether or not we would ever be able to have this conversation."

Lyra's hands suddenly shook. "You're a Watcher?" she asked, before her brain protested at yet another revelation and she quickly retreated once more behind her tea.

"Yes. It turns out that it is much easier to lecture on ancient history when you have lived through it yourself. Do you remember that lecture I gave in the first term of your second year on the Maverick of the Argosan Sea?"

Lyra could almost hear the cogs whirring within her own head. Even before she had finished putting the pieces together, her finger was pointing accusingly towards Virgil.

"Really? Him?"

Karris laughed once more. "Oh yes! That was one of his more interesting phases."

"I never did care for that nickname," mumbled Virgil.

"I wrote a paper on you!" yelled Lyra. "Wait, come to think of it – you helped me write it!"

Dr Schumon nearly spat out her tea. "You didn't!?"

"I just couldn't help myself," Virgil chuckled, watching Lyra's face grow a bright shade of red.

For a few minutes, laughter filled the forge, and for the first time in many months the great troubles of the world seemed very far away.

That is, until three loud knocks pounded away at the forge door. The laughter ceased and Virgil opened the door, watching as two familiar figures strode inside.

"Good evening, Doctor," said Rillo, more than a little surprised.

"Captain."

"Evening all," greeted Aequo, casting a momentary glance across the room. "What a merry gathering we have here."

Dr Schumon's posture straightened and her face adopted its usual coolness. "I'm glad that you think so, Sergeant, because we have quite the night ahead of us."

"Is that a promise, Doctor?" asked Aequo.

"If you hope to kill Nihilo and save the city, then absolutely."

Lyra placed down her cup. "It sounds as if you have a plan?"

"I do," Karris nodded. "Over the past three months my guild has been raiding city guard weapon stockpiles and recruiting artificers who oppose Nihilo's regime. I also have it on good authority that a number of former Vox Militant soldiers have been launching raids on Fereli patrols. Nihilo and his Council have a lot of mercenaries within the city, but after the months of harassment that they have endured, I doubt their hearts will be in this fight."

"I've never known the Fereli to back away from a fight," said Rillo, sharing a knowing look with Aequo.

"And I bow to your greater knowledge of them," continued Karris. "But they did not come to Abys-Luthil seeking a fight: they are fleeing from a far greater threat. They will not wish to bring their families to so hostile a city. If we challenge Nihilo and show that someone other than him wields the real power here, then we may even win the Fereli over to our side."

She observed the pained expression on Lyra's face. "Not all of the Fereli are like those who attacked your home, Lyra. There are good people amongst them, some of which are in my guild, and they may prove to be worthy allies."

Aequo stepped forward, arms crossed across his chest. "Well, they better ally themselves with us quick, because we need to make our attack soon, or we won't be making it at all."

"What makes you say that?" asked Virgil.

Rillo sighed, rubbing the bridge of his nose between two fingers. "Two hours ago, Nihilo had the city guard march into Magister's Square and hang three men, for all the city to see. He claimed that they were guild spies, trying to bring ruin to the city by spreading hateful propaganda, amongst other crimes."

Aequo stepped over to Dr Schumon. "How many men did you have infiltrated within the city guard?"

She remained silent, her expression stone.

"Let me guess," continued Aequo. "They were three young lads from Abys? Ones that nobody would miss much?"

Karris exhaled. "They volunteered, they knew the risks."

"Three young lads from Abys knew the risks? Of course they did, the poor buggers weren't given a chance to know much else, were they?"

"Aequo..."

Ignoring Rillo, Aequo leaned closer. "Funny how none of them were from Luthil, but then again, without a book in their hands, what use would they have been? I bet they'd still die as hard though, wouldn't they, eh? Choking as the rope closed around their throats, right in front of a crowd, bad way to go that. Still, that's all a bit hard to see from the library, isn't it?"

"Aequo, enough."

The former soldier scoffed. "Whatever, that hardly matters now, I suppose. Because straight after stringing your boys up, Nihilo displayed his two new weapons of war."

"What weapons?" Virgil cut in.

Aequo cast his friend a sideways glance. "Bellators. I wouldn't have believed it if I hadn't seen them with my own eyes, but Nihilo has two working bellators standing right outside the Grand Magisters' Chambers."

Lyra could practically hear Virgil's teeth grinding together, and she would have been lying to deny that hearing this news sent a shiver down her spine. She knew of bellators, everyone did. They were things of legend, ancient walking war machines that the Luthil emperors had used to conquer whole nations. She had heard about them many times, reading of them in books and hearing how much Kat wanted to get her hands on one. From what she knew of them, they were magical mechanical monsters of a bygone age.

"Two working bellators?" asked Karris. "Well, that came about sooner than I expected. How good of Nihilo to be so prompt," she said, the lightness of her words betrayed by the slow draining of colour from her face.

"Oh, it gets worse than that. He's just announced that in a few weeks he will have over a dozen bellators ready to deploy across the city to keep the peace," said Aequo, laughing grimly to himself, as he poured some tea.

Dr Schumon shook her head. "That's not possible. A dozen bellators? In working order? No, the city has not felt the tread of even one operational bellator for over four hundred years. Its impossible."

Rillo glanced over to Virgil, "Is it impossible?"

The artificer drummed his fingers along the arms of his chair, his face lacking the coolness of Karris. It was not simply the dread of this sudden revelation that furrowed his brow, there was anger also.

"It's possible, it's very possible," he gave Karris a look, "if you have the right help."

Upon hearing this, her cheeks went completely pale. "Dis?"

"Yes, that's the only way that he could power them," answered Virgil bluntly.

"Dis? What does this have to do with Dis?" asked Aequo.

"Everything," Virgil rose to his feet. "Tomorrow, this has to end tomorrow. You have the chance to destroy Nihilo now. For this brief moment in time, that opportunity is yours. You have weakened his Council, you have shaken his hold over the people of this city. But if he can resurrect even one more bellator, then this city is lost to you."

"We have no army with which to remove Nihilo," said Rillo.

Aequo nodded. "And besides, you're Virgil. Aren't you supposed to be the greatest artificer in the city? Surely you can deal with a few bellators?"

Virgil scowled. "Destroying the bellators wouldn't be a problem if you didn't mind wiping out half the city in order to do it. No, whatever forces from Dis are aiding Nihilo, that's precisely what they want me to do... what they expect me to do."

He turned to Karris. "Your guild must act tomorrow. Nihilo will be sitting in the Grand Magisters' Chambers, hiding behind his bellators. You won't get another opportunity."

"My guild is not an army, Virgil, and I am no general. If we really hope to march on the Grand Magisters' Chambers, then we can't do it alone."

All eyes slowly settled upon Rillo.

"What? Why are you looking at me? I am no longer in charge of soldiers. If we really must strike tomorrow, knowing that we're going to face two bellators, then I have nothing to bring to the table." His voice lowered. "I'm sorry, but in that case Nihilo wins."

"That's not true," said Karris raising a finger. "Captain, the Vox Militant may have been disbanded, but since young Lyra's slaying of members of Nihilo's Council, many of your former troops have launched attacks on Nihilo's forces. If anyone is in a position here to muster an army, it is you. At this current time, where the Vox Militant lead, the people will follow."

Rillo was about to protest, until Aequo cleared his throat. "She's right, mate. I've spoken to more than a few of the Vox who would give anything to put Nihilo in his place, preferably a few feet into the ground. Only you can lead them. A few of the other officers are out there, scrapping for a fight, but if we need to attack the Grand Chambers, we need you at the head."

"Aequo, I..."

The former sergeant interrupted. "Look, no one's more surprised about this than me. But if we're going to charge head-first into a pair of bellators, then I'd rather you were at the front. But don't get me wrong, I'll be right behind you, someone's got to keep you alive."

Rillo looked down at the ground, his face contorted with uncertainty.

"My father once said that the people's voice was their best defence, and that the Vox Militant were the guardians of this right," said Lyra. "I saw him berate magisters, defy the power of foreign kings, and dismiss the wealth of this city's greatest merchants, but never did I hear him once criticise the Vox Militant. My father loves this city and he sacrificed everything to speak in defence of its people, and even when he feared that he would fail, he trusted that the Vox would still stand, protecting those who could no longer defend themselves."

Rillo looked up. "Well, we didn't stand. When Nihilo forced you into exile he tore my order apart. We failed – I failed."

Lyra nodded and held out her hands. "Maybe, maybe not. You say that Nihilo exiled me, that's true, and yet here I am. The only ones who can stop Nihilo are us, right here. You may not be able to control the fate of this city, Rillo, but you can decide what you do, here and now. You can either pursue the good and act, or you can run from it, but I promise you that you cannot escape it."

Dr Schumon gave Virgil a knowing look. "Old words from a young face."

"She's right, mate," said Aequo. "Besides, where are we going to go if we can't stay here? Dargestan? The beer is just awful. As for Aurel, well a man can't live on wine alone."

Rillo grinned, and rubbed his hands together. "True, and I'm not sure that either of us would survive listening to you complain all the way to Aurel." He paused, and a look of grim resignation fell over his wearied eyes.

"You can get everyone together?" he asked, gazing over towards Aequo.

"You give me a few hours, a handful of beer and the promise of your heroic leadership to inspire the troops, and I'll have the Vox standing before you by noon tomorrow."

Rillo rose to his feet. "Ok, if this really is our last chance then I say that we give it all we've got. I can't promise that we'll be victorious, much less that we'll come out of this alive. But I'll be damned if Nihilo is going to rule this city without a fight."

"Excellent," exclaimed Dr Schumon. "If the Vox Militant lead the way I will make sure that my guild is following right behind, and I doubt that we will be alone in the charge. Together our forces might prove to be enough."

"Well it's not going to be dull, I'll say that," muttered Aequo. "I can't say that I've ever gone toe to toe with a bellator before."

Rillo turned to face Virgil. "Those bellators are going to be a problem. I can't see a way of us entering the Grand Chambers with two of them standing guard."

Lyra's thoughts drifted back to her gauntlet. Her memories of wearing it so recently brought a dull ache of shame to her mind. It had been a powerful weapon; she had felt invincible whilst wielding it. However, she had also felt the darkness of it, how it had fed upon the blood and torment of its victims. It had been more than a gauntlet, it had been a doorway, a channel to Dis itself. She had brought about moments, terrible moments, when Dis had been allowed to enter the world, and for that, no matter what her motivations, she was struggling to forgive herself. If the bellators were fuelled by the same power, she could only imagine what terrible monstrosities they must have been.

"Don't worry about the bellators. I will deal with them," said Virgil, his speech laboured as if speaking those words brought him great pain.

Dr Schumon looked into his eyes, and a look of horrid realisation crossed her face. "Virgil, no, you can't. There must be another way – "

"There isn't," snapped the artificer before slowing his speech. "There's only one way that those bellators can be stopped, Karris, and you know it."

"Wait! What's happening?" asked Lyra, concerned.

"Our dear Virgil is thinking of doing something terribly heroic," Karris muttered, her face the very picture of dread.

"There's a first time for everything," replied the artificer.

"Oh, I can think of one or two previous examples," said the other Watcher, "but I won't stand in your way."

Virgil smiled. "This was always going to happen one day or another, and in any case, I doubt that your guild will relish the chance of fighting two bellators."

Rillo stepped forward. "That's a good point. Can you really guarantee that Karrick is going to go along with all of this?"

On hearing this, Karris rose slowly to her feet and placed a hand gently upon Rillo's shoulder. "I think that you, Aequo and I have some things to discuss. Let's go over to the tavern for a bit, we have much to plan and very little time to do so." Dr Schumon led them towards the door, casting one final gaze back at Virgil.

"What was she talking about? What are you going to do?" asked Lyra as the two of them were left alone.

"I am going to do the only thing that I can do, Lyra. I made a promise to my sister that I would look after you, and that's precisely what I intend to do." Virgil walked over to the forge and lifted a small cloth from a nearby work surface. His picked up the gauntlet that Kat had forged, and handed it to Lyra.

"Take this. It's ok," he said, noticing the hesitancy in her expression. "I have learned at least a few things since I first wrote the designs for this particular artifice. Blood was once the easiest way to power it, and back in those days, there was more than enough being spilled every hour. I have placed some rare magic within its core, materials that unlike steel are measured by the ounce rather than the ton. It will perform as it did before, but it will draw its power from Elysium rather than Dis."

Lyra took the gauntlet and placed it firmly across her hand and forearm. As she did so, she could swear that she heard birdsong calling out from the height of tall trees.

"Oh, and you should have this." Virgil pulled up the collar of his shirt and retrieved a delicate locket from around his neck.

"Beatrice would want you to have it, and I cannot bear to take it where I am going."

Lyra looked down at the delicate piece of silver that she now held in her hand and opened its small clasp. Inside she saw the portrait of a beautiful woman with piercing blue eyes and long golden hair. She recognised the face instantly as the same one which she had looked upon every time she walked through the halls of her family home.

"You look so much like her," said Virgil. "She would be so proud of you, Lyra."

Lyra slowly closed the locket and placed it carefully around her neck, tapping it gently as it was brought to rest upon her chest.

"Virgil, where are you going?"

The kindly smile on his face was betrayed by eyes filled with melancholy. "Even if Nihilo had gathered every other artificer in the city and compelled them to help him, it would take them at least two years to restore the power of even one bellator. To have two, fully operational, with the promise of more to come, means that Nihilo is being aided by the forces of Dis. There are many in that terrible place who would be more than happy to see destruction brought upon this city, to further hasten the ruin which descends from the north."

He wrapped a cloak tightly about him and tightened the belt at his waist. "The power for those machines comes from Dis, and if you have any hope of defeating Nihilo tomorrow then I must step into Dis and shut them down."

"You have to go to Dis, alone? You've done that before, right? Once you're done you can just come back like you did before?"

He sighed. "No, Lyra, not this time. We Watchers have some power to step between the planes of this world, Dis, and Elysium. However, in my past I delved deep into the power of Dis, and with each journey, my strength to escape its clutches fades. I now have no materials precious enough to trade for safe passage."

"Then you cannot go. There must be another way, another means by which you can stop the bellators," insisted Lyra.

Virgil shook his head. "There is none. If I do not go to Dis, then many people will die tomorrow, and your own life will be at great risk. That is something that I cannot bear. But, more than this... Dis is my destiny, Lyra. I have spilled too much blood to escape it. It will be my end today or many years from now, but ultimately, it is my fate."

"No, no, you can't go, there must be another way, there must!" Lyra said, her words both desperate and sincere.

"There is not. I must go and do what I can to stop the bellators. But for you there is another path." Virgil stepped forward and placed a finger on Lyra's gauntlet, watching it come to life with a pale blue light.

"It pains me more than I can say that I cannot teach you of the Watcher's history or our power. But in this gauntlet there is the smallest sliver of magic that is so ancient, that for a brief time it will allow you and another to travel between planes. When this is all over, all that you will have to do is squeeze this gauntlet, think of your mother, and you will be able to step into her presence for one hour."

Lyra simply stood there, almost rendered mute. "I – I don't know what to say."

He smiled, "You don't need to say anything, brave Lyra, just seek the good in all things and trust that there is a far greater force at work in this world than either you or I."

Virgil's smile fell from his face and the many shadows that littered the forge began to grow and shift. Behind the artificer the greatest of the shadows grew and opened wide, revealing within its depths a vast sea of cruel eyes and hooked fingers.

Despite the fear rising in her stomach, Lyra stepped forward. "I can't do this, Virgil. Not alone! Castel and even Kat are gone, I can't lose you as well, please... don't leave me here alone."

He looked at her one last time. "No one is ever truly alone, Lyra, and I will always remember you."

The shadow widened and Virgil stepped into the void, disappearing from Lyra's sight in an instant, as the darkness suddenly closed and light returned to the forge.

Lyra stood alone and her heart had never been heavier. The room was silent and still.

She made her way over to the door, holding the locket at her chest with one hand. Before she could reach it, the door opened and Rillo stepped inside.

Rillo cast a wary eye across the forge. "He's gone then?"

"Yes."

"I'm sorry, really. Where's your friend, Kat?"

"She left."

A look of pained sympathy crossed the soldier's face. "I see."

He walked towards her, casually glancing at the vast array of artifice tools hanging from the walls. "Lyra, I am truly sorry for everything that has befallen you."

"No need to say sorry, it's not your fault."

Rillo inclined his head to one side. "Maybe, but there was certainly a time when I could have done more. If I had acted sooner, if I hadn't let the mistakes of my past weigh me down, well then, this might have all been very different." He turned to face her. "But I can't let my past dictate my future, and neither can you. Virgil is gone, and if you can, I encourage you to forgive whatever mistakes he may have made. Tomorrow may be our last day, and it would be a great shame if you went to meet it with any bitterness."

"Even if I know that I am guilty of the same or worse than Virgil?" asked Lyra, as her thoughts wandered back to those who had died upon the docks and in the mud of Lady Aayla's ball.

Rillo nodded. "You must come to terms with that. Each of us must do it in our own way, especially if we hope to succeed tomorrow."

"You really think that we can win?" Lyra asked, meeting his gaze.

"I do," Rillo smiled, "but even if I didn't, I would still do it, because I see now that it is the right thing to do. We can't decide whether or not we will be victorious tomorrow, but we can decide to what end we strive."

"And that's enough for you? That's worth risking your life?"

Rillo nodded. "Yes, I have seen too much death and far too much of life to believe that mine is worth more than the future of thousands of others."

Lyra thought for a moment, feeling a small spark of purpose awaken within her. "Well then, in that case, even if it does all come crumbling down tomorrow. I can think of few places that I would rather be. It would be an honour to fight alongside you, Captain Rillo."

"You as well, Lady Alpheri."

19

Bloody Artifice

"Hold!"

The line steadied, a thousand glinting bayonets levelled at the Grand Magisters' Chambers, every man and woman waiting for the order to charge.

"Well, there it is," said Aequo, breathing heavily, looking across the square towards the Grand Magisters' Chambers.

It had started with a few quiet words. On hearing the sudden call to arms, many had gone to the secret places where they had hidden their former uniforms and weapons. Others had run immediately to their homes in search of comrades who would also want to join the fight. Each member of the Vox Militant, in their own way, had responded to the call to arms. None of them had relished the thought of spending another day living under the shadow of Nihilo's tyranny. All were willing to give their lives for the cause, and many were surprised to find that, despite the immediate danger, this was the most whole that they had felt in weeks.

The men and women of the Vox Militant had sallied ferociously into the streets, each wearing their own token of loyalty to the order. Some bore their military shako or jacket, whilst others wore their complete uniform. Several city guard patrols had been taken completely by surprise, washed away by the sudden onslaught. Soon, the alarm had been raised and every guard throughout the city was dispatched to put down the sudden uprising. The bronze armoured guards had charged headlong at what they had assumed was nothing more than a lawless mob. This had proved to be a fatal mistake. The Vox Militant had cut them down with ease, laying improvised ambushes in the market squares of Luthil and the tightly-packed bridge crossings of Abys. As street after street was taken back and the Vox Militant advanced, the guilds had spilled forth from their taverns and warehouses. Masked faces carrying all manner of exotic weaponry used their stolen artifice devices to harry the city guard, finishing off what few survivors the Vox Militant left behind.

Rillo looked down the haphazard line which was poised to launch the final assault. Its few ranks were composed almost entirely of the Vox Militant, each identifiable by whatever item of uniform they had been able to assemble in the two hours of preparation they had been given. Behind them was a seething throng of bloodied guild members and angry citizens. Rillo had even seen a few academic robes littered throughout the mob. It seemed that Dr Schumon was able to motivate more than just criminals. But he couldn't dwell on that unsettling revelation now. The Pale Star Guild was a problem for another day.

If they saw another day.

Rillo turned his gaze towards the High Magister's Chambers, his eyes momentarily resting upon the towering structure of the Aquino Tower and the statues of the horses of Luthil and Abys that rose above the chamber's entrance. Thousands of armoured city guards stood in rank upon the square before them, flanked by hordes of Fereli mercenaries. The defensive cannons of the High Magister's Chambers were arrayed upon elevated positions behind them, and looming just in front of the greater chamber doors were the two bellators.

Rillo had seen bellators many times before, but only when they were standing idle within the vast city vaults or used as impressive trophies for some of the tribal kings and chieftains of the north. All of these had been deactivated for centuries; the thought of seeing one take so much as a single step still brought a slight quiver to his fingers. Bellators were hulking monstrosities, built like a knight of old, only much, much larger. Their entire body was forged from arcane metal, its various rivets and armoured plates adorned with a strange language written in a red script. Even motionless, they bore an air of malevolent threat, their huge metal hands curled into fists, their slanted helmets staring down at all lesser beings below.

"Here's hoping they stay asleep," muttered Aequo.

"Yeah, but somehow I doubt it."

"You're such a pessimist. Has anyone ever told you that?"

Rillo chuckled grimly, looking out at the thousands of warriors that stood against them.

"Are the cannons in place?"

"Yes," Aequo answered, wiping some blood from his hands, "turns out the guilds had a few lying around."

"I bet they did," said Rillo, rolling his shoulders and feeling his arms move within his captain's jacket. It was like being back home.

"I wouldn't worry, though, I set Corporal Reynes and a few others to... help them out. They'll do what they're told."

Rillo would have smiled if not for the sight of the bellators. There were few people that he would trust to watch his back on this day of days more than Corporal Reynes.

Aequo looked ahead, sighed, and handed Rillo a rifle. Rillo sheathed his sword and took it, feeling his fingers run across the many artifice runes that ran across the barrel.

"I guess it's time," he said, pressing a rune and watching the rifle's bayonet come alive with blue light.

"Seems to be," replied Aequo, holding his own weapon ready. "If I don't make it through this..." he turned to face his friend, "I told the tavern that you would pay my tab, and man, have I run up a tab. You might want to give that place a wide berth."

"I won't worry too much. I'd rather take on a bellator than deal with whatever absurd bar tab that you've built up."

"Ah, well in that case, you take on both of them. I'll provide covering fire from here."

"Yeah, you remain here with Reynes, the cannons and the guilds. Tell me how that works out for you."

"Actually, now that you say it, charging two bellators really doesn't sound that bad."

"The bellators are not going to be a problem." The pair of them turned to see Lyra standing behind them.

"Virgil said that he would take care of them," she said, sheathing her sword and reloading her revolver.

"Well, there they are, my lady, still standing, right in front of us," replied Aequo.

Lyra nodded. "I know. But Virgil walked straight into Dis because he believed that he could shut them down." She stepped beside them. "I believe him. Those bellators are not going to be a problem."

Lyra's voice brooked no room for disagreement or challenge. The noble-woman was not the same assassin that Rillo had met in the great hall of Salaris Bremmer, then driven by hate and savagery. It appeared that losing her friend and her mentor had tempered her anger somewhat, but there was still something there, some purpose, some fire, that burned bright and would not be easily extinguished.

Rillo looked over to the myriad of faces that stood behind Lyra. Vox Militant, guild members, riotous civilians, all stared directly at Lyra with a mixture of shock and caution. Every one of them had heard the stories of her brutal killings of two members of Nihilo's Council. A few citizens had even ripped Lyra's wanted posters from the walls and now waved them around like triumphant banners. These were now flags under which the poor and the rich of this wounded city could unite.

They stared at her with awe, and she looked out across a sea of foes without a hint of fear.

"Nihilo hides in those chambers," she said, just loud enough for everyone around her to hear. "A rabble of cowards and traitors protect him, and they will no longer enslave this city. Today, free men and women will bring that tyrant to his knees. He will no longer silence us."

A swift cheer rose from the crowd behind her, spreading wider and wider amongst the city's would-be liberators.

"Works for me," grinned Aequo.

"Give the order," said Rillo, cocking his rifle. Without pause, Aequo thrust his fist in the air, held it for a moment and then swung his arm down. A few seconds passed before a sudden blast of firing powder roared from the small row of cannons aimed at Nihilo's forces. Plumes of smoke erupted from between the buildings that lined this side of the Magister's Square. Cannonballs went hurtling into the ranks of the city guard, throwing dozens at a time from their feet. Other cannons launched their salvos directly at the Chambers, sending chunks of masonry flying from the great building and crashing into the Fereli warriors below. One shot even scored a square hit on one of the bellators, but it simply bounced from its metallic frame as the ancient weapon of war remained unmoved.

Soon the cannons of the city guard returned fire, and cries of shock and pain ran through the crowd behind Rillo.

"Vox Militant, advance!"

The thin green line marched forwards, out into the square, bayonets lowered.

"Take aim!" shouted Rillo, as he, Aequo and Lyra stepped beside them. Even amongst the smoke and the terrible shriek of cannon fire, a steady line of rifles was now being aimed directly at the Fereli and the city guard.

"Fire!"

The crack of rifle fire mingled with the fury of the cannons, and amongst the smoke Rillo saw ranks of the city guard and the Fereli fall to the ground. But no sooner had this moment passed and the enemy returned fire, than within the periphery of his vision, the Vox Militant captain saw several green uniforms crumple to the ground. Screams of pain filled the air, the blast of firing powder echoed across the square, and the armed host once again stood against him. This was not a scene that was new to Rillo, he had seen it many times before, and he knew that only one final action remained.

Stepping forward, he lowered his bayonet directly at the advancing Fereli.

"For the city! Charge!"

He ran forwards, feeling the sudden rush of a thousand feet following fast upon his heels. Aequo kept in step with him, screaming at the top of his lungs, and ready to take on the whole enemy force single-handed. Rillo could feel the fury of the Vox Militant propelling the men and women behind him. The blood ran fast and hot within his veins, and he allowed the ferocity of battle to take hold of him. His pace quickened, his grip upon his weapon tightened, suddenly his lips curled, teeth bared, and he roared in anger against the foe.

A sudden spark of blue light burst into life beside him and he saw Lyra running with all the speed that she could muster, with a large magical shield emanating from her gauntlet.

A noise like thunder seemed to shake the square, overpowering even the sound of the guns as Rillo lunged with his bayonet and the Vox Militant hammered into the enemy line.

Lyra rolled, allowing a savage-looking axe to swing harmlessly over her head. She kicked out with her leg and knocked the already-unbalanced Fereli to the ground before swiping down with her sword.

The clash of steel and the desperate tumult of battle lay everywhere. The writhing mass of bodies reminded her of the pages of her father's book and the vast caverns of pain that she had seen within the halls of Dis. Though one important difference remained. Instead of the resigned suffering of those who walked upon the sulphurous earth of the fiery plane, here, there was a desperate need to survive, to fight and to overcome.

Lyra stayed light upon her feet, understanding that in this frantic melee, speed mattered more than strength. Her artifice shield swatted away blow after blow, countering both blade and rifle shot. Her sword, glowing with an arcane light, sliced through armour with ease, cutting a steady path towards the doors of the Grand Magisters' Chambers.

She parried another strike, wrapping her armoured fingers around a guard's blade, pulling him forwards, and thrusting her sword into his chest. No sooner was she able to wrench her blade free than she felt a great force slam into her shoulder and send her sprawling across the floor. Her jaw struck hard upon the stones, and within moments she could taste the blood now pooling between her teeth. She spat and looked up to see the towering figure of the Fereli chieftain staring down at her, his lips curled in disgust, eyes alive with malice.

"You will not escape this time."

Where a large tattoo of a sinister bird had once covered much of his face, there was now simply a mass of burned skin. The rough outline of feathers and a beak could be seen jutting out of the scarred flesh, which cut a series of bald patches through the chieftain's once plentiful beard.

"You will pay for what you did to me. Your whole city will pay!"

Lyra's hand reached for her revolver, but failed to grasp it, as the Fereli's boot slammed into her stomach, sending stars shooting across her eyes.

He muttered something else, but Lyra could focus on nothing but the terrible pain that was shooting across her abdomen.

She watched as the chieftain raised his axe, its red artifice stones shimmering through the air. Managing to grasp her Fereli dagger, Lyra struggled desperately to her knees, taking one last breath as the axe reached its zenith.

Suddenly, blood spurted from the warrior's shoulder causing him to stumble, his axe now held limply in one hand. He looked around in bitter rage, barely able to turn his head before another bullet tore through his chest. A terrible rasping sound now spluttered from his lips, and his strength poured from his body, as he tried to raise his axe once more.

Lyra turned, her vision still blurred, to see a tall woman standing to her right, wielding a large rifle.

"This is for Nathan," said Kat, firing her last shot at the chieftain's forehead and watching his head jerk back with disturbing speed, as he fell lifeless to the ground.

"Come on, Alpheri," Kat extended a hand. "On your feet."

She pulled Lyra up, spinning around just in time to shoot at an armed city guard who came charging out of the smoke. Lyra drew her revolver and stood back to back with Kat, firing at any Fereli who came into view.

"You came back."

"Well, I couldn't just leave you here to die," replied Kat, performing a quick reload of her rifle.

"Kat, I'm sorry. I didn't know about the famine, about my father."

"No, Ly, I'm sorry. It wasn't your fault, or Virgil's. I felt so ashamed after leaving, but I needed some time."

"I thought you weren't ever coming back," said Lyra, firing her pistol and sending another warrior reeling backwards.

"Lyra, it's me." Kat cocked her rifle. "I was always coming back."

She looked over to the steps which led into the Grand Magisters' Chambers, upon which several members of the Vox Militant were now advancing.

"Now, let's end this." Without pause the two made their way forwards, even as cannon fire tore into the building before them. The smoke shifted, and screaming figures fell to the ground, but very soon they were within reach of the steps.

Suddenly, Lyra felt the ethereal form of her shield glow hot with energy as the two hulking leviathans standing either side of the steps roared into life. The sound of a great waterfall, the like of which Lyra had never seen, rose to their ears, and the eyes of the two bellators became alive with hot coals. Within mere moments a pair of twin blades erupted from their monstrous arms, seething with a molten heat. The green-coated soldiers upon the steps barely had time to react before the great blades fell amongst them with a speed and ferocity that was terrible to behold. They were all but obliterated within an instant, and the bellators soon turned their fiery gaze onto the isolated figures of Kat and Lyra.

"Well, that's new," stammered Kat.

At first Lyra offered no response, her breath seemingly taken away by the advance of the great machines.

"Where's Virgil? We could really do with the old man right about now!" yelled Kat.

Lyra came to a halt as the bellators strode towards them.

"He's in Dis."

"He's what!? Why?" exclaimed Kat, taking a few steps backwards alongside her friend, as the two war machines loomed ever closer.

"He said that it was the only way to stop the bellators."

"He plans to stop them by walking into Dis?! Not one of his better ideas!" bellowed Kat above the roar of cannon fire, watching as two projectiles bounced harmlessly from the bellator's shoulders.

Soon the shadow of the arcane machines loomed over them. This close, the great machines were nothing less than monstrous apparitions, seemingly birthed within the bowels of Dis itself. Their strides were so great that there was no chance of escape, and Lyra was sincerely beginning to doubt that even her shield could halt one of their blades.

"Virgil better stop them soon!"

Kat's words were framed by the sound of liquid metal falling from the blades tips and scorching the stone beneath.

Yet they continued to advance, and even the sounds of the surrounding battle seemed to die away as the bellators raised their weapons.

"Kat, I –"

The blades halted. The air stilled, and even amidst the nearby gunshots raging through her ears Lyra could hear a terrible sound, like the buzzing of many bees emanating from inside the bellators. They shuddered forwards and backwards as if both of them were now walking upon sheets of ice. Their arms jerked back with alarming speed. The eyes of the bellators fluttered with a multi-coloured light. Soon they both came to a complete halt, and Lyra saw clearly that the eyes of the right machine had turned a dazzling blue. Much to her amazement it appeared to hold her gaze for a few moments, before it spun suddenly around and hammered its former ally with a solid metal fist. The other bellator reeled away, as if struck by a mountainside.

"Virgil," Lyra breathed.

The blue-eyed bellator turned its venerable gaze onto to her once more, before readying its blades and charging the other machine. The crash of steel rocked the very stones on which Lyra stood as the two monsters of war fought at a speed that was impossibly fast for their size.

"Lyra, move!" screamed Kat.

The sight, smell and sting of battle suddenly returned to Lyra's senses, and not a moment too late, she ducked. A smouldering limb of ancient metal filled the space in which only a moment ago she herself had stood. Fire flashed before her eyes, and it was only by a swift raising of her shield that Lyra avoided the dripping, molten residue of the aged blades.

She felt a sudden force pulling her shoulder, and turned as Kat wrenched her away from the battle of giants. The battle for the Grand Magisters' Chambers roared all around her, but it paled in comparison to the two beings before her. It was not long before each bellator bore a series of grievous wounds, marked by many deep cuts in their rune encrusted armour. Their great blades swung and parried with tremendous power, sending up great sprays of liquid metal with each clash.

The blue-eyed war machine stumbled, falling to one knee as the blade of its opponent hammered into its metallic thigh.

"Come on, Virgil, come on," whispered Lyra to herself. The hampered bellator desperately parried a blow aimed directly at its head. The terrible sound of damaged hinges moving at tremendous speed rose through the air, and the machine sprang forward at great speed, shoulder barging its foe. The other bellator reeled backwards, momentarily losing its footing. Its blue-eyed opponent lunged forward, rending its gleaming chest with the tip of its blade.

Slapping its assailant away with the tang of its own great weapon, the red-eyed monstrosity tried to regain its posture, though it now moved far slower than it did before. A desperate struggle ensued, and little by little the slowing war machine was beaten into the very stones on which it had stood. The repeated stabbing of blades reduced the armour of ages to nothing more than molten slag, as arcane runes melted away and steel plates buckled. Without a moment's hesitation, blue eyes shined and a fiery blade descended as the bellator in which Lyra now placed all her hopes pinned the other machine to the ground, before withdrawing its blade and tearing its enemy's head savagely from its shoulders with one mighty pull. Even in the events of the last few months Lyra had never witnessed such a terrifying and almost primal act of violence.

The light drained from the fallen bellator's eyes, its shattered remnants lying smoking upon the ground. The second titan fell once more to its knees, its towering frame scorched with too many cuts and lines of fire to once more bear its full weight. Its blades receded into its arm and it looked over towards the two women, the lights of its eyes now grown pale.

"It's him, Kat. It's Virgil."

"I know, Ly," replied Kat, stepping towards the remaining bellator. The machine cocked its head, staring straight at Kat. With a laboured heave of metal, the bellator stretched forward its arm and reached out its opened hand towards her.

Without speaking a word, Kat placed her hand within the palm of steel and looked up into the war machine's eyes. She shed a single tear, uttering words that were lost to Lyra amid the clamour of the surrounding battle. The bellator gazed down at the young artificer for a few more moments, and just as its head lowered, its eyes grew dim and the power drained from its form.

Lyra made to speak, her mind racing to find the right words to say, whilst her fingers absentmindedly reloaded her pistol as the battle raged around them. Before she could utter a word, Kat raised her rifle.

"I do believe, Lady Alpheri, that it is time for this whole damn thing to end. What do you say?"

Lyra cocked her pistol. "For Virgil."

They charged up what remained of the chamber steps. A host of Vox Militant and guild soldiers swarmed alongside them. The city guard attempted to bar their way but were swiftly overwhelmed by blade and bayonet. Fighting now spread throughout the grand halls and the ornately-furnished corridors of the Grand Magisters' Chambers. The blast of rifles scorched marble and stone, whilst the clash of artifice weaponry shook the very walls of the aged building.

Lyra and Kat advanced at great speed, swiftly dispatching all who stood in their path. Their progress was only halted when they found themselves standing before the door leading to the private quarters of the High Magister. Nine masked figures blocked their path, robed in the purple and silver livery of Nihilo's family guard.

"This far you have come, Mistress Alpheri, but no further," spoke the foremost of their number.

"Move aside," replied Lyra, clenching her gauntlet.

"No. You and your horde of murderers will not win out this day. We shall —"

The familiar crack of a pistol shot rang through the corridor and the guard fell to the floor.

"The lady said move aside," spat Rillo from behind Lyra, lowering his artifice weapon.

"Charge!" yelled the familiar voice of Aequo, and the Vox Militant ran forward. Within moments the room was filled with the harsh glare of artifice weaponry and the desperate rush of close quarters combat.

"Go!" shouted Rillo, pointing towards the door. "Finish this!"

Lyra barely had time to nod before she ducked under the blow of a masked guard and pushed her way to the door. Not a moment later Kat was at her side.

Lyra punched the hand of her gauntlet through the panels of the locked door, the power of her armour forcing apart the hardened wood with ease. She curled her fingers around the lock and tore it out, walking slowly into the room.

"Ah, Lyra Alpheri. I am happy that it is you who reached me first," spoke Nihilo with perfect calm. "This is the way that it should end. This is right."

Lyra had visited the Grand Magisters' Chambers many times with her father. She had never before seen the personal quarters of the High Magister, but she would not have imagined for a moment that they looked like this. The room was large, flanked on many sides by beautiful glistening windows that looked over much of the city. But this was where its finery ended. The room's furniture consisted of three humble objects: a chair, a desk, and a small bed nestled in an otherwise vacant corner of the room. Each object was chipped and scuffed with use, and they were in such poor condition that they looked as if they had once been left abandoned at the end of an Abyssus alley. Pictures and tapestries had been torn from the walls and were nowhere to be seen, and even the gold leaf carvings which lined the room's many windows had been damaged by some desperate scratchings.

"Please, do step forward."

Lyra and Kat walked with caution. The floor was almost completely obscured from sight, lined with piles upon piles of loose pages and opened books. The desk too looked overburdened with many pages and spent candles.

"I do hope that we may speak for a moment, Lady Lyra, before the end."

"I'm not sure that I have much to say to you, Magister."

Nihilo's eyes widened with desperation. This was nothing new to Lyra; she had seen more than a few desperate looks staring up at her over the previous months. But there was something else disturbing the corners of Nihilo's eyes, a desperate need that was something other than fear.

"No, but I have much to say to you."

"Speaking one's mind is a dangerous thing these days," answered Lyra, stepping forward, gun in hand.

"There are many dangerous things out there, my lady, and it is the job of a loving ruler to protect his people from such things, as best he can."

"Love? You call burning the press houses, arresting and killing innocents, love, do you?"

A small collection of tears pooled within the corner of Nihilo's eyes.

"There are no innocents, not really. I see that now." The magister shuffled towards her, his hands clasped tightly together upon his chest.

"I tried so hard, so very hard to do the right thing, as I saw it." He smiled bitterly, "I suppose that is our great problem, each doing good as he sees fit."

Nihilo looked up at her, the tears now falling down his cheeks. "I was so afraid. You must understand, I was so very afraid. I have never known such fear. You may think me a monster for what I have done, for what I have done to you and your family."

Lyra's hands tensed.

"You don't have to listen to this," said Kat. "Good men and women are dying outside because of him. You don't have to suffer his voice any more."

To her surprise, Nihilo nodded in agreement. "Indeed, a free voice is a dangerous thing. You now know my great fear."

Competing voices raged within Lyra's mind. The stain of blood was upon her clothes and the strain of battle fatigue was already settling within her shoulders. She could still hear the flames consuming her family home, but she could also feel the gentle breeze of the wind that disturbed the branches of the Elysium trees.

"Finish what you must say," she breathed, fighting back her own tears. "I will not deny you what you have robbed from so many others."

"Thank you," Nihilo replied, hands shaking. "Redemption is lost to me, I fear, but not for you."

Seemingly laboured by his own breath, the High Magister stumbled over to the table and leaned upon it.

"Yes, I am in great need of redemption. For I have done great wrong, so great. I see that now. I am sorry," he looked back at Lyra. "So very sorry for what I have done."

She did not reply.

"I was consumed by fear, taken whole by it. I learned of what is amassing in old Luthanril, of the powers of Dis itself walking openly amongst the land of the living. Such tortured scenes were shown to me, that even when I slept, I seemed to walk amongst the realm of agony itself."

Nihilo breathed deep. "There is a darkness, a darkness so deep and so all-consuming that it threatens all things. A stand had to be made against it, those willing to fight it need to stand forward. The Fereli flee from it. They send out their scouts south to find a land that will be free from the power of Dis. They saw the great power of the darkness and they ran. They ran to us. They ran to me."

He looked pleadingly over towards the two women. "I thought that I could keep them safe. Keep my city safe. It would require desperate measures, measures which would inhabit a darkness of their own, but with some sacrifice, I thought that a greater victory could be won. Dis feeds on blood, on violence. I was convinced that if I only shed a fraction of that blood which would otherwise pour through the streets if Dis were allowed to rule Abys-Luthil, then I would be serving the good. Monstrous I know, but such was my fear, I did not see. I thought that if I could bring unity to the people, end their division, end their bickering and their hatred, then the city could better arm itself for the battle to come, and in the long term Dis would be robbed of some of its sustenance."

Nihilo leaned harder upon the table, fatigued by either guilt or loss, Lyra could not decide which.

"I was a fool, I thought that to shed a little blood now, I could stem the greater tide. Now, my home is made in Dis, it waits for me. I am made to join that which I strove so hard against, there is no salvation for me. I accept that."

Finally, he collapsed to the ground, tears washing his ink-stained hands. "The visions of horror were too great, but that is not much of a defence for the things that I have done."

He pulled a small vial from his pocket with a sudden speed, breaking off the wax seal and drinking its small contents. Kat stepped back, even as Nihilo beckoned Lyra to step closer.

"I am so very sorry, Lyra. Please forgive me."

She stepped forward, even dropping to take a knee beside him. She still felt angry, almost more than she could bear, and far more than she could ever forget. And yet, Elysium fields still lingered, even in the far reaches of her mind.

"I forgive you."

Nihilo smiled, his eyes twitching as the poison spread further throughout his body. She rose to her feet, walking back over to a speechless Kat, and not turning to look as the last breath fled Nihilo's lips.

You finally have your revenge, my lady."

Lyra spun on her heel and Kat raised her rifle.

"He died better than I expected," mused Chamberlain Silo Rees, now standing in the corner of the room, a space that had most certainly been empty only a moment ago.

"Though he was already beginning to fail me. Small stabs of conscience, I fear. He saw too much the consequences of his work. A task that was meant for a man such as Salaris Bremmer, but alas, you robbed me of him."

"Lyra, what is going on?" hissed Kat.

"Oh, she doesn't have the full picture yet, do you, Lyra?" interrupted Rees.

"I think that I can put the pieces together," she replied.

Rees grinned. "Very good, Lyra, very good. You have performed admirably these past months."

"You're from Dis."

The grin remained. "That I am, but no less happy to stand here in the flesh for all that. It has been quite a while since I walked upon the world."

"You put the visions in Nihilo's mind."

"Indeed. He would not have been my first choice. Too sincere a man, really, too hopeful to achieve good. Tricky," said Rees rolling his eyes. "But after all, goodness is such a variable, it changes with the tide."

Lyra shook her head. "That is not the truth of the world."

"Oh, Lyra," the chamberlain sighed, wagging his finger, "you really must not believe everything that you hear in Elysium. The ramblings of a hermit hiding in a cave are hardly fit teachings to live by, and neither are the so called "truths" of he who rules that dreary land."

"You speak as if you know it?"

A grimace of disgust curled Rees's lips. "I lived there once, long ago, until I found freedom."

"You're a Watcher."

"Indeed I am. I served and I served. I watched, until I was liberated from the drudgery of Elysium."

Lyra felt her anger rise. "You were meant to protect and to guide. Why do all this?"

A note of icy certainty now lined the words of Rees' lips. "Because even my rebellion is nothing compared to the murder that the humans have wrought upon each other. Even your beloved Virgil is not fully to blame. He may have fashioned the great weapons of war, but it was always the humans that were so eager to use them upon one another."

"You be careful in your choice of words, snake," snapped Kat.

"Oh, my dear, it's hard to be careful where Virgil is concerned, the butcher that he is. Or was, I should say. He's not likely to tread this earth again, damned as he is."

Kat's rifle flared with firing powder, but Rees merely looked amused as he gazed upon the bullet that was held perfectly still in mid-air by an ethereal, red glow shimmering around his body.

"You are not the only one who likes to tinker with the arcane," he said, flicking the bullet harmlessly onto the floor. "The weight of the world's sins now march upon you. Abys-Luthil will not survive it, certainly not in light of recent events."

Rees looked back towards Lyra. "Nihilo was not hard to corrupt, and his short reign provided blood and death. Not as much as I had hoped for, and yet, it shall feed the power of Dis all the same. I tried another, but he was too well guarded. But you, Lyra, I had not counted on. You may have halted my plans and cut short some of the greater acts of horror that I had hoped Nihilo would commit, but this is not the end."

The chamberlain pulled forth a small red crystal from his pocket.

"There is a toll of blood on your heart now," he spat, leaning forward, "and it reeks from Dis to Elysium. Your hands are covered in it, and for the life that you have taken, there shall be a reckoning."

He threw the crystal against a nearby wall, not turning to see it shatter. The room grew suddenly dark and within the blink of an eye a great shadow had crept over the wall, filled with sights of a ruinous landscape and twisted faces.

"But for now, I have performed my part. Until we meet again, Lady Alpheri," said Rees with a light nod, before stepping into the shadow, which, after consuming his form, fled out of sight.

20

Path of the Watcher

D r Karris Schumon took a sip from her wine glass.

Lyra looked around at the rubble that filled much of the Grand Magisters' Chambers' meeting hall, seeing little but scorched stone and chipped marble. She could not for a moment understand how her former tutor had managed to acquire wine, a glass and a rather impressive cheeseboard, only one hour after the battle was over.

"So Rees is a Watcher. Well, he certainly was full of surprises," mused Karris Schumon, wiping away some of the dust that had settled upon the arm of her chair.

"How could you not know? I thought that Watchers had been around for thousands of years?" asked Lyra.

Karris gave Lyra a sharp look before finishing off another slice of well-aged cheese. "Not all of us are quite that old. Now do sit down, Lyra, you're making me most uncomfortable, pacing up and down like that."

Lyra sighed and took a seat, turning down a glass of wine. She tried to ignore the sight of the various city guard bodies that were littered across the large room.

"Besides," continued Karris, "many of our number have a remarkable ability to disguise themselves, especially the elders of our people. Those that committed themselves to the power of Dis are masters foremost of the power of deception. If Rees is indeed an ancient Watcher, then he wields lies like you wield your pistol. Do not spend too much time thinking about what he said, it will do you no good."

"What about Virgil?"

Karris paused mid sip, "I fear that he is lost to both of us. He knew what he was doing."

Her eyes began to well up with what Lyra perceived to be genuine grief. "I walked many centuries with that man. We saw many dangers together and trod the paths of many lands. I shall mourn his loss."

"What if there was a way to get him back?" asked Lyra, looking down at her gauntlet.

Karris shook her head. "For that you would need the power to enter Dis freely of your own accord. I'm afraid that such strength is lost to me. I have sworn no allegiance to Dis, but neither can I in good conscience walk freely in Elysium, as I once did. I am now too much of this world."

Lyra sat still for a moment, thinking of her last conversation with Virgil before turning back to Karris.

"Before he left, Virgil gave me this," she said, opening the fingers of her gauntlet and revealing the precious stone that Virgil had given to her.

"He said that I could use it to visit Elysium and see my mother. But now I wonder if it could also take me to Dis."

A second grief washed over Karris' eyes. "What you hold in your hand there, Lyra, is something very special. Nations have gone to war over just one of those. But, more importantly, that stone there can reunite you with a person and a place that should never have been taken from you. Virgil would not want you to give that up."

Before Lyra could respond, footsteps echoed across the large room and she saw Rillo heading in their direction.

"Ladies," he said, wincing with the pain of a small cut that rested just above his chin.

"Captain Rillo," Karris said with some emphasis on his rank.

"My soldiers report that much of the city is now secure. The city guard have officially surrendered and most of the Fereli have laid down their arms. We have allowed others to flee," he said, picking up a glass of wine upon a small table that rested beside the academic's chair.

"Subduing a city is thirsty business," said Karris, her voice once again steady and assertive.

Rillo looked at her for a moment, before helping himself to the wine. "Not as difficult as I expected, actually. I must say that I anticipated considerably more looting and anarchy before the week was out, let alone during this past hour. But to my immense surprise, the city is peaceful, the guilds contenting themselves with stealing only from the bodies of the slain."

"Maybe there's more to the guilds than you yet understand, Captain?" smiled Karris.

He did not smile back. "Maybe, or maybe there are greater plans at work? All I know is that now the future of the city hangs in the balance." Rillo adjusted the rifle that hung on his shoulder. "I was never one for politics and I'm certainly not ready for another battle today, but what I would know one way or the other, Dr Schumon, is what future you envision for Abys-Luthil?"

Lyra felt her hands tense and her thoughts focus. A victory had been won. Nihilo had been cast down, and the remaining members of the Council of Five had been placed under arrest. However the future of her home was far from sure. Both the guilds and the Vox Militant had suffered heavy losses in the fighting, and there was now no clear authority for the people to turn to.

Karris rose to her feet, wiping a speck of cheese from her lips. "It is my estimation, Captain, that for today, our forces are well balanced. But once my guild has composed themselves from celebrating this great victory, then without doubt you will be outnumbered."

A decided look of grim acceptance furrowed Rillo's brow. "Yes, that appears to be the way of it."

"Or," continued Karris, glancing at Lyra, "the people may well shun both of us and elevate their chosen saviour. Her name now carries more weight than either of us."

"That they might."

"So then," sighed Karris, "what is it to be, civil war? Anarchy? Queen?"

Lyra shook her head, standing between them. "I have no desire to rule – and I do not mean to stay here." She gritted her teeth, her mind made up.

"I must find him," she said to Karris. "I cannot leave him there, in that place."

"You understand what you will be giving up?" asked the academic.

"Yes, and I cannot walk those fields knowing that Virgil is abandoned. I must act. Besides, the danger to this city is not over. Regardless of who rules, a great threat comes from the North. Working together is your only choice if you wish to save anything of Abys-Luthil."

Karris Schumon now bore upon her face a picture of such warmth and pride that for a moment Lyra thought her to be a different woman. She stepped forward and embraced Lyra with the affection of a mother.

"I am so very proud of you, my girl, so very proud. You are the Watcher that I should have been and I have no doubt that one day, you shall tread upon Elysium again," she whispered into her ear. "You are your mother's daughter."

"Sorry to interrupt," spoke up Rillo. "But where exactly are you going?"

Lyra gave her tutor one final squeeze before turning towards the great doors that led out of the chamber.

"I'm going to Dis, Captain. I'm going to get Virgil back. We'll need him for the fight to come. As for the city, I trust that you two can work together."

Karris poured Rillo a fresh glass of wine. "Oh, I'm sure that the captain and I can work something out. My guild has little interest in running this city, if anyone should at all. The Vox must stay, of that I have no doubt. But as for the magisters? – Well, I say that we speak to Maellon Alpheri. He may have a few ideas."

"He is certainly never short of those, though I cannot guarantee that he will help you," said Lyra.

Rillo took the wine and gently massaged the sides of his head. "I see that we still have a long day ahead of us, Doctor."

"That we do, Captain," answered Karris, lightly tapping her glass against his. Rillo went to drink, but chose instead to watch as Lyra stepped away.

"I admire your bravery, Lady Alpheri. But you cannot think to walk into

Dis itself alone?"

"I have no intention of going on my own, Captain Rillo," she replied, without turning back.

The alley was dark and quiet, a hive of shadows, hiding from the light of the celebrations that illuminated the streets outside.

"Are you sure about this?" asked Kat, her voice weighed down with the knowledge of what Lyra had said to her.

Lyra nodded. "Yes, I am certain. But I can't say that I know what to expect when we get there. I can't help but think of Father's book. Did Rees try his dark visions on him? Did my father see a vision of Dis as it really was, and put it to page?"

She pulled her half-mask across her face as if to conceal her concern, or part of it.

"I can get us there, Kat, but I don't fully know what awaits us on the other side."

"Lyra." Kat Darrow swung her rifle over her shoulder, bringing it to rest against her bandolier. "We're going to find Virgil, and we're going to bring him back. But, more importantly, we're going to do this together." She placed her hand upon Lyra's shoulder. "Dis is not ready for us, not by a long shot."

Lyra nodded and took a deep breath. She thought about her father, she thought about Castel and Nathan, and yet above all of these she thought of her mother.

She took out the stone that Virgil had handed to her and clenched it within her gauntlet. The power coursed through her veins and shook the very metal plates of the gauntlet. A sudden light burst between her fingertips, and she let go. The stone left her hand and rose higher and higher into the air. The shadows fled from the wall before them as the stone projected a wonderful vision of golden fields and tall trees throughout the alley.

"It's so wonderful," muttered Kat.

"Yes, yes, it is," said Lyra. Even as she observed the spectacle and thought back to the conversation in the cave, she knew that Elysium was not, for the moment, to be their destination. It took every ounce of will, but she clenched her fists together and thought of her father's book.

The sight of the trees faded and the cornfields turned to ash. Shadows crept in from darkness hitherto unseen, and a myriad of twisted faces looked out at the duo.

"You wish to gain entrance to the paths of Dis?" asked a hooded figure. He possessed long, hooked fingers and a cruel row of yellowed teeth.

"No," said Lyra, placing one hand upon her revolver. "I demand it."

A chorus of hideous laughter arose from the shadows.

"You're a bold one," the creature replied. "We don't simply allow the passage of anyone who wishes to walk our land, even Watchers."

Lyra's eyes narrowed. "I don't require your permission and neither do I seek it. I will have access, as is my right. Now, stand aside."

The hood leaned closer. "You will never find him."

Lyra stepped closer still, offering a twisted smile of her own. "We'll see about that. For the last time, stand aside."

The hooked fingers curled into a fist. "You have no idea what you are walking into. We will swallow you alive, never to spit you out. Our fires will consume you and our blades will tear—"

The robed figure looked down to see a small ring of blue fire in its chest, carved by the passage of Lyra's bullet.

"Bring it on." She turned her head towards Kat, not bothering to watch as the hood burst into flames, its form twisted by the revolver's arcane powers.

"You ready?"

Kat swung her rifle down into her hands, advancing, even as the grim faces vanished from the shadows.

"Always."

Printed in Great Britain
by Amazon

65086974R00200